KINGFISHER WEATHER

Kingfisher Weather

PAUL BINDING

GMP

Extracts from *The Waste Land: A Facsimile and Transcript* and *Four Quartets* by
T.S. ELIOT are reprinted by kind permission of Faber and Faber Ltd.

First published November 1989 by
GMP Publishers Ltd,
PO Box 247,
London N17 9QR

World Copyright © 1989 Paul Binding
Distributed in North America by
Alyson Publications Inc.,
40 Plympton Street, Boston, MA 02118, USA

British Library Cataloguing in Publication Data

Binding, Paul
  Kingfisher Weather.
  I. Title
  823'.914 [F]

  ISBN 0-85449-123-6

Printed and bound in the European Community by
Nørhaven A/S, Viborg, Denmark

Typeset by MC Typeset, Gillingham, Kent

DEDICATION: TO EUDORA WELTY
with gratitude and affection

Kingfisher weather, with a light fair breeze,
Full canvas, and the eight sails drawing well.
We beat around the cape and laid our course
From the Dry Salvages to the eastern banks.

T.S. ELIOT from discarded passage of 'Death by Water' in the original *Waste Land*.

PART ONE

CHAPTER ONE: ROB

Four days out from Baltimore, Bill Bentley, one of the eight passengers on board the *Egon Ludendorff*, invited Rob Peters, a young member of her crew, down to his cabin for a chat. Rob was the Assistant Ship's Cook, who also waited at table. The invitation did not altogether take him by surprise. Even before departure, in dock at Baltimore's Coal Pier, Bill had shown a bright determination that the two of them should be friends and had paid him the first of many compliments:

'This ginger pudding's a bit of all right!' he'd said, 'haven't tasted anything so good all the time I've been here in Uncle Sam's country.'

'Well, glad you like it.' Rob had mumbled. What stupid vanity had caused him to add: 'Made it myself, as a matter of fact.'?

'I knew it, I knew it!' Triumph had shone in Bill Bentley's grey eyes and made his voice ring out. 'Of course it takes an *Englishman* to appreciate traditional English fare. The finer points of this pudding'll be lost on the others you've given it to. So . . . you made it yourself!'

Why do I blush so easily, Rob had thought here, why do I like – or need – praise the way I seem to?

'May I be so bold,' Bill had continued, 'as to ask how someone as young as you learned to cook so well?'

Rob, contrary to his usual practice, had given the truth for reply. 'Well, back in England,' he'd said, 'my mum runs a cafe, doesn't she? I got into the habit of giving her a hand when I was knee-high.'

'Runs a cafe, eh?' Bill had sounded all admiration and good-hearted envy.

'Yeah, *The Copper Kettle*; High Street, Foswich, Essex. Do you know it? We live on the premises.'

'Foswich? Foswich, Essex! Do I know it? Of *course* I know Foswich.' Bill Bentley had slapped his thighs here vigorously, '*a dear* little town. And Foswich Forest, what a wonderful, wonderful place! Bet you've taken many a girl there, deep into its whispering glades!'

Rob had blushed again.

'As it happens, I myself hie from a place not so far from you, a little dump in Hertfordshire that goes by the name of Polhamsted. Went to public-school there,' Bill Bentley had laughed briefly but breezily. 'Wasn't much of a scholar!'

You could have hardly been less of a one than I was, Rob had said to himself, and inevitably his mind took him swiftly to sad scenes in his own English life. When he'd looked back up at Bill Bentley, it'd been to see those grey eyes of his fixed scrutinisingly upon him. You could almost feel their beams piercing your face to discover what lay behind it.

Five days later, and Baltimore and the long, meandering Chesapeake like a blurred and distant dream, Bill said to Rob, as smilingly he received his Soup of the Day: 'I've been thinking, Rob, you and me shouldn't be talking to each other only at mealtimes or at the odd moment when we bump into each other. Here we both are, the only two Limeys on the ship and heading for the Old Country, and we've never yet spent any time together to speak of. I reckon we've got a lot in common.'

'Well, Mr Bentley, I . . .'

'*Mr* Bentley! Bill, please, Bill! We two Brits aren't surely going to stand on ceremony with each other! Listen, when you're through with tea this afternoon – why not come down to my cabin? It's Number Five; well, of course, you know that already. We can have a talk then; it'd make me very happy.'

A lot in common, thought Rob, what the hell could that be? Bill Bentley was, Rob reckoned, in his early thirties; he himself wasn't yet out of his teens. Bill was clearly a prosperous bloke, a smart business-man of some kind or other, who couldn't possibly know what it was like being second-cook-and-bottlewasher, working your ass off down in steamy, dirty ship's kitchens. And then – *a talk would make him happy*! How? I've never made anyone happy.

The tea-things washed up, Andy, the Malay Ship's Cook, let him go, and Rob returned to his own cabin to get himself ready for the meeting. He put on a clean pair of jeans, and a blue-and-white matelot T-shirt. He ran a comb through his short-cropped hair and splashed his face vigorously with his favourite *Opium* after-shave. He didn't look half bad, but he was feeling curiously uneasy, a fluttering in his stomach, a tightness at the temples.

It wasn't as if he were frightened of being grabbed at; he was perfectly capable of looking after himself in this respect, and by now he'd had plenty of experience. But something told him that if passes were Bill's intention, he'd have tried days back. And his approach wouldn't surely be as unsubtle as this formal invitation to his cabin. Applying yet more *Opium* to his neck and forehead, Rob remembered the keen, cold way in which Bill's eyes had examined him, and his disquiet intensified. But then he told himself, I've been feeling so strange all crossing, and not without reason. All he could do now was walk upstairs and knock on Bill's cabin door.

'Good to see you, Rob, good to see you,' exclaimed Bill. Then he clearly noticed the look Rob couldn't keep off his face – astonishment at the appearance of the cabin. 'Tried to make the place a bit my own,' he said, 'half-office, half private sitting-room. I decided to travel by ship to England, to give myself a bit of a break. I've got important work ahead, you see. But it never turns out like that, does it?'

Work, what work could it be? Rob asked himself. Bill was using the desk, perhaps for the first time since its installation, for the purpose for which it'd been made. On it stood a portable typewriter, a pile of pamphlets, and a wad of headed writing-paper. Also some framed photographs. Everything was as neat as could be. But that wasn't all. On the walls were posters; one immediately caught Rob's eye, never to leave it all the time he was there. It showed a man in a long white robe, armed with a huge broom, entering a dirty, untidy house from a well-tended, flowery garden. *Do YOU need spring-cleaning too?* read its caption . . . 'Feel like a coke?' said Bill Bentley, 'I've got a few tins in the fridge.'

'Oh, okay, thanks,' said Rob dully. His discomfort was, second by second, increasing.

Bill got up to busy himself at the fridge, and bade Rob sit down: 'There's only the bed, I'm afraid.' This had so creaseless a cover it seemed almost an act of destruction to lower oneself on to it. 'Well, we're not having too bad a voyage, are we? I never expected a sea as calm as this, I must say. Four days, with scarcely a ripple on the ocean.' His smile had the breadth and good white teeth of some TV commercial.

'Yes, it's been exceptionally smooth,' said Rob, who had a distinct feeling that Bill had planned these remarks carefully in advance.

'It's not normally like this in May then?' Bill asked.

'Can't say, Bill, really. Never been across the Atlantic in May before.'

There he went, giving things away about his life, making a present of them. Bill handed him an ice-cold tin of coke, and said: 'Exactly how long *have* you been working on ships, Rob?'

Rob cast his gaze down on the floor, but still felt Bill's eyes upon him, and also those of the white-robed figure on the poster.

'Since last July,' he said.

He didn't want to talk about himself, his life, his intentions.

'Non-stop?'

'More or less.'

'That makes ten months at sea, then?'

Well, you didn't have to be a business wizard to work that out!

'Always between Tilbury and Baltimore – Baltimore and Tilbury, perhaps I should say?'

'No, not at all.' His denial was made in a louder, more emotional tone than he'd intended. You could see interest lighting up the man's face. While the smile disconcertingly left it.

Casually he said: 'Should have known it wouldn't always have been those two ports, shouldn't I? I mean, this is a *German* ship, isn't it?'

'Yeah, one of the Wolfgang Ludendorff line.' Rob couldn't keep the pride out of his voice; he remembered his feelings when they'd agreed to take him on. 'Their boats carry cargo from Lübeck, Hamburg, Bremen, Rotterdam, on the European side to a whole lot of American ports. I've been to Norfolk, Charleston, Mobile, New Orleans and even Galveston, Texas.'

'Sounds as if you've had a really interesting time, Rob,' said Bill, ensconced now at his swivel-chair, and regarding him intently, 'and do they always carry coal like now?'

'Yes,' said Rob, 'or mostly.' He could tell from the way Bill asked that he wasn't really interested in finding out about the cargo-boats. These questions were a carefully prepared way towards other ones. Nevertheless he went on: 'You see there's a European type of coal and an American type, and . . .'

'So *this*,' said Bill, cutting in ruthlessly, 'is your first trip back to England since you started?'

'Yeah!' said Rob miserably.

'The first trip home *in ten months*!'

Well, obviously, said Rob to himself. His pulse was quickening now. 'That's right, Bill,' he said.

'That explains it, that explains it,' said Bill, as if to himself, 'you're not looking forward to going back to England, are you? Told your folks yet?'

'Of course!' But the words didn't deceive Bill. Somehow he sensed that Rob had very nearly *not* done this, that it had required a great and perhaps mistaken effort of will to send off that letter to his parents.

'Yes, that explains it,' said Bill again. 'The first time I saw you, I said to myself, *There's a guy in sorrow!* A good guy, a great guy, one I'd like to be buddies with, but unmistakeably *in sorrow.'*

Rob didn't know what this curious expression of Bill's meant exactly, but it didn't seem at all a bad description of his own state of mind. Uneasily he shifted his bum on the immaculate bed. The broom of the white-robed figure seemed to shake a little, the advertisement smile had re-appeared on Bill's face. Rob suddenly thought how odd it was that beyond the portholes was the limitless, turquoise ocean. He had the feeling of being rather in a consulting-room or a manager's office in a downtown skyscraper somewhere, not traversing one of the deeper areas of the Atlantic. And for all the apparent palliness of Bill's returned smile, he surely had about him the air of a specialist or a company president, with serious business in mind.

'How old are you, Rob?' Bill asked, clearly not disconcerted by Rob's inability to reply to his last observation.

Once again Rob spoke only the truth: 'Almost eighteen.'

'Young to have been ten months at sea without sight or sound of your native heath. Mind you, I can understand it well. I was none too fond of Polhamsted when I was younger; you can probably imagine why not.' And he gave something like a wink, as if to suggest a world of naughtiness that the two of them, despite their different ages, had shared.

Rob tried to picture a younger Bill but could not.

'You've never told me, Rob, what made you choose a life at sea?'

Well, of course I haven't, said Rob to himself.

'It intrigues me. Here you are, Assistant Cook, on a German boat. Whatever brought you to such a position. *That's* what I've been asking myself these last days.'

'Hard to know how to answer you, Bill,' said Rob, addressing the floor.

'I have the feeling,' Bill swivelled himself and his chair round to a positively inquisitorial angle, 'that there was some moment in your life – something you saw maybe, or a conversation you had, or heard – or *over*heard – which made you think "Ah! – *that's* what I must do: go to sea!"'

The guy has a certain insight, conceded Rob, not unimpressed. 'Well, yeah . . . in a way . . .' he confusedly replied, 'I mean . . . I suppose . . . the two pictures.'

'*Pictures*?' said Bill, brightly, rather as a remedial teacher might.

'Yeah, photographs of a ship on the North sea. Of the *William Wilberforce* of Hull.'

Bill Bentley nodded knowingly, though it would have been extraordinary beyond believing had he known this ship. 'Special personal associations?' he asked in his most professionally off-hand manner.

'You could say that, yes,' said Rob. He didn't want to see himself back in the room where those framed photographs hung, specially not back there his first visit. It'd all be so painful. But Bill was wanting him to say more. 'The pictures were in the flat of a great friend,' he pronounced these last words with some difficulty, for behind them lay his pain.

'I see!' Once more the sage nod. 'A friend who meant a lot to you! Perhaps meant more than anybody else . . .'

It was Rob who – not trusting himself to speak – nodded now. Why, we must look like a pair of fucking Chinese mandarins, he thought. Then, partly to lessen the almost threatening intensity of Bill's stare, he made himself explain: 'The pictures . . . they were of a ship this friend's dad had worked on many times.'

'I *see*!' said Bill significantly, though what he saw Rob dared not think. 'Worked on as cook, perhaps?'

'Oh, no,' said Rob, shifting uneasily, 'I've already told you where my interest in cooking came from.' This talk was – already – *about* something, but what he didn't at all know.

'Your interest, *and* your ability,' said Bill, giving Rob now a bland smile broader than any previous one.

'Nice of you to say so, Bill,' said Rob, flushing as he'd done that first time Bill complimented his cookery.

'I only say what I mean,' said Bill softly.

I wonder, thought Rob, I wonder. Yet Bill was surely sincere enough in his praise of Rob's food. Many times now Rob had watched him guzzling it down like a comic-strip schoolboy. But Bill had moved on now to another point he had not caught.

'. . . Am I not right?'

'Eh, sorry! Sorry, Bill!' How many times at St John's School, Foswich had Rob been pulled up to attention by irritated teachers, by indeed almost all of them except Art Master, Laurie Williams? 'I'm afraid I was thinking of something ... Something to do with what you'd just been saying.'

'I was just remarking,' Bill, unlike Foswich teachers, didn't appear at all irritated; if anything his genial smile widened, 'that I'm picking up from you *pretty* clear vibes, *pretty* clear ones, Rob, that you left England in, shall we say, distinctly unhappy circumstances. You'd already decided you'd go to sea; I understand *that*. But, *but* ...' He left the sentence significantly unfinished.

How can he know all this, Rob asked himself, smitten by something like fear. Could it be that Bill Bentley had second sight, that those grey eyes saw past and future? The very idea made Rob shudder.

'School didn't go too well for you, did it?'

'Well, my 'O' Levels weren't exactly brilliant,' said Rob, putting on a rueful grin. 'I failed all the f–' He stopped himself from swearing. 'Failed all of them except Art. I've heard they're going to change the system soon!'

He intended this observation as a means of deflecting Bill's attention from the reasons for leaving Foswich, but, of course, he underrated Bill's perseverence.

'So I understand,' that man replied, 'well, my own 'O' Levels weren't any too hot. As I told you the other day I was no scholar. Yes, we've got a lot in common, you and me.'

Rob tilted back the almost empty Coca-Cola tin to save himself from speaking. He wasn't sure that he wanted there to be anything in common between them. Somehow, here in the tidy, tidy room with his so efficiently-ordered desk, Bill was far less likeable than in the dining-room, happily savouring the dishes brought him.

'So I got things right, didn't I?' Bill had swivelled himself round again, so that his eyes were shining at him from a new angle. 'You went to sea when you did because things had gone wrong, and you're worrying now because soon you'll be having to confront those things again. Buddy, I feel for you; honestly I do! I feel for anyone who's *in sorrow* the way you are.'

'*In sorrow*, Bill?'

'What do I mean by *in sorrow*? That's what you're asking, isn't it? Well, you're right to ask, Rob; you're someone who doesn't shrink from truths, I can tell that already. And I'll tell you something right now: if you give me the chance, I believe I can take you right out of the condition.'

Perhaps the time's now come for him to jump on me, thought Rob. But no, Bill remained calm and controlled in his swivel-chair.

'Of course there's no way I can tell what's brought you to sorrow; I'm no magician. Perhaps you received one of those nasty knocks life can give any of us. Perhaps you did something – or a number of things even – which you're now bitterly regretting. But the *real* reason for feeling bad, for being *in sorrow* can never be, how shall I put it, wholly external. Do you follow me, Rob? Am I making sense? You see, it's been given to us all to survive the most terrible experiences, and even face up to the sins we've committed, if we come *out* of that sorrow and find peace. Do you get me?'

Well, frankly, no, Rob said silently in reply; I haven't a clue what you're going on about: the only thing I know is that I'm sorry I came down here to Cabin Number Five. Outside the window the sea continued to roll serenely and brilliantly on. At this hour of the day some of the guys of the crew liked to pass the time with playing ping-pong. Rob had got quite good at the game, but instead of proving his skill, he was . . . No mistake about it; the beams from Bill's grey eyes were like fishing-lines, and they had him well and truly hooked.

'Let me put it to you like this, Rob,' and Bill bent himself forward a little; the lines were shortening now, working towards the pulling in. 'When we're in trouble, when we're *in sorrow*, what do we usually do?' He didn't wait for, or want, an answer. 'We usually turn to a *friend* for comfort, don't we? Now I'm mighty sure that *you*, Rob, with your likeable personality and your way with people, have a good many friends. And you've told me in the most open way about a great friend you had who's been very important to you. But now you've found yourself another one.'

Rob tried to tell himself: Well, he *is* going to lunge at me after all. Favours a long verbal build-up, like some other guys I've met.

'I'm going to find for you,' Bill was continuing, 'the best friend it's possible to have.'

Pretty conceited way of talking about yourself, huh? Rob thought. Bill's voice had softened now; in fact he was speaking in a kind of twangy whisper that could have belonged equally to an American or an Englishman.

'That friend's name, Rob – haven't you guessed it? – is Jesus. He's better, far far better, than any other buddy we can have, and why? Because he can do things that no one else can. He can take away this *sorrow* that so many of us are in. He can take away sin and even death itself. Isn't that something! He lived – and He died – not just for mankind, but for *you*, Rob, yes, for the sake of one Robert Peters of *The Copper Kettle*, High Street, Foswich, Essex. He knew from the beginning of Time that the day would come when you'd feel the need for Him. Come unto me, He said, all ye that are sore-laden. And you *are* sore-laden, aren't you, Rob? Never forget when you're feeling down that Jesus tells us (John, Chapter 16, Verse 7) that He is our Comforter as well as our Redeemer.'

Eventually Bill Bentley did lay a hand on Rob, but unflirtatiously. 'Put away fear, man!' he told him. 'Look at those photographs over there on my desk. Guys and girls your own age. Don't they all look happy? Those photos were taken in Riverside Park, Jackson, Mississippi. Near my headquarters!' Staring across the room at them Rob had a vague but gaudy impression of smiling faces, healthy bodies, and of trees in the background boughed down and dripping with Spanish moss. 'Yes sirree, I brought all of those young folk – some of them deep *in sorrow*, Rob, pretty damn deep *in sorrow* – to Jesus. And two of them are now doing His Work, testifying to the Lord for our organisation.'

Underneath his large firm hand the neat form of Rob Peters could not stop trembling.

'Put away fear,' said Bill Bentley again, 'and you never

know, Rob, there may come the day when you too will bring people out of sorrow. You won't always want to be cooking on German cargo-boats, you know!'

In the evenings, when the day's hard work was over, Rob liked to stand upon the bridge-deck. He derived a strong but melancholy satisfaction in watching the sun going down, or, as it seemed, dissolving, a molten copper bruised with verdigris. And with it not just the day itself, or America or the West, but freedom and a bearable present. Conversely, what he was heading for, that curved black line ceaselessly summoning the prow of the *Egon Ludendorff*, was the past and all the wretchedness and wrong-doing of his life in Foswich. Most particularly, it was his wicked treatment of his best friend there, Laurie Williams. How right Bill had been to say that he was *in sorrow*. Would anyone looking at Rob – trim-limbed, short to medium in height, with fair hair, brown eyes and a snub-nosed, weather-tanned face – know the depths of gloom and guilt to which he regularly now descended? Most probably not, but *one* person *had* done: Bill Bentley.

Suppose then he was right about other things? Suppose that from before Time God and His Son had known that he would exist and need – was it Them? or simply Him? – that Rob Peters could be rescued from despair and destruction?

Rob could see beneath him – stretching in a double-line towards the masts at the prow – the great lids of the cylindrical coal-containers. They looked like the jacket buttons of some floating giant. Was that what a world without the friendship of Jesus was like? A huge corpse borne towards blackness.

Up in the lofty, nest-like Navigation Room, enveloped in the light, were the Captain (German) and his First Mate (Indonesian). Upon their abilities his own safe arrival in Foswich depended. Apart from them you could have thought the ship abandoned, a phantom under the clear dark sky, supported by the empty liquid darkness of the ocean. But no! For on the deck below him, there *was* another visible, and Rob knew who this would be: Peter, a Filipino boy his own age, a deckhand away from home from the first time, just as he himself had been ten months ago.

Rob and Peter had eyed each other, looked each other up and down, several times before they'd been introduced. (When the boat was still loading at Baltimore Coal Pier.) So when the First Mate had said: 'Rob, I'd like you to meet Peter Rodriguez from Manila!', they'd talked to each other as two boys who knew something, probably something very important, about one another, but were not for a while going to admit the knowledge.

Pete, as he liked to be called, had not been slow to tell Rob his story. Shortly before his twelfth birthday his parents had been killed in a road accident, and he'd grown up in the house of a much older sister, whose photograph he carried in his wallet. But he'd begun to feel a burden to her – after all, she had five children of her own – and work was getting harder and harder to obtain in the Philippines. And the political situation was worsening. The growing movements against the Marcoses were making them, apparently, more, not less, oppressive, and given to arrests and detainments. So Pete had decided to join relations of his in New York. These he hadn't found at all to his liking, and as for New York, 'it's a very dangerous place,' he'd giggled, with a wink, 'for someone like me!' So he'd moved on to another relation, an uncle he had, in fact, never met before, who lived in Baltimore. ('The whole world's full of uncles of mine,' he'd said.) Mooching around Baltimore had been pretty boring, but happily this particular uncle had known guys in Wolfgang Ludendorff's American offices there. So thanks to him he now had a job.

Rob had not quite felt up to responding to these confidences in kind. He knew they were appeals to confirm that bond they both felt existed between them, and that was one reason for holding back. Another was the nature of the confidences that he himself had in his power to give . . . The Filipino boy was now leaning against spray-clammy rails, drawing on his cigarette, the tiny tip of which glowed against the huge night. Then he turned his head. Splashed in the light issuing from the Navigation Room, it was like some illuminated representation of the condition of loneliness. Pete *was* lonely, he'd said so, lonely for Filipino friends specially for one called Ricky. (Rob had been surprised that Filipinos had such humdrum English names.) Yes, of course he needs someone now to occupy Ricky's place, thought Rob, but not me. Not a ne'erdowell, a traitor, a thief and a runaway. Maybe, of course, he shouldn't be searching for earthly friends at all, but for a heavenly one: Jesus.

Rob removed his gaze from the Filipino boy and looked back up to the sky in which tonight the stars were so very bright. Perhaps you should look at the situation of Peter and himself — and indeed of all the passengers and crew of the *Egon Ludendorff* — as you looked at *them*. Each star in the immensity seemed hugely lonely, yet was linked to another to form a meaningful pattern, a constellation. In the same way all the often desperately isolated people of the world could perhaps be connected to each other, through the love of Jesus.

'I'm sure you, Rob, have a good many friends,' Bill Bentley had said. But he didn't really, never had had. He and his elder brother, Philip, had never been close, and as for old Neil Ferris and all the crowd at St John's School, well, he rarely thought about them now. Only Laurie Williams did he care about, did he miss! *He* still shone star-bright in his memories, through all the vast darkness of solitude and self-fatigue. And yet equalling his presence in brilliance was Rob's lurid recollection of his own crimes against him, crimes for which he still hadn't paid.

But, thought Rob now, maybe the feelings he'd known — and expressed — last summer, prior to his sin of July, proved there *was* some good in him, that he was not unworthy of the supreme friend who could change his whole existence. Inevitably then he went back in his mind to a May afternoon in Foswich, Essex, almost exactly a year before.

Foswich is strung along a low ridge which, to the south, connects to that great tract of woodland, Foswich Forest, and, to the north, declines into the well-farmed undulations of mid-Essex. At the foot of this ridge flows a stream called on the large-scale maps of the area the 'River' Fase. Sloping water-meadows seperate the Fase from the town, and at the bottom of them runs a path. This, just below the Parish Church, crosses the river by means of a little wooden bridge, built in Japanese half-moon style, to recall prints by Hokusai or Hiroshige or their French admirers.

Along this path Rob was now once again walking, alone, homewards, from a visit to the Towns Baths with Neil Ferris. While they'd been showering themselves after their swim, Neil had said something that Rob had found very disturbing. Neil was his most regular mate, a stocky boy with dark hair, rosy cheeks and glinting, mischievous eyes. Yet this oldest companion of his had spoken to Rob in a stranger's voice, with a stranger's expression on his face. Why, Neil had asked, had Rob so obviously *not* enjoyed Mike Carter's party last Saturday, Rob who was usually ready for fun. Why had he hung back from all the goings-on? Everyone had remarked on it.

Rob had hoped his behaviour had gone unnoticed. In fact, he'd later congratulated himself on having successfully disguised his reactions. For the truth was that he'd *hated* Mike's party (or 'orgy' as everybody persisted in calling it). In the fug and din of the Carters' 'lounge' a truly alarming transformation had occurred – similar to, though more complete than, that of Neil under the showers this afternoon. Familiar companions had suddenly, dynamically, turned alien, had talked unlike themselves, had moved unlike themselves, had refused to respond to long-used catch-phrases and favourite jokes. And all for the sake of girls who, for the greater part of their school careers, they'd ignored. At one point in the party Rob had seen Mike and Neil and all the others, mates for many years, as a troupe of marionettes, jigging obscenely in artificial, prescribed attitudes. Rob felt that he alone had remained natural, true to himself.

Of course none of all this had Rob expressed to Neil Ferris who'd seemed a little surprised at his buddy's reluctance to defend himself.

It was good to be by himself again. Hawthorn-flower – white may – was profuse, it had blizzarded the hedgerows, had loaded the warm afternoon with its scent. Of course in the non-human world coupling-off took place also – the evidence was to be found everywhere – but it wasn't effected, accompanied, by all the archness, the false excluding laughter, the dishonest chatter that the young at Mike's 'orgy' – and doubtless in every like circumstance all over England – had so horribly indulged in.

How still the Fase valley was! It was a stillness you could feel, hear, smell, touch. And yet, said Rob to himself as he began to mount the Japanese bridge, it's the stillness of expectancy. The fields, the river are in a state of waiting, yet what can it be that's going to happen? Whatever it was, it'd make the stupidities of Saturday's party, and of Neil's questionings after the swim, seem as nothing. He paused on the crest of the bridge, poised to meet whatever event was to be delivered to him, to meet it with both his body and his soul.

And then, abruptly, but with a slow insouciant grace, the kingfisher rose from the rushes of the Fase. A kingfisher! Rob – who was more interested in birds and animals than in anything else – could not believe his luck. For a long time now he'd wanted to see one, knowing that their tunnel-like nests were to be found at irregular intervals along the river-bank. It was blue beyond expectation, beyond beauty; its flight – from one fishing-perch to another – was motion freed from time, was a moment of blue which made nonsense of any clock. When reposing with folded wings the bird is (as Rob knew from natural history books) dullish of hue. Flying as now it rendered everything around it – the dipping willow-trees, the clustering reeds, the sun-like marsh-marigolds, the prolix hawthorn-blossoms, and all the hushed tender greens of the meadow-land – a mere context for its appearance.

The kingfisher, as it hung there, gathered up for Rob other occasions in his muddled young life, occasions when he'd felt that somehow he was being shown something. He recollected the calf he'd seen gradually and delicately being born and then wobbling on its legs, in the muddy March meadow in which it had arrived; the frog that had leaped out at him shrieking from a woodland bank: the mole that one twilight walk he'd surprised digging and that had looked up at him with tiny, quick, bright, near-blind eyes: the toad he'd found under a stone in the backyard of *The Copper Kettle* with carbuncles on its back gleaming like edible jewels; the polarbears he'd watched slowly, solemnly yet tenderly fucking in an enclosure in Regent's Park Zoo. And now he could feel his low spirits being borne upwards and brightened by the Kingfisher's strong, vivid wings.

Then Rob turned his head to look at the path that unfolded on the other side of the bridge. And there stood – plainly, from the look on his face, also a witness of the kingfisher – Mr Williams, the nice, always-friendly art master at St John's. As later with Pete looks had passed between them long before this meeting, looks which spoke of recognised bonds. A minute – probably much less – of mutual apprehensiveness followed. Then Mr Williams gave him a rather diffident smile and, self-consciously began to ascend the rise of the wooden bridge . . .

'I'm sure *you*, Rob, have a great many friends!' No, Bill, he should have said, I've only had one real one, and after a certain day last July he isn't my friend any more.

That night he had a strange dream. He was still in his cabin, though sleep had changed it, had littered it like a school locker, with gym shoes and football shorts, stubbed pencils and tattered exercise-books, as well as with used 'johnnies' and jockstraps. Out of the portholes it wasn't the Atlantic that could be seen. No, it was the hawthorn- and willow-lined Fase. Suddenly – through a microphone? delivered on ticker-tape round the walls? – Rob received unmistakeable and powerful words: 'Do YOU need spring cleaning too?'

Obviously he was expected to answer 'Yes!'; obviously he was expected to open the door. So why was he nervous about doing so? Perhaps simply because to confront Jesus (that's who the white-robed figure was, and no mistake!) must always be intimidating. The only Friend who could take away sin and sorrow. That made him both desirable and appalling . . .

But when he *did* bring himself to turn the knob, it wasn't Jesus at all that he found on the other side of the door. Instead, rising from some dark corner of the corridor, was a kingfisher, his and Laurie's bird, as dazzlingly, divinely blue as on that afternoon last year. It had come to bear away on its bright wings any misgivings about what was happening to him on this crossing, his realisation that he needed, and – wonderfully – could obtain, salvation. Then Rob became aware that someone else was in the passage-way; surely it was Filipino Pete? But before he could be certain he'd woken up – only for a few minutes, minutes in which he made a resolution that he would tell Bill Bentley about that episode upon the Japanese-style wooden bridge . . .

Would morning ever be anything else but a new brightness, issuing from the east upon a seeming limitlessness of water? Sometimes Rob found it impossible to remember what getting up to an ordinary inland English day had been like.

At breakfast Jerry, the Irish Radio Engineer, pantomimed his hang-over (the amount of whisky and beer that he got through off-duty was prodigious). 'Just black coffee for me, Rob, my old pal,' he groaned, 'what a night! what a night!' He might have been referring to an expedition to some kinky and classy club. 'Still, when someone is as saintly as yours truly, making himself indispensable to ships and men, I daresay the good Lord looks kindly on him taking a drop. Even if it's a drop too much!'

'The good Lord' – would Rob ever be able to hear such a phrase again, specially when used facetiously, and not think of the solemn truths that hovered – in the wings – behind it. With rising he'd appreciated just how much his life, so shapeless, so stained with sin, called out for redemption, so that some sort of sense could be made of it. If he could be received by God and His Son, why, both the past with the crime it contained, like a viper in the bosom *and* the future would undergo transformation. All his unsatisafactory seventeen, going on eighteen years could be viewed as leading to this encounter with a man of Christian faith, and after it – well, the road wound ahead to the eternity of joy beyond death, in which, he was relieved to find out, it was possible to believe. Like most young people in their later teens, and like most seamen of all ages, Rob had – these last ten months – thought about death a good deal.

In February and March the great storms which, coming from the fury of the sky, made a greater fury of the ocean, had turned into a sudden possibility (and therefore a reality) what had been hitherto only a realm of occasional nervous fears: Death had seemed all at once as near, if not nearer, than Europe or America. And Rob had not felt ready.

Filipino Pete was sitting next to Jerry. A smile sat lightly, hopefully on his melancholy, gold-yellow face. 'Rob, just hand over all the food you were going to give to Jerry to *me*,' he said, 'I'll wolf it down, I promise you!'

'Greedy guts!' said Rob. And obeying an impulse he rested his hand, with affection, on Pete's neck. How supple, how delicate, and how strong this seemed, what a sensitive conductor of mysterious energies! . . . Rob turned round and saw, from the passengers' section of the dining-room, Bill, his grey, protuberant eyes intent and shining upon the two of them. Colour came to Rob's cheeks – as if he'd been caught out in an indecency. What emotion could be discerned on Bill's face? Disapproval? Almost certainly! Jealousy? That's what it looked like! But why should that be the case?

Rob removed his hand and went about his business.

But when Bill spoke to him it was cheerily enough: 'Four thirty in my cabin still okay for you?' he inquired.

'Sure, sure!' said Rob, adding, 'I've got something I'd like to tell you, something I think you'll be glad to hear . . .'

He meant, of course, the vision of the kingfisher. On and off all day he rehearsed a description for Bill of this experience, though appropriate words predictably fled from him as the appointment came closer. It had been always thus. In class, or writing an essay, Rob had never been able to find the phrases he needed for saying what he felt. Unjustly some teachers had interpreted this as a sign of his not feeling very much.

But when 4.30 came round, to his surprise, an adequate vocabulary did not desert him; he was able to make vivid, at least for himself, the scene by the Fase the abrupt and beautiful flash of blue. It was Bill Bentley's response that Rob had not anticipated.

He was not impressed. He was not even very interested.

'And there I was thinking that you wanted to get out of sorrow. That you wanted me to help you do so!' His tone had a pained gravity about it.

'Oh, yes, Bill,' Rob gabbled, nervously, anxious not to say or do the wrong thing, 'I don't like being *in sorrow* at all. I need your help. Honest! But you were telling me yesterday about how,' he paused, being shy of mentioning the holy name, 'about how Jesus was the best friend we could ever have, and all. And I was thinking – well, I've had a sort of proof of the things He can do!'

'Excuse me,' said Bill, 'but I wonder if you've understood the *seriousness* of the situation, the consequences – yes, the consequences, Rob,' and he made the word sound peculiarly dreadful, 'of being *in sorrow*.' He let his gaze rest on Rob so firmly, so intensively, that Rob had the distinct feeling that the guy was seeing him not just with his eyes but with every bone, every stretch of skin upon his head. Bill was pleased to continue:

'The sight of a kingfisher' (and he pronounced the word with something very like scorn) 'may have been very pretty, but it's – it's – shall we say, hardly relevant to the business in hand.'

'Business, Bill?' No doubt Bill Bentley was right; there was a lot about being taken out of sorrow and 'saved' that he simply hadn't understood. But then all his life he'd been failing to understand things, hadn't he? The 'O' Level examiners, for instance, hadn't formed a very happy impression of his powers of understanding.

'*Business*, Rob!' repeated Bill, 'the most important business there is!'

Yes, he went on, the sight of a kingfisher (Bill was very fond of repetition of this kind; indeed had been encouraged to employ it during his training period with the evangelical organisation in Jackson) had very little to do with the facts that Rob obviously must now face. Indeed you could say it had *nothing whatever* to do with them. Didn't Rob understand that Jesus *alone* was his Saviour, that without Him there could be no eternal life? 'Let's get the whole thing straight, shall we? Jesus wants the friendship of one Rob Peters, yeah, wants it pretty badly, but if Rob Peters refuses to think about *his* part, *his* little bit, and babbles on a lot of guff about birds instead, what can He do, Rob, what can even the Son of God, the Son of Man, do?'

'I'm not sure I quite get you, Bill,' said Rob. No doubt of it: fear was coursing its way from head to loins, where it took uncomfortable repose.

'Thought you hadn't,' said Bill, shifting himself in his swivel-chair so that he was looking out of the porthole towards the ocean. (Where *were* the skyscraper office blocks, the rows of sleek business cars?) And when he swung himself round to confront Rob again, he showed a face without any smile. 'Thought you hadn't,' he repeated, and each syllable was heavy with menace. 'You see, Rob, there's always something within us that kicks against the kind of friendship Jesus wants of us. He doesn't just demand a *lot* you see, he demands *everything*. Everything, Rob – just let that word sink in.'

'But what exactly d'you mean by it?' Rob asked, doing his best to sit still, for in truth the fear now lodged in his crutch made him want to jump and jump about. 'Can't you explain it to me?' He might have been a child about to be left out of a treat.

He wondered whether Bill had ever displayed so stern an expression to those merry, smiling boys and girls in the photographs up there, so healthy in body and mind, so secure – out in Riverside Park, Jackson – in Jesus' fondness for them.

'We'll look at it this way, shall we? Yesterday afternoon we agreed, didn't we? that Jesus is the one Friend who can take unto Himself all a guy's sins. And someone *in sorrow* like yourself is in the best position of all to know what a wonderful thing that could be. *All* those bad actions, *all* those bad feelings, *all* those bad thoughts and words borne uncomplainingly – *uncomplainingly*, Rob – by One who lived

– and died too – for *your* sake! But it's no good for a guy, with this chance in front of him, to start shilly-shallying and beating about the bush with some funny tale of a kingfisher seen on a river-bank. A guy has got to get down to the nitty-gritty.'

'The nitty-gritty, Bill?'

'That's what I said. At this very minute – 4.52 p.m. – Jesus, like the buddy He is, is extending a hand to you, the hand of Friendship. But He also wants *you* to come to meet *Him*, and I kid you not, Rob, I kid you not. How can He be sure that you mean to be His friend unless he hears you repenting of your sins – sins in the past, and, in the present too.'

'I must . . . ' began Rob, miserably.

'I've just told you what you must do,' said Bill.

He's not the only bloke on this ship, thought Rob. I haven't *got* to be spending time with him, though he speaks as if I have. There's that young violin-maker from Cincinnati travelling to London (the world-centre of violin-making, and I never knew it!). There's that funny old guy from Savannah, Georgia, who keeps cracking corny jokes: 'Don't give me any more water, please. Rob! Shall I tell you what I have against water: It's very wet!' And then there were friends among the crew: Andy, his boss, who liked to ramble on affectionately and wistfully about his wife and two children back in Malaysia; João, the almost too handsome Brazilian *mestizo* in his mid-twenties who had more than once asked Rob to . . . And Pete, of course, lonely, appealing Pete with whom, from that time they'd all but bumped into each other in the corridor leading to the kitchens, he'd felt that strange sympathetic bond. But how on earth would he be able to avoid Bill for the remaining days of the crossing?

Bill had now got his Bible out. Apart from Religious Knowledge lessons, Rob could not remember having ever read a page of it, and certainly it played no part in the lives of his parents. Bill was giving him a smile of grim, if restrained, triumph. Like a conjuror discovering upon a member of his audience objects he knows perfectly well can be found there, he'd opened the Bible – as he suggested, by chance – at a passage of apparently peculiar applicancy to Rob and his situation. 'See here, Rob,' he said, 'you just can't get away from it. The Bible has turned of its own accord to that fine, vigorous work *The General Epistle of Jude*. Here we can read what is waiting there, reserved, for those who will not let God and His Son into their lives.

In an assured voice, that of someone who knows beyond doubting the truth behind his words, Bill read out:

'These are spots in your feasts of charity, when they feast with you, feeding themselves without fear: clouds they are without water, carried about of winds; trees whose fruit withereth, without fruit, twice dead, plucked up by the roots;

Raging waves of the sea, foaming out their own shame; wandering stars, to whom is reserved the blackness of darkness for ever.'

'The blackness of darkness for ever.' What could be the difference between that and "darkness of blackness", Rob wondered. But this quibble did nothing to stave off another, and stronger rush of fear.

'See here, too,' said Bill, 'you'll find this very interesting, Rob.' And he compelled Rob by tone and looks to follow him, as he read from the page:

'Behold the Lord cometh with ten thousands of his saints. To execute judgement upon all, and to convince all that are ungodly among them of their ungodly deeds which they have ungodly committed, and of all their hard speeches which ungodly sinners have spoken against Him.'

'Yeah, I think I'm beginning to see what you mean, Bill,' said Rob. Beyond any question his crime against Laurie Williams was an 'ungodly' deed.

'But we shouldn't leave the good apostle at *this* point,' said Bill, and Rob was reminded here of Dad, determined that he hear some extra proof of his stupidity, hopelessness, unworthiness. Bill's finger posed dramatically above the page seemed like a part of the Bible itself, a tumour arising from the text.

'In the next verse we find some very important words about *men crept in unawares*,' said Bill, obviously enjoying his delay of the reading, 'now, it's we ourselves who are unaware of these guys, these intruders; the fellows themselves like as not,' and he gave a grim but bland smile, know the devil's work they're doing.' Hey, what *is* all this about, Rob asked himself; it's almost as if he's speaking about people on board the *Egon Ludendorff*. 'Anyway,' said Bill, 'let's press on:

'*For there are certain men crept in unawares who were before of old ordained to this condemnation, ungodly men, turning the grace of our God into lasciviousness and denying the only Lord God, and our Lord Jesus Christ.*'

'Powerful words, eh, Rob?' Rob nodded, helplessly, 'And true ones, true ones. Attend to the *next* verses, Rob!' As if I've any choice in the matter, said Rob to himself: Bill had him in an aural trap. Both the happy young Americans and the white-robed Jesus appeared to be staring down at him in determination that he should endure the whole horrible reading:

'*I will therefore put you in remembrance, though ye once knew this, how that the Lord, having saved the people out of the land of Egypt, afterward destroyed them that believed not.*

'*And the angels which kept not their first estate, but left their own habitation, he hath received in everlasting chains under darkness unto the judgement of the great day.*

'*Even as Sodom and Gomorrha, and the cities about them in like manner, giving the selves over to fornication, and going after strange flesh, are set forth for an example, suffering the vengeance of eternal fire.*

'*Likewise also, these filthy dreamers defile the flesh, despise dominion, and speak evil of dignities . . .*'

Bill raised his head very slowly after his proud delivery of these sentences – raised it in the manner of his that has become so famous since. Why is there all this pleasure in destruction, thought Rob, and then he had a swift image of himself at his foulest and – yes, perhaps destruction *was* what such behaviour merited. It must truly be abominable to God.

'Be honest with me, Rob, don't these words strike home?'

Why at that moment did Rob have a vision of Pete's supple

young neck? why could he feel his hand upon it? . . . But Bill was continuing – with a kind of smooth fervour: 'Can you, under God, look me in the face and say that what I've been reading *doesn't* apply to you, yes, to no one *more* than you, Rob? Can you truthfully declare that you haven't been one of those *filthy dreamers* who have *defiled the flesh* and spoken *evil of dignities*? Rob, I charge you – look me in the face.'

Rob's mouth was quite empty of saliva, and his pulse was racing so, so fast. Desperate was his desire to bolt out of the room, beyond the porthole of which he could almost fancy the crackling flames of eternal fire, the fire promised in the Book itself for blokes such as him. But of course he didn't bolt. Even in Foswich, however bolshy he'd seemed, he'd usually done what he was told. And so he lifted up his head to meet the eyes of those of his agent of salvation. And? – and he did not like what he saw there. Too late he understood that, far from having found a new friend who could repair his treatment of a dear former one, he'd met yet another person who refused to accept him as he was. But at the same time, even while thinking these things and acknowledging Bill's power, he appreciated that there was – curiously, and as yet indefinably – something of himself in Bill Bentley. That something he was afraid of.

'*Why*, I'm wondering,' Bill was going on, 'was I moved to read from that particular epistle? *Why?*'

' 'Cause there's a great deal of truth in what you've said?' opined Rob.

'Not in what *I've* said, Rob, but in what *God* has said in His Book!'

'Well, in what God says then,' Rob felt – and sounded – like a rebuked child.

'Wouldn't you agree, Rob, that a lot of the things that you've done in your life must be very displeasing to Jesus – horrible things, vicious things, disgusting and dirty things. If you want a friendship with Him, hadn't you better start heartily and manfully repenting at once?'

'Suppose so, yeah!' Rob conceded mumbling.

'And how do you think you can go about this repentence?'

(Anything to be out of this room. Anything to be out of

this *fucking* room!) 'Dunno, Bill!'

Rob knew that he would never leave the cabin till Bill Bentley had granted him permission to do so.

'By confessing to Jesus in a full but humble voice all those foul thoughts and deeds of your past, all that impurity and ungodliness that make you, as yet, so unfit for His company. And by saying, after you've told all, Rob, *all*: I am sorry, my Jesus, I am sorry. And because I do repent me of my manifold sins, please will you take me unto yourself and be my Friend?' And Bill re-applied a smile to his face, while Rob hung his head in diffidence and reluctance and shame.

There was a decided impatience, and a hint too of dark eagerness in the next sentences that the evangelist spoke, breaking the silence that had filled the room and made the Atlantic audible again. 'Rob, don't you think we should make a beginning *now*!'

For the slightly coarse beauty of the lad in front of him, staring down now so wretchedly at the floor, was by no means lost on him. Yeah, what a heart-jerking attraction Rob could be at a Revivalist meeting in, say, his favourite Riverside Park, Jackson, Mississippi.

In a rather gentler voice – for he mustn't frighten his latest find away – Bill said: 'Jesus doesn't much care for ditherers, you know. But a humble and a contrite heart will He not despise.'

Rob was thinking: 'What would Laurie Williams say if he could see me here now. Would he be impressed? I'm sorry he never wrote to me, but, of course, I deserved his silence. Just as I seem to have deserved everlasting darkness ever since.

CHAPTER TWO: LAURIE

Laurie Williams was born in Hull, where both sides of his family had lived for many generations. His father, following his own father, was a merchant seaman, who, however, by diligence and talent, had made his way up to the position of Second Engineer. There is something Hanseatic about Hull – those old grand mercantile buildings; those prospects of a bleak, muddy North Sea estuary – and the ships for which Roy Williams worked were all bound for ports implicit in their place of departure: Gothenburg, Copenhagen, Kiel, Lübeck, Gdansk, Riga, Leningrad. Laurie, the eldest of three sons (his younger brothers were twins) twice accompanied his father on voyages, both times to Copenhagen. The sight of that city's greeny-gold copper roofs, rising above a flatness of water and rocks, became for him synonymous with the word 'adventure'.

On the second of those voyages Roy Williams, a reserved, serious man, told his son that he'd decided to retire from a sea-faring life. His cousin, Reg, knowing his long passion for local history, for rooting around in ancient records, thought he could help him to a part-time job in Tanbury Town Hall, Oxfordshire. Certainly such a job would suit him. Laurie would remember that article he'd had published in the *East Yorkshireman*, the product of six months' research, on sea-shanties and the press-gang.

So, a year later, move the Williams family did. Laurie was

within a few weeks of his eleventh birthday. That summer he found the Oxfordshire countryside strangely lush after the wind-beset wolds of the East Riding of Yorkshire and the Humber mudflats that northwards turned into gaunt headlands of white chalk. The golden stone of so many of the older buildings, both in Tanbury and its neighbourhood, was surprising. It suggested a centuries-long comfort, at once perplexing and seductive. Laurie decided he liked his new surroundings better than those he'd left. Weren't they more suitable for someone of his temperament? Sometimes, though, he'd dream of walking down Hull's Land-of-Green-Ginger, or of bicycling to Beverley with its mighty Minster towering above rows of huddled houses, or of standing by the Willoughby Foreshore gazing at the boats on the chilly water. But the dreams got less and less frequent.

Tanbury had rejected a plan to become a London overspill town, but had accepted the installation of several subsidised light industries, and with these had arrived a fair number of immigrants from London. With these racy, nimble-tongued newcomers Laurie, as another outsider, was apt to be classified by the indigenous young of the town, yet, in fact, their sophistication, their frank, self-seeking hedonism often bewildered him. Laurie had to win for himself a place among both these Tanbury communities, for his was not a nature that thrived on isolation, and win it he did through a conscientious amiability.

Home, though, was not what it had been in Hull. Dad *seemed* contented enough in a circumscribed sort of way, pottering about local museums or Civil War battle-fields, and having an occasional beer with his cousin, though he once admitted missing acutely his times at sea. Mum, however, uninhibitedly pined for the neighbourliness of the North. Not that she liked the other people on the Meadowborough Estate. They were all very common, and often talked of things she preferred not to hear mentioned.

Laurie went to Tanbury Grammar School. He was not a very academic pupil but always well-meaning and eager to please. Several teachers mimicked his East Yorkshire accent which they found uncouth, but his persistent affability, and the inevitable weakening of the accent itself, eventually put a stop to all that. One master, though, was kind to him from the very first: Jonathan West, Head of Art Department. Laurie began to look forward to every lesson with him. Art became his favourite subject and that at which he was best; he became ingenious at thinking of ways of showing his appreciation of Mr West and his kindness, and even tried (much to the amusement of his brothers, Mick and Dale) to emulate the older man's way of talking.

Jonathan West lived with his wife – who was curiously similar to him in looks and manner, white-haired, apple-cheeked, and careful of speech – in a small cottage in nearby Foxton, a little village almost entirely thatched and built in glowing honey-coloured stone. By the time he was fifteen, Laurie – sometimes accompanied by a friend, sometimes alone – would often cycle out there, and the old boy would take him to much loved sketching-places of his own: a descending sequence of lilied ponds in the landscaped grounds of Foxton Manor; a folly built in the 18th-century to house a hermit and now standing above fields full of sheep; an aged bat-haunted stone barn that adjoined the churchyard.

'If you love such places as I can tell you do,' Jonathan West would say to the boy who'd just left a council-house vibrating with the sounds of Gerry and The Pacemakers, The Tremoloes, and Manfred Mann, 'you'll find you belong to a very long and a very wonderful English tradition.' The art master's face looked long and wonderful to Laurie (wonderful because of the conviction visible upon it and its serenity). 'We can look together at the engravings of Thomas Bewick and the paintings of the Norwich School; we can examine the whole marvellous body of Samuel Palmer's work, where bushes and trees can seem like angels; we can explore the Pre-Raphaelites who restored a sense of religion – in its wider, deeper sense – to English art and who have shown us the Great Mystery behind the visible world. And when we move to this century, why,' and the old boy's voice would crack with the pressure of enthusiasm, 'why, there have been – and still are – so *many* working under the inspiration of such things as this!' And here he'd gesture, with a strong, weather-chapped hand, to, say, a lily-padded pool, and the cascade that fell into it, and the almost motionless mandarin ducks upon its surface. 'You won't find anything to beat the English here. There are the Nash brothers (both Paul and John are bright stars in my firmament), and there are the engravings and paintings of Reynolds Stone, Bewick's undisputed successor. All are challenges to the grossness, the greedy, cruel commercialism of our age.'

After such words the very bike-ride back to the Estate – with sulphur-coloured street-lamps breaking upon a sweep of darkening sheep-cropped green – seemed charged with wonder.

One day – Laurie was then in the Sixth Form – Jonathan West took him and a select band of others to Oxford, in particular to the Ashmolean Museum to look at the Pre-Raphaelites. One painting in particular made an enormous impression upon him: Arthur Hughes' *Home From Sea*. A boy in sailor's uniform, had flung himself down upon a grave in a country-churchyard, a girl (one presumed, his elder sister) at his side. The boy made Laurie think of his own ancestors when young, with both his maternal and paternal families having been sea-goers. But it was the whole tenderly rendered context of the boy that made the greatest appeal to him; the sympathy of stone and moss that enhanced the moving plight depicted. And somehow the girl, in her gentle compassionate strength, suggested, as little in art had yet done, the unique comfort that the feminine, the female could give.

When Jonathan West asked Laurie: 'What do you want to do with your life? You *must* have given the matter thought!' his response was ready and confidently given: 'Why, to become an art-master like yourself!' And Jonathan West's rugged, lined face had smiled in gratitude, and Lorna (Mrs West) had pressed upon him a large carrier-bag full of aromatic pears.

Laurie got into the university of his choice, without much difficulty; it was one of the then new ones, built just outside an old cathedral city in East Anglia. Here he would study

Fine Arts, with History of Art. During the summer before he took up his place, he found his interest in the Pre-Raphaelites, above all other artists, strengthening. He learned with delight that they had been greatly beloved by one of the chief figures in his, and his friends', private pantheon; Stuart Sutcliffe, the fifth Beatle, the lost and late one whose very name could start an impassioned brawl in a Liverpool pub. Those hot August and September days of waiting for university to begin were heavy with longings to savour the fuller beauty omnipresent in the world, to effect an entry into the glories of the flesh, a surrender to sensations and a cultivation of awareness more complex than life in either Hull or Tanbury had enabled.

At university surprises awaited Laurie. All were agreeable.

First, almost all those fellow-students with whom he had to associate turned out to admire the Pre-Raphaelites as much as he did. And not just their paintings but their whole attitude to life: their unrepentent sensuality; their hostility to the mechanical and the materialistic; their belief in play; their quest for Mysteries. Laurie felt as though he'd arrived at just the right time in the midst of a wonderful party. Also – amazingly – that he was exactly the kind of guest most in demand at it. For all his recent hunger for sensual experience he'd always imagined that he'd have a difficult time drawing girls to him. Those of Meadowborough Estate, Tanbury, had so very definitely preferred his brawnier, bouncier brothers.

But here it seemed he had precisely the appeal that was most in vogue, beginning with his looks: wavy chestnut-brown hair that soon grew long and flowing, hazel eyes and a willowy body. Nor did it matter socially, as he had feared, that he came from a virtually working-class background, with parents who'd not had much in the way of formal education. For these college girls – from prosperous bourgeois homes – Laurie's provenance only added to his attractions. They even purported to envy him it; they themselves would use what they fondly imagined were working-class expressions, would ask if tea was 'mashed' yet, and say 'Ta!' and 'Coo-hoo!'

It was these girls, of course, who made of this time the

wonderful party it was. Around they floated in swishing, imaginatively patterned, diaphanous dresses, such as Millais or Rossetti or Arthur Hughes themselves would have delighted in. They wore their hair streaming and loose, yet often decked Naiad-style with wild flowers or deftly twisted leaves, or else fetchingly part-covered with bright handkerchiefs. At the least opportunity they'd kick off even their hand-painted sabots to go barefoot. Amanda and Kate, Lucy and Emma, they seemed to have been created for his delectation. They liked pastoral games with a heady innocence to them, Grandmother's Footsteps, The Farmer in his Den, while who could resist on a May morning, forming a double line somewhere on the college campus for: 'Here We Come Gathering Nuts-in-May.'?

When sex came, which, again to Laurie's surprise, it did with some frequency, it more often than not had just that dewy, rapturous quality he'd saluted in the paintings that day in the Ashmolean Museum. It was April Love – and more, and Laurie was often to look back to his college love-makings rather as Adam, after the Expulsion, must have done to the forfeited bowers of Eden. Amanda and Kate, Lucy and Emma were at once so giving and so understanding, so ready in body and so light of heart. Nor was there any need for secrecy; you were expected not only to be, but to present yourself publicly as, a generous lover.

For the lecturers were as much part of this party as the students, or so it seemed. Laurie, before going up to university, had envisaged his future teachers as more intimidating versions of Jonathan West. But those in the Arts and General Humanities Departments were young, audacious, and determined to flout conventions as publicly as possible. Not only did they actively encourage you to go to bed with girls, they shared other prevailing views: that the way into the heart of mysteries could be eased by drugs, that there was Power in Play.

A young lecturer used to go with Laurie to buy the choicest marijuana, and it was he too who gave that famous fancy-dress ball with himself dressed as a fried egg, and who incited Laurie and Amanda to blow bubbles from a child's bubble-mixture tub *within* the premises of the local *Barclays Bank*. The Head of the Faculty got to hear about this escapade and interestedly questioned Laurie about it during a seminar. How, he asked, had the cashiers looked as the bubbles floated towards them? What had the reaction of the other customers been? Could a soap-bubble be seen as the one truly perfect work of art? Such discussions lightened this art-historian's work-load a great deal and enabled him to get on pretty undisturbedly with his book on Constable – which was to sell very well, and procure for him, a few years later, a $60,000 per annum professorship at an American university. When you mentioned examinations to him, the man would peal with laughter, and when he did set work would do so by means of a little flower-bordered notice pinned to the Faculty advertisement-board. It was all very free and benign, and what a drab place home came to seem to Laurie. As did indeed the entire world beyond the campus precincts.

Jonathan West, on the occasional visits that Laurie paid him in the vacations, appeared irritatingly unimpressed by his former pupil's accounts of university liberty and libertarianism. 'It doesn't seem to me,' he'd say, as the two of them walked round the Wests' well-stocked, well-kept garden, all walled round in golden dry-stone, 'that you're looking for what is *good* very seriously. Whatever can be said for or against me and my masters, we never ceased to attend to the question of goodness; where it could be found, where it could be practised.' Here perhaps he would root up a vegetable and begin very gently to remove any slugs adhering to it, touching the glistening, jelly-like beings with a courtesy of the fingers. 'I'm glad you like the girls,' he said, 'but don't like too many. That's a way of not really liking them at all.'

I don't know that I want to hear much more of this cabbage-patch wisdom, thought Laurie. Maybe Jonathan West was part too, when all was said and done, of that vast, indeed infinite-seeming, outer world of unenlightenment and corruption; which should be rejected outright.

Unfortunately it could not be. Inexorably did it present itself, with a cruel certainty. When it came to Laurie's finals, the Head of the Faculty forgot about soap bubbles and presided over his being given a third-class degree. He did, however, as if to dismiss Laurie with a few strokes of the pen, write a reference sufficiently complimentary to ensure his acceptance on a teachers' training course.

And so to his first job, at a South London comprehensive. Laurie could feel little enthusiasm for beginning it. He felt abandoned, jettisoned upon an anonymous, hostile shore, while his mentors of a year ago were smoking grass and discussing sexual liberation with students whose very names were unknown to him. This realisation was rather like resignation – on a long walk from which there can be no turning-back – to the punitive chill of an incessant wind.

When, four years after he'd left the classroom, Laurie entered it again, he couldn't get over how little the mores of both pupils and teachers had changed. Teenagers still shuffled or, worse, hurled themselves into classes; most of them, just as before, regarded art lessons as free periods, of no conceivable relevance to the rest of their lives. Girls still giggled lasciviously, and some of them raised skirts provocatively at the teacher; boys still shoved and swore, made farting noises and had mock-fights in which they'd tear up one another's sheets of drawing-paper. As for the staff, well, there was no Jonathan West among them. After college lecturers they seemed such a stuffy, dour lot. Not one of them would have come to a party dressed as a fried egg!

Some of them said that a return to good old-fashioned notions of self-discipline was what was wanted, and, Mr Williams, for Pete's sake can you keep your bloody classes *quiet*.

True, there were certain sixth-formers, boys for the most part, who responded to Laurie for being so much like themselves. To them Laurie could, and did, talk about Rossetti and Holman Hunt, discuss blends of hash and explore such mental possibilities as the location of the whole solar system within one's own skull. But even these boys couldn't compensate for the exhausting dreariness of his daily round. Luckily Laurie had an escape-route planned.

Those years constituted what was coming to be known as

the Second Golden Age of Children's Books; to the first, in the late Victorian era, members and disciples of the Pre-Raphaelites had contributed (his own Arthur Hughes, for one). Laurie's best grades at college had been earned with bright-coloured book-jacket designs, and now he decided that, with his girl-friend, Isobel, he would create children's picture-books that would bring him a releasing income and also a reputation. After all, Laurie argued, in every London bookshop you went into these days, you'd find books of sumptuous double-page spreads, ostensibly for the young. Well Isobel's story would be as amusing, and his own art-work as luxuriant, as any on the market.

Their idea was surely an engaging one. Laurie had told Isobel about many Tanbury characters (he could now, unlike in his university days, feel occasional stabs of nostalgia for Tanbury and the raw untidy pleasantness of the Meadowborough Estate), and one of these had taken her fancy: Father Lalland, a kindly, bumbling old Anglo-Catholic priest whose great interest was his chickens, particularly a curious breed he called 'the Baggy-Trousered kind'. Talk of him prompted Isobel to remember an old children's rhyme:

> 'I had a hen,
> And she laid such eggs,
> I made her trousers
> For her legs.'

And so *The Extraordinary Walk* came about; a boy and his godfather, a fat old clergyman, took a trouser-wearing hen through the streets of London. Whenever this hen clucked, something marvellous happened: slabs of meat in a butcher's shop became real animals again; Japanese figures standing in an antique-shop window sprang to life, and so on. Laurie's spreads — splash upon splash of brilliant colour matched the inventiveness of Isobel's story. All their friends exclaimed over the achievement — Fanny Datchett, for instance, thought it little short of genius and Lettie Shawcross's opinion was that the Tate Gallery ought to make an offer for the originals. Greatly encouraged Laurie and Isobel sent their book 'out'.

If Laurie and Isobel had not appreciated, when they first sent their book on its way, that difficult, financial times were upon the country and undermining the publishing industry, after their eighth letter of rejection they could hardly fail to do so. Recession – the word, the concept, as well as the economic reality – spread through England like winter fog rolling up the Thames valley towards Tanbury.

When Isobel, after this last letter, markedly less civil than its predecessors, said: 'Honestly, sweetie, I don't really see any point in sending out *The Extraordinary Walk* any more, do you?' Laurie, sadly but unequivocally, agreed with her. Shortly afterwards Isobel left him for a guy she'd already been seeing quite a bit of, someone a year younger than himself, who'd made a very promising start in commodity-broking. The day after her departure Laurie was called in by the Headmaster of his school. 'Much as I like and respect you,' that harrassed man said, 'I think you'd be well-advised to look round for another post. No hurry, of course; take your time over it, take your time! But you've got a bit of a reputation here, you know – poor disciplinarian, a trifle too free and easy generally – and reputations stick, more's the pity! Somewhere new you can put things behind you!'

Somewhere new was Foswich. Laurie went for his interview at St John's School on a warm June day. As afternoon declined into evening, so was the Forest flooded with an incandescent green light. Glade after glade resembled a chapel for the leaf-captured sun. Laurie could never afterwards – in all the dull, dull years that followed – altogether forget this first response of his to the place. Nevertheless the years *were* dull.

At first Laurie tried to reform his attitude to his job. Though it was not in his nature to deal with people formally, he made himself a little more aloof, a little more magisterial than he'd been in Walworth, and consequently order in his classes considerably improved. He read up art history and criticism with a limited success, and tried to broaden his skills so that – for instance – he could teach puppet-making and rudimentary fabric-design. But it was all a little like a farmer holding back a falling hay-rick. The truth was, as he would confess to his old friends, that his heart wasn't in his work, but where could he go to, what could he possibly do instead? There was scant mobility now in the teaching profession, and Laurie felt that the sad history of *The Extraordinary Walk* demonstrated his lack of serviceable talents to lead him away from it.

In Foswich he lived in a rented flat (two rooms, plus kitchen and bathroom), the first storey of a Victorian villa near both the flintstone Parish Church and the County Library. More and more did Laurie spend his leisure-time alone. Amanda and Kate and Lucy and Emma and their friends were far less interested in an entrenched and disenchanted young schoolmaster than they had been in a bashful boy from a Tanbury housing-estate. Anyway the majority of these girls had taken their tresses and their long trailing skirts to offices in publishing-houses or media organisations. They tended to earn high salaries. Laurie's affairs grew sparser and more fragmentary; the days of making love in rich meadows seemed gone, long gone. Yet Foswich was surrounded by a fecund countryside, erupting to the south in the density of the Forest, which should surely have been a landscape for sensual satisfaction. Instead it became the background for increasing despondency. Many evenings he'd just install himself in front of the television, and soon he came to measure his week by its comedy programmes. At weekends, and during the school holidays, he went to Tanbury with a regularity that surprised him.

In fact home now was a far more melancholy place than that he'd known even in boyhood. Dad, retired from the Town Hall and deprived by death of the companionship of his cousin, tended to sit hour after hour motionless in his winged armchair with a far-away expression on his face. Was he seeing conflicts between Roundheads and Cavaliers such as formed his favourite reading? Or was he back upon the seas – hazarding storms in the Skaggerak; watching Elsinore Castle raise itself above the low Danish coast; scanning the wooded Swedish skerries as they presented themselves across the cold vistas of the Baltic. He never let on.

Mum began to suffer from a series of troubling swellings,

beginning in her armpits. They'd puff up, to preoccupy her all day long, then subside as suddenly as they'd come. 'The things I think of!' Mum'd say, 'There was I imagining I'd . . .' She could never finish the sentence. 'But look now. Flat as a pancake.' But for only a while. Up they came again. She refused to visit the doctor. 'I've never been one to take myself to a surgery with every little ache and pain I've had,' she'd say. 'The troubles I've put up with, and have never said owt about: they'd fill a book!'

Dale and Mick mooched about the house. Collecting the dole they could find no congenial jobs, nor even the prospect of one. Dale wondered if they ought to go to 'Aussie'; Mick said he'd be fucked if he'd go 'down under', just to find employment when you could make do with what the Social Security offered . . . Laurie told himself that his family needed him. Really, of course, it was he who needed them.

He started paying regular visits to Jonathan West in Foxton again. His former teacher was kind enough never to comment on, or even to allude to, the infrequency of his appearances earlier. Back they went to familiar sites, those that had once been like doorways into more vivid worlds, telling of what lay beneath self, what 'inscaped' the visible world. Once more that honey-coloured folly built for a tame hermit loomed above a sheep-grazed hillside; once more a lily-padded monastery pond was tranquilly busy with gleaming, peaceable-seeming ducks. One afternoon – a sunny one in October, pungent with the smell of wood-smoke and of damp fallen leaves – Jonathan West surprised Laurie by asking (his gentle voice cutting into the equally gentle air). 'Why are you so listless, son? Aren't you happy in your life?'

Laurie, in reply, took himself by something like surprise: 'How could I be?' he heard himself cry out. 'How could anyone in my position be?' I don't even see how *you've* been able to stand it all these years. Just an art-teacher! Just someone who gives the kids a break – allows them to chatter to their hearts' content, and splash paint about – so they can return, with a bit of steam let off, to the lessons that count. Those that'll prepare them for the *real* world. Which won't employ half of them, just as it isn't employing Mick and Dale.'

It was hard to make out his old art teacher's response to these bitter words. Wise head bowed, he merely paced on up the path that wound through the chestnut woods. 'How have you done it, Jonathan – all these years! Stuck in Tanbury Grammar School yet always so serene. Is it because you're happily married? Is it because you've been able to go on painting where talentless people like me haven't. Or is it some inner faith that's kept you? When I think of my expectations . . .'

'Perhaps,' said Jonathan West, when given a pause by his normally so mild-mannered ex-pupil, 'perhaps it's these expectations which have been wrong. A wise old English man named Sidney Smith said you should take "short views of life – not further than dinner or tea". He also said – he too was trying to cheer up a young friend suffering from low spirits: "Don't expect too much from human life – a sorry business at the best." '

'But what a sad, dreary way of approaching things!' exclaimed Laurie despite himself.

Jonathan West was looking at him quizzically, those brow-overhung dark eyes bright in his craggy, weather-beaten face. 'Maybe, maybe,' he said, 'but I believe that if you follow Sidney's advice and renounce the kind of expectations you've been having, then you'll discover that life *can* present wonderful things to you after all.'

'Such as?' Predictably Laurie felt more tired and more depressed *after* his outburst than before it.

'Such as friendship with a pupil perhaps,' said Jonathan West, wryly. And Laurie was humbled into silence.

In fact personal interest in his pupils – such as Jonathan West had shown him – had never altogether deserted Laurie, even at his most dispirited. Indeed now, two or three years after his arrival in Foswich, this interest was beginning to intensify or, perhaps more accurately, to change into something different. Various boys or girls would arouse his curiosity; he would be filled with longing to have them as companions, interacting, caring ones, who'd let him into the world of their intimacies and secrets. Was it that he was seeking in these pupils – ten, twelve, fourteen years younger than himself – qualities which he felt had gone out of his own life forever? Not, of course, that he consciously chose Anna Blakeney, William Percival, Judith Atkinson, Rob Peters. Rather these seemed, mysteriously and magnetically, to *occur*, to present themselves as challengers of his ennui, as possible restorers of his shredded hopes and shattered dreams.

But, after this October afternoon with Jonathan West, Laurie did acknowledge to himself his need, his quest. This strengthened his resolution where these possible friendships were concerned. At that particular time it was Judith Atkinson who was his lode-star . . .

Of the four pupils mentioned Rob Peters was surely the most unexpected choice, the least explicable. Laurie had seen him about the school for a long while before his interest in him began – mucking about with a bunch of lads tediously like bunches of lads everywhere, with their slouching walks, their cocky little vanities, their ribaldry, their almost stupefying indolence, their ever-ready mockery. Just such had 'twins' been! But even before Rob Peters had invaded Laurie's imagination, and – yes! unwittingly entered his heart – he had noticed some things about him which rendered him sympathetic and appealing.

First, Laurie was struck by the number of occasions, often in the midst of drollerie with his mates, when Rob would become suddenly abstracted. His intense brown eyes would cloud over, as if some poignant or difficult truth had forced its way up from within. Then, in those Fifth Form classes which Laurie taught, Rob was, he observed, though far from diligent or talented, never, even in look or gesture, insolent, as so many, many others were. And from time to time he caught him looking at him as if trying to puzzle out just what sort of bloke his art-teacher could be. When the boy spoke, it was invariably in a light, amiable tone, different from that which Laurie had heard in the school grounds. Lastly Laurie appreciated that Rob had a particular regard for living things. Whenever it came to making studies of plants or zoological specimens (snails, slugs, beetles, caterpillars) – though by no means competent in draughtsmanship – he would approach his subjects with a gentle reverence; he would then proceed to examine them exceedingly carefully, being, in truth, far more attentive, to detail than Laurie himself – for whom Nature tended to be a beautiful and often anodyne tapestry.

'That Rob Peters is rather an interesting sort of lad, isn't he?' Laurie remarked as casually as he could manage to a senior colleague.

'Not quite the word I'd use for him,' said the latter (his name was Dai Griffiths, and he was the head of the Physics Department). 'He's a sullen young bastard, if you want my opinion. And he's got a damn mean temper too.'

'Really!' Laurie's surprise was genuine, and therefore the interrogative in his voice sounded more strongly and shrilly than he'd intended.

Dai Griffiths gave him a kindly smile. 'You're not going to turn into a lame-duck collector, are you, Laurie? It's one of our occupational hazards and, believe you me, it's one well-worth guarding against. I'll grant you that Rob Peters is as good a candidate in the lame-duck stakes as any, so you'd better beware. He's got a bullying sot for a father, a weak, prissy mother, and a brother and sister far cleverer than himself. So I should be *sorry* for him, you're saying.' Laurie had not, in fact, said anything. 'Well, maybe I should, but there's something about him that I can't care for and never have done: you can't trust him. When he was in the junior forms, he used to have what were once called "paddies", and hysterical, vicious little exhibitions they were too. I expect he's grown out of *those*, but he won't have changed all that much, mark my words.'

Surely it was only to be expected that Dai Griffiths had the opposite effect on Laurie to that he'd tried for. Laurie could feel, rising from the very centre of his being, a desire to become friendly with this apparently difficult boy, which coursed through every artery of his body. Someone had once told him that he brought out the best in others. Well he, Laurie Williams, would now show all Foswich that Rob

Peters was amiable, kind, interesting, dependable and, even, talented. So Laurie began to devise plans of how best to establish personal contact with the boy, and once you've started laying plans, then a significant meeting is bound to occur. Not that Laurie could have anticipated its nature.

On the morning of that May Saturday the telephone rang in the communal hall of the terraced house in which Laurie lived. Laurie, not expecting a call from anyone, was surprised on picking up the receiver to hear his Mum on the other end of the line. She was not difficult to make out, for as always she shouted – rather as if she were trying to pitch her voice so it could reach Essex from Oxfordshire. The line emphasized her East Riding accent; it made Laurie think of the sharp tangy winds and the walks along the Foreshore of his boyhood . . . She had some news, not to worry, Laurie, but she'd taken herself along to Dr Cardew after all. Those swellings had been getting worse, you see, and there were others . . . well, no point in going into the whole wretched business. She had the greatest confidence in Dr Cardew, always had had. He'd fixed an appointment for her with a specialist in the Radcliffe Infirmary in Oxford. Dad would go with her; her complaint seemed to have roused him at last from his dreams about the seventeenth century and the buzzing of bees in his bonnet about English folklore, though the Lord knew how long his interest in her would last. Not to worry, Laurie love, she repeated. At first she hadn't been going to tell him anything, then she'd thought that it would be unfair *not* to inform him of the visit to the hospital; he'd always been such an affectionate son; out of the family the only one who'd persistently been on to her to have a proper medical opinion of her troubles. Unlike his Dad who wouldn't have noticed had she swollen up to three times her usual size. 'Twins' didn't know about the trip to the Radcliffe Infirmary; surely they had enough on their plate thinking about their job-situations.

No good Mum telling Laurie not to worry. Anxiety possessed him the moment he put down the receiver. He found himself unable to eat his usual snack lunch, unable too to settle down to any occupation, however trivial. He went for a short walk to the post-office, and then returned to pace the poky flat, arguing nervously with himself. Hundreds, no, thousands of women up and down the country were probably suffering from swellings similar to – if not worse than – Mum's. Women were far more prone to psychosomatic illnesses than men; medical evidence had conclusively established that. Nevertheless, Laurie's disquiet refused to die down. Most unusually he took up a book, for preparation for a Sixth Form lesson; it was one on Rembrandt, and, of course, it fell open at that wonderful, loving portrait of the artist's aged mother. Please God, Laurie found himself praying, let her live to be as old as that. And he tried – with considerable difficulty – to make a mental image of Mum (54) as octogenarian.

Realising now that he was quite incapable of getting on with anything, and refusing seriously to contemplate catching the next train to London and thence to Tanbury, Laurie decided to go out again – for a proper walk this time. He would take the path along the Fase towards the Forest.

In the Foswich gardens all the pear and plum and cherry blossoms were out; in the meadows by the river there'd been a positive snowfall of hawthorn bloom, and here and there among the long, sweet, motionless grasses were proud and fragrant cowslips. Laurie did not believe with Browning's Pippa, as she walked through *her* fine day, that 'God's in His Heaven, All's right with the world', but he did feel soothed by the profusion all about him and reflected that a world that produced it could sustain him when hard times came. Which, pray to God, they would not do right now! If only, though, he had some companion with whom to share both his worries and his response to the beauty of the May afternoon.

Laurie paused at the foot of the Japanese-style woodenbridge. And almost simultaneously he saw, winging between the river's rushes and the opposite bank, a bird, a kingfisher, a flash of blue, and – apparently transfixed upon the crest of the bridge – the boy of his thoughts and dreams. So much was boy concentrating on bird that he seemed almost to *be* the brilliant feathered body which, alighting at the fishing-perch, could also have been an emanation from inside his head.

The kingfisher folded blackish wings over his lucent blue, and the moment passed. Or rather it dissolved its magic into those moments that perforce followed it – to spread back out into comprehensively measurable Time.

Eyes of master and pupil met.

Laurie walked up the rise of the bridge. 'Hullo, Rob,' he said, and in this context the Christian name had a strange, exciting intimacy about it, 'well, wasn't that quite a sight!'

Rob said: 'Oh, hi, Mr Williams. D'you realise how fantastically lucky we've just been? Kingfishers are about Britain's most elusive birds.'

Laurie thought: 'He's got that from a book!' But everything else was genuine – the ecstasy still in his voice and eyes, even in his shallow breathings. Despite the troubling news he'd received that day, Laurie could feel happiness re-entering his life.

CHAPTER THREE: ROB

The words Bill had quoted to him from the Bible echoed in Rob's head as he took up his usual position on the bridge-deck:

'Raging waves of the sea, foaming out their own shame; wandering stars, to whom is reserved the blackness of darkness for ever.'

But the waves of the sea were not raging now, not at all. Four days had gone by since his first visit to Cabin Number Five; three of these had been dominated by his confessions. Inside there was turmoil; outside calm continued to reign. Though the breaking of white-capped tips of the vast oceanic depths upon the ship's side was in rhythmic accord with a terrible interior recital . . .

'What a place!' said a quiet, familiar voice at his side, 'well, it isn't a place, is it? It's nowhere, it's nothing!'

It was, of course, Pete. He must have caught sight of Rob while making his own nightly promenade of the decks. Rob didn't know whether to be pleased at the Filipino boy's presence or not. On the one hand any distraction from his so frightening thoughts was to be welcomed; on the other, not following them through might lead to that dismissal of his need for salvation, of the offers being made him by God and His open-armed Son, of which, said the Bible, Hell was the consequence.

'Do *you* like it?' Peter was now positioning himself beside Rob, leaning against the salt-wet rails, with his head half-turned. Once again a lighted cigarette dangled between his fingers, its tip a tiny travelling beacon bound for the black line of the nocturnal horizon.

'Like it? Like what?' said Rob, pulling himself out of his speculations as best he could, and thinking: No, I'm *not* sorry Pete is here, with me.

'This!' answered Pete, 'the Atlantic!'

Rob shrugged his shoulders. Perhaps he didn't like it! After all what could be likeable about an enormous ocean? But it had become a part of his life (as last year he'd so hoped it would be), and liking was beside the point. It had given him release, freedom, and, as it would seem, the opportunity to be saved . . .

Pete was longing for conversation – that much was clear from his moon-washed face, sad, round, full-mouthed, with a very broad, very flat nose, and eyes that appeared not to have been inset but laid in their dark brightness between the strong bones. Rob said: 'I've got used to it, by now, I suppose. Funny, but the sea seems more strange when it's extremely smooth like now than when it's rough.' Then, something of the real nature of existence was shown to you – all energy and destructive rage.

Pete drew upon his cigarette, considering this. 'No life!' he said, 'That's what I didn't expect. Growing up in the Philippines like I did, I've looked out at the ocean every day of my life. But it's different when you're doing so from land, isn't it? From places with people and living creatures in them. Do you realise that, for a whole week now, we've seen no birds in the sky, no fish in the sea, no aeroplanes, no other boats? We might not be in this world: we might be someplace else completely.'

Rob could tell real fear when he heard it. 'You'll get used to it, Pete,' he said, 'it takes us all at first like it's taking you now.'

Pete put a hand on Rob's arm, 'I like you,' he said, in that voice of his which was – curiously – at once metallic and warm, 'we're pretty alike, huh? . . . you and me.' Don't you think so?'

He wouldn't say that if he knew some of the things I've done, thought Rob, with a pang, seeing the picture of himself he was busy presenting to Bill and Jesus. Particularly if he knew about one hot day last July. To change the subject he said:

'I'll tell you something that might cheer you up – if we *are* the same sort of person. It's a great moment, perhaps the greatest, when you first see the birds. It's almost better than seeing land come into sight, somehow. Just birds, and yet you know that they're bringing you everything else.'

It was virtually as if he could see those wings and hear those calls now, at night in the empty mid-Atlantic.

'*I* like birds too!' Pete said, and you could hear truth where fear had been only a minute or so before. 'In my own country I'm a little famous for my love of birds.' Rob tried to imagine what these would be like: exotic, clamorously brilliant in colour, startling greens and scarlets where his own best-loved bird had been blue. 'In the southern Philippines,' Rob heard Pete continue, 'in the island my mother's family came from, the boys have a dance which imitates the birds. It presents a bird's whole life,' he was looking keenly at Rob to see whether he was being impressed, 'from coming out of the egg to the moment of its death.'

'Is that right!' said Rob, not knowing what else to say. Swiftly he tried a mental picture of Neil Ferris and other Tanbury mates joining together in dance to honour the birds. It was comically improbable.

'I didn't tell you, did I?' said Pete, tightening his grip on Rob's arm, 'that back in my country I worked in a folk-dance group. For two years, after leaving school. My mother had just died (my father'd been dead for ten years), and the company became like a home to me. Then the money ran out. But that bird-dance was one of my favourite numbers.' He gave a nostalgic, rather melancholy giggle, curiously inappropriate for the dark wastes of the Atlantic at which they were both gazing, and made the sadder-sounding for its context, 'I got a lot of compliments for the way I performed it,' he added, with a sort of plaintive pride, and the eyes he turned full Rob were gleaming with wistfulness.

'That sounds pretty interesting,' said Rob. And strangely, though he'd hardly ever thought about folk-dancing in his life, he *was* interested. Partly, of course, because he'd been provided with a window on to the Filipino boy's past, a past so different from his own that it was difficult to imagine it being *fact* for someone else. But also because of the relationship now intimated between Pete and birds. Was that one of the secrets they'd signalled wordlessly to each other that first day on the *Egon Ludendorff*: Pete with his ability to reproduce a bird's movements, Rob with his great debt to the flight of a kingfisher.

'Rob, why don't you,' Pete's voice was an urgent, throaty one, a whisper which the solitude of the bridge-deck did not warrant, 'why don't you come down to my cabin, and I'll dance it for you? I think you'd like it. It doesn't matter not having the music for it. You can appreciate it without.'

How could Rob refuse the invitation without hurting Pete's feelings? Anyway what were the alternatives? A game of cards with Andy (but much as he liked Andy, cards were beginning to bore him). More self-communing and ponderings over his wickedness and the punishment (eternal?) which it might have earned.

'Sure, Pete,' he said, 'I'll come down to your cabin.'

And down they went, Pete's cabin being even smaller than Rob's, and closer to the engine-room. The great vibrations possessed it night and day, animating it remorselessly. But, taking a seat on the bunk-bed – strident-coloured pictures of palmy, moutainous Filipino scenes above his head – Rob was scarcely able to distinguish the thump-thump-thump of the engines from the increasingly rapid thump-thump-thump of his own heart.

Something is going to happen here, he told himself, just as he had a year before on the Japanese-style wooden bridge over the Fase.

Inches away from him Pete stood poised. He was taking deep, slow breaths – of preparation – and blinking, as if to bat away his human personality. Rob found himself blinking too, with anticipation, shyness, uncertainty. When his gaze settled, he saw that Pete was crouching on the floor – or should he say 'ground' – jerking his round head backwards and forwards, opening and shutting his mouth eagerly and nervously, as if grasping at the air with his lips. He was new to the world, was very young.

Now he was beating his arms against his side, while running hither and thither with short, neat steps; gradually he raised himself to his full height. He looked about him. Rob might as well not have been there, nor the cabin's dreary walls nor the photographs that sought to alleviate that dreariness. What was he seeing behind the door, out of the porthole? Huge trees luxuriant with leaves, heavy with gaudy flowers? A jungle creek? A heat-steamy mountainside? Pete wheeled the room, at first tentative, then in a bolder spirit of exploration, then with confidence – faster and faster and faster. And the more rapid and excited these gyrations, the more his long, muscular, golden-skinned-arms seemed a-shimmer with bright plumage. *Were* his soft, agile, yet sturdy feet upon the floor (ground) or, if they were, would they stay there? Surely he might be taking off any minute for an enticing cliff-ledge, a tempting tree-top.

But, little by little, the circles being traced on the floor diminished, convexed upon some as yet indiscernible spot. Their making slowed down; every so often Pete would stop – to strut, to leap, to raise arms high. At such moments parts of his body acquired an existence of their own: taut thighs, crutch, the compact buns of his arse. And then, seconds later, Pete would, as it were, gather them back into his whole body as he spun towards some centre of his being.

Rob never knew how long the dance lasted. Like that Essex kingfisher rising from the rushes of the Fase, Pete had put time into suspension; all was motion and inaudible music and – beauty! But, just as Rob was thinking this, change overtook the dancer. See how the head was slumping! Look how limb after limb was growing numb! The body crumpled until valiant feet took it, bore it, in one solemn ultimate revolution. The arms gave a desperate flap, the mouth gasped, as if air were pain now. A twitch – and the whole sinewy joyous body was still.

Thump-thump-thump went the engines next door; thump-thump-thump went Rob's heart.

'I'm dead, in case you hadn't understood,' came Pete's voice from the floor.

'Oh, I had, I had,' said Rob. 'it was ... you were ... wonderful. I'd never seen anything like it before.'

'I bet you hadn't,' said Pete, 'and now I'm alive again, which could be the best part of all.' *Could* be? ... As swift as a bird's flight was Pete's leap now, onto the bed and beside Rob. 'I *like* you,' he was saying, 'in the way I like Ricky.' That mysterious Ricky!

Rob didn't reply; Pete was kissing his neck. Shouldn't he say or do something? No, because he had nothing to say and didn't know exactly what he should or what he *wanted* to do. Except that it would be something in response: Pete's kisses felt so good, and now he was nibbling the lobe of his ear ... Rob's cry of pleasure, which even as he gave it, seemed to him more bird-like than human, and was more specific perhaps than any statement or initial action could have been.

'We make love?' said Pete.

The question came a few minutes too late for any negative answer. Rob was not only too aroused, he was too tired – after the battering sessions with Bill Bentley – to be able to resist so sweet a pressure, so enjoyable a closing-in upon him as this. ... Besides, hadn't he known that this was how the visit to Pete's cabin would end? Hadn't he known what conclusion to the dance lay ahead of all those pretty and seductive steps?

'You been with João?'

Rob grinned, but shook his head.

'However did you get out of that?' giggled Pete.

'Maybe I didn't want it enough,' said Rob, and this time he turned round and reached out to Pete, to pull him more closely to his own waiting body.

'It's better,' said Pete, whispering into his chest, 'without the clothes, wouldn't you say?'

Of course he was right.

You felt you could consume the whole of the voyage this way, didn't you? All other duties, pastimes and activities dissolved in the embraces of this golden-bodied bird-boy.

Rob made an effort – admittedly, not a very strong or convincing one – to leave the cabin after their love-making seemed to be over. But Pete was adamant. They must sleep together. 'Sleep!' said Rob, with an incredulous smile, for he knew what the night together would be like. But once again he seemed to have no power for resistance. As he lay there enfolded and enfolding the Filipino boy's limbs, he wondered at the places they'd been to, the experiences they contained, the other people who'd known them. About himself and the part he'd just played – no, was *still* playing – he didn't really wonder very much. He'd just accepted his course, hadn't he? He didn't feel in need even of a navigator . . .

Lying drowsily in Pete's arms – not very comfortably, it must be admitted, for the bunk-bed hadn't been built for *two* – Rob wondered if he'd ever known such contentment before. Contentment – which was turning out so fragrant – hadn't been exactly a feature of life before the Wolfgang Ludendorff Line. But then can contentment be yours unless others are – demonstratively and spontaneously – content with *you*?

. . .'No, Rob's *nowhere near* as clever as our other two,' Mum was saying in her faded-sounding voice to some friend who'd dropped in 'behind scenes' at *The Copper Kettle* 'A pity, but there it is!' She didn't give the impression, however, that she was as resigned to the fact as her words suggested, and she would sigh – as if to an invisible audience – on the occasions when she looked over Rob's scrappily-done homework.

'He wants a touch of the S.T.R.A.P.' said Dad. Heaven knows why he chose to spell out the word; maybe it gave him a little stab of pleasure, or maybe, on the other hand, he was ashamed of the instrument of castigation. Of course you could see why Dad thought he merited it. Rob wasn't in total disagreement with him: he'd had the S.T.R.A.P., for instance, when he'd blown brother Phil's stamp-collection out of the window, and so away, scattered, over the yards and gardens of Foswich.

But it hadn't only been given when Rob had behaved badly. Dipping a happy hand into the sleeping Pete's crutch, he remembered the incident of Church Alley, frequenting that walled snickey had been an old black mongrel dog – more spaniel than anything else: Rob had called him Joey, like Pal Joey, for truly they were pals. Rob would regularly nick food for him from the cafe kitchen, but it wasn't a question of cupboard love, for the old dog – always so shamefully thin – had been as pleased to see Rob when he wasn't carrying scraps as when he was. He would lick his face with an affectionate energy Rob had encountered in no other living being. Then one afternoon Rob had seen Alan Linley, that great, crude-mouthed slob, aiming a vicious kick at his friend, who in fact had spotted him and had been coming to greet him as usual. It hadn't been difficult for Rob to pick up a stone and hurl it (his aim was good!) hard at Alan's forehead. When blood has spurted from it, he'd been really pleased, and had laughed aloud and mockingly.

Of course Alan's silly parents had come round to *The Copper Kettle*, and though Rob had not foreborn to describe Alan's cruel and wanton behaviour, he had not been believed – or else, which was almost worse, not sympathised with. He'd been sent up to the room, and there Dad had given him another taste of the S.T.R.A.P.

At times Mum had wondered if Rob were a changeling. And then – odd how one's memory did things one didn't want it to! – it had been Dad, Rob now recalled, who'd reminded Mum how tirelessly Rob worked for them in the cafe, and what a favourite he was with the customers.

Had he been pleased at these words? Perhaps. Had he been pleased when Mum complimented him on the batch of scones he'd made, completely off his own bat? Of course! But on the whole Foswich life was a dismal tapestry. What things were bright-coloured in it? Hot afternoons by the river, swimming in the pools where the great Forest began; drawing maps; looking at all the boats in the Essex estuaries and visiting the harbours of Ipswich, Lowestoft, Yarmouth; mucking around in the showers after games or visits to the baths, when you could have a feel of another boy's cock and balls, all swelling with the effect of water and of another's touch; the birds in the garden and down by the Fase; listening to records usually in the company of Neil Ferris – of *The Police* and *Pink Floyd*; getting a new pair of baseball boots or a slip with a different design or a crisp bi-coloured summer shirt.

And then there'd been his friendship with Laurie. Sometimes he thought there couldn't be a face as fine, or a voice as melodious, or conversation as intelligent, sympathetic and stimulating as Laurie's. Laurie whom he'd lost!

There were times – those times when he dared to think over his past evil – when imaginatively he undid that dreadful day. Together with Laurie – yes, and with Polly too – he re-entered the church at Saxingham Enfrith. Cool in the hot weather, it exuded sanctity. Very reverently did Rob ask Polly to repeat that Saxon prayer, very reverently did he approach the altar, bowing perhaps to our Lord's presence, impressing thereby not only Laurie and Polly, but Julian Lumley Greenville as well . . .

Rob awoke at about half-past five – and really he hadn't slept so very much or so very soundly. The day had already begun: the sea was a burning silver, there was a long pink blush for horizon, and, above that, streaks of translucent milkiness. It was almost certainly going to be the hottest day of the voyage. He was still in the state of contentment – no, more of satisfaction – in which he'd fallen asleep, and seeing Pete at his side, deep in some realm of peace, was a beautiful thing. He had never felt less alone; indeed only now did he realise quite how often he *had* felt this, without daring to confront, let alone change, the condition. The attitude in which Pete lay was more or less that in which he'd finished his dance, the posture of simulated death. Maybe death itself could be as tranquil, as lovely as the flight of a bird, as the being (particularly the sexual being) of a boy . . . *There* was a thought! A happier, more desirable destiny than that offered you by Bill Bentley and the parts of the Bible he seemed so easily to alight upon – where enjoyment of Heaven involved a knowledge that others were being consigned to the 'blackness of darkness for ever'.

Bill Bentley! He had an appointment with him: 4.30 that afternoon. Confession of sins; preparation for the moment when he'd be ready to shake Jesus by the proffered hand in friendship; all to be continued. And how was he to deal with the matter of the night just past? Declare it? – and earn sermons of fire and eternal night from Bill. Or say nothing? – in which case the whole business of admitting aloud the wrong-doings and confusions of the past was somewhat invalidated. But – *did he have to keep the appointment*? Of course not! *Did he want to do so*? No, he didn't think he did. But . . . *but*, he had to concede that he wasn't *altogether* sure. For someone to feel for almost eighteen years that he had no significance whatever, and then to learn that before Time began, he'd been wanted by the Son of the Creator – well, that was quite some deal!

'Where the hell are you going?' asked a voice from just this side of sleep.

'Best to leave now,' said Rob, 'easier if I'm seen at the usual hour leaving my own cabin.'

'Sure,' said Pete, 'but stay a *little* longer! Please. There's still more things we can do . . .' He extended a golden arm. Bollocks to Bill Bentley, thought Rob.

The weather all morning was unsurpassable. Though in dock she had looked such a cumbersome old hulk, the *Egon Ludendorff* was now fairly gliding across the sheen that was the day's sea. So clear and powerful was the sun, and in so unadulterated a blue sky, that you almost felt it pulling the ship nearer to Europe. Passengers sat out on deck – on chaise-longues with magazines or books. That old man from Savannah, Georgia, for instance, basked from breakfast to lunch with a copy of *Your Hundred Best Jokes* on his lap. And even Bill Bentley was brought out from his office-cabin by the sunshine, having smeared his face and neck first with cocoa-butter. As for Peter, he was at work – swabbing down decks and stairways, beautifully stripped to the waist. Drops of sweat coursed down his so capable, so shapely back; Rob longed to lick them off with his tongue – already, and after so short a time, an expert where amorous attentions to Pete were concerned!

It was while watching Pete that Rob came to his decision. Absurd for him to be nervous about it. Nevertheless how to carry it out troubled him throughout the preparation of lunch, which was today, by arrangement, principally *his* concern. The menu was Shepherd's Pie with carrots (a dish that even the dour German captain could be seen to enjoy) followed by a jam roly-poly with vanilla sauce. As he brought this last to Bill's table, Rob told himself: 'It's now or never! His mouth emptied of saliva, but he forced himself to say aloud: 'Sorry, Bill, but I shan't be able to make it to Cabin Number Five this afternoon!'

He hardly dared look Bill in the face, stared confusedly instead down at the newly starched white table-cloth. Bill, he'd realised, had an iron will. His work was God's work; he was not someone who took matters lightly, who would be easy-come, easy-go in his dealings with people. But Bill's tone as he replied: 'Got something else on, eh?' could scarcely have been more affable, and when – almost timidly – Rob brought himself to turn round and look at Bill, he found an expression on his face as unperturbed as the voice.

'That's right,' said Rob. He wasn't going to blush, was he?

'Fair enough; always another day!' beamed Bill. His eyes appraised his plate. 'The good old English roly-poly, huh?'

'Yes!' said Rob, in a rather meek sort of voice.

'This is the stuff to give the troops, eh? This is what made us Britons great!'

'Yes,' said Rob. This jauntiness was really quite disconcerting. Perhaps *Bill* was tired and needed a rest, too. Evangelising must use up energy like anything else, and even Christ – if you believed the Gospels – required occasional holidays.

But back in the steam and bustle of the kitchen another interpretation of Bill's behaviour occurred to him. Maybe he'd given up on him? Maybe he'd understood what had happened between himself and Pete, and, as a result had decided that he was morally quite beyond the pale? At the recollection of the activities of the night a very pleasurable stirring came into his crutch, but also a twinge of – what? apprehension? fear? It was impossible to have spent the last days as he had done, spluttering over sins he'd all but forgotten about, and remembering always that crime of his which had still gone unexpiated, without feeling in need of some climax to them. Just as, on the bunk with Peter, it would have been cruelty to himself to break off just as the 'coming' was imminent, so now he was agitated – against the wishes of one part of himself – by a decidedly uncomfortable sense of incompletion.

When he came back into the ship's dining-room to take away the pudding-plates, he could not forebear saying to Bill: 'Hope you don't *mind* about this afternoon?'

'Mind?' said Bill Bentley, all smiles still, ' 'course I don't. There's the best sun outside that we could have the good fortune to see. Be out in it, boyo, be out in it!' (But his *eyes* aren't smiling, realised Rob, those dreadful grey bulbous eyes that are beginning to haunt me as those images of defilement and death used to haunt me back in England.) Bill was going on: 'I've got to congratulate you on an even better pudding than ever. You sure are some cook!! "Thanks for the nosh!" as they used to say in the old country.'

When the usual hour for their assignation came round, Rob judged it best to be prominently visible upon the main deck: *that*'d show Bill, wouldn't it? Rob had only a handful of books with him – he'd never been a great reader – so, his choice for a read in a deck-chair was a restricted one. He decided upon an old Pelican book, *Watching Birds* by James Fisher. Sitting rather self-consciously in the full sunlight but avoiding the scorching glare from the ocean surface, Rob happened on the following section:

> 'We have no philosophical justification for imagining that, because we recognise differences between a male and a female bird or between two different sorts, the birds themselves recognise these differences by the same characteristics . . . In the snow-bunting Dr Tinbergen found that it was mainly the attitude and movements of the bird against which the threat display was directed that determined

> *whether the threat should be continued as such or transformed into courtship display. This explains some of the occasional cases of apparent homosexualism in birds. If, by some upset of its sex-glands, or another cause, a male bird goes into a female attitude, it will be often accepted as a female, even though it may bear male plumage – the displaying male may even try to mate with it. Among the ruffs and reeves in the Waders' Aviary at the Zoo there are many more males than females and some of these often take up female attitudes. The consequent attempts at mating have often led onlookers to suppose that reeves bear ruffs.'*

Interesting and assuring too! Though really was it necessary to talk about *female* attitudes? Why not simply say that there were cases (and quite common ones) where a horny male bird got excited by one of his own sex and presented himself accordingly.

Birds mingled with memories of Pete and himself, till wings and limbs as in that Filipino dance, were happily fused. And then a shadow fell across the page, separating Rob from the sea, from the sun.

'Nothing like a good read, is there?' said Bill Bentley.

'Oh, hi Bill!'

'What's grabbing you?' Bill went on, breezily. Rob – not without an inner smirk of satisfaction – held up the worn old paperback. No doubt Bill had imagined him wrapt in some pornographic work; he certainly seemed surprised by the title, and could, of course, have had no idea of the thoughts the matter behind it had prompted in Rob.

'Always good to have a hobby!' Bill pronounced. Rob couldn't help but remember how dismissive he had been about the kingfisher by the Fase. 'Bet you know all the birds you can see from this ship?'

'Well, right now you can't see any,' Rob said, not without a touch of truculence, 'we're in the mid-Atlantic.'

Bill gave him a rather piercing smile, then said: 'While we're on the subject of reading, I thought,' and now Rob noticed some sheets of paper in his hand, 'I thought you might care to have a copy of the good work that's been meaning a lot to both of us – at least, I *think* it has – these last few days. Discovered I had quite a few photocopies of it, and you're more than welcome to one, buddy, more than welcome.'

Whether it's welcome as far as I'm concerned is another matter, said Rob to himself. Aloud, however, he merely muttered, 'Thanks!' then, 'You've marked it, I see.'

'Oh, I'm a real devil for underlining,' said Bill, broadening his – it now seemed alarmingly – amiable smile.

Rob could feel – and smell Pete – again, as he'd lain in his arms last night. Remember how good it was, he told himself, remember that *always*!

But, needless to say, he couldn't resist casting his eyes down at the passage that Bill had so vigorously honoured with red ball-point. Not that he was really in any doubt as to what it was:

> *'Even as Sodom and Gomorrha, and the cities about them in like manner, giving themselves over to fornication, and going after strange flesh, are set forth for an example, suffering the vengeance of eternal fire.*
>
> *Likewise also, these filthy dreamers defile the flesh, despise dominion, and speak evil of dignities.'*

'Well, better be on my way,' said Bill, 'mustn't keep you from your birds any longer.' His smile was menacing. Does he know, or has he just guessed? wondered Rob. Though he'd spoken so much about the Son of Light, and of the angels who served Him, Bill Bentley seemed just now (as he had himself facetiously suggested) to be of distinctly diabolical company. Only the black arts showed you another's intimate secret.

He mustn't be kept from his birds! Bill who knew nothing about them and had been so unappreciative of the kingfisher. Rob wondered how his co-witness of the bird would have reacted in this situation. But it was hard to imagine Laurie Williams, ever being enmeshed with someone like Bill Bentley of Jackson, Miss.

CHAPTER FOUR: LAURIE

'D'you realise how fantastically lucky we've been?' Rob's words referred, of course, to seeing the kingfisher in flight, but weren't they equally applicable to the two of them meeting up like this? After all that eye-contact, curious, eager, embarrassed, appreciative, in corridor and classroom now they were confronting one another alone and uninterruptable, with only the hushed Fase valley for witness.

'I don't know as much about wild life as you do, I think,' said Laurie, 'I've always noticed in art lessons how well-informed you are about it.'

'It's my biggest interest,' said Rob, turning his river-dazed eyes full upon Laurie now, 'but I don't know one half, one quarter of what I'd like to. But it's always like that, isn't it?'

What do *I* want to know twice, if not four times as much about, wondered Laurie. He was aware, all of a sudden, of a dreadful lack of enthusiasm pervading his life, a lack which could be extended backwards, for his past too had been marked by it. And yet when he was Rob's age, he surely *had* known what ardour meant: those visits to Foxton, those porings-over the Pre-Raphaelites. Or had he not cared even about those as much as once he'd thought?

Before he'd time to reply to the boy, he was being asked another question: 'What's *your* great interest, Mr Williams?' It was like a disturbing half-reading of his mind. 'Art, I suppose?'

'Well, that most of all,' said Laurie, uneasily.

'We all certainly get the feeling that you're very bound up with it,' said Rob, 'your classes make *us* enthusiastic too.'

'Really?'

'Yes, no kidding! They're great!'

Laurie had often fantasied about such words of praise, and from precisely this quarter. But now they made him feel unpleasantly unworthy. He ought perhaps to reveal himself as the fraud, the sham he was. What in fact he did say, however, was: 'Well, it's nice of you to say so. Every teacher dreams of hearing such things ... If you're not doing anything else, would you like to come back to my flat for a cup of tea?'

'Well, thanks, Mr Williams,' said Rob, almost effusively, 'but won't I be taking up too much of your valuable time?'

What a grim discrepancy between his vision of me and me as I really am, thought Laurie. He had come really to envy those who have to struggle against the clock. For him the expression 'Time hangs heavily on his hands' had come to have an almost literal meaning. Even *Fawlty Towers* or *Dad's Army* on television alleviated Time's weight only slightly. As he retraced the path back to his Victorian terrace home, the youth of his recent thoughts and longings at his side, Laurie searched his mind for things to say to him, and could find only the dullest of questions: What have you been doing this afternoon? How many lengths of the Town Baths do you normally swim? Are you a good diver? As he walked along, he trailed fingers through the passing hawthorn blossom as someone sitting in a boat might through water; no wonder that ever afterwards these white, heavily-scented flowers were to prompt in him thoughts of the beginnings and endings of all relationships.

His flat was rather a mess. By nature tidy Laurie had extended his lassitude of late to where he lived. The basic furniture was his landlady's (she was a Mrs Hargreaves, a solicitor's widow) – poor quality versions of the low, linear and self-consciously utilitarian furniture of the Thirties. But here and there among them, like eruptions of dahlias and gladioli in a vegetable garden, were possessions of Laurie's own, bits of Victorian bric-à-brac that he had delighted in pouncing upon in junkshops: a glass case full of mounted butterflies; a clock the face of which was painted with a Kate Greenaway scene; a harmonium with elaborate stops now more of decorative than of musical significance. Not one of these but needed a good dusting. Indeed it seemed to Laurie that the whole place had – almost without his noticing it – acquired a distinctly forlorn air.

'Nice place you've got here, Mr Williams,' said Rob, and Laurie took the remark as the compliment it was obviously intended to be.

And another compliment was forthcoming. 'This one of yours, Mr Williams? It's got to be! I can tell your style! I must say, I like it a lot.'

Why, the lad means what he's saying, realised Laurie, amazed. 'This' was one of the original double-page spreads for *The Extraordinary Walk*, not hanging in the Tate as Fanny, that friend of Isobel's, had suggested it should do, but merely decorating a dreary room in a cul-de-sac in a smallish Essex town. But now that he looked at it again – with Rob's eyes – wasn't there a certain something about it, a sort of coiled and waiting happiness? The fat old priest and the trousered chicken had arrived in a park, one of those small walled and building-dominated London parks that he and Isobel had been so fond of. The chicken was causing a stone lion, the support of a drinking-trough, to raise its head and roar.

'Glad you like it,' said Laurie, 'I did it a long time ago – to go with a text written by a girlfriend of mine.' He noticed a quickening in his visitor's eyes at this last phrase. No doubt his sex-life had been extensively speculated upon by Rob Peters and his coarse-minded layabout friends. Not that there was very much for them to know nowadays . . . But somehow paying attention again to the colour-spread made his past erotic days and nights seem nearer than they'd done for so long, for *too* long. What inventive love he and Isobel had made; he could feel again his own tongue working through the scented shrubbery that was his lover's bush to penetrate the sanctum of the cunt . . .

'Lions interest me, you know, Mr Williams,' Rob was

saying, while Laurie was in the kitchen hunting for something more exciting than a packet of extremely stale digestive biscuits. 'I had one when I was younger, you see – I mean, in my head I did. Most nights, before going to sleep, I'd imagine setting out with him somewhere. Sometimes I'd be riding him, sometimes I'd be walking by his side. I pictured how people would react when he lifted up his head to roar, just like in your painting.'

'And how *did* they react?' asked Laurie. His search had been successful: in a cupboard he'd some across an unopened box of shortbreads.

'Terrified, for the most part – what d'you think!' replied Rob, with an almost salacious chuckle. 'Get the scene, Mr Williams. I'd take Leo – sorry, it wasn't at all an original name – right into the middle of Foswich market, and coo-hoo! everyone'd scream and run away, and all the stalls would be overturned, and fruit and vegetables and ironwear and heaps of clothes would go flying all over the pavement, and several people would have fainted, and there I'd be, cool as a cucumber because Leo was *my* friend. It was great!'

'Yes, I can see that,' said Laurie. It wasn't hard to reconstruct the boy's fantasies because he'd been so plainly reliving them while talking. He didn't appear concerned with what he was going to be offered to eat or drink.

'Some nights,' Rob went on, the sight of the picture having evidently effected a change in him, for there was no sign of the shyness there had been on the walk, 'some nights I'd send myself to sleep with visions of what the lion'd do to people who annoyed me. He'd tear them to shreds with his mighty claws, wouldn't he?, and eat them up, slowly munching one limb after another.'

'What . . . what sort of people?' asked Laurie, a little taken aback. For his part he could recollect no violent fantasies of childhood, and did not believe he'd ever had any.

'Horrible people,' said Rob in a matter-of-fact voice, 'my *dad*, for instance.' A most curious gleam, provocative yet satisfied, came into his vivid brown eyes. Laurie recalled Dai Griffith's words: Mr Peters was a 'bullying sot', and his son was capable of meanness and viciousness. He offered him another shortbread.

'And what about *those* then?' exclaimed Rob, suddenly, 'those photos?' The interest in his voice had a nervous, eager quality.

'They're of a ship my father worked on,' Laurie told him, 'the *William Wilberforce* of Hull. One of the Ollerman Line.' The name could mean nothing to the Foswich boy here, but there were circles in Hull were it spelt everything, the certainties of the past, the precariousness of the present, the glumness of the future. It was on Ollerman Line boats that great-uncles Tom and Will, had been employed.

There was a different kind of light in Rob Peters's eyes now. He got up and gazed hard at the framed photos, as if to turn the imaged waves into real heavings of foaming salt water. Laurie remembered his own choppy crossings on that ship on her way to Copenhagen; he saw his dad all of a sudden younger and more energetic; he heard the gulls' plaintive, lovely cries, and saw their swooping movements about the prow of the ship.

'Your dad was a sailor then?'

'Yeah! Second engineer. And that ship you're looking at – I travelled on her myself twice.'

Rob's face suggested that Laurie had just admitted to having made a journey by magic carpet to the Baghdad of the Arabian Nights. '*I* like the idea of a life at sea,' he said quietly, 'always have done. It's what I think about when I go to the coast – Lowestoft or Yarmouth. What's the point of mucking on here, on land?' I ask myself.

Laurie was obscurely touched by this, as if he personally had been paid some sort of compliment. What more was he going to hear about the lad's inner life, his fantasies and dreams? It was almost too good to be true that he'd heard so soon so many.

But maybe these hopes of a life at sea were too present and urgent; Rob did not speak of them again that afternoon. He returned silent to his chair, and Laurie poured out the tea. When conversation started up again, it was more conventional, but fluent and fluid. Rob was interested in the butterflies beneath the glass dome and could identify most of them ('That's a Lulworth Skipper, that is! Coo, they're *very* rare! You can only find it in one corner of England.') He liked the harmonium and tried to pick out tunes on it; then he persuaded Laurie himself to play, as he used to in student days gone by. Recollections of all that merry 'camp' Victorian music-making, pretty girls all a-ripple with silvery, self-indulgent laughter, swiftly passed through Laurie's mind as he sat himself down to wheeze out for the perky-expressioned boy some old favourites: 'Villikins and his Dinah', 'I Wouldn't Leave My Little Wooden Hut For You', 'My Old Man Said "Follow the Van!" ' and 'Knocked 'em in the Old Kent Road!'.

'Thanks for the tea and talk, Mr Williams,' Rob said, eventually, 'I think I'd better bugger off home now. I mean . . .' Disarmingly he blushed at the mild obscenity he'd used, 'I mean, I'd better be on my way now. Today's the day I help with the washing-up at the cafe; there's usually a hell-of-a-lot on Saturdays.'

'How about one more cup of tea for the road,' urged Laurie. After the boy had left, the room, indeed the whole flat, would fill up with loneliness again – with boredom, anxiety about Mum, fears of the future (and, too, of futurelessness).

'No, best not to . . . Thanks all the same! Next time' (and though Rob didn't specify when this would be, wasn't it something for him to have spoken these words?) '*next* time, *you'd* better come and have tea at *our* place – *The Copper Kettle*. Can't recall ever having seen you there. There are folks who reckon it's the best place for lunches and teas in the whole South Essex area; a bloke has even said so in a guidebook. You'd be welcome there *any* time, and on your first visit,' and his whole face veritably shone at the prospect, 'your tea will be "on the house", as they say. Old Rob'll see to that!'

What real sweetness of expression he's capable of, thought Laurie. He could almost feel the proverbial melting of the heart. (How can a boy who smiles like that deserve the nasty things that Dai said about him?)

What's more Rob had put him in mind of his Hull

great-uncles, Tom and Will. Laurie felt he had known these men personally – they'd long been dead – for his mother's rambling talk had made him more intimately acquainted with them than with many whose flesh-and-blood forms he'd encountered. Today, perhaps because of the bad news from home, they acquired a sudden poignancy that made them fuse with the boy with whom surely a friendship had just begun.

Tom and Will, both fair-haired, blue-eyed, lean, Viking-like. Tom had stowed away on a ship when he was only fifteen, a trawler bound for the Dogger Bank. All voyage he'd been terribly sea-sick, but all those endless-seeming days of spewing on a tossed-about boat hadn't put him off a life at sea. A life that took him to Narvik, Hammerfest, Murmansk, Archangel; several times the ice threatened to close in upon his ship, and maybe it was the howling Arctic climate that developed the tubercular tendency of his boyhood.

At thirty-five he began to die – at home in Hull. 'Don't let me die with my boots off!' he'd implored his sister, Gran, Mum's Mum. 'Whatever I do, I must die like a *sailor* – with my boots *on*!' And on his thirty-sixth birthday Gran had realised that the end was at hand, and had pulled him up from his bed and pushed his feet into sea-boots that were needed for only an hour or so.

Will worked on ships that travelled not to the Arctic ports but southwards. His greatest interest as a boy had been animals and birds, and in the Middle East and North Africa he was able to become an enthusiastic collector of them. Back to Hull he'd brought monkeys, chameleons, geckoes, parrots, lizards, tree-frogs; the chameleons had lived on the sitting-room curtains, the monkey in the scullery: His name had been Prince Albert.

Will also died when he was thirty-six, though not on his birthday. A freak storm hit the ship shortly after she left Lisbon; Will was among the drowned.

For some reason Laurie felt a pricking behind his eyes as he 'remembered' these two relations. When he'd been younger, he'd often thought – indeed at times had assumed – that he'd follow them in the kind of life he led. After the move to Tanbury he had *not* thought thus; they had grown remote from him in spirit as well as in time and place.

Yet they had never altogether left him. Perhaps Rob would be their successor.

When Laurie arrived home from afternoon school the next Monday he did so just in time to answer the telephone.

'Laurie, it's Dad here!'

Laurie could not remember his father ever having rung him up of his own accord. He fought down a panicky notion that Mum had died, that she had visited the Oxford specialist too late. Controlling himself, he asked: 'Nothing the matter is there? You and Mum've come back from the hospital, have you?'

'Yes, Laurie, we have!' Dad's gravelly Yorkshire voice had never sounded more portentous and slow.

'And what was the verdict?'

'Good and bad, Laurie, good and bad!'

'What's the good?'

'That your mother's growth isn't malignant . . .'

'Growth – who's said anything about a growth before?' But we've all been thinking about one, he had inwardly to concede. So often what we actually manage to say aloud is unimportant . . .

'Dr Cardew had X-rays done here in Tanbury, you know, and they were sent to the Oxford specialist for analysis. He's a clever man is Dr Cardew, but that man in Oxford . . .' Dad allowed his sentence to trail away in sober, awed admiration of a surgeon's expertise.

'So what's the bad?'

'That your mother has to have an operation. There's no proof that this . . . this growth between her right breast and her right arm-pit will *stay* non-malignant. Something's got to be done about it at once; she'll be going in for the operation next week.'

'I see.' Well, the news did seem more good than bad. 'What do *you* feel about the situation, Dad?' he asked.

'Oh, just a little bit of rough weather,' was the reply, 'a minor storm in the Skaggerak, as you might say!' As I certainly *wouldn't say*, thought Laurie; Mum's so frequent irritation with Dad was easy at times to understand. Still there did appear comparatively little reason for worry . . .

'Oxford's a very wonderful place,' Dad was continuing, 'your mother and I had the privilege of watching, and then meeting, some Morris dancers in St. Giles . . .'

Half an hour later Laurie had talked himself into optimism. So he went along – as all weekend he'd intended – to *The Copper Kettle* for tea; he was determined to be sanguine.

The cafe is accommodated in the ground floor of a mostly 17th-century cottage, pink-washed and stuccoed, with lattice-paned windows and a moss-patched pantiled roof. Inside the nostalgic tea-searching traveller can find all that he would wish to – flagged floors, a low oak-beamed ceiling, a huge inglenook fireplace above and around which many much-polished old brasses shine. Chintz curtains hang at the windows; each oak table is graced with a slender vase containing roses or charmingly arranged wild flowers. There is a perpetual smell of pot-pourri and lingering woodsmoke. A latched door connects the cafe proper with the rest of the house.

Rob's mother, Beryl had about her an air of strained calm, her face so taut with this quality that you half-expected it to crack. She seemed almost desperately anxious to avoid any topic which admitted of disagreements, and spoke banalities in a miserable, soft monotone. In features and colouring Rob had taken after her more than had dark Philip and red-headed Anne. The moist, brown eyes set below fair brows were her younger son's.

Today, Rob waited on his art-master with transparent pleasure, talking the while, letting him into culinary secrets and gossip about the cafe's regulars. And he wouldn't let Laurie pay a thing!

Very soon, *The Copper Kettle* became part of Laurie's personal landscape. Too often, though, there was a disconcerting presence in it, one that Laurie encountered even on that very first visit. This was Rob's father, Geoff Peters, the 'bullying sot' of Dai Griffith's description. Laurie was just pouring himself out a fourth cup of tea, to go with a second slice of the delicious chocolate sponge-cake, when he became aware of a red-faced man in a sheeny blue suit lowering over his table.

'I don't believe we've had the pleasure of introducing ourselves to one another,' came the man's voice, hearty yet consciously ironic, 'I have the honour to be the husband of the good little woman who runs this outfit,' here he gestured at the tea-shop's array of pretty tables, 'and the dubious distinction of being the father of the nipper in whom I gather you're now taking an interest.' (So that's what Rob's told his parents, said Laurie, pleased, to himself). 'Geoff Peters!' And Rob's father made a half-parodic inclination of his large triple-chinned head, and proceeded to extend to Laurie a clammy hand. 'I suppose we should have met at one of those parent-teacher evenings you have up at your show!' Mr Peters went on, 'but frankly I tend to leave all that sort of thing to my lady-wife. I'm a bit too busy doing my bit to keep British commerce on a reasonably steady path.'

No answer to these somewhat haughtily delivered sentences occurred to Laurie; few parents on the occasions Mr Peters had alluded to bothered to come to talk to members of the Art Department anyway.

'I expect you're aware of my other two, aren't you, Mr Williams? Philip, my elder son, is now articled to a bloody good firm of chartered accountants *in town*, and my daughter, Anne is studying Home Economics (like every right-minded female) – at the Tech. in Walthamstow. Rob – he was an accident, I'm afraid – is what you could call the odd'un in the family, the changeling of the brood.' And to Laurie's great regret Geoff Peters lowered his great bulk on to the wicker seated chair opposite his own. Gusts of liquored breath emanated from him as he did so, entering, so it seemed to Laurie, the remaining chunk of his wife's sponge-cake.

'How d'you mean, Mr Peters?'

'I should've thought it was only to obvious.' Geoff Peters gave a mirthless bark of laughter. 'My elder son and my daughter have always worked hard and well. Though I says it as shouldn't, they're the stuff this country of ours needs to take it out of the decline it got into.' And he surveyed Laurie with his veinous eyes as if to ascertain what stuff *he* was made of and appeared not to like what he saw. 'Yes, Philip will go far in the accountancy sphere, and Anne'll make some chap a really first-class wife. They're *serious* young people, you see. Rob is totally different from them, totally! Has never done a day's work in his life! At least not what *I* would call a day's work, for naturally I discount helping in this cafe.'

He gave at this point another bark-like laugh, suggesting that in his world of roaring commerce and manly politics *The Copper Kettle* could count for little. It was only later that Laurie appreciated that in the several long periods of Geoff Peters's being 'between jobs', the tea-shop had counted for a very great deal. 'So much for the "work" side of Rob; the less we say about the "play" side the better, eh? Just good for mucking about in the most mindless kind of way! Obviously he's not going to do well in his 'O' Levels, so we'll all have to put on our thinking caps to find him some occupation for next year. It's occurred to me to send him away – to one of our public schools,' he stressed the possessive pronoun, as if he'd played a significant part in these schools' creation, 'for frankly I'm not much of an admirer of the state system, particularly the comprehensive game! Or we could try and persuade Her Majesty's Army to find room for the lad. In any event,' and his stare over the vase of roses was far from kindly, 'while I'm delighted that someone's at last interesting himself in my nipper, I should make it quite clear from the start that I shan't be best pleased if he's encouraged to go in any artsy-fartsy direction. In my opinion that's a way young Britishers would do well to avoid, and I am sure,' he paused with rhetorical satisfaction, 'that Maggie Thatcher herself would agree with me.'

And Laurie wondered at the paradox so frequently met; lazy, blabber-mouthed slobs like Geoff Peters championed the enforcement of standards (so-called), while diligent puritans like his colleagues at school espoused a liberalism they'd never avail themselves of. 'Any idea of my line of business?' Geoff Peters was now asking him.

'I did have . . .' began Laurie, almost nervously, for it did not take much perspicacity to perceive that Geoff Peters was a man of what is euphemistically known as an 'uncertain temper'.

'I work for Sleepwell,' said Geoff Peters, proudly.

Laurie did his best to assume an impressed smile.

'Makers of just about the most prestigious mattresses and pillows on the face of this ruddy globe.'

'They certainly do have a good reputation,' improvised Laurie.

'And *I* am their Eastern Counties Representative,' said Geoff Peters.

Laurie left *The Copper Kettle* that afternoon strengthened in his desire to enter into friendship with Rob, whose sufferings at home were all too easy to imagine. Had Rob heard his father's remarks about him or not? Had he heard the warning given to Laurie against leading him in an 'artsy-fartsy' direction? Probably; and with his son too. Geoff Peters had succeeded in accomplishing the very opposite to what he'd wished. At school the very next day Rob stopped Laurie in the corridor which connected assembly-hall to staff-room. He was wondering if Mr Williams were going to have tea again in their cafe; if so did he feel like a walk afterwards? There were some things he'd like to ask him.

There were indeed! How had Laurie's father begun his seafaring career? What shipping companies did he think most highly of today? Particularly among those which still operated across the Atlantic? Maybe it was because he'd spent his life in the east of England, but the West, and the great continent that lay behind the setting sun, had always had great appeal for him. Many times Rob had dreamed of arriving by ship on the virgin shores of America . . .

Laurie's answers were perfunctory, if friendly and interested-sounding. When he went home to Tanbury again – which he would do the weekend after next, to visit his mother in hospital, and then see her safely out of it – he would ask his dad the questions Rob had just put to him. 'Gosh, *thanks*, Mr Williams,' said Rob. 'Don't mention it!' said Laurie, 'and please, call me "Laurie" now.'

They were walking through fields framed by thick flowering hedgerows; as in walks of adolescence, each field seemed to sing out its own particularity, its own uniqueness. In one a rivulet, crossed by planks, flowed; in another dairy-cows were grazing in a corner. Cow-parsley had appeared in that which best commanded a view of the Norman church of Mapping Green; and a hollowed old oak stood, isolated and proud with fresh leaves, in the enormous meadow which could lead you back, townwards, to the main London-Foswich road. A country walk in English early summer in pleasant company can produce a feeling of well-being as little else can, and that day, as nearly every day for the next fortnight, Laurie would arrive back in his uninteresting flat with that feeling he'd known in adolescence: that the visible world was immanent with beautiful Spirit which could pass into and re-animate one's self, and even assist one beyond this life. Fitting that the sight of a kingfisher had been the prelude to this recovery of joy!

Such thoughts inevitably brought Jonathan West to mind, and partly for this reason, partly because – in truth – he did not really find Rob easy to talk or to listen to, Laurie found himself describing to his own pupil, during their walks together, the benefits, the lasting, incalculable benefits, he had derived from the company of his old artmaster.

'He gave one a kind of assurance that life was *good*,' Laurie would remark, perhaps while scrambling over a stile into a little bosky outpost of the Forest, 'just to be in his company was to believe that you could make something of your years upon this earth, even if all you did was look more closely at the trees and flowers around you. He'd show us – me and my friends – paintings which were like acts of worship in honour of Life: we'd look at . . .' but then he'd recollect that the very names of Samuel Palmer and the Pre-Raphaelites and the Nash brothers would be unknown to Rob, 'many paintings, including some done by himself,' he'd try without much success to recollect exactly what these had looked like, 'and we'd all return to our homes somehow enheartened.'

'Sounds rather like you, Laurie,' Rob would say, with a sweetness of tone and expression that was almost alarming.

'Oh, no!' said Laurie truthfully, 'Jonathan West and I aren't a bit like each other. I haven't *any* of his strength of character.' I haven't even any of his beliefs, he might have added, for he hadn't, hadn't really beliefs of any sort.

'Like you in the way *you*'re able to relate to one of *your* pupils?' Rob hazarded, '*I* always go back home after one of our walks together feeling the better for it . . . able to think more positively about life.'

And what on earth can that mean, wondered Laurie, though he was pleased, indeed touched, by Rob's words. He would resolve to speak less about Jonathan West and his own past the next walk, but the conversation always seemed to revert to the man, perhaps at Rob's instigation. It was as if, for all the patina of memory that had accrued round Jonathan, talking of him was a way of uniting himself and Rob, rendering them both two questing adolescents, for whom the adventure of existence was still to be canvassed.

When the time came round for Laurie's weekend in Tanbury, it seemed to the two of them that their friendship quite defied measurement both in terms of time past and time future. An eternal present of communing walks through a countryside tangible in its well-being was theirs. Rob even walked down to Foswich station to see Laurie off that Friday; the station, at the farthest end of the Central Line, stands apart from the town, seeming to serve fields and woods. Yet on its platforms the bustle and hum and dirt of London can seem imminent.

'I hope your mum's okay, Laurie,' said Rob, 'and . . . and don't forget to ask your dad those questions about shipping companies, will you?'

In every relationship there is self-seeking, thought Laurie sadly. *I* have needed someone young and confused yet capable of eagerness and excitement to restore my flagging spirits; Rob still requires an adult alternative to his father, to Phil, his pompous brother, and to an assortment of censorious schoolmasters. And who can fail to feel close to someone when there is the abundance of an English early summer all round about him, harmonising with – and eliciting – his most tender emotions? But when all is said and done, what have the two of us in common? Very little really

... As the train took Laurie past the small villas that mark the beginning of the capital, Rob's substantiality diminished somewhat, and he began to ask himself what he would find when he arrived in Oxfordshire ...

In fact the operation – so the surgeon had told Dad – could be counted a success, though deep-ray treatment would be necessary afterwards, 'just to be on the safe side'. Dad himself did not seem to be troubled, but would he have been so even if the news had been less good, wondered Laurie. He realised, alone with his father for the first time since their voyages to Denmark, that he had no idea what emotions the man entertained for his wife, what their intimate moments had been like, whether in truth, Dad was as bored with Mum as she purported to be with him. But then there was so much he didn't know ... about others, about existence, about himself. 'Oh, fuck it!' said either Mick or Dale, 'the funeral hasn't begun yet! What're you looking so long-faced about?'

In the hospital Sister Anderton said: 'We've been a model patient. We've never complained once, and we've done everything we've been told. And we're very grateful for all that's been done for us, too, aren't we, Mrs Williams?'

To her family, however, Mum was disgruntled and disconsolate. She dismissed Dad's rather awkward words of solace with 'How can you possibly know that, Roy? Who's been on the operating table, you or me? And I don't know how you've the nerve to talk to me as you're doing when you've let twins have an all-night party, just to celebrate me being out of the house?'

'Milly, it wasn't an all-night party,' Dad protested in that slow-churning East Yorkshire voice of his, 'it was just a question of a few friends round, to cheer themselves up.'

'To cheer themselves up! From *what*, may I ask! *I'm* the one who needs cheering up, I'd have thought. *I* can tell you, that it's been more difficult coming to after the op., *knowing* about that party, than it would have been had you been like a normal man and put your foot down where your sons are concerned. I've been lying here thinking of all the hoovering I shall have to do – fag-ash and God knows what else all over the fitted carpets ...' Her gaze suddenly fell upon Laurie who was standing rather abstractedly behind his father inwardly lamenting the lack of cards and flowers round the bedside; all the others in the ward had so many more. Really it was true, Mum had made next to no friends in Tanbury. 'Thank heavens there's someone here who cares for me, who doesn't put his own pleasures in front of a woman's health.'

Laurie felt that he didn't deserve such praise, felt too a sudden estrangement from the petulant, morose woman in the bed, whose former prettiness was now showing like a skeleton behind the fleshed body. 'Mum, when you come home tomorrow,' he said, 'you'll find everything spick-'n'span; the old vacuum cleaner will never have done work like it!'

His mother pealed with laughter as if he'd made the funniest joke she'd ever heard; this ostentatious amusement at what he'd said was, Laurie sadly reflected, principally another way of paying Dad out for what she felt was his failure in real concern for her.

In the train that chugged across the rich Oxfordshire pastureland towards Tanbury, Dad said: 'Your mother, you know, can be a little difficult at times, Laurie, a bit hard on me . . .'

Laurie, truly sorry for him, admired his father's courage in at last saying what for him had probably long seemed unsayable, but he did not feel up to the intimate conversation that should surely follow. So, remembering Rob, as hawthorn-decked hedgerows and smiling lush fields outside the train windows made it easy for him to do, he said: 'Dad, I wonder if you could possibly help me, or rather a young friend of mine – one of my pupils actually. . .' And he presented his father with Rob's predicament and wishes. Before he left Tanbury that weekend, he had in his pocket the address of the Ludendorff company of Hamburg, with whom the Ollerman Line had been affiliated . . .

For what reason he never knew, but he decided, on arrival at Paddington Station, to look up an old university friend of his, Colin Eastman who lived with some other blokes in a flat near Notting Hill Gate. 'Lazarus – raised from the dead, that's what you seem like, Laurie,' said Colin, 'to what do we owe the pleasure, the honour of your visit?'

'I just felt like seeing old familiar faces,' said Laurie simply, 'faces of friends.'

In truth Colin himself had – for Laurie that evening – a Lazarus-air, as did the large, ramshackle flat in which he and his mates lived. Indian cushions instead of chairs, kites suspended from the ceiling, joss-sticks burning, Javanese music pounding from expensive hi-fi, a miscellaneous brightly dressed group of people sitting relaxedly about smoking joints – it all belonged to a life the other side of the tomb. And, as if to confirm, to heighten this impression, there sat a girl whose Pre-Raphaelite looks were exactly those he'd most admired in his amorous student days. Copper-coloured hair cascaded down her back; she was slim with a sharp, sensitive, freckled face and gentle, inquisitive, green eyes.

'I don't believe you've met Polly, Laurie,' said Colin, 'she's Nick Keating's sister.'

'I feel as if I *have* met her,' said Laurie, almost a-tremble with delight at the beautiful girl in front of him, cross-legged and dressed in a shaggy oatmeal jersey and tight pale blue jeans, 'how *is* Nick these days? Is he still interested in Tibetan dancing?'

'Would that he were!' said Polly, giving Laurie a rueful – but grateful – smile, 'he doesn't have time for all that sort of thing in the Inner Temple, though.'

'He's taken his Buddhism as far as actually joining a *temple*?' exclaimed Laurie, thinking that Lazarus *could* hear pleasing, assuring news.

Polly laughed and laughed, and as she did so, her glinting glorious tresses shook and sparkled with the play of evening sunlight from the huge curtainless windows. 'The Inner Temple – Lincoln's Inn – the Law!' she said, 'If only he *were* saffron-robed; if only!'

The misunderstanding drew them together, made subsequent conversation easier than it might otherwise have been. The strain of Tanbury – of fractious Mum, helpless, lonely Dad, and feckless twins – fell from Laurie like some oppressive coat that shouldn't be worn in summer. Polly told him that she was a Ph D. student at University College, London; her thesis-topic was Anglo-Saxon ecclesiastical architecture and how it epitomised certain fundamental and distinctive aspects of that people's culture, more particularly their religious culture. It was a matter to which Laurie had quite literally never given a moment's thought before, but he was prepared to do so now because . . . because he wanted to know Polly better, to see her again, and soon.

'Perhaps you might like to come to Foswich one weekend,' he said, 'it's not a bad sort of place really, with the Forest to hand and everything.'

'And many Anglo-Saxon churches in the vicinity,' observed Polly.

During the train ride home – assuming that Foswich *was* home for him – Laurie thought about Polly a great deal. As in some Pre-Raphaelite painting she had been for him the very centre of her surroundings, irradiating all the people and objects about her. The Central Line surfaces at Stratford East; the wash of light of this early summer evening made even the heterogeneous rash of houses of this part of Outer London acquire not just dignity but charm. Villas presented themselves bathed in roseate colours, and it was possible to see, in what relieved their dull lines, a Gothic spirit of beauty that – for Laurie – Polly summated. The stained glass windows, the mock-ecclesiastical arches, the sham turrets, the patterned brickwork which broke up the monotony of this subtopia all suggested Polly to Laurie. And as the countryside forced its way into the straggling boroughs, and Foswich Forest became mile by mile more detectable, Laurie's thoughts about her became overtly sexual. Indeed their force, their stubbornness took him by surprise: it made him wonder at the abstinence, the emotional and libidinous barrenness of these last years. He could all but *feel* her breasts sweetly cupped in his hands, his tongue running along the delicious rift between them.

Rob was there to meet him on Foswich station.

'However did you know which train I was coming on?' asked Laurie, for some reason irritated rather than pleased to see the boy there.

'I didn't know, of course!' said Rob, a positively canine fidelity showing in his eyes, 'I've just met every train that's come in from Liverpool Street since late afternoon.'

That seems to be carrying friendship rather far, thought Laurie, but he tried to smile at Rob. How young, how ingenuous he both looked and sounded! Whatever was wrong with him that neither friends nor family, neither hobbies nor revision for 'O' Level couldn't occupy him, and he had to come bothering a man thirteen years his senior at the end of what had been for him a psychically exhausting weekend?

'How was your mother?' said Rob, as the two of them began the steep climb up the ridge on which Foswich is situated, towards the High Street.

'Oh, well enough, all things considering . . .' said Laurie dully.

'And your dad?'

So that's it, that's the reason for the obsessive waiting for the London trains, said Laurie to himself. What appalling egotists teenage boys are! Aloud he answered, 'Busy and worried, of course, as anyone would be whose wife's had a major operation. But don't worry! – I've got an address from him for you. Of a shipping company in Hamburg that plies boats between Northern Europe and America . . .'

'Gosh, *thanks*, Laurie,' breathed out Rob.

Every bird in South Essex seemed to be singing in the declining light to welcome Laurie back to the town where he'd lived so uninterestingly for so long.

Before he went to sleep that night he'd picked up the telephone and dialled Polly's number. He'd so enjoyed meeting her, he said, couldn't get the conversation with her out of his mind. He was wondering . . . had she been serious about coming up to Foswich one weekend? She had? Well, how about next? . . . Lovely, said Polly, that would be lovely, Laurie.

Polly arrived the following Friday. She was carrying a bright-coloured folkweave bag that she'd bought in a Moroccan souk. Her hair could have been that of Janey Morris as painted by Rossetti – russet, and spangled by light.

She professed herself delighted with Foswich from the start: those glimpses of the Forest the train afforded; those fields sun-yellow with rape; these pretty colour-washed, stucco-walled houses. Not that she was going to forget work while she was here: she had brought maps and topographical books with her. What a treasure-trove for someone interested in the Anglo-Saxons! . . . .

'Rob, I've got a visitor for the weekend,' Laurie said, answering the doorbell and seeing the boy standing, smiling and expectant, and fetchingly dressed in jeans and a *Talking Heads* T-shirt. He ought to have told Rob about Polly's coming to stay with him, but somehow hadn't brought himself to; besides, he'd argued, what business was it of a mere pupil's?

'Oh, I didn't know,' said Rob, and the smile died upon his eager face.

'Do you want to come in and meet her?' Laurie asked reluctantly, but how could he do otherwise?

'Her,' repeated Rob, '*her*?'

'Polly Keating,' said Laurie.

In the sunlit shabbiness of the flat they confronted one another, and straightaway the boy lost to the girl, becoming gauche and confused and a touch dreary. 'Pleased to meet you!' he said, ungraciously.

'Laurie teaches you, I gather,' said Polly.

'S'pose you could call it that,' said Rob, 'I'm not much of a learner.'

'Not a shining student then?' said Polly, green eyes all flirtatious challenge which Rob did not take up.

'No, I'm a thickie,' said Rob, 'can't draw to save my bloody life!'

'Oh, come off it,' said Laurie, 'you don't do too badly. But, Polly, Rob and I got to know one another because of something we both saw.'

And – rather more self-consciously than he would have liked – he began to relate the episode of the kingfisher. He didn't do this particularly well, being too aware of the determined smile of interest Polly was wearing and the scowl that Rob was.

'How riveting!' exclaimed Polly, 'I expect you both know that passage in Eliot's original version of *The Waste Land* where he talks about *kingfisher weather*'.

It was *just* possible, perhaps, that Laurie might have known it (in fact he did not!) but Rob . . . poor old Rob had not even heard of poet, let alone poem.

'Next week,' said Polly, 'or whenever-it-is that I next come to Foswich,' (*next week*, said Laurie to himself, can it be, can it wonderfully be, that she is as keen to begin a relationship with me as I am one with her?), 'next week I will bring down a facsimile edition I have of the work, and I'll read the lines to you.'

That night they made love, Laurie and Polly, and it was like a return to that fragrant, dewy, prelapsarian bower he'd left such an age ago. He was an Adam on what was still the threshold of the Eighties recapturing, if not reenacting, scenes of a late Sixties Eden. To wake up with her affectionately beside him was like discovering a morning of sunshine after weeks of drizzle and mist.

Polly did come the following weekend, and, having an excellent memory, brought with her the volume of the complete manuscript of *The Waste Land*. Never did Laurie (nor, he later realised, Rob) forget the gnomic, charged lines which Polly read, as if animated by some sibylline spirit:

> *'Kingfisher weather, with a light fair breeze,*
> *Full canvas, and the eight sails drawing well.*
> *We beat around the cape and laid our course*
> *From the Dry Salvages to the eastern banks.*

Polly paused.

'Go on!' It was Rob who asked.

'We-ell,' Polly looked dubiously, imploringly at the two of them. 'I will if you want me to. But I'm afraid the voyage doesn't turn out at all well. The *kingfisher weather* doesn't last, you see.'

'It never does, does it?' said Rob. It was more of a plea than a question. He was sitting on the very edge of his chair, as if dreading what further events were about to be presented to him, yet helpless against their enactment. His eyes, Laurie noted, were fixed with a nervous fascination upon the picture of Dad's ship, the *William Wilberforce*.

Polly gave Rob a concerned though condescending little smile. It was clear, to Laurie at least, that she rated the boy's intelligence rather low. Taking a deep breath she read on to the conclusion of the passage . . .

It's almost, Laurie thought, as if the seas are raging outside these dull Foswich rooms of mine. As if we three are bound on some rough, if not disastrous voyage, with Mrs Hargreaves' house as the frailest of ocean barques. He turned to look at Polly, who had laid down the edition of Eliot in a dramatic gesture. Her hair, caught in a sudden shaft of sunlight, was a hundred gleaming tints, all the way through from red to a fluid gold. I shall soon be in love with her, he said to himself; indeed I am perhaps already.

CHAPTER FIVE: ROB

Rob and Pete made vigorous love that night. Rob went down into his mate's cabin as one who'd consciously rejected Bill's bringing of 'good news', who'd spurned that appalling *General Epistle of Jude*. But the act of having spared himself information about just how wicked he was, and about just how inexorable in vengeance Bill's God would be unless . . . freed him into a warmth and an inventiveness of physical expression surpassing anything he'd shown the Filipino boy that first time.

Beyond the cabin was a very clear night-sky; stars beyond counting were even brighter than previously, and seemed more numerous, though Rob had read that the most you could ever see on one night was about two thousand. Maybe, for every star, for every planet that revolved round it, there was a way of loving someone: old Jude, whoever he had in fact been, had mentioned the stars and the sea, but in a very different spirit. He hadn't thought of *that* possibility.

And now – with Pete – there was so much to do, so much to enjoy, so much to feel a kind of gratitude for (and to some force beyond the cabin, beyond the visible).

This was what was establishing itself as perhaps their favourite position: Pete would lift his legs so that the knee-joints rested on Rob's shoulders. That way Rob could slowly, pleasingly work his member up Pete's arse, while clasping hands tightly round his neck, gazing into his all but black-irised eyes, and kissing him on his aromatic full lips. At such times, you really felt part of someone. And at the coming, you hardly knew which of you had fountained forth where; rather it seemed one great explosion of delight.

About two-thirds of the course between the American coast and the English Channel, ships are likely to encounter a current which causes a frequent vigorous swell. The *Egon Ludendorff* struck it during the second night that Rob spent with Pete. When a boat is moving as slowly as the cargo-laden German vessel, this convergence – far from pleasant – can last up to thirty-six hours. That May it was to affect lives.

When ship met swell, Rob was in the middle of a dream. His head resting peacefully against Pete's sexy but hairless chest received – in its shifts of interior scenery – a most baffling and alarming vision of Laurie Williams.

Rob was back at St John's School, Foswich, was walking across the grass to where – standing apart from the main buildings – the not very prepossessing Art Block stood. It was its south-facing window that confronted him now (the north-facing ones looked out over the playing-fields to where the Forest began); they were full of the usual kind of masks and puppets that pupils made, yet it seemed to Rob, as he neared them, that each one of these wore a decidedly disagreeable and mocking expression.

It was very cold, with one of those sharp, remorseless winds which blow across the East of England for so many winter days. Rob realised that he was naked (as indeed he was in reality, snuggled against Peter) and therefore increased his pace so as to get inside quickly. He had the greatest difficulty in opening the Art Block doors, however; they simply would not yield to his hands and had to be shoved very hard. Inside was confusion; canvases, easels, objects assembled for studies, brushes, papier maché heads, had all been thrown about, and many had suffered maltreatment. Here a clay model lay smashed, here were strewn drawings, torn or shredded. There was the usual smell of oil, turps and chalk, but, far from striking Rob pleasantly, there was, on this bleak day, something oppressive about it all.

Strangest of all, though, was the absence of people. No boys or girls, no teachers. 'Mr Williams,' Rob called, 'Mr Williams, you there?' No response. Rob began to run hither and thither inside the Art Rooms which now seemed, with every frantic movement of his, to be expanding, and changing shape as well as size.

'LAURIE!' Rob then yelled, 'I know you're here. I know you're somewhere in this fucking place!'

Then it was that he saw him. He was naked too – naked, and unmistakably dead. Taller than Rob remembered, Laurie Williams hung from the rafters of the ceiling, nailed to a great cross like Jesus Himself. Blood was dripping from his riveted fingers, from his wounded palms, from his tortured feet, from his thorn-pierced head – drop, drop, drop onto the linoleum floor. And above him was a placard bearing the words: 'Never forget Saxingham Enfrith'.

And then Rob knew, with that certainty dreams uniquely can confer, that the only way to bring the crucified Laurie back to life was to bend down in self-humiliation, to lap up all those little puddles of shed blood.

So, down on the floor he went! And down on the floor he, in truth, was, when, after a nasty bump (his forehead hitting the bunk's supports), he woke up. At first he could not understand where he was, or why. Painfully trying to right himself from his strange position like a worried puppet-master, pulling all his senses together into service, he made out beyond the porthole window a rising dark wall unlike any view it had offered all crossing. What could it be? Not the beginning of that blackness of darkness which lasts for ever, surely?

Then, of course, he understood that they'd reached that north-east Atlantic swell. Rubbing his forehead – on which he could feel an unpleasant growing bruise – he raised his head. There were Pete's dark eyes, hanging brightly in the still shadowy room, shining with incomprehension.

A sky of sea, than a sea of sky, then, with giddying rapidity, that sky of sea again! Even for the experienced it was difficult moving about the decks or along the corridors. The passengers – most of whom had woken up, some hours before day-break, to shock and nausea – slipped and slid about like nobody's business. Pale, anxious and irritated they had to cling – when making their way anywhere – to walls and door-handles.

'I just *don't* understand it,' said Mrs Van Asdalen, a nervous New York lady, 'there's no bad weather in sight. The sky and the sea are the same beautiful blue as yesterday. So what's gone wrong? We're swinging from side to side as if we were in a goddam *funfair*.'

Rob tried to explain about the swell-creating current in this area of the Atlantic. Clear explanations were not Rob's strong point, and Mrs Van Asdalen looked unimpressed. She'd have to ask the Captain about the matter, she said pointedly. Presumably she did, and heard from the gaunt, laconic Captain Shreider what in fact she'd already heard from the Assistant Cook.

'Well, all I can say,' she resumed, 'is that there's one *hell* of a surge *just* where this boat is moving, and nowhere else, but nowhere!' Her eyes moved anxiously to the vehemently rising and dipping horizon. 'Seems mighty strange to me,' she went on, 'and it makes me wonder if you guys know what the *fuck* you're doing. And can you please tell that dago steward to bring me a stiff brandy *pronto*.'

Only two passengers made it to lunch. One was the old man from Savannah, Georgia, even more determinedly jokey than ever: 'Tell you what,' he remarked to Rob, patting him on the shoulder,' I don't reckon it's the boat that's rocking about, I reckon it's the *sky*. I always did say that we shouldn't have gone in for space travel the way we have.'

The other passenger was – who else? – Bill Bentley. Rob had not, in fact, dared to hope that the ship's lurching would have confined him to his cabin, and clearly he'd been right not to do so. Rob presented him with a bowl of Chinese soup. Slices of mushroom and water-chestnut floated in it like paper flowers. Bill's eyes met his, challenging him to be the first to speak, to show his temerity:

'Swell not bothering you too much, Bill?' Rob asked. His manner was just a touch impertinent, and maybe he deserved the reply he got:

'The . . . oh, the *swell*!' It was as if he had to think a bit to know what Rob was meaning, even though he'd been shooting glances out of the window whenever the ship heaved herself particularly violently from port to starboard, and back again.

'Yeah,' said Rob, for some reason wanting to tease him, 'the movement of this ship?'

'No,' said Bill, 'it takes more than a little to-ing and fro-ing to put me off my stroke!'

'Glad to hear it, Bill,' said Rob. And no sooner had he spoken than there was a wrench to starboard so forceful that everyone, not excluding the Captain, had to reach out for stability, and a number of plates and glasses went crashing down onto the floor.

'Let's hope all this doesn't last too long,' said Rob, as if significantly. (Wouldn't it be better to leave Bill alone? There he was, wanting nothing to do with him, and yet here he now was voluntarily protracting conversation!)

'Last too long?' There was now in Bill's eyes precisely the look Rob desired. An unmistakable whip of alarm passed across large irises, dilating the pupils. 'Maybe,' he was thinking, 'I shouldn't have made this sea-crossing at all.'

'You never know, in these parts,' said Rob, lying, of course. He had had plenty of experience of the Atlantic (or so it now seemed) and, besides, there was Irish Jerry's meteorogical report, only recently picked up: the swell would have subsided by late evening. 'But don't you worry, Bill!'

The ship momentarily steadied itself so Bill could pick up his soup-spoon with a nonchalant gesture, and reply to Rob: 'I haven't said I *am* worrying, have I? And *you* don't seem to be worrying either. Full of energy, full of go, aren't you?'

Rob didn't care for the tone of this remark much. 'Oh, we don't get any allowance for rough seas when we're signed on,' he said, 'the officers and crew all have to eat and drink even if –' he glanced at all the empty places, 'others don't want to.'

Bill said: 'I wasn't just thinking of your work.' And his tone was meaningful and the glance from his bulbous eyes knowing.

Rob thought: 'He *is* aware what's happened between Pete and me. He *has* somehow been able to see it, just as he's seen all the badness in my Foswich past. The black arts!' He felt frightened. Was this why he said – against his better judgement, against his wishes, or so it seemed: 'Did you . . . did you want me to come down to your cabin this afternoon? At the usual time?' He hoped the way in which he asked this would elicit a denial. 'Oh, I hadn't thought ahead as far as that,' Bill said, a little loftily, 'I've had so many things to be getting on with – several matters I should have attended to in Jackson and didn't . . .'

He can't have cared about my immortal soul and its dangers as much as he made out if he's willing to let me go *this* easily, thought Rob. Memories of the fervour of the cabin sessions instantly swarmed into his head, however, as if to refute this conclusion. It was all very strange. Strange too that he felt nettled, if not actually hurt, by Bill's present indifference.

'Oh, well, see you around. Must tend to the others . . .' And Rob slouched off almost reluctantly.

Though the forecast picked up by the Radio Officer was surely to be believed, the swell increased with the afternoon; relentlessly, cruelly indeed, that process of the elevation and descent of the horizon against the equilibrium of the ship advanced until almost everybody was adversely affected by it. Maybe the serenity of the previous days of this voyage had created a false physical security: Rob was surprised to find that he himself was beginning to feel queasy. 'Of *course* I'm not sea-sick! he told himself, 'the idea's just been put into my head by all these silly passengers.' Be that as it may, the idea as sensation would not leave him, and a dampness broke out all over his face and in great splodges upon his body. He hadn't known anything like this since those dreadful storms of March, and yet it was true what Mrs Van Asdalen had said; the sky and sea continued an unsullied, healthy blue. The kingfisher's wing still prevailed . . .

Rob went into his cabin. Yielding to nausea he gave himself a drink of water, followed it with another, and then threw himself down on the bunk. What was the *real* explanation of Bill's acquiescence in his stopping the visits to Cabin Number Five, he wondered; how, knowing – as disquietingly he did – that Rob was defying the particular moral law which he espoused, could he permit him to go on and on till death and perdition?

Could the truth be that – yes, say it! *He was too wicked for any Redemption* . . .? Possibly – no, *probably* – the reason he'd handed Rob that photocopy of the *General Epistle of Jude* was that he wanted Rob to realise the futility of any spiritual rescue-operation. He, Rob Peters, was 'one of those' who were 'before of old ordained to . . . condemnation.'

If this were the case – if no amount of salvation-work could alter his plight – what should Rob do? What indeed was there for him to do? . . . He could enjoy himself, with Filipino Pete and a hundred, a thousand others. He could put aside all the guilts that he'd been encouraged to let surface these last days – guilts that had made him want to assault his own body as a very temple of evil – and just get on with – with what? With life, he supposed. With being busy and having a good time until the day arrived when he died and was transported to an eternity of fire, an eternity of blackness, from which no one – not even Jesus, Son of God – could deliver him. You would just have to hope that you lived a long time, for this moment, dreadful beyond any words or images, to be delayed . . . And just then the ship rolled on its port-side so savagely that Rob wondered how it could ever restore itself. The end might come – well, today. Another hour and he would see and hear the flames – no, not see them, for he'd be in the blackness of darkness, he who as a boy had refused to go to sleep unless he could see a chink of light through the curtains, who dreaded those moments in railway trains, when they charged through tunnels without putting the lights on, and all was like pitch, and you seemed suddenly to have been robbed of the power of sight . . .

It was hard to tell now whether the waves of nausea that broke over him were due to the workings of the current or to his own new understanding of Bill's view of his condition. But strong, lashing waves they were, and Rob, face-down, clutched the sides of the bed, and moaned. Bile dribbled from his mouth and salt-water was squeezed, by some inner pressure, from his eyes onto the pillow-case.

And then there was a knock on the door.

'Bill,' thought Rob, almost relieved, 'it's Bill come to arrange a session for this afternoon after all!' 'Come in!' he cried. And the door – very slowly – opened, and there was Pete.

'Rob,' said his companion, his lover of the past two nights, 'Rob, help me – I feel so bad.'

Indeed Rob scarcely needed to be told. The boy was doubled up and trembling, and his marvellous golden colour was gone; his was now a greenish hue. His quivering mouth hung open, his eyes were watery yet lustreless, and a bitter aroma clung round him, him who smelt, as no one knew better than Rob, normally so very sweet . . .

'It'll pass,' said Rob, finding somehow the strength to lift himself up from his bunk and stumble towards his visitor, 'it'll pass. I've never known the swell *this* bad – outside storms, of course. But it *will* end, and then *you'll* be better! Jerry reckons that by 8.30 p.m. we'll be out of it. Or at least the worst part.' Pete was now – like some collapsed puppet – in his arms, and – heaven help him! – even though threads of recent vomit adhered to the boy's lips, Rob felt a sudden and strong surge of desire. Obeying a will of its own, his penis stiffened. 'One of those who were before of old . . .' Stop, Rob silently shouted to himself, stop, stop, stop!

'I want to . . . to lie down,' Pete spluttered out, and flung himself down on the floor in precisely the attitude he'd adopted as the dying bird. And with a sort of desperate creature-courage he tried to sustain himself against that tilting to first one side, then the other, that tilting which did indeed seem like some sadistic elemental sport . . . 'It feels . . . feels good to be staying with you,' Pete spoke into the dun-coloured carpeting. 'I can't tell you how good. I'm going to die . . . I know it, I'll never see my friends and family again. But at least *you'll* be there. I like you such a lot . . .'

Rob could not but be moved by these words. He made no reply to them, but then Pete wasn't in any position to appreciate one, fighting his sickness, contorted on the floor. On and on, first this way, then that way, rocked the ship, like a cradle that was bearing you not *into* a world but out of one. I ought to face up to the fact that Jerry may have misinformed us, said Rob to himself. Perhaps this isn't the famous current after all, but something quite different. Some nautical danger I haven't yet learned about. Still what Pete just said goes for me and my feelings about *him*! If the end is coming, I'm pleased he's nearby . . . Death could maybe turn out as beautiful as a tropical bird or an English kingfisher, as the taking of a bird's spirit into a human body.

But almost as soon as he'd thought these things, the *Egon Ludendorff* gave her greatest shudder of the day, and then – *then*! though the horizon didn't exactly remain still, its heaving and plunging ceased. Minutes went by. Eventually Rob dared to turn himself gently over so that he could look the better at Pete. And Pete, for his part, was now lying on his back, his eyes fixed, affectionately, gratefully on his companion.

'I think . . . think she's stabilising now,' said Rob.

'I can't believe it,' said Pete, 'I can't believe we're ever going to move straight again.'

But the rattling of objects all over the deck was all but over now. A certain harmony was re-established between one thing and another, and between the interior of the ship and what lay beyond the porthole. 'Thank God!' said Rob to himself. And then he wondered if the Being that Bill Bentley was trying to present to him really did – or *could* – care about the fate of a few unimportant people and a load of American coal upon the Atlantic. He was feeling stronger by the second; before long his eyes were able to rest again – without distress – on the line of sea meeting sky.

'Rob?'

'Yeah?'

'Help me!'

'But it's subsided quite a lot, Pete, can't you *feel* it? A few hours and the whole experience'll have become part of the past.'

'I said "Help me!" Look!'

The black eyes gleamed with urgency. And Pete was unzipping himself and letting a cock emerge that was expanding to the ready . . .

'What are you waiting for?'

'Nothing.'

Rob climbed slowly off the bunk, in the grip of the greatest sweep of desire he'd ever known. He let Pete undress him. When they embraced, it wasn't simply that they went to each other as intimates, with the courage of familiarity. It was more, now, that each felt himself the question to the other's answer.

'How long will you be in England?'

'Depends on my family,' said Rob; they were lying side by side now, and Peter was smoking a Lucky Strike, 'and of course, on *me*. I don't get on too well with my folks, you see. But there's someone in Foswich, my home-town, I have to look up'.

'A friend like me?'

'I've told you, I've *no* friend like you.' And Rob stretched out a hand and, with nice tenderness touched Pete's prick, still moist, still stiff, the foreskin still down a bit so that the whole resembled a spring-time bud.

'But he's important to you?'

'The most!'

'And when you've seen him?'

'Back to Germany, I suppose. To sign on in Hamburg!'

'We can go back to Germany together perhaps. And before that the two of us can enjoy ourselves in London. I've heard you can have a *great* time there. Fun! Love!'

'Hmm!' How beautiful Pete's bony face seemed! The smear of bile, the sweat that had enveloped him had only made him the more exquisite and desirable . . . And simultaneous with post-coital calm and with response to the movement of the ship came images of a Saxon chapel and of the grinning, haughty face of its 'owner', one Julian Lumley-Greenville of Saxingham Enfrith.

Half-past three, and back to work! Some passengers hadn't recovered from their nausea, while the swell, though greatly reduced, was still palpable. Mrs Van Asdalen appeared for tea and a slice of Madeira cake. *How was she doing*? Well, she was a seasoned traveller, you know. She'd merely taken a medicinal glass of brandy, had had a short nap, and then . . . she didn't understand what all the goddam fuss was about. So the boat swayed from side to side! Big deal!

Among the passengers who did not show up for afternoon tea, however, was Bill Bentley. His absence cried out at Rob in that room he had as good as furnished with his healthy, confident form. 'I think,' said Andy, 'it might be a good idea to take some tea round to those passengers who aren't here. João'll probably need some help.'

Thus it was that Rob found himself knocking at the door of the horribly familiar Cabin Number Five. Could the tremulous voice that said 'Come in!' really be Bill's? Rob entered to find the stalwart evangelist prone on the bed, the anti-human hues of sea-sickness clear on his bronzed face.

'Hey, Bill, you poorly?' said Rob. As if he needed to ask! 'Andy thought absent passengers might appreciate a cup of tea, so I've brought you one. It's our English remedy for everything, isn't it?' A brief vision of *The Copper Kettle* came to him.

'That's mighty good of you, Rob, mighty good,' said Bill Bentley, and his sincerity was patent, 'I'm afraid the sea got the better of me after all. I'll be all right in a while.'

Somehow, as he spoke, Rob could imagine Bill his own age. What *had* he been like then? A sinner apparently. But mustn't he always have realised that he was going to know the Lord – at least realised this in some deep region of his being?

'I'm sorry you're poorly. Here, let me hold the cup for you!' All that was capable and kindly in Rob was crystallised in his next action – holding the teacup in his steady young hand for the suddenly enfeebled but still dignified Bill. Whom he did not like, would surely never like. But making love with Pete had given him such a sense of well-being that he would have performed any kind office for anyone – even his dad.

'You're a good kid,' said Bill, and let us hope he was speaking from his heart! 'I miss our sessions!'

'Take another mouthful,' urged Rob, pressing the tea-cup closer again, 'I can see a bit of normal colour returning to your face even now. Give us a few hours, and we'll be back on completely smooth seas again.'

'It's a terrible thing to let a friend down,' remarked Bill, when he'd done what Rob had bidden him, 'a very terrible thing indeed.'

Cold hands suddenly seemed to clasp Rob round the waist.

'Do you . . . do you think that *I've* let *you* down then?' he asked. He did not want to repeat those terrible afternoons – retchings far more painful than any the ocean could cause – but maybe he could visit the bloke from time to time, just to show that he meant him well.

'I'm not talking about myself,' said Bill, 'surely you've understood the gist of all our talks. I'm talking about the One Friend who *really* cares for you, who *really* needs you and will look after you . . .'

'You mean, Jesus?' said Rob.

'Come off it, Rob, who else could I mean? Of course I've been around, I see how things are with you. Another friend, another *kind* of friend, shall we say?' and he paused significantly, 'seems far more exciting than the steadiness I've been trying to bring home to you, the steadiness that *Jesus* offers when he becomes our friend . . . An earthly buddy will let you down, Rob, specially if, believe you me, specially if he is one of this . . . this certain *kind*. Just as you yourself have let people down, Rob, even someone you valued and still, in fact, value . . .'

It was quite pointless even to attempt incomprehension. Quite how Bill knew about Laurie (as well as about Pete) Rob felt too frightened even to guess: possibly in all his confessions he must have implied the worst deed of his life, the one he so far had been unable to articulate aloud, so fearful an indictment of himself was it.

'Why . . .' stammered Rob, preferring to think about the friend of a *certain kind* than about the man he'd betrayed in Foswich, 'why can't you have both? Someone on *earth* who means a lot to you – even in a particular way' – he tried not to blush here, 'and then also someone in Heaven as friend for those sides of yourself that the earthly one can't reach.' It suddenly seemed so reasonable – and feasible – an ideal that Rob wondered why he had not thought it before, wondered too that it was not the ideal of every man, woman and child.

For answer Bill, laying down his cup on the bedside table, gave Rob the hardest, most challenging stare he'd ever been subjected to. For reasons he as yet could not understand Rob realised that this double friendship he proposed wasn't 'on', as far as salvation was concerned. He saw rather that the pendulum of a dreadful, and surely unnecessary, either/or was being swung in front of him.

And Saxingham Enfrith – house, grounds, chapel – was, all in a trice, surreally, horribly clear to him.

'Have you got calls on other cabins to make?' Bill was asking him.

'Yeah! One other!'

'Couldn't you come back here afterwards? I'm sure I'll be feeling better then – thanks to *you*, Rob. And we haven't so much time left to follow up the stuff we've talked about earlier. We've got rather more work to do together than I'd appreciated. We're dealing with eternal issues, Rob, eternal issues!'

Bill gave him here a much-rehearsed, much-employed smile – of comradeship, of cheer in the face of known hardship, of congratulation on the meeting of a strenuous challenge. Rob was not proof against smiles; he'd been given too few of them in his life. Obviously he'd been wrong about Bill; the guy did care what happened to him, had just been waiting for an opportunity to re-state his case. 'Well, Bill, I reckon I could look in for a short while, yes!' he said.

Stepping out in the corridor, however, he encountered João, whose handsomeness the day's swell had not in the slightest tarnished. João also gave him a smile – one of breath-taking charm and flirtatiousness. 'Hullo, beautiful,' he said, 'been calling on that old sugar-daddy of yours.'

Rob laughed, 'He's not old,' he said, 'and he's certainly not a sugar-daddy of mine – or anyone else's.'

João threw back his great black bull's head and laughed. 'I love your innocence, Rob; man, I swear I love it. Where did

you pick it up? I wouldn't mind a bit of it myself!'
'I was born with it,' said Rob, though to himself he said: 'But I've lost it now.'

CHAPTER SIX: LAURIE

Polly Keating, it soon was clear to Laurie, was as keen for a boy-friend as he himself was for a girl. She had only just got over a long, and mostly unhappy, affair with a married man, a Keeper of Anglo-Saxon and Early Norman manuscripts who had once declared himself willing to leave wife and three children for her sake. Laurie found it flattering, as well as unnerving, to be following so sophisticated an individual. How uninformed his conversation must seem, and how dull his emotional past, compared to those of Fenton Carmichael. His very name sounded distinguished, and it was one that Polly spoke really rather often, though always in comparisons to Laurie's advantage. 'Oh, Fenton would never have thought of *that*!', 'Imagine *Fenton* being kind enough to do such a thing!' And she would give Laurie a grateful, plucky if bitter little smile that made him feel that truly he'd entered the army of the world's lovers again.

The weekends of Polly's visits to Foswich followed a very definite and, for Laurie, reassuring pattern. She would arrive early on the Friday evening, say around half-past six. After the embraces of glad reunion she'd say: 'And now I'm going to really *do* your flat for you. At the end of a whole week of Anglo-Saxon religion I've a real need for some practical occupation.' 'Doing' the flat was not just a matter of sweeping or dusting or tidying, it meant a re-arranging of furniture, the installation of some gadget that might well, she thought, transform Laurie's life, the positioning of trailing house-plants or bonsai which she'd come across in some special shop. Then came a light supper cooked by Laurie, talk usually of a confiding retrospective nature (it was then she would reveal the callousnesses and acts of exploitation that Fenton Carmichael had been so abundantly guilty of) and, after this, love-making and sleep in each other's arms. Polly's sleep was like some flimsy veil she'd throw over herself: the least thing could disturb it.

They'd get up at a conventional hour the next day. Polly 'adored' Saturday mornings in country towns, and was very talkative to the people she encountered in Foswich shops, displaying that bright, self-conscious curiosity that English middle-class tourists like to display to the permanent residents of foreign towns they stay in – asking questions of a local florist or greengrocer and listening to the replies with a wide-eyed raptness.

After shopping, lunch – perhaps at a pub, perhaps at *The Copper Kettle*; both presented dangers. In the High Street's two busiest and most cheerful pubs – *The King's Arms* and *The Crown and Anchor*, there was the virtual certainty of coinciding with colleagues, parents, and ex-pupils. While Laurie was pleased for them to see him in the company of so pretty a girl, he couldn't prevent himself being irritated at the amount of time Polly was prepared to give them all. She remembered so much more about each person than Laurie did, nor did her interest in these Foswich folk end once encounters with them were over. Later Laurie would have to listen to a kind of analytical synopsis of the progress of their lives, rather as if they were characters in a soap-opera, as perhaps indeed for her they were.

The problems of *The Copper Kettle* were, however, graver. For he had to confront Rob and the Peters family. He had – somewhat diffidently – told Polly that he had an out-of-school friendship with Rob different from that he enjoyed with other pupils at St John's. 'It's hard to explain why . . .' he'd said, with complete truth, for it didn't submit very well to serious self-questioning. 'But *I* can understand why, perfectly,' she'd exclaimed after that first meeting, 'those intense brown eyes (with that fair colouring too!) and that look of adoration he turns in your direction when he thinks you aren't looking!'

'Oh, I'm sure he doesn't,' said Laurie, disconcerted, though in fact he'd caught Rob giving him these looks several times.

'And why shouldn't he?' asked Polly, 'there's such a charming ingenuousness about boys at that age; it's so very, very lovable. I'm sure *I* shall come to like him a lot, too.'

Despite this certainty she was not at all keen on including him on any of the Saturday afternoon excursions. This was perhaps the principal reason for *The Copper Kettle* seceding to the hearty, genteel, populous pubs as summer progressed. Rob was more often than not serving the meals, and would be apt to hang around their table, both during and after the lunch itself, as if waiting, indeed expecting an invitation from them. Polly always made much of Rob's forthcoming examinations, for which, in truth, he was doing remarkably little work. 'Poor you, Rob! I feel for you, I really do. A Ph.D. in Anglo-Saxon religious history is *nothing* to 'O' Level Maths, you can take it from me.'

Rob's eyes would cloud over; maybe he was thinking, as Laurie was, that even to *speak* of him in connection with a Ph.D. thesis was preposterous – and also somehow, probably unintentionally, mocking.

Meanwhile Beryl Peters would have scrutinised them from the kitchen doorway with a refined malignance, or Anne – whose burnished hair rivalled Polly's own – might have called out: 'There *are* other customers in the cafe, Rob!' Or Geoff Peters, on a half-sozzled yet haughty inspection of the premises, could have glanced in Laurie's direction and then explored Polly with his veinous lecher's eyes. What's such a good-looking girl doing with an artsy-fartsy fool like him, he was obviously saying to himself.

These trips from which Rob was more often than not excluded frequently had as their destination one of the Anglo-Saxon churches in which Essex is comparatively rich. Polly's Renault seemed veritably to be borne, these warm, langourous June afternoons, over the billowing pastureland –

rich green broken by the brilliant yellow splodges of rape – towards where some stubborn squat tower reared itself to show where more than a thousand years ago Christians had believed ardently enough to erect a sober, stolid tribute to their God. Sometimes, while listening to Polly explaining some point of architectural history and how it corresponded with creeds and social ideals, Laurie would let his mind wander, or perhaps better, to drift up to God. He didn't believe in Him, at least that's what he'd always said. But stepping out of a quiet, damp, little church into the thick, animated silence of a yew-dominated graveyard, Laurie would wonder if maybe, in a sort of way, he could. He would even formulate a prayer to himself which the country peace seemed to suggest would be granted; it was always the same prayer: 'Look after my mother. Make her properly well again, and live to a ripe old age – just like Rembrandt's mother in that painting.'

If the operation had left Mum tired, troubled and subject to weepy glooms, having to go into Oxford three times a week for deep-ray treatment induced a deep morbidity which she was loath to shake off, despite assurances and good reports. The rays burned and bruised her black and blue. Mum told Laurie that, locked in a hospital room with a huge machine that, though curative, was nevertheless terrifying in its power, she would pass the time of enforced capitulation by a singing all the old songs she knew: 'Dashing away with the Smoothing-Iron', 'Bobby Shaftoe', 'On Ilkla Moor Baht 'At', – Laurie had forgotten she'd known them all, but now, of course, he remembered her singing them to him in his infancy, to soothe away his pains real and imaginary. He found the image of Mum's repeating the songs in such different circumstances – when the breasts he'd once suckled were wounded and sore and stitched – peculiarly affecting, and, in Essex churchyards, he commended it to God's attention. It had to be admitted that others in his family still didn't appear particularly worried. Dad, in a private phone call had expressed laconic satisfaction with 'your mother's progress', and either Mick or Dale had said: 'Oh, Mum's going to be *perfectly* all right. I mean to say practically every woman in the country's had the op. she's had, hasn't she? Why don't you start bothering yourself with the problem of when the *fuck* yours truly's going to find himself a job?'

The exploration of an Essex village and its hoary church over – and maybe notes on the latter written, in Polly's copybook-worthy italic hand – there would arise the matter of where to dine that evening. Polly always carried a surprising amount of money with her (at least it was surprising to Laurie) and she also was the proud (if casual-seeming) possessor of several credit-cards. *The Good Food Guide* lay in the front of the car like a talisman; no St Christopher could have been treated more reverently. Dinner was always 'on' Polly, and she was heedless of its price; in fact Laurie suspeted her of preferring it to be expensive. Here she was very unlike Amanda and Kate and Lucy and Emma. She was not at all indifferent to what she ate, however, knew exactly when a sauce wasn't piquant enough or of the requisite creamy consistency. Once or twice she sent wines back – not cold enough or insufficiently *chambré*! Such behaviour embarrassed the easy-going Laurie until he noticed the look of sycophantic admiration that every waiter gave her, and then he too felt a glow of pleasure at a pretty young Pre-Raphaelite-visaged girl acting with such authority.

Sunday morning they got up late. Often as late as mid-day, though the windows would have been opened wide to let in the splendid June sunshine and the fragrance of the roses that positively crowded the neat Foswich gardens. They would make full love a great many times. Polly liked Laurie to take the lead, something to which he was by no means averse. She would often exhibit a shy gratitude for this that quite touched Laurie. Here was another way in which she differered from Amanda et al. Probably this was why he told himself that he was in love as never before.

Throughout Sunday lunch and the walk that always followed it – along the Fase, into the easier reaches of the Forest – separation was imminent. Polly liked to be back in London for the whole of Sunday evening. 'Otherwise Monday becomes all tainted, and my Anglo-Saxon religion will suffer, and I'll be full of regrets.'

'But you're tainting *Sunday* by leaving so early,' protested Laurie, clasping her imploringly to him, 'isn't that as bad?'

But Polly was not to be budged. So, from twelve o'clock onwards, Laurie would feel a physical tightness, a sinking in his stomach, intimations of mortality which vitiated even the most interesting and forward-looking of conversations, even the most idyllic of strolls through Foswich and its surroundings.

The sudden arrival of Rob could also do this, indeed, later in the summer and the relationship, the very prospect of it. Rob Peters – what on earth was Laurie to do about Rob Peters? None of the other pupils Laurie had taken up had turned out to need him in this sort of way, to make him into an object of such pathetic and hopeless obsession. The duties promised his mother in *The Copper Kettle* apart, Rob appeared willing to sacrifice absolutely anything – work for 'O' Levels; activities with other boys and girls; family peace – for the sake simply of physically being with Laurie. That Laurie might be paying attention to someone else cut no ice with him at all!

The doorbell might ring at – let's say, half-past-twelve on Sunday morning. Should it be answered? Well, it *might* not be Rob. But it always was ... *This* time however, Laurie would say to himself, I'll be firmer, make it clear to the lad that, much as I like him, I want to be on my own with Polly.

Was he prevented from doing this by remembering how, only six/seven weeks ago he'd have been delighted to find Rob Peters on his doorstep. Or was it the beseeching, doting look in Rob's eyes that made truth-telling so difficult?

'Hi, Laurie, beautiful day, isn't it?'

'Hullo, Rob. Actually Polly and I ... we've only *just* got up, I'm afraid.' Despite his being able to feel the play of the boy's brown eyes – stripping him of his so recently donned clothes to see back to the love-making attitudes of less than an hour ago – Laurie would persevere: 'Disgustingly late, but then it *is* Sunday. Day of rest and all that!'

Rob would look unconvinced. 'You and Polly thought of going for a walk this afternoon? I was just wondering if either of you'd ever been over to Durrant's Mill; it's really great up there, with an old mill-wheel and all.'

Laurie would feel rather as if he were denying a dog a bone he'd just shown it – and then maybe half-beating it in exasperation at the (aroused) vexatious interest it was showing. 'Quite honestly,' he'd stammer out through his uneasy conscience, which possessed the entire doorway like a miasma, 'we haven't decided *what* we're going to do after we've had our lunch. Polly has to leave early and . . .'

Sometimes there could be no getting out of inviting Rob with them. On such occasions Laurie would deliberately walk with his arm firm and amorous round Polly's waist. That surely would demonstrate to the lad that he was together with Polly in a way that he could never be with him. And the demonstrativeness might even embarrass him! Some hope! Rob revealed himself as thicker-skinned than his manner at other times would have indicated. He prattled on (once did so while Laurie and Polly stopped for a picturesquely-sited kiss), giving them a whole heap of facts about flowers and birds and animals and Essex lore and topography. He didn't mind repeating himself either. More than once did Laurie and Polly hear how kingfishers tunnel narrow passages, in the banks and create nest-chambers at the end of these; more than once were they told of how 'centuries ago' the Fase had been different in its course, and how (as if one didn't know!) Foswich meant Fase-wich, the town on the Fase . . .

'He gets a bit wearing, doesn't he?' said Polly feelingly after a walk through water-meadows on the far side of the Japanese bridge, 'I'm afraid – when time's running out between us – I can't help wishing him away.'

'Me too!' said Laurie, 'anyway he should be working for his exams now.'

'Sweetie,' said Polly, unwinding her pretty, pink gauze scarf, '*whatever* do you talk about when I'm not there? Does he still go on regaling you with the nesting habits of every bird in sight?'

Laurie puckered his brow in thought. 'No, he doesn't do *that* so much when we're alone together. But the funny thing is, Polly, now you ask, I can't remember. I suppose he talks mainly about himself. This week I'll try and take note of what he says, and I'll answer your question next Friday.'

For Laurie's visits to *The Copper Kettle* still continued, as did the strolls he took with Rob afterwards. Rob spoke principally, Laurie registered, about his fantasy of the moment. Now that he had received from Laurie the address of the Ludendorff company in Hamburg (to whom, to Laurie's surprise he'd already written), his mind seemed taken up to an almost feverish degree with the prospect of voyages – across the North Sea, up and down the Baltic, from one side of the Atlantic to the other. He wanted to hear as many anecdotes of Laurie's dad's life as possible, and Laurie's own experience aboard the *William Wilberforce* never failed to interest him, he'd obviously accompanied him to Copenhagen many time in his imagination. What kind of birds had Laurie seen from the boat? Had Laurie's dad ever caught glimpse of a whale?

'Maybe we could make a voyage *together*?' he suggested almost rapturously – they were once again upon the Japanese-style wooden bridge. 'But I suppose if you made a voyage now, you'd want Polly Keating to come with you.'

'With or without Polly, I don't think my life admits of a voyage right now,' said Laurie, he trusted dismissingly.

The other boys and girls from St John's School whom Laurie had befriended had engaged lively relations with their fellows and their community. Not so Rob! Laurie and no other was the member of the school staff for whom he cared; all the rest could go hang, and he didn't know that he had much in common with his old mates any more. As for his feelings about his family, well, he'd made those fairly explicit that very first tea-time they'd spent together, and everything that Laurie had heard or witnessed since confirmed the fact that Rob was in no way warmly disposed to his home.

'Sometimes,' this was two days after the walk on which he'd talkatively 'played gooseberry', 'I wish we were all born out of single eggs on a great plain. Aren't there some birds or primitive creatures who have simply to make their own way out of their shells? Think of it! We'd all have to fend for ourselves, strike up relationships if we wanted to, but with nothing to join, nothing to belong to, nothing to escape from. Wouldn't that be great?'

'I suppose so,' said Laurie. The question had to be asked: after that fortnight which had seemed to deliver them both from loneliness, that fortnight heralded by the kingfisher, didn't he find Rob – well, something of a bore? Rob was a mere boy, he reminded himself, thirteen years younger than himself.

'But I suppose even in those circumstances there'd be pairing off,' said Rob, as in glum refutation of the validity of his own fancy. Laurie took these words as a sort of rebuke to himself for his relationship with Polly. It was, once again, extremely hot; the sun had been tireless and staring in a cloudless sky, and even now that it was declining, its power lingered, making all walls warm to the touch, and all interiors airless ... He wished Rob would leave. Later tonight – sweating, a little tired and fractious – he would mark some Art History essays. Before that, a bath, a glass of beer, without the egotistic ramblings of this *kid*!

'... You didn't hear what I just asked you obviously!'

'Sorry: my mind was on the work I've got to do this hot night. Just as *you've* got to, Rob. 'O' Levels are not that far off, you know. You can count the days now ...'

'I bloody *know* when 'O' Levels begin, Laurie, thanks. But maybe you just didn't want to answer my question.'

'Not at all,' said Laurie, 'I was merely hot and tired and inattentive. I'll get us some cokes from the fridge, shall I?' (Rob, perhaps because of the example of Geoff Peters so constantly before him, never 'fancied beer' as he put it, and Laurie didn't like to drink it in his company.)

'Thanks! Laurie, what I asked you was – how old were you when you first made love with someone?'

'I ... I really can't remember.' For some reason, which he didn't understand, Laurie was both vexed by the question and unwilling to answer it.

'Oh, come off it, Laurie. Don't tell me if you don't want to, but don't give me that for an answer. It's something that *everyone* must remember – their first time.'

'I don't know that it really appears quite like that,' said Laurie, yanking up the lever of the coke tin, principally to avoid looking into Rob's face, 'I mean, *technically*, well, of *course* there's a first time. But it's often followed by months, years maybe, of imagining your way round a girl's body. So that when at last you do the deed, as it were, it's not quite the event you might imagine. Nevertheless,' he couldn't forebear adding, 'once it's entered your life – real love-making – it's not something you want to do without again.' How, he wondered, *had* he endured all those empty years in Foswich? What dullness had possessed him? Why, now it was intolerable just to have to wait for Polly's next visit!

Rob was visibly giving these words thought – while tilting ice-cold coke down his throat – as, could he have understood them, he might have done dicta by Freud or Reich. 'I see what you mean. Perhaps I should have asked you a different question.' He looked up and his eyes burned across the room, so stuffy, so unsuitable for summer weather, with a daunting intensity. 'How old were you when you loved someone so much that you . . . you wanted to make love with that person?'

I don't see why I should reply, thought Laurie, not if I don't want to. And if he takes the hedging as a rebuff, well, perhaps so much the better. 'It quite escapes me,' he said, for him, slowly and coldly. 'If one believes the psychiatrists, I was probably five or six years old, only not "up" to it.' The vulgarism – really quite out of character – surprised them both; indeed Rob had to re-apply himself to the coke tin to hide his embarrassment. Presently he took his leave. Laurie was relieved to see him go; maybe he'd made it clear that he now wanted no more probing intimate questions. Strangely however he could not forget Rob, his intensity of expression, all evening. He went to bed late – marking those essays took longer than he'd expected, and tired, threw himself down on the bed naked, needing neither pyjamas or coverlet. Sleep was elusive, but, through its grey counterfeit veils, he kept on seeing a kingfisher of dazzling virginal blue, rising from the river Fase. And nearby, on the bridge that spanned this, stood an ardent boy whom he'd long wanted to know . . .

Laurie went to Tanbury the next weekend, while Polly attended a family reunion in Putney. The train moved slowly up the Thames valley as if combatting the heat that had rolled so copiously all over the country: it seemed to drive the haze before it, from off fields, hill-slopes, the great river itself. Tanbury wore the aspect of the most intense days of Laurie's adolescence; the glow of the golden stone of its older buildings, the shimmer of its gardens, the tantalising faintness of the line of the Cotswolds in the distance, all brought back to him those days when Jonathan West had opened the world to him as a place of adventure and beauty. Jonathan West – he must see him again!

Adventure and beauty were singularly lacking in the house on the Meadowborough estate. Mum was as wrapped in depression as Oxfordshire was in the recently so relentless heat. She was sitting miserably outside in the small, much over-looked garden when Laurie arrived:

'Your dad seems to think that being out of doors is going to change me,' she grumbled, 'though whether he means my spirits or my disease, I can't quite tell. Daft idea! I've always loathed the heat! We Yorkshire folk aren't used to it.'

That was certainly very true, thought Laurie; in his childhood memories a savage wind blew almost continuously from off the North Sea.

'What d'you mean, your disease?' said Laurie, 'you know that the doctors' reports are excellent.'

'Why am I having to spend day after day locked up in a room with a brute of a machine, then?' asked Mum defiantly, turning her still pretty yet exhausted face to her eldest son's, 'tell me that, Mr Know-all?'

'It's been explained to you,' said Laurie, putting his arms round her, '*and* to Dad, *and* to me. It's a precaution – to clear up anything that might not have been removed with the operation. Do you think the doctors would have lied to Dad about the whole matter?' He quickly answered the question; for, alas! it was one that several times had occurred to him, 'Of course they wouldn't!'

'Ah,' said Mum, 'but how can I know that the whole lot of

you aren't fibbing, because you think I'm a hysterical woman who isn't able to accept the truth.'

'What truth?' asked Laurie deliberately, though he knew.

'That I'm dying, of course,' said Mum, with a smile at once bitter and flirtatious, 'that I shan't be here to see next summer.'

Laurie could not avert a sudden current of fear and sadness. What if his mother were right? She had been so constant a presence in his life, always the same mixture of warmth and contentiousness; for her not to be in the world would be for the world to be other than itself. It would have turned into another planet.

'Mum, you're letting morbidity get the better of you. Why don't you and I go down into Tanbury and have a drink at one of those pubs which has a nice garden to it?'

'There you go; you're as bad as your dad. What's so special about gardens for heaven's sake that all the world expects me to be *in* one, the whole time?'

'Well, it *is* rather exceptional weather,' said Laurie, feeling that he must be sounding like a particularly patronising matron, 'it seems a shame to be indoors on an evening like this!'

'Indoors, outdoors, as if it makes any difference when you're dying,' said Mum. She looked away from Laurie now, towards that gap which showed Tanbury proper below, dominated by its cupola-crowned church and spreading out towards an industriously farmed Midlands landscape.

'Mum, if you use that word again, I'll take the next train back,' said Laurie, unable to think of any more effective threat.

'I'll use it *one* more time,' said Mum provocatively, 'and then I *might* – *might* let up for a while. *As* I'm dying, I have a right to ask something of you, I think. After all, you wouldn't be here if it wasn't for me!'

'What is it?' Laurie could not but be apprehensive.

'I want you to have married someone by the time I go – that is by next summer. I can't believe you're not seeing some girl or other right *now*. And it's time you stopped your silly bachelor life – waiting around for Miss Wonderful to appear. Who never will, because she doesn't exist . . .

Laurie suddenly felt a quickening throughout his body. 'I don't know about that,' he said, 'about Miss Wonderful – to use that awful expression – not existing. I think she does. I *have* met a girl, you see . . . whom I like very, very much.'

And – the confiding teenager again – he began to talk about Polly.

That weekend he did go over to Foxton and the cottage of Jonathan West and his wife. Would there ever come a moment in the whole march of Time when Foxton didn't stand serene and compact in its hollow, its cluster of thatched, honey-stone houses suggesting the repose given by harmonious work and well-adjusted living? Yet maybe that was yet another illusion, thought Laurie, as on his old bicycle, he sped down the lane, past the churchyard, to the Wests' home; there was every sign that these cottages that so proclaimed old English husbandry were increasingly the property of slick young businessmen and their socially pretentious wives.

Jonathan West was watering flowers from a huge old can, rather like the one which Beatrix Potter shows Peter Rabbit as having to hide in. He and his wife appeared pleased to see Laurie; they always liked, they said, a surprise visit from an old friend. Mrs West produced tea – as good as that produced by *The Copper Kettle* – a huge pot of Darjeeling, and, to eat, lardi-cake and a plate of chocolate buns. When this had been appreciatively consumed, she absented herself, in that almost pathologically diplomatic manner of hers, to bustle about some bucolic, domestic task or other – leaving Jonathan and Laurie to talk, as for so long they had done, as affectionate master and pupil. Laurie found himself able to express his worry that there might be foundation to Mum's worries about herself, that it was not impossible that she could die from what the Oxford specialist had discovered in her; he also, to his even greater surprise, could articulate both his warm feelings – well, *love* – for Polly and, too, anxieties about their relationship he'd scarcely known he entertained. The difference in social background, in financial position and expectation, would this perhaps increase, widen with the intertwining of their lives rather than the reverse? Laurie did not exactly say that he'd noticed an irritation, a weariness within himself at certain family stories of hers that seemed to him to suggest a smug unwitting exclusiveness. But he allowed this to be inferred from his sentences of hesitant but unfeigned criticism.

'And there's another thing that's been bothering me recently,' Laurie went on, 'you remember how, when I was going on against my life as schoolmaster, you reminded me of the pleasure you can have through a friendship with a pupil. Well, not so long afterwards, I did become pally with a fifth-former, Rob Peters.' Somehow the word 'pally', with its hearty yet casual connotations, seemed peculiarly inappropriate to what had been established between himself and Rob, and he was astonished how difficult it was saying his name aloud in a deliberately matter-of-fact way. 'He's an unusual combination of qualities, I suppose: not at all academic or artistic, hangs around with a pretty ordinary sort of bunch, but somehow he's got something inside him that's very sensitive and appreciative and independent . . .' He was not at all satisfied with this description, which surely applied to the majority of schoolboys in the country. 'He's not happy at home, and I suppose he was very pleased to have found an older person who took an interest in what he was doing and feeling, and who liked spending time in his company.'

'Just as *you* were to have found a *younger* one in that position,' said Jonathan West.

'Well, I didn't take to Rob *because* he was younger, did I?' objected Laurie, a little vexed by this unnecessary interruption.

'Didn't you?' said Jonathan West.

'Well, of course, not,' said Laurie, 'I mean, literally every single pupil at St John's is that.'

'Oh, quite, quite,' said Laurie's former teacher, 'but let's put it this way: can you imagine Rob as older than yourself? If he was himself at say, thirty-five, would you have been so keen on his company.'

'It's surely not possible to say,' said Laurie, realising that Jonathan West found it all too possible.

'But it can be beautiful, I think,' said Jonathan West, 'the friendship between an older person, a teacher in particular and a younger one. Each can give to the other such precious things!'

This wasn't what Laurie needed to hear; he didn't want to think that what he'd in fact solicited from Rob was a 'precious thing'.

'I remember how you, when you were this boy's age, brought me such happiness,' said Jonathan, 'I used to see even my favourite sketching places with new eyes. I'd feel: well, perhaps, I can paint them better now.'

It had never occurred to Laurie that there'd been this kind of reciprocation in their relationship of so many years ago. And of course he felt moved by this revelation, the more so because he had given Jonathan his 'precious things' unwittingly. Just by being young and innocent and ignorant and pleasant-looking, most probably.

'And I like to think that what I was able to show to you, the kind of introductions I made, were also not without value.'

'Oh, indeed!' said Laurie, hoping there was the sincerity he in fact felt in his voice. He was embarrassed by the turn the conversation had taken, and not greatly pleased either.

He had come here wanting confirmation *against* Rob Peters more than anything else, the advice of an experienced schoolmaster in how to cope with difficult pupils. And all he'd got was reminders of his own youth and indebtedness, and – as a result of this – a jogging of his memory that had tried to gloss over very recent sentiments.

For, of course, he had longed to know Rob Peters with an intensity that these last weeks had come to seem incredible. And he too had felt, during the few days of their unsullied friendship, that he was seeing things with new eyes, that the whole Fase Valley from the Japanese bridge upwards and downwards had been magically changed . . . Really Jonathan West, like Rob himself, was a bit of a bore (however kind and generous his last words), with this perpetually moral way of regarding things. He looked round the Wests' sitting-room, wanting to find fault with it, and, through it, with the whole way of life Jonathan and his wife had built up. Wasn't it all a bit shabby-genteel and self-conscious and puritan, he asked himself, greatly wanting to find affirmative proof of these qualities, which was surely not hard to seek. But, as so often happens, he found himself smitten with precisely the opposite emotions to those he desired to feel. What met his eyes filled him with admiration, with gratitude for past experiences, with the envy that relates to respect. The pretty china on the dresser seemed like a regiment aligned to fight on behalf of the spirit of calm; all the handmade wooden bowls and pitchers proclaimed themselves as worthy of the brush of Chardin; and Jonathan's own paintings on the walls formed a chain of gilt-framed prelapsarian worlds, an alternative solar system of freshness and tenderness, as desirable and lovable as they'd seemed when first he'd seen them. The truth was, a life such as Jonathan and Lorna West's was inexpressibly appealing to Laurie; it was what deeply he still would most like, and he felt angry with himself – and with Fate – that it eluded him.

He sat there ever more sourly, but talked on:

'To continue,' he said, 'for some weeks of this term Rob and I did a lot of things together that brought both of us pleasure. Walks to a country pub, excursions to one or two places in the neighbourhood, nothing very out of the ordinary!' Then . . . I met Polly, and naturally the two of us wanted – well, we *still* want – to be together *alone*. But Rob doesn't appreciate that; he's for ever angling for invitations, for ever hanging about and making us both feel embarrassed and guilty . . .'

'Excuse me, but I don't quite follow,' said the exasperating older schoolmaster; 'why should either of you feel as you've described? *Polly* can hardly know him, if you've been as excluding as you've implied.'

'Why *indeed* should we feel these things?' exclaimed Laurie, 'it's all a bit ridiculous! It isn't as if . . . as if I've ever had any feeling for this boy that wasn't totally straightforward. I've no interest of that kind in boys.' Yet the remark did not come out as the simple, denial he'd hoped for.

Jonathan West did not reply to this directly. Instead he said: 'Let me ask you something? In the days when you were a *young* friend of mine – for you are not *quite* in that category now – did you ever feel jealous of my wife Lorna?'

'Well, of course not,' said Laurie, almost crossly. The idea was preposterous.

'Precisely!' said Jonathan, 'which is to say that *this* friendship is a little different from that you enjoyed with me, and you should realise it.'

'What do you think I ought to do?'

'I think,' said Jonathan West, and Laurie couldn't altogether avoid the suspicion that his former teacher was enjoying this mantic role, 'that you must – just *once* – go out of your way to include him in something. You and Polly.'

'You mean invite him for some outing or other?'

'Something like that.'

Laurie tried to picture the occasion – with some difficulty. 'Well, *I could*', he conceded.

'You *should*,' said Jonathan West.

Shortly afterwards Mrs West appeared with a white picnic-box: 'Just a bit of summer-pudding,' she said, with disingenuous modesty, 'for your mother. With our very warmest wishes.'

These days the position of the sun seemed scarcely to affect the heat; Laurie's home on the Meadowborough Estate felt every whit as hot as when, a few hours of fuller daylight back, he'd left it. Mum was sitting inside, watching yet another showing of Alfred Hitchcock's *Rebecca* on television with a disturb-a-sick-woman-if-you-dare look upon her plump, tired face. 'Mrs West has given you *this*,' Laurie ventured to say, presenting his mother with the white box. Mum remained unimpressed, however. 'What on earth would I want *this* for?' she said, 'a lot of old bread and squashed-up fruit!' There was no pleasing her.

Dad was sitting in the garden with some fusty tome of Oxfordshire history on his lap. He plainly did not want to be interrupted. If Mum's operation had galvanised him into a rather livelier relation to his family, to the humdrum world about him, it had also plainly exhausted him. On his face could be read that pining for some remote anti-domestic existence which Laurie had always suspected. Why, he's elderly and discontented and too tired even to *try* to kick against the pricks, thought Laurie. He had a lot of his father in him. And nice though he was, he did not provide a very inspiring example of a man advanced along life's highway.

G.C.E. candidates came to school only for the examinations. In they'd slouch with something of the air of youthful combattants returned from the battlefield to a much resented parade-ground. Now and again Laurie would see the neat but dejected figure of Rob among them. No need to ask him how he was doing! But he *had* glanced at the lad's art exam and found it not at all bad; that was one subject surely that he'd have passed.

The weather made no kind of work easy and most people – Laurie included – unusually tetchy. It was Wednesday before Laurie spoke to Rob: the classes had seemed interminable. At the end of afternoon school Laurie went along to *The Copper Kettle*. All the world knows that on a very hot day a very hot cup of tea is the best restorative. Besides he had to act on Jonathan's advice. This was the last week of exams, Rob would be free at the weekend, and so he could give him the invitation to join Polly and himself on a visit to Saxingham Enfrith, a Suffolk country house.

The Copper Kettle was very full, so full that not only was Rob serving but his sister Anne also, tall and with a shock of red hair. She and Rob were dressed almost identically, white T-shirt, pale blue jeans, though unity wasn't what they suggested; every time they passed one another, weaving ways through the crowded room, they were exchanging obviously cross words and almost audible scowls. Rob looked drawn, pale, tense. 'But it can't be a case of too much midnight oil with him!' said Laurie to himself. So far Rob had only perfunctorily acknowledged him, and when at last he came to Laurie's table, he showed none of his customary (and unflagging) anxiety to please.

'My usual!' said Laurie with a near-flirtatious smile. Only a few days before he'd been saying that Rob was an intrusion in his personal life; now he was setting out to bring back the boy's affability, being pained by its absence.

'*What* usual!' said Rob gracefully.

'We-ell,' began Laurie, taken aback, but Rob cut in: 'I mean you don't have the same thing every bloody time, do you? We *do* try to vary the menu here, you know.'

'Steady on!' said Laurie, 'have I said you didn't?' He didn't succeed in meeting Rob's eyes which had narrowed and were lightless. He attempted a little joviality: 'What I'm after is the biggest pot of tea possible. God, how I need it after the ordeal of 4A.' Though, he reflected, 4A would be no worse than a stuffy cafe where sweat and cigarettes had successfully worked against the fragrance of all the sweet-peas and the pinks arranged in little vases on the oaken tables.

Rob made no reply.

'Lot of people here this afternoon,' Laurie went on – fatuously, he immediately realised.

'Yeah, I *had* noticed!' said Rob sarcastic. Then in an aggressive undertone he added: 'Stupid cunts! Don't think waiters are human beings, do they? I could teach them a thing or two.'

When – quite five minute later – he returned with the tea and scones, his hands were – Laurie observed – trembling slightly. 'You've been overdoing it!' he said to him.

'Maybe!'

'Well, let's hope it's produced the goods. Only one more exam to go!'

Rob's eyes widened. He gave a mirthless bark of laughter. 'You don't think I've been *revising*, do you?' he said, 'Bloody hell, what'd I want to be doing a pointless thing like *that* for? And when I was in the exam room I took it really cool, I can tell you.' His expression was quite malevolent here.

But then, suddenly he leaned over the table, and said, in a very different tone: 'Laurie, Mum says I can get off from here in about twenty minutes. My brother Phil's back early; he apparently doesn't mind giving a hand. I've been at it since 12 o'clock . . . There's something I'd really like to talk to you about.'

I suppose that means more questions about a life at sea, thought Laurie. Really the boy's egotism was pretty enormous: not a question about *Laurie's* problems, about the sad situation in Tanbury which he knew all about. Nevertheless: 'Okay, when I've finished, we can . . .'

'We can go for a stroll by the river,' said Rob, and how uncertain and nervous and charged his voice sounded.

Almost exactly twenty minutes later – Laurie had settled up the bill with Anne Peters – Rob appeared beside the table; his hair sprinkled with water and thoroughly combed, and with a different t-shirt. 'You ready, Laurie?' he asked, and the words had an oddly ominous ring to them.

They walked along the Foswich streets in virtual silence. Laurie's attempts at conversation (he tried Tanbury, school and the weather as topics) were not taken up. The town was very, very still, the sky also, a glaze of blue which you felt you could stroke. Its vividness emphasized the brilliance of the yellow rape and the tired quality of the greens of field and wood.

They crossed the river by the main bridge – then, down the steps to take the path that follows the bank to the Japanese half-moon bridge that had been so significant for the two of them. And it was like walking into a further dimension of quiet, a quiet of midges and quavery exhalations of warmth from both land and river-water. And there's something he badly needs to talk to me about, thought Laurie. Well, if it isn't going to be him that raises the matter, it'd better be me, hadn't it. 'So, Rob,' he said, 'what's up with you then?'

The answer could not have astonished him more. Spoken in a rapid, low, intent manner, it was: 'Laurie, I really believe I'm a bringer of destruction and death.'

Laurie had no words for so bizarre a statement. Rob was obviously disappointed at this (not only egotists but exhibitionists also, these adolescent boys, thought Laurie); eventually he said: 'You heard me?'

'Yes, but I don't know what to say to you. How *can* you be these things?'

Rob shook his head, as if Laurie had asked a wholly different question.

'You don't know me, I reckon. I have to face that,' he said. 'Shall I tell you something, Laurie?' He didn't wait for a reply. 'Sometimes I think that what I wish for most in the whole world is for you *really* to know me. But I reckon if you did, you wouldn't like me. Even less than you do now!' Those words are a gauntlet he's made himself throw down, realised Laurie; I'm going to refuse the challenge.

'I don't seem to want what most people want, do I?' Rob continued, his gaze not upon Laurie or the path but on weary ducks asleep on the water among the rushes. 'I mean that's one reason why I've not been working at these exams, isn't it? I don't give a monkey's for them!'

'Well, I don't see that's so very odd,' said Laurie, 'even Foswich must be full of people who don't give a monkey's about 'O' Levels.' No sooner had he said this than 'What a schoolmaster I've turned out to be!' he told himself, emphasizing how no one's as special as he thinks himself, that he's not the only pebble on the beach etc. etc.

Rob shuffled dust and stones before him. 'But most people see 'O' Levels and everything they lead to – college, a job, a position – as a *part* of life. I just can't see them that way; life means something quite different to me, different from what other people make out it is.'

Laurie saw the Sixties/early Seventies rise before him like a mosquito-cloud. The swift, brief vision included Polly's brother, Nick, inveighing against all the impositions upon body and spirit made by institutions and the conventions they embodied. And what was he now, a rising young barrister who had just announced his engagement to an admiral's daughter?

Such thoughts – and a *real* swarm of mosquitoes, with their fast, stinging, singing attentions – obscured from his attention what Rob said next; when he re-caught the flow of his talk, it was at the point of these words:

'Shit. And blood.' They were not uttered at all loudly, indeed the reverse. But they seemed to reverberate all over the heat-filled valley.

'You'll have to forgive me, but I didn't quite get all that!' said Laurie, 'what were you telling me?'

'I was telling you,' said Rob slowly, and now he did turn his gaze full upon Laurie, and very sharp, very penetrating the beams of his eyes felt, swivelled there on him, on the dull, familiar pathway. 'I was just telling you, Laurie, how it's been like that ever since I can remember – or just about! Certainly ever since I was five or six and understood how hopeless people thought I was, how I was a no-gooder compared with Phil and Anne.'

'Been like what?' said Laurie, and why was it he felt afraid all of a sudden? In truth what Rob had said was correct: he *didn't* really know the boy.

'Been seeing shit; been seeing blood,' said Rob, 'as if they always *had* to be everywhere, always part of the world.' His voice was fatigued and regretful upon the hot afternoon air. 'See here, Laurie, you remember when we first talked together friend-to-friend, when you invited me back to your flat for a cup of tea after we'd met on *this* bridge?' For they were in sight of the Japanese half-moon now. It still seemed a fair way off, though, the distance increased by the muffle of temperature. 'I told you about Leo the lion, didn't I? and a few other of my thoughts. But it wasn't so very significant, what I told you then, and even when I was speaking, I knew you were getting a false impression. You'd have chucked me out of your rooms before you could say "knife", if you'd known what my mind really makes.'

What his mind *makes*, repeated Laurie silently; what sort of talk was that?

'Do you want to explain more,' he said aloud, 'I'm afraid I'm a bit in the dark.'

'Oh, I'll enlighten you!' said Rob, with an odd, uncomfortable laugh, 'often – and specially when's something's bothering me a bit, something at school, something with parents – I'll see between me and the outside world great steaming mounds of shit. I'll see it coming from someone I'm talking to, or from a picture or a book or even a wall of a building. But . . . but there's worse than that. *Other* times,' and he paused, but Laurie had to admit that it was *not* for effect, 'other times, it's blood that I see. Coming out of holes in the side or head, coming out of cuts and gashes and wounds, and flowing just everywhere. Imagine it, Laurie, almost always having your peace disturbed – just wanting to be quiet and happy, and then having these sights before you all the time.'

'*All* the time?' Laurie had lowered his voice without realising it.

'If I'm in a bad way, yeah!'

'Like . . . *now*?' Laurie dared the question that had obviously occurred to him.

Rob nodded. 'Yes, Laurie, like now!'

'Is it . . .' But to finish the query with 'shit or blood' sounded grotesque, like asking someone whether he wanted coffee or tea, jam or honey? Rob, however, did not need the sentence finishing, nor did any grotesque qualities seem apparent to him.

'Now – today –' he said, and you could truly hear a great weariness in his voice, the greater because he seemed, this afternoon, so very young, scarcely past childhood, 'it's blood, Laurie. Blood just about everywhere! This morning when I woke up, I thought I could feel it on my hands. If I touch my palms with my fingers, I said to myself, they'll be warm and red and sticky. Who have I . . . who have I . . .'

'I'm sorry I didn't get that,' apologised Laurie.

'Who have I *killed*?' said Rob, in all-but-a-whisper, 'that's what I asked myself *this* morning – and *every* morning this week. Who have I murdered?'

'You . . .'

'I get out of bed like a killer,' said Rob.

And now the wooden bridge rose in front of them. More than ever did it look like something out of Hokusai. Heat wrapped it round, as it did the motionless, overgrown yet drought-dusty banks it spanned. The water-lilies below it looked firm enough on the dark sunken river to stand upon; ducks, for the sake of shade, had turned themselves into statues between the arches; the still rushes seemed engraved upon the air.

Back where – only weeks ago, but how much longer it seemed! – their friendship had begun, Laurie looking at Rob saw the trembling of his lips, the teardrops that hung upon his eyes. He felt more moved than he knew how to deal with; he had not expected *now* to be moved by Rob Peters. He put out a hand to touch him lightly upon the arm. 'You know it's all morbid fancy,' he said, 'you haven't killed anybody; there's no blood.' (But people did kill, a voice told him, and blood does flow . . . Just as every human body so regularly produces *shit*!)

'That's what I tell myself,' said Rob, 'but it all seems real enough to me. That's why I said I was a bringer of . . . well, you remember what I said. I'm different from other people, I'm a marked man – or marked boy, whichever. I've been thinking a lot these days – and nights, 'cause it's too hot for much sleep, isn't it? – and I now don't know which came first in my life, thinking of myself as in a separate band from most others – or seeing this shit, this blood before my eyes . . . I hardly know one from the other.'

They climbed the rise as older had to younger so many weeks before. I would never have guessed all this then, Laurie thought, and how could I?

One thing was certain: there could be no kingfisher's flight today. Too weightily did the afternoon lie on everything for such keen and irradiating movement to be possible.

Yet something was occurring, was breaking the stillness. Rob had taken hold of him by the shirt: 'Christ, Laurie, what am I to do?' he cried, 'I don't *want* to be this . . . this bringer. But when the pictures come on full and bad, then I don't now how I *can't* be. Do you understand what I'm trying to say, Laurie? Do you understand how *true* it all is, for fuck's sake!'

And now it was head not hand that was upon Laurie's breast, a heaving head, and tears were wetting his candy-striped summer-shirt, and also the hairs of his chest and his nipples, and he was strangely stirred – and stirred in that most intimate place where you'd think Rob Peters and the likes of him could have no power at all.

A little awkwardly, diffidently, Laurie patted Rob's head. Well, perhaps it didn't matter all that much if anyone were to see them. Still – he had to admit it – he'd rather no one did.

'You're done in, Rob,' he said, 'that's what it is!' (And he felt he honestly believed this.) 'In this weather you shouldn't be working in the cafe as well as . . .', he fumbled for words, 'as well as worrying about school stuff. I'm surprised at your parents.' And indeed this was not the first time that he'd noticed their extraordinary indifference to their youngest child's welfare. Blaming them for this odd – and really wholly unanticipated – outburst somehow put it on to a matter-of-fact level. And a matter of fact too was the arousal in his crutch; his blood seemed to be mocking those words he'd spoken to Jonathan West last weekend. *Jonathan West*! Good that he had come into his head. No involvement with pupils had led in *his* case to this sort of embarrassing thing! Now was the time to act on his counsel ...

'And you've still got a French paper on Friday morning,' he went on. Rob, however, was saying in an imploring, intimate voice:

'You don't despise me, do you, Laurie?'

' 'Course I don't. What could give you that idea?'

'Knowing Polly?'

'*Knowing Polly?*' He attempted surprised indignation.

'She hates me!'

'You really are overwrought, aren't you?' said Laurie, 'how could she hate you? Why should she?'

'Give me a proof that she doesn't!' said Rob, now lifting up his head. With the boy's hands still round him, Laurie found the meeting of their eyes like that of a pair of lovers. And – Jumping Jesus, thought Laurie, as he stared at that young face so full of anguish and non-comprehension, he's *beautiful*! Why have I never thought that before?

'A proof, Laurie!'

'A proof,' echoed Laurie foolishly. And then, gratefully recalling Jonathan West again, he said: 'Why, Polly was saying only the other day how much she'd like it if you could come on one of our expeditions.'

'Bit vague, isn't it? Not much of a proof!'

He must know what he's doing to me, Laurie exclaimed inwardly; why, any minute now our lips will be meeting in a passionate kiss! 'Not vague at all, Rob!' he said in a firm, sensible but warm voice that over the years he'd developed for certain situations in the classrooms (usually with an emotional girl!). 'Polly was suggesting,' and gently but unambivalently he extricated himself from Rob and turned upon his heel to indicate a return home, 'was suggesting that you come with us on rather an interesting expedition. Next Saturday. To a rather famous house with a Saxon chapel. Saxingham Enfrith.'

Something plopped in the river. An unseen stone? a frog? neither would ever know. Laurie wished that the kingfisher *could* make a suden vivid appearance, but wishes were things that were only dubiously granted, weren't they? Fairly-tales told you *that*!

And then Rob said: 'I'd love to come, Laurie.' Then, 'Tell me how your Mum is. I know how you worry about her!'

'. . . Darling, I felt I had to,' Laurie said to Polly the morning of the Saturday they were due to visit this Suffolk country-house. Not only had he not told Polly that he'd extended the invitation to Rob to join them a week before, but he had said nothing whatever – for obvious reasons – about the discussion he'd had with Jonathan West of the problem the boy posed. 'I really felt I had to! Of course I too don't like having the little time we've got together intruded into, but . . . well, Rob's feeling pretty wretched after his 'O' Levels. I'm sure he's done very badly in them.

'And he's probably got a lot of nastiness at home to contend with. Poor Rob mustn't think of himself as excluded.'

'But he *is* excluded,' said Polly, 'by me – except for passing the time of day with, when it'd be rude not to. Would it be normal for a couple – who've only just formed a relationship – to want a muddle-headed adolescent in permanent attendance . . . ? It's not even as if he can provide interesting conversation of any kind!'

'Oh, come! That's *bit* hard!' said Laurie, for he felt there could be an implicit criticism of himself latent in this remark; he was not as clever, as intellectual as Polly, and the sooner they both faced up to this fact the better.

'And you seem to have forgotten,' Polly continued, 'that Saxingham Enfrith belongs to a connection of Uncle Cosmo's and therefore to a sort of cousin of mine, Julian Lumley-Greenville.'

Laurie had indeed forgotten this fact, and reminded, found it didn't at all please him.

'I'd been *so* looking forward to seeing Julian; do you know that I haven't seen him since he "came into" his house?'

'I'm afraid I can't see what possible difference Rob Peters's coming with us can make to your seeing Julian again!' said Laurie, though of course he did see this. 'Whether you'd seen him before or after he'd "come into" the house.' The last phrase, though he'd intended it sarcastically, did give him a certain pleasure.

Polly didn't give a direct reply. 'And we'll have to put up with the boy's company for dinner tonight,' she sighed, 'I'd found in the *Good Food Guide*, you see, the most smashing place we could eat at, only ten miles from Saxingham Enfrith. It's really too bad!' She was obviously as much annoyed by Laurie as by the situation itself but luckily circumstances – standing by the market in the busy High Street – inhibited fuller expression. For then – '*There's* old Mrs Ickeringill!', indicating an old crone in a William Morris patterned dress hobbling towards a flower-stall, 'I *must* ask her how her cat is. Tomkins had an operation last Thursday – do you remember, Laurie? – and the poor old girl was dreading, absolutely *dreading* it.' She wore her expression of amused concern.

Suddenly, in the cheerful bustle of Foswich's Saturday market, Laurie felt an unprecedented tiredness drench him, as if he were standing beneath a waterfall. He did *not* want to go to Saxingham Enfrith and run into some classy relations of Polly's, to whom he would have to be somehow accounted for, however nicely. He did *not* want to have to act as mediator between Rob and Polly, even though he knew perfectly well that their being in one another's company this hot afternoon was entirely *his* doing! And what he was tired of by no means ended there! While Polly chatted with sympathy to Mrs Ickeringill, by a stall brilliant and fragrant with cut pinks and carnations and sweet peas, Laurie realised that he was tired of *people*, with all their thrusting egotisms! St Sebastian of the arrows was he, with Dad's retreatism and Mum's melancholia and twins' slobbishness and Rob's narcissism and Polly's wilfulness and snobbery accosting him again and again. Nor could he absolve *himself* from what produced this tedium, for who was more the slave of half-understood egotisms than himself?

He would like a life of tranquil busy contentment such as the Wests had been able to lead. And yes – with all that could make her at times so exasperating, he wanted Polly to share such a life with him. What he'd said to Mum had been true. Only with the girl beside him now could he spend the years stretching ahead the girl now saying, 'It's a pity it has to be *Saxingham Enfrith* that Rob accompanies us to, but I'll try and put up with him – for your sake, Laurie!'

'Thanks – thanks a lot, Polly!' The sweat was profuse on his forehead. 'Gosh, it's hot!' he said, superfluously, 'I really think the weather might break today, don't you? There's a tension in the air, as if all hell could break loose in the sky!'

Polly glanced upwards to the parchment of the sky. 'Maybe, maybe,' she said, 'but they've been promising storms – for so long, haven't they? Anyway, let's hope – even if one does come – that we're at least able to see the famous Saxon chapel.'

CHAPTER SEVEN: ROB

In truth Mrs Van Asdalen didn't look at all well, and Rob couldn't help feeling sorry for her. She oughtn't to have had anything to eat at tea-time; doing so had led to her being copiously sick. Hot tears were hanging on her very large and tense-pupilled eyes, and her breathing had that shallow, exhausted, gasping quality that often follows retching. This didn't deter her from talking, however, from giving Rob a remarkably graphic account of how and what she'd thrown up.

'... "I'm not haemorrhaging or something, am I?" I said to myself. And then I realised: I was vomiting up some cherries from one of your goddamn cakes.'

A bit much to blame me for that, said Rob to himself. Aloud he replied: 'I'm very sorry about it all, Mrs Van Asdalen. Anyway have a sip of brandy, and then I'll pour you out a cup of strong tea. I'll sugar it well too. That did the trick for Mr Bentley down in Cabin Number Five.'

'You seem to be seeing a lot of him,' said Mrs Van Asdalen, taking from Rob the proffered glass of brandy rather as La Dame aux Caméllias might have taken her final draught of medicine. 'I'm glad you cured him, but let me tell you something; his constitution is *not* the same as mine. I doubt he's had the trouble with his neck that *I've* had with mine, and he *certainly* hasn't had his uterus removed.' She pushed a slightly stray lock of blue-rinse hair back into place, and then applied the brandy-glass to her heavily made up lips. 'He's a preacher, isn't he?'

'Well, yes!' said Rob.

Mrs Van Asdalen looked proud at herself, as if she'd just seen through a conspiracy. 'Thought so!' Then she gave a mysterious half-smile, the ironic vision of the gravely ill, and said: 'You two got a thing going then?'

Rob thought she must be talking about his possible conversation to Jesus, and answered: 'Maybe – a bit!'

Mrs Van Asdalen gave him a most peculiar look. 'Well, *chacun à son goût*, as our friends the French say. Not that they're *my* friends!' A little tragically she took another mouthful of brandy. 'In fact I just can't stand that people, you know. I went with my second husband to Paris once, and you cannot believe,' and here her tearful eyes glared at Rob, as if she were seeing again all the offending French people, and expected him to do something about it, 'you cannot *believe* the rudeness the two of us had to put up with. It was always *non – non, madame*! *Non*, we couldn't have iced water with our meals; *non*, we couldn't have the room service we required at seven o'clock; it was too early! *Vous êtes americaine* – one waiter said to me – I forgot to mention we were staying in a five-star, but a *five-star* hotel, right by the Jardin du Luxembourg – so I said, "*Oui, je suis americaine*. I come from the country," ' and Mrs Van Asdalen shook both her blue curls and her brandy-glass in recollected emotion, "who got all you guys out of the mess in 1940. I come from the country that paid all your godamn bills and set you all on your feet just so you could sneer at us, and *not* bring us iced water, when we're guests who are handing over to you I don't know how many bucks" God, I feel awful!'

'Have a cup of tea!' said Rob. Then, because he felt that some comment on this immensely boring story was required of him, he said: 'Just as well then isn't it? that you're going to England now, and not France!'

'Is it?' Mrs Van Asdalen looked at Rob with a kind of mocking sorrow, 'well, let me tell you something! You English guys aren't any too hot on manners either. All my life I used to hear about one hundred and fifty million times a day: the English charm, the English charm, the English charm. And what do you think I said when I came back from your country the first time, *and* the second, *and* the third? . . . Don't give me any of that dog-shit any more! *That's* what I said.'

'Did you?' said Rob, maybe not as politely as he thought.

'You are all *so* dull,' said Mrs Van Asdalen, '*so* godamn dull! Have I been bored by English people? Have I ever! "Terribly nice weather we're having, Mrs Van Asdalen. Isn't it simply spiffing?" ' She spoke these words in a strange throttled voice. ' "Do have another scone!" "Sure! . . . and how's your sex-life?" "Oh, it's going *frightfully* well! Thanks most *awfully*!" '

Mischievously Rob could not resist asking her, while she sighed and moved her mouth from tea-cup back to brandy-glass: 'Do you know many English people well, Mrs Van Asdalen?'

Mrs Van Asdalen spluttered liquor and biley saliva back into her glass. 'Do I know any English people well?' she echoed, 'my godamn daughter went and married one. That's what I'm going to England for – to spend a little time with my girl. And let me tell you something – Minty didn't just go and marry any old normal Brit. She got herself hitched to a member of the aristocracy. Can you beat it! A jerk by the name of Julian Lumley-Greenville, if you please.'

Some coincidences seem cruel almost beyond bearing. Since he'd first made love with Pete, Rob had felt more released from guilty apprehension than he would have thought possible, more ready to confront England. Now – hearing the name of a man, in two important ways responsible for his being out on the Atlantic, *here* in this cabin, as he was calming the nerves and easing the nausea of a stupid, arrogant, insensitive and unknown woman – Rob experienced something close to terror. God moves in a mysterious way, the hymn said, His wonders to perform, and who would have thought that a reminder of that day of wickedness, of his crimes against the good Laurie Williams, would have come to him while giving brandy and strongly sugared tea to one Mrs Van Asdalen.

'You mean Julian Lumley-Greenville of Saxingham Enfrith?' he asked, just to be sure.

'Oh, you *know* him!' But it was more an exclamation than a question; perhaps Mrs Van Asdalen thought the whole of England knew Julian Lumley-Greenville, and therefore it wasn't very surprising that this Assistant Ship's Cook did.

'Yeah, I've met him. I've been to –' He could hardly pronounce the name of the Suffolk country-house, where he'd listened to a diabolical voice and acted on it too.

'To Saxingham Enfrith. Yeah, it's some house, though let me tell you something, the draughts there are no joke. If you've had the trouble with your neck that I have had, you wouldn't be pleased when Siberian, but *Siberian* winds come whistling down the passages. But Julian's such a stick-in-the-mud, even though he *has* been such a traveller. Get him to change the heating system – get him to do something about the godamn cold in his country seat – why, he won't move his ass one inch!'

'Yes, he was a great traveller, wasn't he? He'd been up and down the Baltic, knew Hamburg where the Ludendorff company is headquartered,' said Rob, knowing he must be speaking strangely, nervously. Yes, indeed, a coincidence can be a cruel and, in certain circumstances, a terrifying thing!!

'Oh, yeah, the English are always saying how they are people of few words, and yet I've never known folk who talk as much. Julian Lumley-Greenville would bore the boobs off you with his tales, particularly those of his sailing adventures. Thank the Lord I've never *listened* to *one* of them!' Almost in the same breath now, she said: 'I guess I'm tired and better have a sleep. It's one thing to be brought brandy and tea, it's another to have to cope with conversation and other people's problems.' Rob couldn't quite make out what these might be, unless it was Julian Lumley-Greenville's propensity to talk of his travels. Certainly he himself wasn't at all sorry to be dismissed.

Mrs Van Asdalen closed her blue eyelids theatrically, and Rob put glass and tea-cup back on the tray. There's someone on this ship, there's been someone on this ship ever since we left the Coal Pier at Baltimore, he told himself, trying to stave off panic, who's been to Saxingham Enfrith, who's seen where I succumbed to sheerest evil! . . . Mrs Van Asdalen was mumbling something now: 'Always been my trouble,' she could be heard to say, 'as my husband Walter said: "You think far too much about other people and far too little about yourself." I think I've got to remember *me* for a change . . .'

By the time Rob knocked again on the door of Cabin Number Five, he was unable to stop trembling. But then, hadn't the Apostle said – according to Bill Bentley – that one must work out salvation in fear and trembling? . . . Well, he certainly knew those emotions now.

'Take it easy, Rob, take it easy!' said Bill Bentley, 'all this is quite natural at this stage of the procedure.'

'What stage?' asked Rob. Chattering teeth made the absurdest sound!

'Drawing towards the moment when you can say: "Jesus, take me as I am! I'm ready for your friendship!" '

'I can't believe *I*'d be acceptable to Him!' said Rob, reverting to the phraseology of earlier sessions.

'Take it easy!' said Bill, yet again, 'we'll listen to the singing of some young friends of mine back in Jackson, Miss.'

And he pressed a button on his Sanyo recording machine, and there burst into the cabin this revivalist song. Banjos strummed and guitars twanged an accompaniment to it:

'One day I fell into the hands of Satan,
My soul was wandering out in chains;
I knew my only hope was Jesus
If I could only reach His hand!
One day on my knees I was praying,
Then God reached down and touched my hand.
NOW(!) I'm walking with my Saviour,
On the sunny side of life again.'

Rob began to sob convulsively. 'Bill,' he said, 'one day I did fall into the hands of Satan. It was at a place called Saxingham Enfrith . . .'

That morning Rob woke up very early – perhaps as early as five o'clock – after a dream only too like many a one he'd been troubled with before.

He was standing on a jetty, about to take a small boat that would carry him to a larger one proudly and enticingly visible in the harbour. But before he could jump into it, a figure stopped him, a man whose face he couldn't see. Desperate, for the larger vessel would be leaving any minute, Rob threw himself upon him and tried to force him into the water. Had he got a knife? He seemed to be hacking at flesh and bone, and much issue of the human body was upon him, urine and shit, saliva and snot, semen and blood. Who won the struggle Rob didn't know, but he was panting like a frightened dog, a hunted fox, when he found himself awake and in his bed – or on it, to be more accurate, for the night had been far too hot for sheets and blankets. *The Copper Kettle* was inadequately ventilated; it became very stuffy in the summer. The yard below the window was still filled with the silvery haze of the imminent day, when once again – surely – the weather would not break, the heat would not be dispelled. And the haze was thicker still down in the Fase valley, would be smothering the Japanese bridge and the river-banks it connected.

The Japanese bridge. That made him think of Laurie. Now since Wednesday he *knew* Laurie's feelings for him! That was wonderful just as the sight of the kingfisher, the bringing-together kingfisher, had been wonderful. And today, Laurie had invited him out – to this place in Suffolk. True, there would be Polly, and it was all somehow bound up with the bloody Anglo-Saxons, but, now that Rob appreciated the depth of Laurie's affections for him, there was surely no need for him to be jealous of *that* bitchy upstart! Indeed he would show this by being particularly nice and attentive to her.

He slipped back into an hour and a half's tranquil if light sleep.

Nowadays he tried to intercept the postman. Or if that was not possible to get to the letter-box before anyone else did. And this morning – as if to celebrate the fact that all exams (however little he cared about them) were something in the past, and a new life had started – the letter he was waiting for was plopped in the box, before his eyes. The German stamps danced at him; he was all thumbs as he undid the envelope to read the following communication:

'Dear Herr Peters,

We thank You for Your letter, which it was our pleasure to receive. Herr Wolfgang Ludendorff is gladdest to hear news of the good Roy Williams whose memory is most valuable to him.

It is, of course, difficult to say what vacancies on our ships are available to You, or which posts, if any, would be most suitable or acceptable to You! Arrangements between the Bundesrepublik and the United Kingdom do not make us anticipate any particular difficulties in employing a young British, and, of course, a sentimental connection is always greatly to be esteemed.

Perhaps if You are able to come to West Germany and visit us in Hamburg, we could pursue this matter further.

With cordial wishes,

Ursula Mayerhofer, Secretary.

What a stroke of genius it had been to mention Laurie's dad like he had (as an old and revered friend). Why, now he as good as had a job! Here was yet another proof that life was going to be good.

His happiness must have been apparent at breakfast-time. 'What's come over you then?' said Dad grumpily; he was never at his best in the mornings, but then when *was* he at his best? 'Smiling away to yourself like a prize fool!'

'I was just thinking of the life ahead of me!' said Rob with conscious mystery.

'I sh'd have thought that'd make you miserable rather than anything else,' said Dad, 'it's certainly making *me* miserable I can tell you. Such a different story from my own schooldays,' he drew himself up a little proudly as was his wont when mentioning his education.'

'Examinations don't matter to me,' said Rob provocatively, 'I'm bound for the ocean wave.' He was not, of course – or at least, not yet – going to mention the letter from Germany.

Thank God only *he* had seen it.

'You're bound for no such thing!' Dad's main objection to the idea which Rob had several times gently mooted seemed to be that it was Rob's own. Otherwise it surely corresponded to all he claimed to want for his son; what could make a bloke stand up for himself more completely than work on a cargo-boat? 'No such thing! I'm not having you give in to every daft whim that comes into your head. Why, when I think of myself at your age . . .'

'It doesn't worry me that I've probably failed every exam,' said Rob, 'and when you find out that I have, you'll be glad that I'm away, being tossed about by Atlantic storms.'

. . . Storms! the word was hopeful on everyone's lips. Sooner or later this cruel parching weather must end: the sky was stretched tight, it seemed, like canvas above the thirsty countryside, and the air it imprisoned lay heavily on all shoulders. For several days now meteorologists had forecasted that the drought would end with a bang – and heavy rain; the B.B.C. had invited a man learned in Red Indian lore to perform a rain-dance on a television show, and Colchester and Chelmsford councils were debating whether emergency measures should be taken. A vicar had described watering flowers in gardens as being 'at this moment in time' not only an anti-social but an anti-Christian act.

Rob's happiness took him through morning and lunchtime (when he waited at table in the cafe). Then, meal and duties over, he took a bath, a long one. Dad had a taste – not, in fact, uncommon among men of his blustering, self-vaunting kind – for bodily luxuries, and Rob found some expensive pine-essence of his which he poured liberally into the hot water, filling the bathroom with aromatic green vapour. Then he lay luxuriatingly back, and contemplated his cock stiffening into an upright position, with the urethral eye winking at him. Think what life the two of us could have together, it seemed to be saying . . . And maybe at sea they would. For that he would be in the near future, on board a ship he had little doubt: 'Arrangements between the Bundesrepublik and the United Kingdom do not make us anticipate any particular difficulties . . . in employing a young British.'

But then away at sea he would be away from Laurie. Maybe that wouldn't be altogether a bad thing; it'd make Laurie see more keenly how they needed each other. He'd return from his voyages, a stranger but still in his heart the same person, and Laurie – who had tried to do without him – would feel his pulse race and his eyes moisten at the sight of him. Wednesday on the Japanese half-moon bridge had changed much in Rob's mind. What he'd ventured to hope had received confirmation.

If Laurie could see him now, stretched out with prick stiff, how would he react? He'd held him in his arm, hadn't he? What was *his* cock like? Rob had, of course, felt it – through his clothes, against his skin, and known that it had expanded and tensed at the contact. It would be what Rob called of 'the swinging sausage' kind, and perhaps one day, one night, when he was home from sea . . . Rob lathered his right hand with Dad's Imperial Leather soap, and then applied it to his bum. It felt so good working the arse-hole clean and tingling; he was sorry he couldn't see it and the lines of dark silky hair below which it opened, those rows of secret corn.

Rob hadn't, naturally, believed Laurie when he'd said that Polly had thought of his coming to Saxingham Enfrith, that she'd been planning some little post-examination treat for him. But he realised his coming on the jaunt was important to Laurie, and so he'd accepted the invitation. He'd make a go of the day; from now on he was going to succeed at things.

Yes, thought Rob, sinking himself deeper in the bath, my failures are behind me now. That letter from Hamburg had really set him up. He sang. His hand was still attending to his arse, and the thought occurred to him from the steam, like a genie speaking through the lamp-smoke? From the other side of the window where, even in the thirstiness of midday the blackbirds were singing? – that for him, 'failures' and 'behind' were not always to be linked . . . In a strange sort of way, as it turned out, the afternoon ahead provided the first proof of this.

After the bath a meticulous, slow shave, which he

concluded by smacking on to his smooth, scraped face a delicious lotion called *Antaeus*. Then he put on his smartest clothes – a lemon and grey summer shirt, a scarlet slip (though who would see this?), newly pressed white ducks and cream-coloured Gucci sandals. A final raid on Dad's toilet cupboard produced a bottle of Eau de Portugal, and he sprayed this on his – now close-cropped – brown hair, making it glisten fetchingly. Indeed, he told himself as he scrutinised himself in the mirror, he looked quite a dish! Even Polly Keating (jealous bitch that she was, in need of a hot poker up her) might find him acceptable today, and – well, he was doing Laurie proud . . .

To be honest, a trip to a country house wasn't at all his idea of an interesting afternoon. To go a long walk through the countryside, and scramble into the woods and gardens of some estate – that was another matter, but Rob wasn't much interested in history and hated having to listen to guides. Occasionally in childhood Mum and Dad had taken Philip, Anne and himself on visits to one of 'the stately homes of England, of which we should all be darned proud', to use his father's words. Those visits had been tedious almost beyond bearing, the 'grounds' a mockery of nature with all their regulated 'walks' and troops of tourists meandering along them, their interiors an endless-seeming sequence of horrible old portraits, uncomfortable, unused and unusable furniture, and collections of no possible interest to himself – of guns, coins, antique dolls, etc. Just remembering such excursions gave Rob a headache – the ache of fatigue. He saw no reason to suppose Saxingham Enfrith would be any different, but naturally he would pretend to enjoy it – more, to relish it – for the sake of Laurie, his good friend who in his view, had very probably defied Polly's wishes and *insisted* on Rob's accompanying them.

He was to be vindicated in this latter opinion sooner than he expected. Polly – perhaps she was suffering from the heat – made no attempt to be even conventionally welcoming. 'Hi, Polly!' Rob used his cheeriest voice, 'how are things?' He had to concede to himself that she looked particularly pretty today, wearing a dress of lime that suggested at least the possibility of coolness. Perhaps Rob should compliment her on her clothes, but he knew he'd not be able to do this well, would trip over ill-chosen words and please neither Polly nor himself. So instead he breezed: 'Had a good week, I hope! Your researches been going well?'

Polly's glance at him was a cold one. 'My supervisor seems to think so,' she said snubbingly, 'and how about your 'O' Levels?'

Rob blushed. (How he wished he didn't blush so easily. He'd read somewhere that you could go for cures for doing so.) 'Well, they're *over*!' he mumbled. 'Behind', 'over' – what magic lay dormant in these words, the magic a Hamburg shipping company possessed perhaps, sending out lines all over the world . . .

'So I gather!' said Polly.

She doesn't mean me well, Rob said to himself. She's furious that I'm coming with them today. What should I do? It's not too late to get out of it . . . He glanced at Laurie who was standing there, smiling at the two of them, as if they were having the most amiable of exchanges. Old Laurie! thought Rob, how he likes everything to be peaceful! – no quarrels, no aggression of any kind, just friendliness and calm. There could be no doubt as to what he should do: he must go to Saxingham Enfrith because Laurie had asked him to. That was sufficient reason; in fact no better reason could there be.

I must act as if I haven't noticed her bitchiness, Rob admonished himself. 'This place we're going to,' he persevered, 'this Saxingham –' and its second name deserted him, as names so often had in class at school, so he made a gulping noise to cover over the missing syllables, 'sounds most interesting. I've been hearing a lot of good reports of it.'

'From customers at *The Copper Kettle*?' asked Polly nastily (at least in Rob's ears the question seemed to have been asked thus), 'well, to me Saxingham *Enfrith* is certainly most interesting. You see, it's got in its grounds, an Anglo-Saxon chapel of great significance to my researches.' There was a detectable mockery in her pronunciation of this last word, and Rob remembered that you usually used it in the singular.

'And besides,' went on Polly, 'the house itself belongs to a connection of my family's, to a sort of cousin of mine, Julian Lumley-Greenville!' Her hazel eyes delivered a challenging look here. Match *that* if you can, it said, you nobody you! 'Julian is one of the most fascinating characters of his generation.'

'Is he?' said Laurie languidly; he didn't sound as if he believed her, 'in what way?'

'In a great *many* ways,' answered Polly, implying that her audience wouldn't be able to understand if she explained any more particularly, 'and now, as the driver, I say that, if we are to go to Suffolk at all, we ought to leave *now*. I was expecting Rob to show up half an hour ago.'

And neither of them has even noticed, let alone remarked on, my chic lemon and grey shirt and my white ducks, thought Rob sadly.

They drove through a toasted countryside. Whole fields had shrivelled under the sun's oppression. Villages were dozing the day away. Often you saw, in farmyards or outside cottages dogs lying exhausted in the shade, with reproachful expressions on their faces, and their tongues hanging so far out of their mouths you fancied they might drop. Here and there were stream-beds through which only the smallest trickles of water ran. Trees looked tired too, coatings of dust dulling their leaves. As they neared Suffolk, the churches grew bigger, with massive towers and flintstone buttresses. Almost more than age or faith they proclaimed the power of assuaging your discomfort; they would give you shadow not glare, a cool moistness not a hot aridity.

'I wonder how kingfishers manage in *this* weather,' he said, phrasing his question so that Polly would be able to tell that he'd remembered the lines she'd read them, 'what *can* they do if their stream or river dries up?'

Talk hadn't been flowing at all well; perhaps mention of this bird might unite them all, as it had done in the past.

'I'm *amazed* you don't know,' said Polly acidly, 'you've been talking these past weeks like a walking ornithological encyclopaedia.'

When my sister Anne says thing like that, Rob reminded

himself, I pull her hair, her auburn coloured hair that blends with Polly's. I pull it even now that Anne's become what Dad's pleased to call 'quite a young lady'. I pull it very hard until I have the pleasure of seeing warm tears come into her eyes and of hearing her squeal despite herself. That's what I'd like to do now. For a full minute he had to fight against his right hand which wanted so badly to reach out cruelly for those copper-coloured tresses. Blood glowed on it – again! Or was it some other effluence!

Polly turned on the car radio – perhaps to prevent further attempts at conversation. An announcer told them that in Thanet and the Isle of Sheppey storms had already broken, and were expected to occur north of those parts later on that day. That meant *them*, thought Rob – and in his heart, as he stared at the backs of Polly and the more-than-usually-passive Laurie, he felt a storm was imminent too. Then a light glowing tenor began a recital of popular American folk-songs, singing to a guitar:

> *'I know a gal that you don't know:*
> *Lil'Eliza Jane!*
> *Way down South in Baltimore!*
> *Lil'Eliza Jane!'*

In his hot sweaty misery the phrase 'Way Down South . . .' gave Rob a shiver of delight, of expectancy, and he was to remember it, when, a matter of months later, he saw Baltimore for the first time, raising its sky-scrapers and proud brick mercantile houses above the reaches of the tree-lined Chesapeake. And in his mind's eye the sweltering interior of Polly's Renault was once again clear and real, the three of them cooped up unhappily together, and above their journey the parchment sky being stretched, it seemed, tighter and tighter over the weary countryside . . . 'Way down South in Baltimore . . .' that, or somewhere like it, was where he should be.

In the right-hand back pocket of his ducks Rob could cracklingly feel – carefully folded – that letter from the Ludendorff Company of Hamburg. He was longing to tell Laurie about it, but though Rob had opened his mouth several times during his car-ride to announce the good news, words had not come to him. Maybe best to wait until he and Laurie were by themselves. (Laurie and he by themselves! would that beautiful state of affairs ever arise again?) . . . Rob had done more than merely re-read the sentences of the letter now in his hip-pocket. He had let them enter the passages of his brain, until they had undergone a chemical change, for they now seemed to speak of places and persons he *knew*. He *knew* that the company's premises was a tall gabled old house with a prospect of cranes and a lime-tree outside the front door; he *knew* that Ursula Mayerhofer was in her fifties but still blonde, with a gentle voice and large bosom. He knew that Wolfgang Ludendorff had a shock of white hair and wore flannel waistcoats and smoked a fragrant pipe and in the evenings liked to play melancholy waltzes on the piano. And he could see the great forms of some of their ships, ships on which he would soon be working (but in what capacity?), bound for the west, the setting sun, America, liberty!

'Are you keeping your eye on the map, Laurie?' Polly said sharply, 'I don't want to miss *another* turning.' This had happened five minutes ago, while the American tenor had been singing 'The Blue Ridge Mountains of Virginia'.

Laurie's eyes travelled nervously back to the Ordinance Survey map on his lap. 'Yes, of course, I am, darling,' he said. (Darling, repeated Rob, *shit* to your 'darling'.) 'According to this we should be seeing a signpost to Saxingham Enfrith in about two miles.' He sounded for all the world like a small boy trying to please teacher with a bright answer.

To arrive may well be far worse than to travel, thought Rob. Once more the country houses of childhood were vivid to him – tiresome cordons to keep you from touching things (assuming you wanted to), guides that droned on and on, visitors who gave little sycophantic laughs and asked questions to show how cultured they were, and, above all, a great and demanding house that seemed to deny the very idea of 'home'.

However Saxingham Enfrith did not resemble Rob's expectations at all, any more than did its proprietor, whose pedigree and exact relationship to herself Polly had explained at considerable – and exasperating – length.

The lane got narrower and narrower, and its hedgerowed banks steeper. Presently it began to descend – dropping from cornfields and into a woodland, and then, there, at the bottom of the hill, protected by two great chestnut-trees and with a narrow ragged lawn in front of it, stood a long, low, yellow-washed house with tall old chimneys. Behind it, like a large grazing sheep turned into stone, the little chapel was visible.

At this afternoon hour everything was drowsy, weighed with heat, as motionless as in some painted landscape. The bell hung without swaying, the branches of the trees were static heavy lines against the intensifying sky.

'To View! Please knock on front door,' read a notice, which then listed the hours between which you could do this. Certainly it was all very unlike the large car-park, the coaches, the tea-booths, the regimented paths of Rob's dread. Whatever guide-book had proclaimed Saxingham Enfrith's charms had not done so very efficiently, or maybe the entire east of England was too enervated, for there was no sign of any other visitors, and truly it was hard to imagine that there would be any others. Almost in awe at the stillness, the silence, Polly, Laurie and Rob walked through the thick, heavy heat and up the short front garden path to the main door, the one pointed to by a hand painted on the notice-board. No matter what faults he would find with the place later on, Saxingham Enfrith could not be censured for lack of homeliness. Its proportions were such that almost anybody would happily imagine himself living there.

'Jonathan West would love this house,' said Laurie.

Polly, pleased at this praise, smiled at her boy-friend, her first amicable look of the day. 'I'm sure he would. From what you've told me about him, I can see that Saxingham Enfrith would be just his sort of place. Maybe, one day he'll even come down and paint it. Julian's awfully keen on the arts . . .'

But *I* am the one Laurie's told about Jonathan West, Rob angrily said to himself. He confided this great youthful friendship to *me*, long before he so much as knew Polly

Keating existed. She obviously got jealous of me knowing things about Laurie's past, and after one of our walks together, realising what I'd been told, dragged from him information about his old teacher. It's the most obvious thing in the world that my relationship to Laurie and his with Jonathan West have a great deal in common, and have absolutely no resemblance to that he 'enjoys' with Polly.

These thoughts had taken him right up to the oak-studded front door. A window open above them told them of the house's occupation; otherwise you would have assumed that it had been abandoned intact, like somewhat in a fairy-tale. Nevertheless when Polly took hold of the great iron knocker with the lion's head and thumped it against the door, it did seem rather like trying to break a spell. The noise it made had a violence about it in the afternoon sleep of the land, and was almost blasphemous in its brutality.

Now footsteps were ringing out over the flagstones in the interior. When, rather slowly, as if rolling back the layers of heat outside the house, the door opened, Rob experienced another sensation of violation. For the man who stood before them was not the grave, mellow nobleman of Rob's imaginings, but a vigorous if febrile-seeming individual – florid-complexioned, with very dark hair and dark eyes so bright you suspected them of having been polished. He was by far the tallest of them all and also by the far the shabbiest-dressed: a tennis shirt filthy with the stains of sweat, grass and soil, light grey flannel trousers with no pretence to creases, and ill-tied tennis-shoes of matching splodges of dirt to the shirt. Round his neck, though, was a rather natty red handkerchief; this, together with something in his whole demeanour, gave him something of the air of a party-going 'county' pirate.

'Julian!' said Polly as if in surprise, as if she'd acccidentally encountered him in Picadilly rather than driven forty miles in hot weather in the hope of seeing him, 'Julian Lumley-Greenville! you remember me!'

'My *dear*, of course I do!' To Rob it was as if the gleaming eyes were speaking; sun-dazed at first, they now came into focus upon the girl with the red hair and the green dress, 'you're Polly, Edmund and Diana Keating's daughter.'

'I wasn't sure that you'd recognise me,' confessed Polly.

'As if I could fail to recognise so lovely a relation,' said Julian Lumley-Greenville, in a mannered, self-confident voice the like of which Rob had never heard before, 'why, when I used to see you a few years ago, I used to have the *maddest* fantasies about you, my dear. Kidnapping you from that Putney home of yours, and galloping off with you – well, to *seduce* you, my dear. But I fear,' and he looked at Laurie here, 'that I'd be too late now. Anyway I'm a married man – married a girl from New York last year; she's away at the moment – but, of course, when the cat's away . . .'

'I'd had visions of lots of tourists swarming round your house,' said Polly, 'I hadn't imagined it as quiet and beautiful as this. I'd have rung up if I'd known . . . I don't like the idea of intruding . . .'

'You *intrude*, my dear!' exclaimed Polly's cousin, 'nothing exquisite can intrude upon *me*. As I've just said, I'm on my own, and I was feeling all grouchy and miserable, and so I'm perfectly delighted to see you – *and* your friends. And, my dear, have you *heard* the weather forecast? Have you *looked* at the sky? I think there's going to be the mother-and-father of a storm, and – whisper it not to Edmund and Diana, your good parents, or to any other of our kith and kin – but I am just the *weeniest* bit frightened of thunder and lightning, and so I'm terribly, terribly glad that someone so attractive as you has arrived in time to hold my hand!'

You affected old sod, thought Rob, you're no more frightened of thunder and lightning than I am. In fact I doubt if you're frightened of *anything*! And when are you going to take any notice of the two males on your doorstep?

But at that moment the preternaturally bright dark eyes did alight upon Laurie and himself. 'Polly, you must introduce me to my other guests.' He turned beamingly to Laurie, 'My dear, I *do* hope you're Polly's lover,' he said, 'I love meeting people's lovers!' And he gave here a sophisticate's laugh which made the porch and the wooded hollow in which the house stood resound strangely.

Laurie said: 'Pleased to meet you!' and extended a hand.

From the expression on Polly's face Rob realised his friend and mentor had not done the right thing; socially he felt sorry for him, and his feeling of hostility for Polly and Julian increased.

'And this?' asked Julian Lumley-Greenville, as if indicating an object for sale in an antique show-room.

'Oh, he's Robert Peters,' said Polly, somewhat begrudgingly, 'an art-student of Laurie's in Foswich.' Rob blushed – not out of shyness, but at the lie, or misrepresentation of the truth, that Polly had presented to her relation. For clearly Laurie must not be an ordinary schoolmaster, and therefore *he* couldn't be an ordinary all-subjects pupil. 'How d'you do?' Rob said; he did not proffer a hand.

'An art-student. How audacious!' said Julian Lumley-Greenville, 'well, I find it moving to the point of tears,' truly he didn't look as though he'd ever in his life shed any, 'that you've come all the way from *Foswich*,' he made this sound like John O'Groats or Land's End, 'just to see this paltry house of mine that I had the dubious luck to come into two years ago. Anyway, in you come, dearest all.'

Gladly they followed him into the shadowy interior of the house. The harsh unremitting sun of the afternoon had given Rob a pain behind the eyes, which were, anyway, slow to adjust to the half-light of inside. Rob noted nonetheless thick old walls many of them papered with Indian or Chinoisereie patterned paper and profusely hung with pictures and prints. He noted rugs prolix on the floor, and corners interestingly filled: with a grandmother clock, a cupboard full of china figures, a cheerfully crammed bookcase.

'Julian, how *stunning*!' Polly cried, and Laurie was moved to reiterate his conviction that Jonathan West would really take to such a place.

Meanwhile Rob, a few steps behind, entertained destructive images which he scarcely tried to fend off and which, in his days of repentance aboard the *Egon Ludendorff*, were to recur to him as reminders of his moral health before he'd been introduced to the saving friendship of Jesus. He imagined smashing the pieces of Dresden or Nymphenburg china into a thousand pieces; he saw his hands scratching the surfaces of old kysts and tables, and his urine staining the pretty rugs, and his feet making holes in the old paintings that Polly and Laurie were now cooing over. Nor did these fantasies cease when they all arrived in the large, comfortable, lavishly furnished drawing-room, the french windows of which gave onto the lawn that separated house from chapel.

'I shall get Annie – no, I've not been left *completely* alone; Minty, my wife, choc-a-block with faults though she is, would never do *that* to me – I shall get Annie to make us a pot of tea, and then I will give myself the great pleasure of showing you round the house and grounds.' ('Grounds!' groaned Rob, and there was I thinking that Saxingham Enfrith didn't have any. He did not feel in the least like sightseeing, partly for the usual reason, lack of interest, and partly because there was a painful uneasiness in his stomach, the result probably of a car journey in heat.) 'I *am* right in remembering, aren't I, Polly,' Julian Lumley-Greenville was continuing, 'that you're what's grandly called an Anglo-Saxonist. The chapel here probably isn't anything so very special, but I think you *should* see it, my dear. It's a poor thing, perhaps, but it's mine own. Well, mine own and Barclay's Bank's, and my wife's – for Minty is a *millionairess*, my dears, – and, last, but not of course least, old God's.' He gave another sophisticated laugh. It was obvious that he had made this joke many times before. It wasn't funny, anyway. But Polly laughed at it, and so, to Rob's disappointment, did Laurie. And him with a few rented rooms in old Ma Hargreaves' house!

Julian Lumley-Greenville noticed that Rob had not shown amusement, and his bright face did not look pleased.

But now he was pressing a bell concealed under the carpet. 'I'm most anxious for you to meet Annie,' he said, 'a perfect example of Silly Suffolk. You can't describe her as bird-brained, because birds are so *vastly* more intelligent, but she has a heart – well, not of *gold*, no, I don't think you could call it gold. Let's say rather a gilded Suffolk clay.' And once again he laughed at his own wit. He must be a very happy man, thought Rob, to find himself so continually amusing. Then he glanced across the room, and appreciated that, of course, he was not. He was a restless, bored, nervous man, and who knew what things – good and bad – possessed his mind while he was indulging in his compulsive, inane, high-spirited and decadent babble?

Annie, a slim, pale, somewhat sulky-looking girl, appeared, and tea was asked for. Efforts to draw her out failed; perhaps she'd been the victim of too many. Rob sank himself deeper in the exceedingly easeful armchair, partly because the region from the small of his back forwards to his abdomen was so very uncomfortable, in places tighter, in places looser-feeling than normal. He was also very tired. That he wished he had never come on this excursion went without saying: shouldn't he try to 'put himself away'?

'Putting himself away' was a skill he'd acquired when he was about seven or eight years old. In boring and uncongenial surroundings – a meal-table at home, a dull or demanding classroom at school – Rob had been able, so it felt, to free himself from his body and let his spirit float over a preferred landscape – which he could, it seemed, create at will. Today he should try to free his soul from the body that, tense and stomach-aching, was a prisoner in this elegant room, and drift towards Hamburg. There to embark on a ship of the Ludendorff line, which would cross the Atlantic for the virginal-appearing coasts of North America . . . But, alas! his abilities were not what they were, and, hard though he tried, he remained unpleasantly tethered to a chair in Saxingham Enfrith.

'And are you writing another book, Julian?' Polly was asking, adding in a reverential whisper to Laurie: 'Julian's a budding author.'

'My dear, you are too kind and too flattering,' replied Polly's cousin, 'but this time, I have to confess, my agent *does* think I'm on to something'. His eyes seemed to have fixed again on Rob, who was finding it increasingly hard to sit still. A treacherous softening sensation in the intestines was now spreading, tube by tube, downwards; already a noiseless but very malodorous fart had escaped from him. Putting himself away not proving possible, he was beginning to feel quite pierced by the beady eyes of his host. 'My dears, I hope my book's title won't shock you too much and cause you to go dashing out of this house back to your car in puritan but righteous indignation.'

'Whatever can it be?' asked Polly.

'*The Perfect Brothel*', said Julian Lumley-Greenville, 'what I'm doing, my dears, is going round my neighbourhood asking everybody – simply, *everybody*! – from the highest,' he all but pointed at himself, 'to the lowest,' and here, beyond doubt he switched his temporarily strayed gaze back to Rob, 'to describe to me his or her idea of a really naughty bordello. My dears, you should have heard some of the replies! There was a sweet old lady living near here in a *bungalow*,' he emphasized this word, as if there were something peculiarly comic about it, and she said to me,' and here he gave an animated, if not very convincing, rendering of an elderly 'common' voice: ' "Oh, that's one of them houses where the gentlemen takes off their trousers the moment they gets inside the door!", "Mrs Jeffries, sweetheart," I said to her, "there may have been just such a house in *Ipswich*, but I rather think elsewhere that the gentlemen have to wait a *little* longer before divesting themselves." '

And to think that I *put on* my best trousers, as well as my lemon-grey T-shirt and my Gucci sandals, thought Rob, just to associate with a man like this. In fact he *was* shocked by his conversation, greatly disliked the idea of his consuming hours with a book about a perfect brothel. He turned to Polly and Laurie; both were smiling as though privileged to have heard some real jewel of humour ... That softening, treacherous sensation in his guts had travelled if not actually into the bowels, dangerously close to them. Not since childhood had he known anything like this, childhood days of 'accidents in your pants', days when he'd been able to put himself away. He must have one final try at this ... Annie came in with the pot of tea.

Talk now moved back to Saxingham Enfrith itself and what could be seen there. My dears, everyone one knew had a better house than this funny little one, but there were one or two things ... Inside, a fine collection of samplers, some water-colours and drawings by Girtin, Crome and Churchyard, a small secret-room hidden behind a panel in the library, and outside – well, above all, the chapel, of course, but we mustn't forget the rather adorable little eighteenth century folly, the dogs' cemetery of roughly the same date, and a glasshouse, believe it or not, built by *the great Paxton himself*. Why, at this rate, we're going to be here forever, thought Rob. And then – after a particularly vicious twitch in the lower regions – his will-power was rewarded: he *was* put away.

He was standing on the bridge-deck of an old freighter. Coal was what it was carrying: that, he knew, was what lay in the cylinders far beneath him on the cargo-deck. Besides, he could see – and feel – coal-dust mixed with salt-spray on the railings by which he'd placed himself. It was night. Cloudless and very starry was the sky; serene and moon-dappled black was the sea. And near him was a boy, a boy his own age, whom, he knew, he not only enjoyed talking to, but touching – yes, and holding and hugging and (the awareness sent another sliver of disquiet coiling down to his colon) and . . . kissing!

And when he came to: '. . . my time at sea,' Julian Lumley-Greenville was saying.

At sea! Could Rob have heard right! Even in the most accomplished days of childhood 'putting himself back' had always been much more difficult than 'putting himself away'.

'Your time at sea?' Rob couldn't be sure whether he'd spoken these words aloud or not, 'did you spend time at sea, Mr Lumley-Greenville.'

'My dear, that *has* rather been the theme of my conversation these past five minutes!' Both tone and accompanying facial expression were unfriendly, cold.

'You worked on a ship, did you, like Laurie's dad?' Rob asked. (He could see Laurie blushing here, but why?) When the subject of the sea arose, there was just no way he could find of stopping himself asking questions, even to the point of making a fool of himself.

'What's he like, this student of yours, that he doesn't take

151

in what's been said?' Julian was asking Laurie. Who looked kindly but pleadingly at Rob: Don't show me up, his gentle eyes were surely saying, don't make things difficult for me.

'I'm sorry,' Rob mumbled, 'you see, I'm having a bit of stomach-ache . . .' In fact he was amazed that the others hadn't caught the smell of the foul gases he knew he'd been emitting. 'So I wasn't concentrating as well as I should have been.' He'd thought he'd put this rather appealingly, and indeed the two men did look won over, but Polly shot him a fed-up and fiery look. Why the hell did you have to come, it all but shouted at him.

'My dear, I was just being excessively and unforgivably boring about my past. Remember that I'm rapidly approaching my dotage. We oldies are prone to nostalgia like you young are to pimples.' (This was an unfair dig; Rob hadn't suffered from this complaint for eighteen months!) 'You see, as I was explaining to those present who were kind enough to *listen* to me, I did the maddest possible thing when I left school, left it a little betimes, I might add. My dear, I joined the *Army*! Can you imagine it? And I was stationed in Germany. To say I didn't like being in Her Majesty's Army would be rather like saying that the Himalayas were high. But, being as I was in the north of Germany, I managed to do a lot of sailing. I got to know many German and Danish ports and islands – the Friesians on the one side of Jutland, Bornholm and other islets on the other, and then of course the great old centres of Hanseatic commerce, from Bremen to Lübeck . . .' The stylised languor of Julian Lumley-Greenville's voice had quite vanished, and it was all at once easy to imagine him a vigorous young man with tangy salt winds blowing upon him and ruffling his dark hair, all a long way in place and time from Saxingham Enfrith and his American wife's millions.

'That's very interesting, Mr Lumley –' for the second time that day Rob couldn't produce the second part of a name, 'because, well, you see,' he was speaking, he was aware, in the furious, incoherent gabble of one who has been silent for a long time – but what the hell! Julian Lumley-Greenville (yes, that was his full name!) might well know the Ludendorffs of Hamburg. The time had come, obviously, for him to tell them all – and Laurie in particular, naturally – about the letter he'd received, so full of kindness and promise, from Germany, that very morning. 'You see,' he went on, while Julian gave questioning (yet knowing) glances at both Polly and Laurie, 'you see there's a possible job . . .'

But Polly was not going to let him finish. 'Rob,' she cut in like an adder shooting its venom, 'has only just finished taking his *'O' Levels.*' Whether she'd forgotten her implication of Laurie's being an Art Lecturer rather than a school-master, or whether she thought this worth sacrificing in order to shut up an embarrassing boy whose Essex accent excitement had made more than usually strong, Rob wasn't sure. But she succeeded in her wish to snub him. Rob's cheeks instantly began to burn, and there was burning too in his bowels, worse even than before.

' 'O' Levels!' drawled Julian Lumley-Greenville, 'how I *feel* for you, my dear! 'I remember that I *masturbated* throughout mine. It helped me a lot.'

'Oh, Julian,' laughed Polly, 'only you could make a remark like that!' (Let's hope so, thought Rob. A look out of the corner of his eye at Laurie revealed his friend as looking as ill-at-ease with such wit as doubtless his host had hoped.)

'Did *you* masturbate throughout *your* exams, my dear?' Julian Lumley-Greenville was asking him with undisguised malice.

'I wouldn't tell you if I had,' said Rob, rather to his own surprise.

'My dears,' Julian Lumley-Greenville cried to Polly and Laurie, 'This protegé of yours has *spirit*! He isn't going to be *angry* with me, is he? I get so afraid when people are angry with me. I'm only a poor old Lord-of-the-Manor who means nobody any harm.'

'Are you as afraid of anger as you are of thunder and lightning?' Rob couldn't prevent himself from asking. Outside the window the sky, he could see, had changed; huge dark stains were creeping over the parchment.

If anyone showed anger, it was Julian Lumley-Greenville himself. Clearly he was not accustomed to being answered back, had been the hero of all conversational exchanges that he'd set up. 'You were speaking, my dear,' he said malignly, 'of a job!! Now what kind of job could that be? What have you *qualified* yourself for?'

Polly was obviously delighted that Julian disliked Rob as much as she did, and was only too willing to join in the baiting of him. 'As far as I know, the only job Rob could have is the one he already – more or less – has; helping in his parents' cafe, a tea-shop in Foswich.'

'As Assistant Cook and Bottle-washer?' laughed her horrible cousin.

'Well, why not?' Rob was bold enough to reply. Why, oh, why, he asked himself, does Laurie not say something? He's eaten enough good teas in *The Copper Kettle*.

Julian had turned to Polly. 'I've never met anyone who actually *worked* in a tea-shop before. I always assumed that they had a sort of robot staff of manufactured genteel ladies.' (Polly was obliging enough to laugh again here.) 'What a richly comic tapestry life provides! Is there a tea-shop keepers' union, I wonder? One wouldn't want a *closed shop*, though, would one?' And he threw back his head in mirth, and Rob wondered if those polished-seeming eyes of his might fall out.

I loathe you *all*, I really do, thought Rob. And as he did so, three things happened: First he was afflicted by a pain so lacerating in his colon that it was all he could do not to scream; second, there came the indisputable roll of thunder. The forecasters were at last going to be proved right; the storm *had* moved north-east from Sheppey and the Thames Estuary. Third, Polly's bitchiness and Julian's snobbish superciliousness had given him an answer to that question that had been bothering him for some while, but most of all today: *what* work, *what* skills could he offer the Ludendorff company that would make them want to take him on? And the answer should surely have occurred to him from the first: he would put forward his considerable and tested abilities and experiences as cook and as waiter.

Perhaps only his acute gut-ache stopped Rob from jumping up for pleasure! Where there had been the haziest of lines, his future now appeared a firm and straight path.

'My dears,' said Julian, 'I heard Thor striking his hammer. He means business today, I'm sure. So let's go out and do our sightseeing now, and then we can return to the house to look at the pictures and have our "sippies". ('Drinks,' he translated for the bemused Laurie's benefit.) 'I shall show you everything I've told you about, starting with the Saxon chapel, and ending with the Paxton greenhouse. And there's the prettiest little cottage awaiting occupation by a loving couple.'

Rob would have liked to have asked for the bog, but he was too shy to do so. He didn't know what word would be most socially acceptable to Julian and Polly, and Julian might well make an unpleasant joke at his expense. So, queasily, he followed the three of them outside. In the garden a stillness yet prevailed, but the deepening of the sky, the aftermath of that first rattle of thunder, had made it different in quality from that which had struck Rob on arrival. Now he felt, surveying the chapel, the chestnuts, the formal gardens beyond, that he was quite possibly looking his last at them; they might soon, violently and speedily, dissolve upon the elements.

It was still, however, very hot!

Julian Lumley-Greenville unlatched the chapel door and held it open for his visitors. 'After you, Assistant Cook and Bottle-washer!' he said to Rob, with a taunting smile and a wink at the others.

Rob stepped into the muskiness of the little church – so compact, so sturdy, and appealing in its plainness – with a hatred and desire to do harm gnawing at him as cruelly as waste matter was in his rectal passages. Even so he did not fail to respond to, the gentle nobility of the place, the gravity that its stones had held for thirteen centuries, its almost comforting severity.

'It's a perfect example of the Saxon screening off of the altar with a thick wall,' said Polly, 'of course, as always happened, the later generations opened it out a bit, but even now two-thirds of the holy area is protected . . .'

'*Procul este, profani*,' suggested Julian.

'Not exactly,' said Polly, 'though I suppose there's a suggestion of that. The pious could always look through the slits in the walls to the right and to the left of the altar . . . *These* slit windows are very fine specimens!'

'My dear, you should live here always and be our resident guide,' said Julian 'beauty and scholarship combined in one person. I believe you could do more to save the place than all Minty's ample stocks!'

Polly gave him a look of flirtatious gratitude. Why don't she and Julian pair off, thought Rob, and then Laurie and I would be free to be friends again . . . The movement of fire towards his arsehole was accelerating now, and he had no alternative but to sit himself carefully down in one of the pews.

Yes – maybe, despite himself – he liked the chapel well enough. It was low-ceilinged, its four pillars were like the wide boles of old trees. The woodland atmosphere was enhanced by the leaf-light from beyond the plain glass windows. The walls had, long ago, been plastered over and cream-washed, except in one place, where faint outlines and blurs of faded colours told of a mural many hundred years old. It was, said Julian Lumley-Greenville, a fourteenth-century representation of the Last Judgement, and if you looked very hard you could make out crowns and thrones. Judgement? wondered Rob. Of whom? for what? . . . This ancient little place of worship suggested resignation and acceptance, not judgement and consequent rewards and punishments.

'And here, my dears, is an inscription of an old Saxon prayer,' announced Julian Lumley-Greenville,' and no doubt a scholar such as you, Polly – there's no such word as "scholaress", is there? and doubtless if there were and I'd used it, all those tiresome feminists would upbraid me – no doubt a scholar such as you can translate it for us.'

In the musty shadows of the church Polly strained her eyes to read the carved letter and then rendered it aloud to the others – in that intelligent, mellifluous voice in which she'd read the sequence from *The Waste Land*. And Rob, for all the havoc in his bum, could not but be moved by the lines she spoke:

> 'Now we must praise the author of the heavenly kingdom, the creator's power, and counsel, the deeds of the Father of glory, how He, the eternal God was the author of all marvels – He who first gave to the sons of men the heaven for a roof and then, Almighty Guardian, created the earth.'

Above the old hammer-beam roof of the church, and above that a drumskin sky about shortly to be ripped. What, Rob asked himself, had prompted God to make Heaven and Earth in the first place? Had He got bored or lonely just being by Himself? How long had He been around ('forever', he knew was the meaningless answer) before the idea of Creation occurred to Him? Was He happier now that He'd acted upon His idea, or was he pretty tired of it all now, and would be very pleased when the Last Judgement could take place.

These thoughts – frightening ones – helped to loosen further Rob's bowels, and were to return to him when reviewing his life and spiritual position on board the *Egon Ludendorff*.

'A lovely prayer for a lovely chapel!' sighed Polly, and Rob could not dispute her sincerity. 'I must make some notes. Like the good Anglo-Saxonist I am!'

'And so you shall, my dear!' said Julian Lumley-Greenville, a summer-time Father Christmas, 'but not until we've seen all the other sights that the grounds of Saxingham Enfrith have to offer. I'm most anxious you should see the cottage – it'd be the snuggest love-nest. Thor's bringing that old hammer of his nearer and nearer, I rather fancy, but we can get our tour in, if we're nimble about it, *before* the storm begins.'

'Please,' said Rob, his words coming, he felt, from the knot of vipers that was his guts, 'd'you mind if I don't come with you. I'm not feeling too well. I'll meet you here when you return from your walk, when Polly comes back to make her notes . . .'

Maybe both his face and his tone of voice proclaimed his truthfulness; or maybe all three of them were merely very relieved to be independent of Rob, a tiresome appendage, for a bit. 'But of course you should stay here!' said Julian Lumley-Greenville. 'Sit and think holy thoughts to take back to your tea-shop!'

And before leaving for the loaded heat of the afternoon Julian and Polly exchanged further grins.

Alone Rob shifted his position in the pew, and buried his head in his hands. His arse felt like an inverted volcano, about to erupt. Indeed the process was already underway; his recent farts had been liquid affairs, spraying his underpants with disgustingly warm spurts of excrement. But it wasn't discomfort or shame that was causing him to cover his face but simple grief. Grief not merely that he'd been humiliated but that such meanness of spirit, such destructive spite as had caused this existed, and that among people who had the world at their feet and whom no one would dare to criticise in the way they would a shambling young waiter at a tea-shop. Tears moistened his hands; from every orifice there was issue . . . Someone entering the church now would have taken Rob for a boy deep in his devotions. And maybe that wouldn't have been a complete mistake.

Thunder could be heard again, closer still now.

It was like the answer to an unspoken prayer; it had a decisiveness about it that was irresistable. His bowels were on the point of evacuation. He *could* stumble out of the church and relieve himself behind the trees; he *could* – somewhat less easily – make his way back to the house and find the bog there. Or he could – and it was all the fantasies of years uniting for one dramatic possibility – *shit here right in the chapel*. He removed his hands from his face, and all but cried out in joy. Right here, on Julian's property, inside the object of the horrible Polly's rhapsodic admiration, in the 'house' of the 'author of the heavenly kingdom' who'd fashioned such a wretched one on earth, so chock-full of suffering and yet presided over by heartless bastards and bitches! Yeah, he'd drop shit just about everywhere he could! And his laugh at the idea was like a gladsome psalm sent up to the rafters of the hammer-beam roof.

Rob unzipped his white duck trousers, and let them tumble to his feet. Next he pulled down his brown-stained and damp red slip. He exchanged the pew for the aisle, and, crouching down, let fall from his bum a considerable amount of steaming, stinking dung. Fire went on flickering within, though he hadn't done yet. Clutching his abdomen and staggering forwards, more like some simian being than a human one, Rob moved towards the Holy of Holies that stood protected from the marauding by that so interesting stone wall. Shit was positively slipping out of him now. Nevertheless, he managed to hold back enough for the altar. Below the Communion Table, so that it could not fail to hit the eyes of any entrant to the chapel, he dumped a prodigious heap, with a smell so foul that it made him himself choke, and more tears came to his eyes.

At last he had nothing more to give. His intestinal pain had ceased, though his whole body, guts, arse, back and head, throbbed with the exhaustion of it all. Exhaustion too perhaps that images of defilement which had long racked his life had achieved reality – external, visible reality – at last!

He had strength enough to quit the chapel, to scuttle across the lawn to where it met the lane, to pass stealthily by Polly's Renault, and thus gain the fork that led uphill back to the outer world. And now what should he do? what the *fuck* should he do? Forty miles separated him from Foswich, and he could legitimately regard himself as a hunted man for whom to be seen was to be undone.

(Laurie! what would Laurie think not just of what he'd done but of him as a friend? Surely he'd never want to hold him again, to soothe him with touch and words?)

He now noticed on the right side of the fork a path leading through the woods, woods he recognised as having been passed during the descent of Saxingham Enfrith. That'd be safer far than the road; no one would go looking for him there, and, if by any chance they did, he could always hide in undergrowth or behind a tree. And eventually the path must connect with a road; the direction was the right one, and – cautiously – he could try to hitch a lift homewards . . . Crikey, how sore his arse was now, and his head didn't precisely ache, rather it seemed at once suspended and light, as though it couldn't contain acknowledgement of the crime its owner had just perpetrated.

The very air felt worn out.

The woods received him in an eerie stillness; no birds sang, no bough or twig rustled. It was not unlike a religious building. Which did God, 'author of all marvels', prefer – the woods *He* had made or a chapel dedicated to Him but really serving the snobbery and self-satisfactions of the odious Lumley-Greenvilles and their like?

But no sooner had he thought this than the little Saxon church he'd just desecrated aroused in him a curious stab of pity. He imagined over the centuries men and women and children creeping out of the woodland and marshes to think good thoughts and ask for good things in its prim solemn coolness. He imagined even the animals from banks and burrows going there – awesomely, yet tranquilly too. It would be odd, you had to admit it, if God were pleased at his deeds there.

The going was rough, at times extremely so, for the path would all but disappear under pressure of ferns and willow-herb. Where did that confidence come from that urged him on, that told him that the path would not in fact trickle out but would arrive at the road – and so take him home. (Home! what a mocking word. He *hadn't* one!)

Perhaps it came from the same source that had enabled him to see a kingfisher at its most radiatingly lovely?

Rob sang as he pushed on forwards, no song of the greenwood but of something quite other. He'd had to learn the verses at school, and even in the dullness of the music block, they'd moved him, and were to return to him again when he lay near the sick Pete Rodriguez ten months later:

' *"O bury me not in the deep deep sea!"*
Those words came slow and mournfully,
From the pallid lips of a youth who lay,
On his cabin couch at the close of day.

"O bury me not in the deep deep sea,
Where the ocean billows will roll o'er me;
Where no light can break through those dark cold waves

And no sunbeams rest upon my grave.'

He pictured himself calling out these sad lines, and Laurie and Polly and Mum and Dad and Phil and Anne somehow hearing them and feeling sorry at how they'd never appreciated him. Terrible to think of the ocean claiming your body, but maybe it'd be better than any other end. Personally he'd exchange any day both in Foswich and Saxingham Enfrith for the wastes of water.

Singing is both a release and a tiring activity. Perhaps that is why Rob, thinking again of his achievement this afternoon, laughed, laughed as if he'd just discovered the facility. His laughs were as long and ramified as bindweed, as the sweet threads of honeysuckle in the woods. They were hard to call a halt to, however, and every now and again Rob had to pause, to clutch at a bush or an overhanging bough to recover his breath. His bum was as sore as hell now, but what he'd just done with it, well wasn't that rather terrific, as well as funny? Rob was in danger of laughing a-fresh.

In the end the path *did* reach a road, and here came a Volkswagen.... And Rob knew his appearance had an innocence about it that made people always willing to give him lifts. But, today, the driver might be less keen to do so did he or she catch a whiff of him; how the drying shit on his person and his clothes must smell!

The driver – slowing down now – was a woman in late middle-age. She had straggly grey hair and just the suspicion of a beard....

'Where are you wanting, laddie?' she called out.

'Foswich – but anywhere in that direction will do!'

'You're in luck. I'm going to Chipping Ongar! Are you harmless?'

'I believe so!' Rob gave the woman his most ingenuous smile. Of course he knew he wasn't.

'Not got a knife concealed on you?'

'No?' But a knife would have been good this afternoon he thought: he could have pretended that he was about to cut the throats of Julian and Polly, might even have been able *actually* to cut them both a bit and make them bleed....

'And no other lethal weapon?'

Only my cock and my arse, Rob could have said but didn't. Oh, yes, and my temper – which I've never really quite lost as I'd like to; those frenzies at school were nothing!

'And what might your name be?'

Perhaps best not give the correct one. 'Jonathan,' Rob said, 'Jonathan West!' Why not, after a deed of depravity such as his this afternoon, assume the identity of the best man his best friend had known.

'And mine is Nesta Coolidge! A nice name, eh?'

'Very!' said Rob, realising that there was something unusual about the woman. Her face was wrenched to one side, as if, not so long ago, she'd suffered a minor stroke. Her tongue appeared a little too big for her mouth; sometimes it was more of an obstacle to words than an instrument for them. 'Jump in then, Jonathan, she said, 'but in the front seat, please! There's a friend of mine in the back.'

The door-handle burned to Rob's touch. He peered into the rear of the car, but could see no one. Then he discerned the form of an animal (but what?) asleep on the seat. 'Fat Anna!' said Nesta Coolidge, 'I have twenty friends back home – goats, that is – but Fat Anna has always been my favourite.'

'Really!' said Rob.

'She and I were a bit bored this afternoon, so I thought we'd go out for a long drive. Really she likes the seaside best, but no, I said, it's time you had a little culture. You and I together, my friend, will gaze upon the wool-churches of Suffolk. She wasn't too pleased, after all wool equals sheep, and sheep and goats are age-old rivals. But I really think she enjoyed herself, even so. Anyway she's sleeping the sleep of the just right now, bless her heart!'

I've picked a right one here, thought Rob. However I needn't have worried about smelling bad; Fat Anna reeks high to heaven. In the sullen sky ahead the whip-crack of lightning cut – once! twice! thrice! 'I think I shall drive very fast and very recklessly,' announced Nesta Coolidge, 'my friends who live with me in Chipping Ongar don't like thunderstorms one bit. How they'll butt, how they'll bleat!

I'd like to be home to make them a nice dinner before the worst comes, so let's rip! . . . And,' she giggled, 'if we have a little fatal accident, we'll never know, will we?' Her tongue veritably bounced on her lips.

Certainly the way she took corners didn't make the idea of an accident at all improbable. The abandon of her driving made no difference whatever to Fat Anna who snoozed and snored regardless, and Rob decided it was best to emulate her nervelessness. Had he not survived so much this strange day! . . . 'Do you know many goats?' Nesta Coolidge was asking him.

'No, can't say I do,' said Rob. Then to be nice to her, he added: 'But I wish I did.'

'Oh, your life would be so much fuller,' Nesta Coolidge said, and with such enthusiasm it was a real wonder she didn't drive smack into a passing van. 'There are times, you know, when I wonder whether goats won't inherit the earth.'

It was a bit hard to think of a reply to this. Lightning flashed again across the ever-darkening sky. 'Is,' Rob asked, for want of any better question occuring to him, 'is goat's milk good in tea?'

'We-ell!' Nesta Coolidge waggled her tongue so energetically it was surprising it didn't fall out, *'we-ell*, I wouldn't thank you for a cup of tea with cow's milk in it.'

She'd better not come to *The Copper Kettle* then, thought Rob, or, for that matter, to any other place I know . . .

'What are you thinking of me, Jonathan, I wonder,' Nesta Coolidge asked a few miles further on, 'a bit doolally-tap?'

'No, no!' protested Rob. In fact he was liking her; after the callousness of Julian Lumley-Greenville and his cousin, Polly, such tender devotion as she manifested when talking of her goats was almost moving. But to deny that she was odd . . . Rob was almost glad – perversely – that his arse was still palpably filthy and smarted, for without this discomfort the journey would have seemed almost phantasmagoric: the chiaroscuro of the Essex landscape against the storm-pregnant sky, the coarse breathing of the goat on the back-seat, the weird gaiety of Nesta Coolidge and the complete lack of restrain in her driving, rather as if she were at a fair rather than on a Class 'A' road.

'I've got quite a reputation in Chipping Ongar, you know, Jonathan. I didn't go unremarked in my pre-goat days, you know!'

'Is that right!' said Rob.

... But what do I do when I get home, Rob was asking himself. Sit and wait all evening for a call from Laurie? What on earth could the poor bloke say? 'Excuse me, Rob, but I've got a question to ask you!' It *was* you who shitted all over Julian Lumley-Greenville's chapel, wasn't it? Polly was most upset. It quite put her off taking notes for her researches.' Rob had here to bite back another fit of laughter such as had seized him back in the woods.

'So, recently, I invited my friends – my *human* friends, that is, round to my house. Sit down all of you, I commanded, for I can be very bossy. I'm going to sing you the goat version of *Oklahoma*. You know that old musical, don't you, Jonathan?' (Rob nodded). 'It lasted about an hour, and was a howling, or shall we say, a bleating success?'

'Yeah, I suppose it would be!'

'I *like* you,' Nesta Coolidge dug him almost roguishly in the ribs. 'I like you so much I'm going to bestow on you the title of Honorary Goat: H.G. Like H.G. Wells.'

'Well, thanks!'

'So now,' and for no apparent reason Nesta Coolidge pooped her horn very loudly, to the alarm of the driver of a passing car, 'so now for another performance of the great Rodgers, Hammerstein and Coolidge production: OKLA-GOATA.' And she proceeded to sing to Rob in an oddly true and sweet voice such numbers as 'Oh, what a beautiful udder!' ('Oh, what a beautiful morning!') and 'The billy with the horns on top' ('The surrey with the fringe on top').

Maybe Rob had never been told before that anyone *liked* him. He felt surprised and grateful. They made of him as good an audience as Nesta Coolidge could ever have had. But, curiously, the principal result of her farouche amiability was to increase Rob's resentment against Polly and Julian – and – yes, why not admit it? – against Laurie Williams also, who had failed to defend him from their condescension and contempt. No, Rob could not be sorry for what he'd done in the chapel, really not. Moment by moment he felt more proud of himself.

By the time that Nesta's recital had come to its (perhaps overdue) end, a loud clap of thunder overhead, of shuddering ferocity, announced the downpour the whole county had awaited so long. That Anglo-Saxon prayer in Saxingham Enfrith had spoken of God's having given the Sons of Men 'heaven for a roof'. Well, now that roof was collapsing. It was intimidating, the speed with which darkness engulfed the countryside. Rain came down in remorseless straight lines, making visibility poor; you were travelling through a no-man's-land of black falling water, and even Nesta Coolidge was shocked by the change into driving like a normal person.

'I can't let you fend for yourself in this,' said Nesta, intent upon the near-desperate movement of the windscreen wipers against the torrent, 'there are occasions — please forgive me, Fat Anna,' the goat had, in fact woken up after the storm had begun, 'but there really are occasions when people have got to come before goats, and this is one of them!'

The goat made a snorting noise, half of disbelief, half of resigned annoyance.

'Tell me where you live in Foswich, Jonathan, and I'll take you there!'

Because of the false personal name he'd given her, Rob felt it perilous to say *The Copper Kettle*. So he gave Nesta Laurie's address. Polly and Laurie would not have arrived back, could not possibly have done so, with all the fuss he'd arranged for them. And anyway they'd been planning on a dinner at some swank restaurant in the vicinity of Saxingham Enfrith; Rob even remembered its name: *The Saw Mill*. Laurie's landlady, Mrs Hargreaves would surely let him in . . . She'd seen him there often enough! It was hard to tell one familiar Foswich street from another. The rain had translated all houses into tremulous squares in which lights shimmered.

'Mrs Coolidge, thank you very much for all your kindness,' Rob said, 'one day I must come over to Chipping Ongar and see all your friends!'

'You'll be more than welcome. And now make a dash for it, Jonathan, as quick as you can!'

Rob, an athletic boy, ran very fast to Mrs Hargreaves' front door, but even so the rain had drenched him by the time he reached it. The lights were not on in Laurie's flat. Maybe Polly was at this very moment having hysterics, and Julian was deliberating whether or not the police should be called in . . .

'Why, Rob, whatever are *you* doing here – in this tempest?' said Mrs Hargreaves, a plump, perpetually abstracted elderly lady, 'I thought you'd gone out for the day with Laurie and Polly.'

The action of running to the door – and maybe a certain relief at being out of the claustrophobia of Nesta Coolidge's Volkswagen – had brought on again the scalding pains in the guts. He found himself panting as he replied to Mrs Hargreaves 'Oh, no we changed our minds about that; Polly and Laurie went by themselves to see some relation of hers. But Laurie said I could get something – something to do with art, and – well, a friend I've been seeing in Chipping Ongar has just dropped me here, instead of home. But, of course, Laurie forgot to give me the keys . . .'

'Oh, don't worry about that; I've got two spare sets,' said Mrs Hargreaves, 'if I were you, I'd stay there a while. The worst of the storm's not over, and you could get your death just trying to walk back to *The Copper Kettle*. Go upstairs and make yourself a cup of coffee or something. Laurie'd hardly mind! I know we've waited long enough for this storm, but somehow I can't like it now it's come; it's *too* violent! Makes you think all the wrath of the gods is unleashed against us.'

Julian was afraid of it, goats in Chipping Ongar were afraid of it, and now Mrs Hargreaves. But Rob rejoiced in it. What could suit his mood better – the mood of giving vent to long pent-up feelings – than this evacuation of dark water from the sky?

But back again in the so intimately familiar flat – where hung those marvellous photographs of the *William Wilberforce* upon the North Sea, and that captivating painting of

Laurie's of a stone lion coming to life – Rob knew both the most acute agony of the day in his already tried and tormented bowels and also his most unadulterated burst of rage against Laurie. Here in this room they'd talked so fondly, so easily the two of them. Remember that first visit he'd paid to it? – the day that the kingfisher's wondrous flash of blue had presented itself. So much had been heralded by that lovely bird, so much between him and Laurie. Something had begun to develop. And then along had come Polly, and the development had painfully ceased. And it wasn't *his* fault. He had always loved Laurie, had shown him that love too . . . And last Wednesday, when he'd broken down on the bridge, he had understood what Laurie felt for *him*. Why, why then, this being the case, had he chosen to take him, so clearly against the wishes of his hard-hearted girl-friend, to the house of a stuck-up, evil-minded bastard called Julian Lumley-Greenville? It was all too much.

Outside it was as the middle of a barbarous night. What had opened as a hot dry summer's day was now offering water whooshing down gutters and cascading into the dark from off the eaves. Suddenly Rob knew what he wanted to do, what he *must* do. Bent double with this new assault of pain in his colon, Rob crept into Laurie's bedroom. He pulled the duvet off the bed so that the sheet-covered mattress was exposed, and then upon this, slipping down his trousers and scarlet slip, he emitted from his anus as copious an amount of shit as he'd deposited inside the Saxon chapel. To shit *in the bed itself*, at the very centre of Laurie's present love, was a desecration – that important word – as great, as delectable, as his crapping upon the altar of God's house. Then came another explosion of thunder.

Perhaps only with a rain-storm such as he'd been describing could Rob's convulsive sobs be comparable. Bill Bentley watched in the grip of these with a cold astonishment. 'Don't you see it now,' he was crying out, this lad with the soft, light voice that put passengers so at their ease, 'how I was then in the hands of Satan just as your hymn says? I was possessed by evil, I'm sure of it. I can remember just how I felt when doing . . . doing what I've told you about, I was rejoicing in my foulness, I laughed and sang in diabolical glee . . .'

At the beginning of his narrative Bill had found Rob exceedingly hard to follow. Was it really necessary, he'd asked himself, to attend that closely to all the splutterings and chokings and stammerings: more likely than not this pantomime was over nothing so very dreadful or, for that matter, important or special. Guys often got pretty conceited about their sins, as Bill knew from many years of experience. They had no sense of perspective. Oh, yes, the lad was clearly going through hell – Bill half-guessed the accompanying desires to his tale, to take hold of a knife or sliver of glass and hack his criminal body into the bloody shreds it deserved – but he was probably getting a bit of a kick out of it; the confession was making him feel significant as little else could.

'Jesus!' Rob called out in a terrible voice strong enough, it seemed, to bring down the walls of the cabin, 'I know my fate should be the blackness of darkness for ever, but have mercy on me! Be my friend, just like your servant Bill Bentley here says Thou wilt be, and I will be Thine for ever and ever . . .'

I never would have imagined this boy (and him British too!) capable of such hysteria, said Bill Bentley to himself. It was a most unattractive exhibition. True, Rob had been *in sorrow*, but really – well, you couldn't help wanting the coming out of it to be attended by a little less hullabaloo, could you? It wasn't . . . wasn't quite *manly*! Bill was a little irritated with *himself* too; he'd thought there was little he didn't know about 'saving', but he certainly hadn't marked Rob down in his mental note-book as one who'd come to the Lord with a lot of tears and histrionic clamour. Well, it just went to show, didn't it? He guessed, for all his years of service at Greater Glory, he still had a lot to learn. And Bill permitted himself a grim little smile at his own exemplary – and surely exceptional – modesty.

Rob interpreted the smile as one of forgiveness and encouragement. He wasn't seeing things so very clearly, anyway, through his veil of tears.

'Thank you, Bill for showing me the way, the light! I'm

glad to be going back to England in *this* condition. I *am* truly repentant, aren't I? I *am* fit company for Jesus?'

He's already asked me that about two hundred times, said Bill Bentley to himself. 'Have you told me all?' he asked in as impassive voice as he could find, 'I have the feeling that your story hasn't come to an end yet.'

It wasn't really that he himself wanted to hear that much more, though maybe he did feel greater curiosity than he cared to acknowledge. It was that he would not have exerted his power to the full – that power bestowed upon by Jesus Christ and those good and mighty organisations which did His work – unless he exacted a *complete* penitent confession. It was an axiom in Greater Glory that you made guys tell *everything*! Besides it wasn't unpleasurable, reducing someone to shivers and sobs, repellent though actually confronting these undoubtedly was.

'There *is* a bit more, of course,' said Rob, 'but,' he asked piteously, 'do you really want to hear it?'

'It's *Jesus* who does,' said Bill Bentley, 'Jesus can't be satisfied with an unfinished task!'

'But He must know what happened Himself!'

'That's hardly the point!'

Rob realised that Mrs Hargreaves would be bound to tell Laurie of his visit to his flat, and therefore, assuming that any doubt persisted in his mind, his great friend would before long know the identity of the double desecrator. Would he inform Mum and Dad! Think what an inferno his life would be at home . . . Dad would not perhaps try to beat him but he knew many other ways of making his younger son's life a misery.

There was no alternative, Rob knew, as he entered *The Copper Kettle* from the unremitting rain, from the night where no night should be (it was not yet six o'clock!) to putting Foswich behind him.

Unusually Mum and Dad had been invited out to dinner. Alone in the house, hearing the pantiled roof assaulted by rain as by arrows in some medieval war, Rob braced himself for another crime and for escape.

In the café's till he found almost ninety pounds. He put these in his wallet and then wrote his parents the following note:

> 'Dear Mum and Dad,
>
> I've decided to go to Germany to try my luck with that company I told you about, that runs cargo-boats between Northern Europe and the United States. In order to get over there I need more money than I've got, so I've helped myself to the till. Rest assured you'll get your £88.60 back before Christmas. I'll write to you when I've got the job I'm hoping for, and when I have an address of one sort or another.
>
> I'm sure you – and everybody else – will be better off without me.
>
> Your son,
>   Rob.

It would not have been truthful of him to have apologised either for the theft or for the flight.

Making his way to Foswich Station was perhaps the hardest part of the ensuing journey. He was terrified of being seen, canvas bag in hand, not that there were many people likely to be out on this wild evening. Once aboard the Central Line train, on which, thank goodness, was no one he knew, he felt a certain peace, a certain strength steal over him, exhausted though he was. It took him about two and a half hours to reach Harwich. Unbelievably he found near the station a terraced house advertising Bed and Breakfast, and the owner not only answered the doorbell at this comparatively late hour but welcomed him in. He described himself as a student (as earlier on Polly Keating had done) on his way to Germany (wholly true, at least as far as intentions went!). 'I've never seen anyone who could *truly* be described as a dying duck in a thunderstorm before!' laughed the amiable Mrs Benton, 'when you get upstairs to your room, take your clothes off, and when you're decently in bed I'll come and take them away and dry them for you. They should be all right by morning. I'll bring you up a supper-tray, if you like. You have the look of someone who's still in need of your evening meal.'

To Rob, awash with a sense of his own capacity for wickedness, Mrs Benton appeared the very embodiment of human virtue . . .

Sleep was not difficult, as he'd feared it would be. Thoughts of Laurie and Polly discovering the shit in their bed, of Mum and Dad coming home to find his note and the rifled till did not disturb him seriously. His dream was a pleasant one; he saw a ship on a summer sea, and crew and passengers alike were goats. The name of the ship was the *Nesta Coolidge* and it was going to make its way up the Fase to where the kingfisher nested.

'But the Fase isn't navigable,' protested Rob, 'it couldn't take more than a small canoe at its very widest . . .'

'As if *that* would bother us!' said Fat Anna, 'are you, or are you not, H.G. Peters? If you are H.G., have faith!'

He woke up to a clear day. The pretty Dutch-like port of Harwich had a freshly-painted air. The world had been redeemed by rain. The sky was a kingfisher blue in which clouds and gulls showed very white. There was a boat going to Hamburg that afternoon, and Rob had no difficulty in getting himself a berth on it.

Church-bells swung all over the town. Their clanging was perhaps what jolted Rob into his one act of the weekend that later was to seem worthy of his better nature. He stepped into a telephone box.

It was Laurie himself who answered.

'Laurie, it's me, Rob!' He could barely hear himself above his heart-beats.

Silence.

'Speak to me. Speak to me, Laurie, *please*!'

'What – what *can* I say to you, Rob?'

'You can say "Goodbye!" I'm not ringing from Foswich, but from somewhere else. I've already left my bad old life behind me, you see.'

'I . . . I just can't understand you. I suppose you've just gone to pieces after the examinations! Even last Wednesday you were in a bit of a state, weren't you? I ought to have realised how bad you were feeling. And this afternoon's been a climax.'

Well, that's a rather convenient way for you to look at the incident, Rob could not stop himself from thinking. The line was very bad, crackles and hissings blocking whole sentences; maybe it had been affected by the storm of last night. 'Polly was absolutely *devastated*!' he heard. I shan't be losing any sleep over *that*, he said to himself.

'I want you to know something, Laurie,' he said, through all the separating noises.

'Sorry, I couldn't hear you!'

'I said – I want you to know something!'

'And what's that!'

'That I'm your friend!'

Whatever Laurie said by way of reply – which was probably not very much – was lost; more easily could he hear the seagulls mewing above his telephone kiosk.

'So . . . I suppose the truth is,' Rob said as loudly and clearly as he could, 'that we can't *be* friends any more, can we? after . . . after all this?'

And then Laurie's voice came startlingly loud and distinct. 'I wouldn't quite say that,' he answered, 'but I certainly can't see how things can ever be quite the same again between us.'

'Of course they can't! I understand that! So, when I go away, as I'll be doing very soon, this very day, it's best that we don't communicate, isn't it?'

A pause: the crackles were resuming.

Then – 'I'm not sure I'd go as far as that!'

'Okay, let's make a pact, shall we? *I* won't write to *you*. I'll assume that you won't want to be hearing from me, that you'll be relieved at not having me around any more . . . But, if *you* feel like writing, well, I'll be glad . . . you don't need to be told that, do you?'

'That sounds like a fair enough arrangement. We ought to shake hands on it. Pity we can't do so!'

. . . 'Can you wonder,' Rob said later, 'that I've always thought and spoken of Laurie Williams as a *good* man. Can you match such forgiveness, such magnanimity?'

Laurie's words had delivered him – temporarily – from the evil of guilty brooding; indeed for most of that crossing he felt a light-heartedness, a desire to embrace all of the animate and inanimate world that he could see, such as he could parallel only with that moment on the Japanese bridge over the Fase. He played the juke-box, ordered himself lagers (illicit, for he was still under-age), chatted to a whole assortment of folk, both his contemporaries and his elders, behaved in other words, as he rarely did, as an ordinary, but happy, youth for whom the imminent future is the most important tense ... The New Jerusalem of his later Bible readings could not have looked more wonderful to him than did the banks of the Elbe estuary, and its prosperous merchants' villas with gardens proudly going down to the water.

And late in the afternoon – not forty-eight hours after his sufferings and crime at Saxingham Enfrith – he was calling on the Hamburg offices of the Ludendorff company, for all the world like the hero of a fairy-tale who has come to seek his fortune.

Rob was as good as his word. His parents received ninety pounds two weeks before Christmas. For many months he thought he had nothing to feel even rueful about, let alone guilty. He had not read his own character right. But it was only when England became again a reality – somewhere he would soon *be* – that he knew anguish, that his past arose with demanding horror.

'... Jesus! I've told it all now, I've revealed myself in all my wickedness, you have to take me now. "Just as I am!" I beg you, I implore you ...'

Time to put a stop to all this carry-on, Bill told himself. On the one hand he was pleased that the moment he'd been working hard for all crossing – working his ass off for, you might say – had arrived. He was not someone who countenanced defeat, and the Greater Glory Tabernacle down in Mississippi didn't either. He now had to pronounce the shrieking youth in front of him 'saved', no doubt of it! You wouldn't want to get anyone – particularly an obvious hysteric like Rob Peters – saying that he'd been brought to the point of knowing the Lord and then denied His healing, redeeming hand. When the time came – and Bill Bentley was en route to England to organise such a time! – to stand up and be counted, well, the more the better, and Rob Peters was not unwelcome to be among the testifying throng (testifying, that is, to the power and goodness of Greater Glory). But as for being a figure on a platform, an associate ... Well, *that* was a different story. He must think over the whole matter of Rob again, and most carefully.

Anyway – to get it over with! Bill said: 'Well, Rob, this is it, I reckon. I can *feel* Jesus very close now. I can see His hand reaching out for yours in friendship – the friendship of forgiveness. How proud I am that I have played a part – only a very small one, I know – in your coming to know Jesus Christ!' ...

Shut up! Belt up, can't you! he'd so nearly said. Shucks, it was worse than a panic-stricken kindergarten, all the blubbering and boo-hooing this now quite uninteresting boy was making.

'Thanks ... thank you, Bill!' For a moment Bill thought that Rob was about to embrace him. 'I don't know how to ... I can't ... I mean, how shall I ever ...'

Bill handed Rob a large, monogrammed handkerchief and told him to go into the bathroom adjacent to the cabin to give his face a good wash. When he'd done this, Bill asked him to kneel down, and they would say a prayer together. In his most sonorous voice (while Rob bit back further sobs) he delivered an appropriate one, thanking God that Robert Peters had been brought to Him. From now on he could surely be numbered among the Select, the Saved, for he would pay tribute to Jesus and His goodness wherever he went ... The weeping Rob nodded agreement.

It is surely a pity that Rob didn't look up at the face of the agent of his salvation. He would not have liked the expression upon it, any more than he had the last time he'd done so, an occasion he'd now forgotten. He would also have realised that he knew nothing about the temperament of the man bringing him to the Creator of the Universe, a man who in truth despised sensitive, introspective people. The self-absorption of shame, and of the need to escape from it, had made Rob accept Bill's presentation of himself as almost outside – or beyond – personality. Of course that couldn't really be any the truer of him than it could be of anyone else – of Filipino Pete, or Mrs Van Asdalen, or Rob himself. Rob was unable to see Bill the English failure-made-good, Bill the money-man, Bill the lecher.

After the prayer Bill pressed knobs on his smart Sanyo machine, and the two of them listened to – and joined in with – gladsome singers from Mississippi. They sang 'I'm H.A.P.P.Y. because I'm S.A.V.E.D.' and:

> *'Jesus, lead me evermore*
> *To that last eternal shore*
> *Where my home will be with You*
> *And those I love.*
> *I will rest upon Thy throne*
> *With my Lord to lead me home!*
> *Take me to the golden gates*
> *Way up above!'*

Rob saw those golden gates – shimmering in their beauty – just a little beyond the porthole of Cabin Number Five. The sea that stretched on the other side of them was serene again. The ship had left the troublesome current well behind, and he – oh, he had joined that privileged multitude of those who had Jesus as their Friend, whose sins and cares were borne by Him, who had loved him and all those others, since before the creation of sea and land, before worlds, before Time . . .

Incredibly normal life asserted itself. He was due back shortly in the kitchen. Bill Bentley said that while, of course, he was free to come in and have a chat any time, the best thing in his opinion was for Rob to spend the remaining free time this trip praying and reading the Bible. And, so saying, he handed Rob a copy of the Good Book – from his desk cupboard, a buddy's Christian smile upon his lips.

'Gosh, thanks, Bill,' said Rob, 'I'll . . . I'll certainly do as you say.'

How stupid, how sad, how terrible that Rob didn't understand that he was being dismissed.

Bill'd found all the mooning about Laurie little other than 'soppy'; *he* had never felt thus for anyone in his life; it belonged, he thought, to the pages of schoolgirl stories. More important, though, were the acts in which Rob's confession had culminated – they were absolutely disgusting, so much so he scarcely felt like seeing the boy again. If there was one thing that Bill set store by, it was hygiene.

CHAPTER EIGHT: ROB

Tonight the ocean was once again a silken spread played upon by star-light. The swell was over as if it had never been. Britain was palpably nearer. And Rob would be landing there – yes, Robert Peters, ne'erdowell and criminal – as a Friend of Jesus, with the power to bring others to the same wonderful condition.

For – and he knew he wasn't deceiving himself – Rob *felt* saved. 'Now, come off it,' someone like old Neil Ferris might say, 'what on earth do you mean by *that*?' And this is how I would answer, Rob told himself, gripping the salt-sprayed rails of the bridge-deck. For the first time this crossing the black rim of the night horizon holds no fears whatever for me. I'm truly ready to meet whatever my destination has to offer, be it rejection, be it pain, be it violence.

He closed his eyes so that the cool Atlantic wind could caress his now weary head and maybe deliver thoughts, images, hopes acceptable to God. Momentarily sightless he could the more easily imagine himself floating into the great void – which was, if the Bible were true, not a void at all but an infinity of majesty and love (with somewhere inside it dark fire for those who had repudiated their maker). Yes, let's say he was dead, dead like Pete at the end of his dance. Being dead meant travelling on the instant through space that wasn't space and through time that wasn't time to the source of all life. And there he'd find a white-robed friend with arms extended.

'. . . Lost in thought, eh, Robbie?'

Here was something as pleasing to the eyes as the figure he'd been trying to conjure up: sinewy, athletic, golden-skinned Pete, sexy, bird-boy, lover and companion.

'I've got so much though to be lost in,' sighed Rob. Life would be much simpler if he hadn't, but then it would end in the blackness of darkness for ever.

'Lucky me, then! I'm a guy of very few ideas,' giggled Pete, 'and right now I'm a guy with only *one*!' And he put a beautiful arm round Rob's neck.

Rob didn't at all want to remove himself from Pete's attentions, and though gently he did so, it wasn't with the decisiveness that would have communicated anything to the Filipino boy.

'What idea is that?' he asked, though he knew perfectly well.

'Do I really need to tell you! . . . I smoke another cigarette up here, and then we go down to my cabin, eh?' Pete, hold loosened now, gave a deep contented exhalation that somehow, seemed to Rob to be his also.

'God, it's good to see the ocean itself again, isn't it?'

God . . . good, thought Rob fearfully. Just like Bill said in one of our sessions, we pay tribute to Him all the time without knowing what we're doing or why. 'Pete,' he said, 'being quiet doesn't make the ocean become itself; it's itself also when it's rough. Sometimes, like I once said, I think it's more so.'

Pete shrugged his shoulders. 'This is the way things *should* be!' he said, 'and don't think I don't know about the dangers of nature. Remember I come from the tropics. You ought to have seen from my bird-dance that we Filipinos accept *everything*!' That bird-dance! – even the word made Rob feel horny . . . 'Well, how about it?' Pete was now saying.

'Pete, I'm sorry,' Rob forced himself to say, and truly he was, 'but I just can't make it tonight!' Did he realise that he was using virtually the same words to this lover-boy as he had to Bill Bentley when trying to wriggle out of a commitment to him.

'Tired, huh?' said Pete, 'well, so am I! Ricky says I never seem to get tired doing you-know-what, but right now a night's good sleep wouldn't do me any harm, I grant you.'

Rob looked away from him, so supple, so desirable, so suggestive of kisses and a great deal more. 'Pete,' he said, trying to draw strength from the solemn black Atlantic below and around them, 'don't get me wrong, please! I like you, like you a *lot*. But we mustn't . . . *mustn't* do what . . . what we've been doing again.'

Pete drew apart from Rob. '*Mustn't*!' he said, as if the word were a stranger to him; there was an injury and a sharpness in usually so light and amorous metallic voice, 'what d'you mean, Rob?'

Well, Pete can't think of love-making with his own sex as wrong, thought Rob. Any more, he added to himself, than I can when I do it. (He was almost afraid of this admission which his honesty compelled from him). So what should he say? 'Mustn't, because I've got so many things to sort out about myself, Pete,' he said, 'I just shouldn't have any interruptions right now.

'Thanks a lot,' said Pete, 'thanks a fucking lot! It always does a guy good to know he's an interruption.'

'I didn't mean it like that,' protested Rob, 'honest, I didn't. I'll always be ready for a chat, a game of ping-pong or cards, any time you want, any time you're feeling lonely and blue.'

'Gee, that's *great* of you,' said Pete sarcastically, 'and what are these things you've got to sort out about yourself? Whether you're gay or straight? I could give you an answer in one second flat . . .'

Best not to rise, Rob told himself. 'No, I've got to think hard about all my sins, all the things I've done in the past, and how I can undo them.' Above all, he could – and should – have added, by bringing Laurie Williams to Jesus.

Pete's face showed his complete inability to understand. 'Things you've *done*!' he said, with a not particularly amiable laugh, '*what* things? I knew a hundred times more at *fourteen* than you do *now*.'

Rob blushed: the conversation must stop. And did Pete really think, as his talk suggested, that having sex was the most important thing in life?

'I know what it is!' Pete was crying out, with a look of mocking triumph on his almost perfect face, 'you've been listening to Bill Bentley, haven't you? He's "got" you, hasn't he? Come on, admit it!'

Rob's pulse raced. 'What if he had?' he asked, 'I've a right to listen to who I choose.' Words from The Bible had come into his head. 'Get thee behind me, Satan.'

'He talks bullshit, that man,' said Pete, 'in fact he's the biggest bullshitter I've ever known. "Get thee behind me, Satan", indeed!'

'He's preaching the one true gospel,' said Rob.

Pete was lighting a cigarette. When he'd done this, he turned slowly to confront Rob. 'Is he now?' he said, 'is he now? Oh, *I* see what's happened, okay, I ought to have been wise to it sooner.'

'It could happen to *you*, Pete!' said Rob, almost beseechingly. For within the body that showed an appetising stiff cock and a delightful arse dwelled an immortal soul with a destiny . . .

'Like hell it could!' said Pete.

'Don't speak like that!' cried Rob, for now, thanks to Bill, he knew what hell was like: the blackness of darkness forever in which blazed fires beyond quenching.

'I'll speak exactly how I want to,' said Pete, and you had to admire his guts while fearing the spirit driving him to his replies.

'Pete,' said Rob, 'let me explain!'

'No,' said Pete, 'all you'll do is repeat Bill Bentley's guff. And I can hear *that* any time I've a mind to.' He gave a strange giggle here. 'So I'll . . . leave you to your prayers.' Should I let him blaspheme so, thought Rob, noting with alarm the quizzical grin on the boy's face. 'And,' Pete added, lit ciggy dangling from his fingers, a symbol, so it seemed to Rob then, of his sex-fiery cock, 'and let me tell you, if *you* don't want me, there's others do; yes, right here on board the *Egon Ludendorff*, including some who'd surprise you!'

Shortly afterwards, lying down on his bunk for needed sleep, Rob found himself crying, crying hard for the tender affections of a boy he'd known for only a very short time and whom he'd now alienated. More alone now, more lacking in others' care, than ever was he now: he felt robbed of a birthright, the warm proximity and demonstrations of another human being. But he must accept his loss. Didn't a Christian have to make sacrifices? Wasn't it indeed expected of him! And in the infinity of life after death, who would have the happier time if not he-who-was-saved?

That night he dreamed of Laurie again.

He was standing on that jetty, as Rob arrived in a smaller boat from a larger one anchored back there in the harbour. As he got nearer shore, Rob saw that his art master and friend's arms were open for an embrace of welcome. The boat drew up alongside the pier. And – horrible! – as he clambered out onto the wooden platform Rob watched the flesh roll off the loved figure, so that what stood there to greet him was nothing but a skeleton, the skull of which was fixed in a ghastly and humourless grin . . .

CHAPTER NINE: LAURIE

Thinking about Rob – who was in fact voyaging towards him – Laurie took himself to *The Copper Kettle*. He hadn't been there for quite some while. The pleasant balmy May weather had brought a fair number of visitors to Foswich, and therefore to the teashop. Beryl and Anne Peters were waiting at table, the latter of these serving Laurie. (This naturally brought to mind the afternoon of Rob's dark confidences down by the river.) He was aware as never before of Anne's resemblance to Polly Keating, that tumble of red hair, those freckles on her fair-skinned face.

Why, he asked himself as he knew he would, had Rob never replied to his two letters? That first visit to *The Copper Kettle*, when the delicious and capacious cream-tea had been 'on the house', those endless meals with Polly – how very long ago both seemed now! His life was surely bathed in an altogether different light; it was as if he'd stepped from one kind of painting, a watercolour, into another: an oil canvas with heavy dark colours. Death had brought this about, Death that had looked up at him before it actually delivered its master-stroke – triumphant in weary eyes set in a loved face that was now sagging over bones, while the body below was noisome with the effluents of its conquest. Sitting by a death-bed was to lose a virginity that you hadn't appreciated was yours. And yet . . . strangely and stubbornly quotidian life continued, just as if you'd never been offered – and met –

that supreme and ghastly challenge. Think of this afternoon! A first-form class, an attempt to catch up with overdue correspondence, Foswich as pretty with blossom and flowers as it had been last year, *The Copper Kettle* still providing scones and clotted cream and homemade raspberry jam. At the tables, laughter, the lowering of voices for scandal, the raising of them for the announcement of news of which the speaker was proud: a husband's promotion, a new house, a new car – all as if the terrible axe-man did not exist.

Yet if his life were acquiring shape at last, and so it seemed to him, particularly in the light of this month's developments, it was Death that had to a very important extent made it. Death and – well, that was what Laurie found so difficult – to understand; Rob Peters. What Rob had done that July day had had an extraordinary effect on him, To deny, as to himself, just an hour back, that Rob had played only a small part in his life was to be dishonest. And, though it seemed more likely than not that he would not play another one, you could not be quite sure of even *that*. Ladling the thick cream on top of the delicious jam, Laurie thought: There's some power in Rob, at least as far as I'm concerned, that I haven't yet come to terms with. But what is it?'

Perhaps a sudden desire to be offered a key to this question, this riddle, was why he decided, by way of settling up the bill, to step into the kitchen-quarters of the cafe. Beryl Peters was spreading a chocolate filling over the halves of a sponge-cake.

'Excellent tea again, Mrs Peters,' Laurie said, 'I don't know why I haven't been here more often recently.' He laid the bill and the money on the kitchen-table with what he thought of as his boyish smile of gratitude and friendliness.

Whether it was or not, it certainly didn't elicit a return smile from Mrs Peters: 'Well, *I* don't know why you haven't been here, do I? The cafe's near enough!!!'

Perhaps one reason I haven't come is *your* conspicuous lack of friendliness, even more noticeable *after* Rob went away than before, Laurie said silently by way of answer. Aloud he said: 'Any news of Rob?'

'I should think we have had some, yes! We are his parents,

after all, though I must admit you wouldn't necessarily think so from his behaviour.'

'Good news?' Laurie persisted. Quite often Laurie attempted to construct a picture of Rob's life at sea – and it was easier for *him* to do this, than for many another, what with Dad's anecdotes and his own childhood voyages to Denmark. But he'd never succeeded in seeing Rob in relation to others on a ship. Perhaps because of imaginative modesty. ... Beryl Peters, now back at work on the sponge-cake, couldn't have heard him, so he asked again: 'Good news, was it, from Rob?'

'In my view,' said Beryl Peters, 'no news that comes from a life on a cargo-boat can be *very* good.'

'I was wondering whether the lad,' using this word somehow made his relationship with Rob more normal, more schoolmaster-like, less mentally troubling, 'whether the lad would appreciate another letter; he didn't reply to the last one.' Beryl Peters, rather pointedly, didn't look up at him here, and Laurie thought he noticed a certain crimsoning of her cheeks. Therefore he added: 'I hope he got it safely?' For he'd delivered it personally, stamped, for the Peters' to send on to Rob's P.O. Box number one rainy evening in February.

'Shouldn't think he did, no!' said Rob's mother quietly.

'Why not?' asked Laurie, 'some trouble with the postal service?'

'Not as far as I know,' Beryl Peters monotone had not changed, 'I mean you're more likely to know that kind of thing than me, Mr Williams; I don't have time to catch up with the news.'

'I'm quite busy too,' Laurie couldn't resist saying, 'I wrote that letter because I had something – well, two things, actually – to tell Rob that I judged were very important.'

'Well, my husband *didn't* judge your letter important. We only send Rob communications that are a hundred per cent necessary. As my husband, Mr Peters often quotes: "Sharper it is than a serpent's tooth to have a thankless child," and we got that serpent's tooth, yes, Mr Williams, we got it all right. So why should we send Rob letters – here, there and everywhere?'

'But is it for you to judge?' Laurie cried; not since some unfairness from a master at Tanbury Grammar School, had he felt so angry at injustice, 'what about the feelings, the rights of those who've actually *written* the letters.'

'I've just explained to you Mr Peters' views,' said his wife, 'I do not choose to go against him. Mr Peters did not think your letter came in the category of those of a hundred per cent importance.'

'He read it?' This was about the nearest Laurie – so mild of manner – had ever come in his life to shouting.

'If you make another insinuation of that kind, I'll thank you never to come to *The Copper Kettle* again,' said Mrs Peters, 'my husband is a gentleman; he would never dream of opening another person's letter . . .'

'But he would dream of holding it back,' said Laurie, recalling the agonising news it had contained, the difficulty – emotional and verbal – he'd had in writing it, 'Mrs Peters, *I*, the author of the letter *did* consider it a hundred per cent important, if not two hundred per cent. And anyway isn't a letter from an old friend a thing of *immeasurable* importance, whatever its actual content may be?'

'Oh, Mr Williams,' sighed Mrs Peters, 'you won't think like that when you get to my age. You'll have reached the point when it doesn't matter a tuppeny damn whether you've heard from an old friend or not.' What appalling sadness, Laurie could not but think, lay behind the genteelly delivered reproach. 'And now if you don't mind, I'll have you remember a little proverb: "You're never the only pebble on the beach." In case you were too engrossed in wondering how Rob was, I'll tell you that there are a lot of customers in *The Copper Kettle* today . . . Very good afternoon to you! Much obliged!'

Anger at the behaviour of Beryl and Geoff Peters gave way, of course, to pity for their son. It was an emotion he had, so to speak, forgotten how to feel for Rob. Yet now that he re-experienced it, he recalled that right from the beginning – from that afternoon visit to his flat when the boy had been so ready with confidences and compliments there had been something about him that had moved Laurie. He had sensed a vulnerability, a lack of certainty about the external world – at least as manifested in other people – and this awareness had surely been vindicated that July day, when the pity these qualities should have called forth had been stifled by other reactions. . . . The re-awakening of tenderness he was now knowing for Rob was stimulated by the incorrect and uncharitable things he'd been thinking about him, under the impression that he would have received February's letter. And perhaps, he admitted to himself, recollecting Jonathan West's wise words to him that afternoon of last year, that is not the only way I have been unjust, judgemental and unsympathetic to Rob. He could suddenly see him again so vividly – appearing at the door of his flat that hot, tense July afternoon, wearing his lemon-and-grey summer shirt and gleaming white ducks, hope and anxiety to please radiant on his tired, young face. And how had he, Laurie, behaved that day? Had he even tried at all hard to make Rob feel welcome? In his cowardice he'd let Polly vent her irritation so that the lad had thought he was wholly unwanted.

What else could he do, his mind running thus, but make his way down to the path that ran alongside the Fase. It was just such a day as that of last year. Then he'd tried to find in the serenity of the countryside, fragrant, bathed in the soft light of the late afternoon sun, some kind of assurance – that could be his in the event of his mother's death. Well, that death had taken place, just as its victim had many times prophesied, and it was a different kind of serenity that he was surveying and contemplating now, and he was in search of a different kind of assurance. Today's Laurie knew what physical and spiritual torment the calm of the countryside could co-exist with. And with such mental torment as Rob had confided to him there! What he wanted it to tell him now was that the force which animated so much that was beautiful and lovable was – in some way that escaped any kind of definition – *stronger* than pain, than the ghastly landscapes of remorse and grief.

By now he had reached the Japanese half-moon bridge. Behind his eyes he could feel a pricking of tears, yet he dared not shed them. He would weep too much; if he did Rob, Polly, Mum were all gone from him, and with them, states of being which he could not but mourn. After Rob he had never made a friend of a pupil again, never would. He and youth had parted company now. He had not, in fact, turned celibate after he and Polly finally broke up, but the subsequent affairs had been short-lived, emotionally tepid, not meaning much either to himself or his partner. With Polly the idea of a shared *life* had vanished, and Laurie had now, he felt, to face a solitary future. As for Mum's death, he felt less than himself after it: his identity had been chiselled at, and he would have to learn to adjust. As for 'home', for all her petulance and lethargies Mum had created an entity in which he belonged, had a prominent, fixed position which one could gainsay or undermine. Of course physically 'home' remained: Dad was touchingly grateful for his visits, and Mick and Dale were still there, mooning about and doing nothing with increasing langour. But they, in their different ways, only enforced the dereliction of Mum's permanent departure.

He leaned upon the balustrades of the bridge, in much the same attitude that Rob Peters had chosen that May afternoon last year. And, standing there in Rob's attitude, Laurie saw it! – as he'd never expected to again. From the right-hand bank of the Fase the kingfisher rose. It was a flash of blue that seemed to contain eternity, and to bestow at least the shadow of this upon the tranquil, flowering countryside. The blue dazzled and delighted and balmed the eyes and raised the spirits. Nothing and nobody can completely end, thought Laurie; even wasting into the void, which was poor old Mum's apparent fate, may *not* be ending. And there was something else the kingfisher's flight proclaimed to him: something he should have learned – and taught – years ago. That the being is most beautiful and has most to give when it is unsullied, when it can move with a splendour that is the greater for its being done to gratify no one's will, to serve no imposed purpose. *Being for the sake of being* – and that must lead to the profoundest Love of all.

CHAPTER TEN: ROB

The remaining days on the *Egon Ludendorff* Rob worked with the diligence that often follows, and is an antidote to, exhaustion. And when not working he applied himself to the Bible.

Some people back in Foswich – his family above all, and such school-teachers as Dai Griffiths – would have been maliciously amused to see Rob so engrossed in a book. One could easily – and without taking up much space – list all those books that Rob had read from cover-to-cover, for there were not many of them, in truth, and of these – Agatha Christies or Mickey Spillanes left about the house by his brother, Phil, he couldn't even remember the titles now. Most works set at school – *Lord of the Flies*, for instance, and *Animal Farm* – he'd never bothered to finish, though in point of fact these two had interested him more than others. Chiefly he preferred dipping into natural history and alighting on a few facts which he'd try to memorise. Thus he could tell you that a hare has been known to cross a river 183 metres wide in order to reach a field of carrots on the opposite bank, and that squirrels will often convert the nests of crows or magpies to make their own dreys . . .

The gospels were of course, to a certain measure familiar to him from those tedious R.E. lessons through which he'd fooled and slumbered, but, sitting on deck or down in his cabin, he was rather surprised by how little he'd remembered. Even now it was hard, since he found considerable difficulty in reading more than three or four pages consecutively and his attention so easily wandered. But it was interesting, what a lot of ill people Jesus had come across, and what a lot of energy he'd spent on them: a great great many with devils whom He cast out and who would have spoken because *they* knew who Jesus was; also lepers and the blind and then a paralysed man lowered through a roof, and, most interesting of all, a man who'd broken the chains put upon him. This guy lived among tombstones, where he sang and cried and then cut himself with stones, and he told Jesus that his name was Legion because of the many devils inside him. Anyway, Jesus sent all those devils packing — into a herd of pigs. It was rather as if, thought Rob, all the nastiness he'd been possessed by at Saxingham Enfrith had suddenly left him and entered one of Nesta Coolidge's goats, Fat Anna. But then Nesta would have grieved, and besides Fat Anna had been a nice animal. He must have got the story wrong. Anyway it was good of Jesus to cure so many people, to summon out the devil and forgive their sins. And Bill Bentley said that even now among the saved there were those who could do these things. After Jesus' death, when He appeared to the Eleven, He told them that they had to preach the Good News to the whole of creation. (And Rob could not but think at this point of preaching to — well, his and Laurie's kingfisher.)

> *'Those who believe it, and receive baptism will find salvation; those who do not believe it will be condemned. Faith will bring with it these miracles; believers will cast out devils in my name and speak in strange tongues; if they handle snakes or drink any deadly poison, they will come to no harm; and the sick on whom they lay their hands will recover.'*

If she needed it, why, Rob might be able to lay a hand on Laurie's Mum. Bill said, though, that he doubted that this talent would be his yet. Asked about the other things in this surely very important ending to the Gospel of St Mark, Bill said — yes, he did know folks who could speak in tongues, and that up in the mountains of Tennessee and the Carolinas, a day's journey north-eastwards from Jackson, Miss. you could find believers who handled the most dangerous snakes possible during their services, though he himself held that the Lord visited the ability only on a very few.

Rob very much liked the idea of the band of friends: first the Disciples and then the greater group after His death. They all seemed to be sure of each other and of their Master's affections; Rob wished you could know more about them all, what each one had been like. They must have had points in common, he presumed; Jesus had chosen them fairly swiftly. Would he, Rob, have liked Andrew and Philip and Bartholomew and Matthew and Thomas and James the son of Alphaeus and Thaddaeus and Simon the Zealot, about whom the Gospels didn't tell you much, though they gave you a good enough idea of what it must have been like to have been around them. Rob was not ashamed, rather he was proud of the tears that filled his eyes, making ship shimmer and ocean blur, as he read the beautiful words that Jesus had spoken to his buddies at the Last Supper – and he read and let tears drop a fair number of times:

> "This is my Father's glory, that you may bear fruit in plenty and so be my disciples. As the Father has loved me, so I have loved you. Dwell in my love. If you heed my commands, you will dwell in my love, as I have heeded my Father's commands and dwell in his love."

So beautiful did these words sound to Rob that he could imagine himself there – among the close and loving friends – when Jesus spoke them. In fact Jesus often implied that, in a sort of way, you *were* there. Even the unborn. And He was pretty adamant on the point too, that for those who were 'chosen' trouble was often in store, in fact almost definitely *was* in store. The world would hate you, it would persecute you; there would be many a place to which you came, telling the good news in simplicity and enthusiasm, and you would be laughed at and worse, and from those spots you had to shake the dust off your feet. It might even come to that in *The*

Copper Kettle and Foswich.

For this earth was full, chock-full, of bastards, and Rob got a certain kick out of realising how Jesus had found this to be so. Think of the Pharisees and scribes and doctors of the law. More ordinary people turned out no better: the crowd roared for Jesus' death, and it was they who shouted for crucifixion. Soldiers made mockery of Jesus by dressing Him up in purple and weaving a crown of thorns to put on His head. They then jeered at Him, and hit him on the head with a cane, and spat at Him, and paid Him mock homage, and then stripped Him of clothes, and then, when He was actually nailed to the cross, taunted Him and reviled Him and this even included the two poor sods who were being crucified beside Him.

And yet He told you to love everybody. Knowing they were like that!

But – and here Rob got further satisfaction – He'd already said some pretty strong things about those who didn't love Him, and His disciples were to say stronger things still. He asked you to be merciful, but if you weren't, if, for example, you went on being angry with your brother you could end up in the fires of hell. That's where you could go, too, if you were led to undue lusts with your right eye. The same applied to the man whose hand was his undoing! Certainly the saved person was saved in another sense from a very great deal of terrible things. And Rob Peters would be among them . . .

First came the gulls. Their wide white wings fill the voyager with gratitude and excitement, a feeling of imminent rebirth . . . Then the ships appeared, one after another, out of nowhere, large, small, gaily-painted, or battered-looking and rusty. By the time that a smeared green line had come into view – the coast of France – the *Egon Ludendorff* had gently changed identity. No longer could it be regarded as solitary worker of an elemental furrow. Now it was but one of many – a mere vessel, and in a double sense of that word! For the ship and her fellows seemed like offerings to some god of humanity, indeed for some, to God Himself, to prove man's capacity for sway over sea and land alike.

Everyone became palpably happier. João's winks became more promiscuously given than ever; that old man from Savannah, Georgia, who took a lot of convincing that the coast of France was not that of England, was a-bubble with even cornier jokes than he'd told before. And Mrs Van Asdalen still gazed upon the French shore, and then said: 'Well, at least the godamn *voyage* is over. Now I've got to get down to the serious business of persuading my daughter to get herself a divorce from that asshole of an English aristocrat she married. Our dollars can go all over the planet, but I *don't* want them bailing out a god-awful place like Saxingham *what's-its-name*?'

Pete joined Rob one time by the rails of the deck. It was early evening; blobs of light were coming up, like speeded flowers, on the coast and on the waters of the Channel too.

'Glad your first crossing's over, Pete?'

Pete shrugged his shoulders: 'I'm indifferent,' he said, 'though quite a few things have happened to me on board. But then,' he giggled, 'I'm a guy to whom things happen to, aren't I?'

Probably, thought Rob, but then so am I. On this voyage I have lost another kind of virginity and found Jesus . . . He wanted to tell Pete how much he'd missed him, particularly in the solitudes of the night (never had he so ached with sexual desire!) but he felt it would be tactless to do so.

'Are you going back to Baltimore with this ship?' asked Rob, 'Have you made up your mind about that? You haven't a contract with the company, have you?'

Pete shook his head. 'Apparently the *Egon Ludendorff* will stay about three or four days in dock. I'll go to my Filipino relations in London, and wait for a call from the ship. I think they'd take me on again; they're pleased with my work. But do I want to commit myself? That's the question, isn't it?'

'What might you want instead?' asked Rob, who had, after all, spent most of ten months on cargo-boats.

Pete gave a fetching wriggle. 'Fun, I guess,' he said, 'isn't that what everyone of us wants.' He gave Rob a quick appraisal with those bright, saurian eyes of his: 'No, I don't suppose it's what *you* want particularly . . .'

Rob felt obscurely rebuked: 'Don't you think I like fun, then? Didn't you think we had it . . .' He wondered how best to finish that question, 'together?' Like lightning flashes came vision of acts performed in Pete's cabin – enthusiastic gropings for the stiff organ, 'rimming' with accelerating rhythm . . .

'Not *fun* exactly, no!' said Pete. 'Anyway your mind's on other things now, isn't it?'

Rob said, indicating the lighted boats to their left, 'By morning we'll be seeing England. Though I've been up and down the Channel many times this last ten months, this'll be the first time since I left England that I'll have seen the coast properly. We've always been travelling so much nearer the European shore before.'

'Looking forward to it?'

'Dunno. More than I was – since,' but he felt shy of saying "since I've been saved", 'since the change that's come over me,' he finished. Pete looked at him oddly, maybe he thought Rob was alluding to their love-making.

'How can that be?'

'Because I've got more confidence in myself,' said Rob, adding privately; not that that would be difficult! 'Also because there are people there I want to bring to . . . to my way of thinking, of looking at things.'

'Why?' Pete asked this gently. Standing there beside him, confronting him in the light-dappled, boat-punctuated waters, and the soft pile beyond these of nocturnal cloud – Pete was arousingly attractive to Rob. He remembered how earlier he'd expressed a wish that they could always find themselves on the same boat. A picture of it was strong in his mind, all at once; a little older, a little more seasoned-looking, their arms lightly about one another's necks, they'd walk up the gangway back from the night out together, in traditional easy-going male style, in, say, Mobile or New Orleans, two sailors returned from fun, in a port. But in closer proximity . . .?

'*Why* do you want to bring people to your way of looking at things?' Pete was asking him.

'Because I believe it's what'll make them happy in the end.'

'Why haven't you been trying with me then? Don't you want *me* to be "happy in end"?'

Rob had not thought of this. 'Well, of coure, I do, Pete!'

Pete laughed, and put a hand on Rob's shoulder. 'What a funny guy you are, Rob. So simple in many ways; well, perhaps in *every* way . . . Anyway there wouldn't have been any point in your trying. Like I told you before I think all that kind of thing is guff.'

Had not the feel of the hand been so particularly good, Rob would have eased himself out of contact with Pete. He didn't want to hear him blaspheme . . . 'Please don't say that kind of thing, Pete; you know it must offend me *now*. And I want to be friends with you, honest I do! Believe me!'

Pete laughed again, and rubbed Rob's shoulder ' 'Course I believe you,' he said in his sexiest voice, 'I want us to meet up in London. Have "fun" – if you *can* – together. I've heard London is a great city for people like ourselves.'

Rob didn't at all care for the 'people like ourselves', though, curiously, hearing it sent the blood coursing into his loins. 'Yeah! It'd be good to be in London with you, Pete,' he said. He implied that he could show the Filipino boy round the city; in fact, near it though he'd lived all his life, he'd spent very little time there. His tastes had always led him away from it and its tentacles, into the country.

'Well, that's a deal,' said Pete, 'I wonder what we *will* do there together,' he mused a little flirtatiously, 'I must say – I've *never* met anyone like you, before.'

Rob didn't know whether to take this as praise or criticism. But Pete Rodriquez was surely speaking correctly: Rob's part in his life was wholly unique.

'You'd better give me your address there,' said Rob.

'Yeah! of course! Come down to my cabin some time,' the very invitation had amorous undertones, 'and I'll give it you!'

Rob indeed went round to Pete's cabin twice that evening, but to receive no answer. Irrational, ridiculous that he should have the feeling that Pete was in fact there – behind the door – but have this feeling he did. He called the next day, and this time Pete responded to his knock. The house where he would be staying in London turned out to be in Earl's Court, a part of the city Rob had never visited. Holding the piece of paper with Pete's address scribbled on it was like holding some magic totem; it all but burned Rob's fingers with stored-in power.

England presented herself across the gleaming water as seagull-white cliffs topped in green and laden like a tray with so many things that added up to the country as you dreamed of her: cottages, castles, stone-towered churches, hedged fields, copses, terraced houses, buses, Martello towers.

And now it was Bill who was standing beside him. Bill with the smiling, confident face of one who knew he was to set his mark on his destination.

'Our own country, Rob,' Bill was pleased to say, 'and remember that you're not returning to it the same as when you left it. Remember you're coming back to England as a Christian, with a Christian testimony to give. Let your light shine forth before men; hide it not under a bushel. A city that is built on a high hill cannot be hid.'

'Yeah, I really see all that now,' said Rob, 'I only hope I can be worthy of Jesus' trust and friendship.'

If only – if *only* the lad hadn't committed quite so disgusting, neurotic and unmanly a crime, Bill thought. If only he hadn't this decided hysteric streak. He really does look most attractive with the sea-breeze playing in his fair hair, and those unexpected brown eyes of his scanning the English shore with an innocent yet broody expression to them.

'Where are you staying, Bill?' Rob was asking, 'I mean there might be some point about my life as a Christian that I wanted to ask you.'

Well, I can always be 'out' if it suits me, thought Bill. Indeed he had behind him many years of practice of fending off unwanted visitors. He was not, though, by any means loath to give the name of the hotel Greater Glory was putting him up in; it showed the economic magnitude of that organisation, doing Jesus' work all over the South and beyond! 'I'm staying at The Dorchester,' he said, 'I daresay you know it. A little hotel in Park Lane.' Could he have heard himself Bill Bentley might have realised that he spoke in both the accent and vocabulary of his stockbroker father, Harvey Bentley of Polhamsted, Hertfordshire.

Unfortunately, he was not addressing a sophisticated youth by any standards, and Rob understood by Bill's reply that he really *was* staying in a little hotel. 'The Dorchester,' he said, pronouncing the name for the first time, 'I'll remember that.

He then turned back to the prospect of his own and Bill's native-country.

'Doesn't it remind you of that hymn you introduced me to?' he asked.

'You mean –?'

'Jesus, lead me evermore.'

'Yeah, you're right, Rob, it does!'

They both hummed its lilting, stirring melody:

> *'Jesus, lead me evermore*
> *To that last eternal shore*
> *Where my home will be with you*
> *And those I love.*
> *I will rest upon the throne*
> *With my Lord to lead me home,*
> *Take me to the golden gates*
> *Way up above.'*

Back in England, set upon that greensward tray on top of the cliffs, Rob would try to bring to Jesus, well, Neil Ferris, and any of his old mates from St John's School; his family – yes, even including Dad whom he'd got on with so badly; any neighbours of theirs or visitors to the cafe that he could engage in serious conversation. But above all – Laurie Williams, he almost *was* England to Rob, the good man to whom he'd done bad and who had apparently been unable to forgive him. But Jesus forgave all who tried to love Him; there was nothing but endless peace beyond His golden gates, and it was Rob's mission to make Laurie see that Jesus' way must be his also.

PART TWO

When Laurie came back from afternoon school that Friday, he found that the midday post had brought him a parcel. Of course he recognised the handwriting on the label. He made himself a pot of tea, and then undid it. He wasn't due in Tanbury until supper-time, and he preferred to wait until the worst of London's exodus traffic was over. He had a car of his own now, had bought Polly's Renault from her.

What had arrived was an edition of Eliot's Collected Poems. Polly was the sender – who else? In the fly-leaf she'd written:

> *'Dear Laurie,*
> *Isn't it your birthday one of these fine days. This week? I hope I'm not too late? Even so . . ., Many, many happy returns!*
> *May your thirties be all you deserve them to be!*
> *In memory of kingfisher weather,*
> *Love, Polly.'*

It was very dear of Polly to have remembered him and to have given him this book; it revealed a generosity of spirit he hadn't always granted her. It also showed, he reflected sadly, an over-estimation of his own intellectual capabilities and inclinations. In truth he would be only just a little more likely to sit down seriously to read a poem by T.S. Eliot than would Rob Peters (who hadn't even heard of the man, this time last year). Idly he turned over the pages as he sat at the table by the window, wondering at so many dense, cerebral lines that apparently meant so much to Polly. And then his eye caught the following ones:

> 'Time and the bell have buried the day,
> The black cloud carries the sun away.
> Will the sunflower turn to us, will the clematis
> Stray down, bend to us; tendril and spray
> Clutch and cling?
> Chill Fingers of yew be curled
> Down on us? After the kingfisher's wing
> Has answered light to light, and is silent, the light is still
> At the still point of the turning world.'

He stirred the sugar in his mug of tea. The lines could have been written for *him*, this afternoon; and he read them again slowly. It proclaimed the present season: had he not recently seen a kingfisher? . . . and was clematis not visible, cheerful and trailing, down in Mrs Hargreaves's garden? The burial of the day by 'Time and the bell' made him think – as Eliot could not have known it would – of Mum's death, since which the very quality of daylight, of its movement into the dark night and subsequent recurrence, had changed for him.

Time had stopped for Mum, though not for her family, who had had to stagger on through it, those days following her death possessing a burdensome heaviness, as the atmosphere was said to do on certain planets. As for the bell, it was for Laurie that dismal clanging in the funeral procession, was Dad and he, Mick and Dale stumbling up the aisle behind the coffin in which lay Mum's lifeless, unthinkable body – while the priest whom they didn't know intoned words they didn't quite understand in a building neither the dead woman nor her living descendants had ever visited . . .

Jonathan West and his wife had been in the congregation, and Laurie had felt so glad to see them. Had that cold January morning been the moment when Jonathan had conceived the idea of how Laurie's life could be altered, restored?

'Fingers of yew' made Laurie see again those churches he and Polly had explored partly in furtherance of her Ph.D. He remembered how the ancient solemnity of the trees had prompted him to prayers – prayers that Mum might live to be old, like Rembrandt's mother, but the prayers had not been granted, and who knew of petitional prayers that ever had been?

Imaginatively within a churchyard, he could not help himself now from stepping inside a church – that little Saxon chapel in the grounds of Saxingham Enfrith. What peace it had spelled – the Last Judgement on its walls faded to pastel colour, the altar protected by thick cream-washed walls and graced with a little bowl full of musk-roses, and plain glass windows admitting a green light – the light of chestnut and oak leaves. All this was, of course, upon the *first* entry! Upon the second? . . . For months Laurie had tried not to think about what had met them there, and later in the intimacy of his own bed. For the same months he'd tended to dismiss it – as a bizarre occurrence of no real importance. Now he knew better! 'The black cloud carries the sun away . . .' Well, wasn't that an almost literal description of what had taken place that afternoon in Saxingham Enfrith when the storm had at last prevailed, and night had fallen in the middle of the afternoon. And thus too had the dark emotions within Rob swamped, to the point of extinguishing, the light of the true personality. Where had the joy gone to but behind a dire and destructive black cloud? And yet that afternoon upon the Japanese half-moon bridge he had surely shown himself, in his private rejoicing over the bird, as *of* the sun, sun-like. Oh, now that Laurie had been privileged to witness the kingfisher again, alone, he understood so much that had hitherto eluded him, or that he had wilfully evaded.

The kingfisher's wing answered questions that Laurie had hardly dared formulate, yet alone ask.

'Time and the bell . . .' Laurie almost believed that he had conjured up the sound of the door-bell through his speculations upon Eliot's words. In the calm of the afternoon it had a nervous, if not frantic timbre. Laurie pushed aside the volume of Eliot and his tea mug, and hastened down the steep, lino-covered flight of stairs to answer its call. Often he was to ask himself later whether he'd known who was standing at the other other side of the door, wanting him. Who else had ever given his bell that anxious jabbing?

Rob looked stronger, sturdier, far more aglow with health and trust in self than he had when last he had seen him – on that blackened day. His fair hair had been bleached and made wavier by the sea-winds and sunshine, which had also bronzed his face. He was wearing dark blue jeans and a light blue towelling shirt. His brown eyes were bright with diffident but determined inquiry – and, much to Laurie's surprise, he was carrying a largish canvas bag.

'I reckon I don't need to introduce myself,' Rob said, and to Laurie his voice too had changed with absence, it was the firmer for it, some Essex twang had departed from it, and a mid-Atlantic poise had entered in its stead.

'Of course you don't. It's a . . . a *great* surprise seeing you,' Laurie used the adjective 'great' as members of his generation had tended to, in its American and honorific sense. Rob flushed with gratitude. Do we shake hands, wondered Laurie; do we kiss? In fact they did neither. 'Come on up,' he said instead, as throughout the May and June of last year he'd been wont to say.

'You don't look too different, Laurie,' Rob said, 'nor does this place! Can't tell you how many times I've seen both – in my mind's eye – since I've been away!'

'Well, *you* look different, Rob,' said Laurie leading him into the flat that last he'd entered to wreak mayhem while outside a tempest raged, 'you've grown up, if that doesn't sound patronising.' You certainly couldn't imagine him now tearfully confessing to obsessional images of shit and blood!

'I guess I had a lot of growing up to do,' said Rob sadly, 'gosh! this room.' His brown eyes showed tears. 'Do you remember that May afternoon I came here – after we'd seen the . . . the kingfisher, and you showed me that painting of the lion coming to life, and these photos of your Dad's ship?'

'How could I forget it?' said Laurie, deciding that he would not tell Rob about his own second glimpse of the bird until the time was exactly right.

'And a pot of tea ready too!' Rob exclaimed, 'it's as if you knew I was coming.

'I've got something stronger than tea if you want!' said Laurie, wondering what habits this changed youth would have acquired in months of a life utterly different from any Foswich had to offer. 'Beer! Some not very good red wine! I've even a bottle of Scotch somewhere . . .'

'Tea'll do me nicely,' said Rob, sitting himself in that shabby armchair by the window, opposite the photographs of the *William Wilberforce* of Hull, the chair that had always been his favourite and in which he'd been sitting while Polly read those haunting lines of Eliot's about 'kingfisher weather'.

'I'll just get you a mug then,' Laurie said, and he dashed into the kitchenette to pick up another of those National Trust Nursery Rhyme mugs. How, he reflected, does Rob now regard his past conduct? Is he even at this moment reliving his arrival there, when the clouds were black and rain was streaming forth out of them, to *shit* just where Polly and I would make love.

When he re-entered the sitting-room Rob was regarding him with a tender, pleading, quizzical smile. 'I didn't know, Laurie,' he said, 'I didn't know at all! I thought you didn't want to contact me again. Recall that bargain we made over the phone. If Mum and Dad had forwarded the letter you wrote me in February, I'd have written you right away. You *must* believe me?' The fear that he wouldn't was visible on his tanned, nut-like face.

'Of *course* I believe you,' said Laurie, 'I know for a fact that they didn't send on the letter, because they told me themselves.' He could see Beryl Peters' intent brown eyes clouding over with resentment, hurt, savage incomprehension, so, pouring Rob out tea from the old willow-pattern pot, he said: 'Anyway, now you know what I had to tell you.'

'Accept my condolences,' said Rob, the formal phrase ringing oddly on his lips, 'about your Mum. That must have been very sad for you; I remember how you used to worry about her. I'm only sorry for *your* sake, of course! For her – it's *wonderful*.'

'You mean,' said Laurie uncertainly, 'to be out of pain. I imagine I wrote to you about the misery she was in during her last days.'

'Not just *that*,' said Rob, 'there are other ways in which a death must be a wonderful event, don't you think?'

'I'm not sure I'm with you,' said Laurie, 'don't you want sugar, Rob? There's some here.'

Rob helped himself to two spoonfuls. He didn't choose to follow up that strange utterance. Instead he said: 'There was other news in the letter.'

'Yeah, there must have been!'

Blushes – those famous blushes of Rob's – suffused his healthy cheeks. 'I reckon I've got to congratulate you,' he said, 'I don't expect congratulations on that subject can be very welcome from *me* –' he gave his mug a nervous, vigorous stir, then continued: 'But congratulations all the same. You're not actually . . .?'

'Actually what?' said Laurie. So much had happened since his letter, he couldn't quite make out what Rob was referring to.

'Married?' Rob all but spoke this word through burning skin.

'To –'

'Well, to Polly, of course!' And if he'd sounded more adult before than the Rob he'd known, now his words had come bursting out of him as they might have done in his infancy.

'Polly,' said Laurie, feelingly, 'was extraordinarily good and kind to me when Mum died; I'll never forget her thoughtfulness. But we'd finished – she and I – long before that.' Not so very long after the havoc *you* caused, Rob, he thought, and it would be impossible to deny that what you did played a part in our going separate ways: we were never the same again with each other afterwards. 'At the time when I wrote you my letter, I was seeing another girl, Laura. I fantasied a bit about marrying her, I don't know why, we weren't *that* serious, and I suppose it must have been her I was thinking about when I wrote whatever bit in my letter you're referring to.'

'I *see*!' It would be impossible not to describe the look that Rob now gave Laurie as one of relief. 'I obviously misunderstood. Typical me!' He tried a grin, but obviously grins were not what the subject of Polly Keating aroused in him. Once again the words came out in a childlike tumble: 'I understand *now* why I behaved as I did, Laurie, last July; I've gained understanding into that, and into a whole lot of other things besides.'

He isn't talking as he used to, Laurie said to himself, his words are at once more stilted and more excitedly delivered. And that light that I'd been imagining Rob generating, well, in a sense he still does manifest it, possess it, but it isn't the pure sunlight of my memories – well, more, of the *old* Rob, it's something lurid. Lightning, not light.

'Look, Rob, don't let's start on about that almost as soon as you've come in through the door,' he said. 'Let's talk about your travels, shall we? I long to hear where you've been.' His eye fell upon the canvas bag that Rob had brought with him, and which he was now prodding, fidgetingly, with his right foot. The bag looked very full – packed for a journey, you might say. Why, then, was it here? Rob had – presumably – only returned to Foswich a day or so ago, and he'd certainly been back to *The Copper Kettle*, otherwise he couldn't have received the unforwarded letter. Truly there *was* something odd about Rob . . . 'I'll go and get my atlas,' he said, 'my geography isn't a hundred per cent by any means, so I'll have to have the various routes and ports pointed out to me.'

'I'd be glad to show you them,' said Rob, ' 'cause it's you I've got to thank for where-all I've been, isn't it? You and your Dad – who, I hope, is bearing up in his bereavement.' He didn't wait for an answer to this; he really is still pretty self-centred, thought Laurie, 'I mean, if I hadn't looked at those two photographs in front of me now – the *William Wilberforce* of the Ollerman Line,' he pronounced the name as though it were some sacred mantra, 'if I hadn't looked at them, and you hadn't told me the story behind them, in that interesting way in which you tell *everything*,' he gave a sudden, disarming smile, 'well, I'm sure I'd never have had all the adventures, the experiences I have had. And there's one that'll surprise you enormously . . .'

Laurie thought: there's something menacing about him. Perhaps there always was, and I refused to recognise it; perhaps that was what made him stand out among other pupils at St John's. To Rob, he said, refusing to accept the challenge behind the last remark: 'Come on, I'm all agog for your travellers' tales!' He produced his old school atlas: 'Here's Hamburg; here's the American coast – now you tell me about things that you saw going from one to the other.'

And truly for the duration of his stories Rob was again the ardent boy, eager if not desperate, to share things, to whom Laurie had been so drawn last summer. He spoke of the ancient mercantile cities of Antwerp and Ghent; of storms that had wickedly arisen when the Channel was opening out into the Atlantic; of the time when a steward, a good friend of Rob, had been thought to have been washed overboard; he spoke of humps that had appeared in the near distance and then had spouted water, his first sight of whales; he described an iceberg glimpsed, horrid but beautiful upon the horizon, and, almost stranger still, right out in a calm mid-Atlantic, after days of solitary journeying, the sight of a children's inflated ball, brilliant orange in colour, floating hundreds of miles from any likely hands or feet. Rob tried to evoke for Laurie the excitement that had been his when he first saw the low wooded American shore, a virginal quivering green line, light-picked with promise. And then he went on to what he'd seen, what he'd thrilled to in America – the great harbour at Charleston with Fort Sumter in its middle, and the elegant brick houses there too proud for the present, too proud for the past; trees hung with Spanish moss, islands in Mobile Bay, flooded with azaleas, Mobile itself with its grid of straight streets and dusty Latin plazas, and the serpentine complex of road-bridges that connected the city to the Alabama mainland. And then of course New Orleans, magnificent beside the Mississippi, the wrought-iron-decorated Bourbon and Royal streets vibrant with jazz and booze and clamour and offers of street-drugs . . . Rob's voice faltered here, as if there were episodes here he could relate but preferred not to. You're no longer a virgin, that's for sure, Laurie said to himself. Was *that* what Rob had meant by the experience that would surprise him enormously?

The majority of Rob's contemporaries tasted the pleasures of sex in Foswich. Out among the temptations of great ports like Mobile and New Orleans – come off it, the surprise would be if he had remained chaste . . .

'And then we had a day or so to spare, so two friends and me, we went by paddlesteamer into the Bayou country,' Rob was going on, smiling almost shyly, at having to give an account of something that had delighted him so much, 'we saw alligators. A boy we met at a Cajun village we landed in had caught one – swung it round and round by its tail. Now *I* wouldn't do that, no animal should be treated like that, but the funny thing was the 'gator didn't seem to mind. You could almost swear he was enjoying it . . .'

'Well, you have had a time,' said Laurie. His words might sound schoolmasterly but his tone did not. It was his own from way back in his Yorkshire childhood when he'd managed to coax out of taciturn Dad stories of *his* travels. Longing – but for what exactly? perhaps just for the strange combination of mutability and realisation of alien permanences which travel brings – filled him now, this late May afternoon, as disturbingly, as pleasurably, as physically as in his remote past: he almost felt like giving himself a glass of Scotch to calm himself down.

'Thanks, Rob, you really brought all those places to life for me,' he said, 'well, I've got one change to tell *you* about – I was going to write to you and let you have the news – but when I realised that your parents hadn't sent on my first letter, I decided not to.'

'Change, Laurie? But *not* marriage?' There was a flash of something very like fear in Rob's eyes. What on earth can he imagine I'm about to tell him, Laurie asked himself. In all truth it was nothing very dramatic, though he, until recently, until perhaps now – listening to Rob's tales – had discovered drama in it. 'I'm leaving Foswich, leaving it in July, at the end of this term. I've got another job, and guess what it is!'

He didn't give Rob time to do this, though. 'Jonathan West is retiring from my old school – which has been comprehensive for some years now – and, well, I've been offered his job. Of course the whole thing happened democratically, but I'd been seeing an awful lot of Jonathan after Mum's death, and – well, I suppose it'd be dishonest of me to think that he didn't use his influence to get me appointed. I can't say I have too much guilt over the matter; I'm amply qualified. So come September I'll be back in Tanbury . . .

'Be taking boys (and girls now) round the grounds of Foxton Manor, on sketching walks through the Cotswold countryside, introducing them to the numinous beauties not only of Nature but of the English painters who served her, from the Norwich School through the Nash Brothers and Reynolds Stone. I'll be arranging trips to Oxford and in the Ashmolean Museum I'll show them the Pre-Raphaelite collection . . . He then saw, with a near-hallucinatory vividness, that Arthur Hughes painting that hung there, of the lad throwing himself down on a tombstone in remorseful distress. *Home from Sea* it was called, and who was 'home from sea' but Rob? And wasn't there a sort of emotional disturbance about him, an air of plight, that made him kin to that sailor-boy from the last century?

'Well, congratulations, Laurie,' said Rob, 'I know how you admired that Mr West. I always used to think that there was a similarity between you and him, and you and me.'

'Maybe,' said Laurie, who did not think this. At least not now.

'So,' Rob set down his mug of tea with an almost melodramatic gesture, '*So* – you won't be in Foswich again, not to any extent, after July. That means that I for sure won't come back here, not ever!'

There was such conviction in his voice that Laurie felt – again – distinctly apprehensive. His eyes went another time to that packed canvas bag. 'But you can't not come back to Foswich because I'm no longer living and teaching here. Your family and friends are here.'

'I have no family, I have no friends,' said Rob, 'my own have received me not.'

A bit grandiloquent, that Biblical phrase, said Laurie to himself.

'I've been back among them and they've known me not,' Rob said, varying his words.

Best to deal with these strange statements head on! Laurie looked surreptitiously at his watch, hoping that Rob did not see him do this. Really he should be leaving for Tanbury in half-an-hour's time! Twins were getting supper ready; he did not want to keep them waiting too long ...

'I'm afraid I don't quite get you,' he said. Had he known it, he was speaking much as Rob had done to Bill Bentley on board the *Egon Ludendorff*. 'Didn't your family make you welcome? Haven't they forgiven you for running away?'

Rob gave a grim little smile. 'The answer to both those questions is "no",' he said, 'but that isn't what I was talking about. It's that they were all completely deaf to the good news I tried to bring them!'

'Good news?'

Suddenly he thought again of the kingfisher; *that* had been good news, if you like.

Rob said: 'Give me another cup of tea, and I'll try to tell you!'

'It must be pretty stewed by now!' said Laurie, 'change your mind, and have some alcohol. How about some bad red wine!'

Rob nodded, did not smile. Obviously the good news was the gravest possible matter. Laurie went to the fridge, took out the bottle and poured two glasses full. In the sunlight of the sitting-room bay-window the cheap wine was translated into gentle molten rubies: it made the drinking of it better.

'You stopped me, Laurie, when I tried to speak about what I did that July day; in a way, though, it's the key to what I've got to tell you!'

Laurie made an assenting noise (at least that's what he thought it was) through a mouthful of the vinegar-like wine.

'You see, like I said, a few minutes back, I *understand* – completely – why I did what I did.'

This statement was delivered so much like a question that Laurie felt obliged to ask: 'And *what* do you understand?' He had to work hard to banish images of lumps of shit in Saxingham Enfrith's quiet chapel, of the diffused heap that had greeted him and Polly as they'd rolled down the coverlet of the bed in which they were to lie in one another's arms.

'That I'd fallen into the hands of Satan,' said Rob in an oddly simple voice, 'that I was possessed by the Devil.'

Laurie very nearly dropped his glass in horrified amazement. *'Satan?'* he repeated as if it were a name he'd never heard before.

'Yeah! I said you were going to be surprised by the one really *great* experience I've had while I've been away.' Rob looked up at Laurie with elation in his expressive eyes. 'I've been *delivered* from Satan, you see. And once I'd been delivered – "saved" as we call it! – then it was clear what had befallen me before.'

'Oh!' said Laurie. He had no words ready. 'Who . . . who delivered you?' He asked.

'Now, Laurie!' said Rob, 'have a think!' *He* was the teacher now, the expert, to Laurie's baffled ignorance.

'I'm afraid I don't see how I can know. I mean, I wasn't there when it happened, was I? I've been here in dull old Foswich!' Better to make a bit of a joke out of it than take this weird confession too seriously.

'Who else could save me but Jesus?' asked Rob rhetorically, 'it was *Jesus* who delivered me!'

'You *saw* him?' asked Laurie, nervously. It really was possible – as awful old Geoff Peters obviously thought – that the boy wasn't right in the head.

'In a manner of speaking, Laurie, in a manner of speaking!' Rob was talking nervously too, with the wine glass shaking in his hand.

'Well,' said Laurie, pursuing the matter, perhaps despite himself, 'you either did or you didn't!'

'I had the honour – the good fortune – to encounter someone doing Jesus' work on one of the boats I've been working on!' Rob didn't wish to let Laurie know how recent his conversion was. 'He brought me to the light; he has made me of the company who can call Jesus a friend.'

Strike a light and fuck a tiger! thought Laurie (it was a

favourite oath of twins'), what can I possibly say in reply? Who would have thought that Rob Peters would have gone and got religion.

'Who was this "someone"?' Laurie asked.

'Bill Bentley of the Greater Glory Tabernacle.'

'Rob,' he said in his gentlest voice – in fact it was far more charged with conviction, and even passion, than he realised, 'it's no good telling me any more! I'm glad that you've got faith, but it won't wash with me, not at all, and there's no point in *trying* . . . I've got my own beliefs, you see, and I think they'll conflict with yours.'

'Those who are not with us are against us,' said Rob, miserably, 'that's a very true saying. But I think you probably don't know what "salvation" means. Why won't you give it a chance?'

'Because I don't want to,' said Laurie, 'have respect for me, please, Rob. I think what I think, I believe what I believe, or don't believe, as the case may be!'

'Well, then give *me* a chance!' besought Rob. Laurie feared he could see tears in the lad's eyes.

'If I let you talk on,' said Laurie, not wanting to hurt his feelings, 'it would only be to please *you*; I wouldn't be in the least likely to respond to what you were telling me.'

'You've closed your mind against the Lord!' said Rob, regretfully and perhaps a trifle angrily. But had he really expected any different?

'Let's talk about something else!' said Laurie. Perhaps now was the moment to describe how he'd seen the kingfisher again. Even sitting here, in the increasingly intense atmosphere of the room, was to be mindful of the beauties of Nature – of *God's* world – if you chose so to call it: the cherry and pear and japonica in the garden directly below, the lilacs nearby full of singing blackbirds and thrushes, the newly fledged woods on the opposite bank of the Fase, and, beyond these, dappled meadows and glowing fields of rape . . .

'But *I* don't want to, Laurie,' said Rob, and for a moment the older man thought that the younger was about to throw his arms round him imploringly, 'I want to talk about that time I did you wrong, that time I succumbed to the sheerest, blackest evil, which demands the fire, the torments of darkness for ever and ever.'

So rarely do I assert myself, my age, my status, my opinions, my liberal education, said Laurie to himself. I decline responsibility, in other words. Well, now it's time to accept it, to act with it!!

'Rob,' he said, 'can you *really* not see another way of looking at your behaviour that day. I honestly don't think there's any need to go leaping about to Satan for an explanation.'

'You don't?' said Rob, 'you deny his awful power, then?'

'Allow me to speak in *my* kind of terms,' said Laurie, 'and let's just stick to one subject – what you did that day and why.' The boy's eyes were surely beseeching him not to go on. But which would ultimately be the worse – knowing the murky reasons for his murky actions, or swallowing a whole lot of rubbish about diabolical possession and deliverance from hell? 'You must surely,' his tone was as gentle as could be, 'know your sexual orientation now.' The phraseology was pompous and schoolmasterly, he knew, so to make amends, he added: 'I mean whether you're straight or gay.' He tried to look Rob in the face, but he'd lowered it; nevertheless it was apparent that the deepest blush Laurie had ever seen on him was suffusing his cheeks. 'Doesn't matter to me which way you are,' he said, he thought warmly, 'but you've got to be honest with *yourself*; that's for sure.' And what's having sex but being honest, thought Laurie ... 'Don't you understand that what you did in Saxingham Enfrith and –' but he couldn't bring himself to mention the terrible visit to this very flat, 'and everything,' he went on lamely, 'was bound up with all that! It was a sort of symbol.'

He was using Polly's words, was following Polly's interpretation. But there surely wasn't another.

And now Rob did look up. Laurie saw from the hunted, frightened expression in his eyes – which all at once seemed larger and more lustrous – that he had comprehended completely what he'd said, comprehended it indeed beyond the actual diffident words used. He'd seen – and here enlightenment must also be torment – that he'd *desired* Laurie, had wanted to offer him his bum, his arse-hole. And because this was not possible, because he'd seen that Laurie's feelings and sexuality were elsewhere, had used that – so to speak, spurned – part of him to deliver filth, filth that first had desecrated a place of worship dear to Polly, and then had made repulsively impossible another shrine, that of Laurie's heterosexual love.

He might have felled the boy with a club, for there followed a long, ghastly silence as if indeed the victim were emerging from a painful daze. It seemed to Laurie that Rob might never speak again, but, of course, after strained moments he did, and his words weren't in the nature of a reply:

'You don't want my help then?'

'Your *help*?' But I mustn't be unkind, Laurie told himself, just firm.

'Yeah, help. Because I *could* help you, Laurie, and undo what I did to you, honest I could, truly I could. I don't really care about my folks; it doesn't really matter to me that they didn't listen to me. But *you*, Laurie, I care like anything about *you*. I don't want *you* to fall into the hands of Satan; I don't want *you* to go to the blackness of darkness for ever.'

'I've told you,' said Laurie, and yet, despite the strength of tone he was still finding, he was just a little afraid, 'I've told you what I think about all that.' Hunched up, wine glass in hand, Rob looked, for all his obvious health and vigour, like a cornered animal. Yet the cornered animal might pounce.

When he next spoke, it was very, very quietly: 'What you said just now about me and what I – what I did last year, that was wicked. When I was telling you about Jesus and trying to give you His message!!'

'I can't see . . .'

'Maybe then I'll have to *make* you see,' said Rob, and there really could be no doubting now that menace in his so soft voice, 'because it's not only me you're insulting but the Lord, who doesn't want to hear that kind of thing. Perhaps you've got a devil in you, Laurie, perhaps I know some words that describe what you are being to me – you with your horrible ideas that that foul Polly put into you, I've no doubt.'

As this was true, Laurie could not bring himself to deny it, as possibly he should have done. Any more than he could bring himself to order Rob from the house. What prevented him was not pity nor yet past friendship but – yes, admit it! – fear, yes, sudden real fear of this young sailor 'home from the sea'.

'You want to know the words?'

'I suppose if *you* want to tell me them . . .'

' *"For there are certain men crept in unawares who were before of old ordained to this condemnation, ungodly men, turning the grace of our God into lasciviousness, and denying the only Lord God, our Lord Jesus Christ."* There, what d'you think of *that*?' Rob had delivered the text so fast that Laurie had caught only its hostile righteous drift.

'I hoped I'd made it clear . . .' said Laurie as certainly as he dared, because Rob had now got up from his chair, holding his glass in his left hand, was coming towards him with a wildness in his eyes such as Laurie had never seen before on anyone. He felt obliged, as steadily as he could manage, to get up from his seat himself and to edge towards that wall on which hung the two framed photos of Dad's former ships.

'So you deny the truth of those words, Laurie?'

'In a sense, yes!'

'Because you don't, in fact, believe in the Lord Jesus Christ and my salvation?'

'I didn't say that!' But wouldn't it be better quickly to do so? . . .

'No, you didn't, did you? You'd really prefer it that I wasn't *in* Jesus, taken *out* of *sorrow*, wouldn't you? You'd prefer it if I went to Hell!'

Laurie, his back hard and straight against the wall, spluttered out: 'Rob, I just can't, I mean, I don't know how to . . .'

The glass full of wine came nearer still, filling his vision. And the room was all at once rent by a terrible, an unearthly shriek. '*Raging wave of the sea!*' Rob cried, his face surely as feral as any boy's could be, 'the blood of Jesus must be shed again that the sea be calmed!!' And with this he hurled, with all his force, the wine-glass, not at Laurie himself, but higher up, at the picture of the *William Wilberforce* making its stubborn way across her Northern sea. The object shattered with a tinkle, and its ruby-red contents flowed down the wall and onto the floor.

'Blood, blood!' Rob was laughing wildly now, 'that's what it's all about really, isn't it? Blood and the Lord's need for it!'

And his laughter continued – a deathly waterfall of sound – while he bent down, picked up Laurie's glass and threw that too, hard upwards, at the second picture.

Neither of the one-time friends was injured, yet, this second act of anger over, it seemed to both of them, in that quiet room, as if a great injury had been done. Rob stood contemplating the wine pooling on the floor as if it were indeed the issue of a corpse. Finally, surprising himself, Laurie discovered – somewhere within – the ability to say: 'The wheel's come full circle now, hasn't it, Rob? The *first* time you came to this room, I showed you the photographs of the two ships, and *then* you could say, there was something in the making. Now – it's your *last* visit, and you've tried to damage the pictures, and there's nothing but destruction . . .'

Rob, all spent now, was crouching on the floor, stooping over the puddles of wine, choking with sobs, sobs more impassioned even than those that had been brought about by his confessions to Bill. 'I *know* what I must do now,' he was saying, but to himself rather than to Laurie, 'I must humble myself. I've crucified my friend; I must drink up the blood that's been shed . . .'

For a dream had returned to him – a dream of Foswich he'd had on board ship – and he began, trying to cherish the humiliation, to lap up the wine.

'And *I* also know what you must do,' said Laurie, moving away from the wall. 'You must leave. You must leave at once. I can take no more.'

He'd spoken half like a schoolmaster, half like a wronged lover who's hardened his heart against his former loved one. And consequently his words had a direct effect – Rob scrambled to his feet, his face red with the blood-like fluid, and said in a child's voice, piteous, injured, innocent and quite innocuous: 'You really want me to go now? At once?'

'I do. Here!' He threw Rob a napkin from the table so that he could mop up his face, and the gesture both restored – as much as it could be – the humdrum to the room and made the younger feel his years, his inferiority.

'I'm due somewhere this evening,' Laurie went on in as business-like a voice as he could muster, deliberately avoiding naming his destination, 'and incidentally,' the oddity of the canvas-bag must be accounted for, 'why did you bring *that* with you?'

'Because I've left home for good,' Rob was whispering, almost whimpering now. All rage seemed to have gone from him.

'But you've only just arrived back!'

'I've spent long enough time here, though. I shall never go to my own again. They're my own no more. Foswich is like one of those cities of which Jesus speaks. Those who turn their backs on people who try to do the Lord's business. I've vowed to go away from my folks for ever . . . I didn't know, you see,' and, though he had to bite back a sob, his voice was 'normal' again: 'I didn't know whether you'd be with Polly or not. If I find Laurie alone, I said to myself, I'll ask him to be merciful and put me up for the night . . .'

'And if not?'

'There can be others. In London. A mate or two who'll have me to stay until we know where the *Egon Ludendorff*, the ship, is going!'

'Fine!' said Laurie, 'I'm glad to hear it!' Pointedly he walked over to the all-purpose cupboard and got out a mop and a dust-pan an brush, to deal with the mess. 'You'll just have to throw yourself upon the mercy of these friends of yours. Because, as I said, I've an appointment for this evening. But even if I hadn't . . .' He took a deep breath, 'I wouldn't want you here!'

Now he would never tell Rob how he'd seen the kingfisher.

Rob said: 'It's goodbye for ever then, is it, Laurie? People'll say strange things, won't they? They'll say that I tried to damage those two lovely pictures of the ships your dad sailed on. But they'd be wrong. Rob Peters would never do a thing like that. It wasn't him. It was Bill Bentley!'

Rob left Mrs Hargreaves' house so emotion-dazed that he didn't know where next he was going or should go. But his feet decided for him. Where else could they take him but down the hill, over the road-bridge, and, then, via a descent of stone steps, onto that path that runs along the far bank of the Fase until it reaches the Japanese bridge?

He mounted the bridge, and then – as so often formerly – leaned over the wooden balustrades and, closing his eyes against the cheerful blue sky, tried to 'put himself away', back into that significant afternoon of last May. Perhaps he should pray; yes, *certainly* he should pray, though not, he thought, to the God of Bill Bentley. Please, Almighty One, he mouthed, make the kingfisher reappear, send him in brilliant blue just *once* more from bank to bank!

He opened his eyes, and it seemed to him that the film had gone as suddenly as it had established itself, and that the Fase beyond was shining and aquiver with promise. How long he waited he never knew – before he was aware, as on that first occasion, of a stirring out of all that intense stillness. There came a flutter of wings, a whirring of a bird making across water – water which audibly rippled and shook and plashed against the reeds.

But, for all this, *with* all this, no bird, let alone the longed-for kingfisher, did he see. Instead, strangely, a flight took place inside him, within his own mind which seemed to be breaking, bursting upon the summer afternoon quiet. In a way you could say that his prayer had been answered, for the sureness of last year upon the bridge was matched with another sureness. He knew how he should go about things now. It was in the nature of a wager.

He made for the telephone kiosk at the top of Station Hill. Presumably this was the last time he'd make use of any of Foswich's facilities.

'Is that the Dorchester Hotel?'
'It is, sir?'

'I'm wanting to speak to a Mr Bill Bentley.'

'A Mr *who*?'

Rob was unaccustomed to the phone. He had to take a deep, nervous breath before answering: 'Mr Bill Bentley!'

'Could that be Dr William Bentley of the Greater Glory Tabernacle?'

A doctor, eh? How distinguished his converter was! 'Yeah, that's right! That's *just* who I want!'

'I'll try his room for you!'

The line went dead, and Rob thought – with a sudden stab of panic – that he'd been cut off. Should he put the receiver down, and try again? But then there came, all loud and vibrating in his ear, the porter's pompous voice: 'Sorry, but the doctor isn't taking any calls just now.'

'I'm sure he *is*!'

'Sir, I'm telling you what I've been told.'

'But I'm *positive* he'd take mine if he knew who it was.'

'And who *are* you, sir?'

That's a good question, said Rob to himself, but aloud he replied: 'Rob Peters. A friend from the *Egon Ludendorff*.'

'All right, Mr Peters,' the guarded voice conceded, 'I'll try him again.'

'Thank you, *thank* you!' Apprehension made him effusive and child-like.

Once more the line seemed to go dead. But – and again very loud:

'I'm very sorry, sir, but you're *not* on the list of people Dr William Bentley wishes to see!'

'But I *must* be; you've made a *mistake*!' Rob cried. 'I just don't believe you when you say he doesn't want to see *me*. He . . . he "saved" me!'

'Can't help it if he got you off the "Titanic",' was the nice answer. 'I have Dr Bentley's instructions! A very good day to you!'

Rob thumped the receiver very hard against the box, hoping to break it. Then he kicked the kiosk door several times savagely. Blood danced before his eyes, issuing from wounds and apertures he couldn't make out.

Anyway the wager was lost. He had to go the other way.

He took the crumpled piece of paper out of his pocket and dialled his second London number. Perhaps it was all for the best. Good job he *hadn't* smashed the phone!

'Tagalog Tourist Agency!'

What the fuck . . .? 'I'm *sorry*?' he brought himself to say, though he was quite ready to kick and break things again.

'This is the Tagalog Tourist Agency.'

'I was wanting to speak to a Mr Pete Rodriguez.' Rob was certain – sure that he'd both taken down *and* dialled the number correctly.

A voice almost identical to the first, high, metallic, impersonal, came over the wire. 'You're talking to,' it paused importantly, 'the Tagalog Travel Agency.'

Oh, the blood that was gushing out now! But he must take a grip of himself.

'Please, I was wanting to speak to a Mr Pete Rodriguez,' he said. He was as polite as at his best when waiting at table – in the cafe or on board ship.

'Ah, Pete, my *nephew*. This is a business house, you know, though we're shutting up shop in about an hour: I was anticipating an important call from Luton. Do you want me to get him for you?'

'If you'd be so kind!'

Pips sounded abruptly in Rob's right ear. He shoved more coins – this with some difficulty – into the slot.

'Hullo?' came a husky version of Pete's voice.

'Pete Rodriguez?'

'Speaking!'

'Pete, it's me, Rob!'

'Oh, hi, Rob!' Pete sounded neither pleased nor surprised, but then – extraordinary thought! – it was only yesterday that the two boys had last seen each other. 'How're you doing?'

'Not too good, Pete, to be honest! My folks! . . . and my friend!' It was pretty hard-going keeping the tears at bay. 'I just don't seem able to communicate with either of them.' He gulped with the misery of it all. 'I came back to England with so many hopes . . .'

'Where are you now?'

'In Foswich! But down by the station; I thought of coming

into London, you see. . . . Pete, you haven't any news of the ship, have you?'

'Matter of fact I called this morning. Three more days in dock, then she takes a cargo back to Norfolk, Virginia.'

'You going to sign on?' If so, *he* would too. What was so special about paid leave?

'I reckon I am. Though, Rob, this is sure one fun city. I've only just landed, and I don't believe I've ever had a hotter time!'

'Is that right!'

'And if that's what I say *now*, what d'you think I'd say after a whole week here, or a whole *month*, for Christ's sake!'

'For Christ's sake,' sighed Rob. Poor, benighted Pete, he didn't know what it was to do things and then suffer, for the sake of Christ, for the sake of Jesus, Son of God . . .

'I've never had a . . . a hot time in London,' he said almost plaintively.

'Come round, and I'll fix it so you do. We can go "cruising" together and be the toasts of the town.'

It was a plan certainly at variance with any intentions he'd entertained for the shape of his life. But loneliness – and maybe another emotion also swept through him, and he said: 'Pete, would it really be all right if I came round *now*, tonight. And could . . . could I stay with you until the *Egon Ludendorff* is ready to leave?' He had to stifle a sob once again, as he said: 'I honestly don't think there's anywhere else to go.'

'Sure! How couldn't it be all right! My uncle was going to prepare a bit of supper, Filipino-style, for us – and then he's going out somewhere. So it can be "Go, man, go" for us, to whatever gay spots we want, and boy! this area is teeming with them.'

'I'll take the next train into town from Foswich Station. We're Central Line out here, you see,' the details would, he realised, mean nothing to Pete, and why had he said 'we'? Nevertheless he went on: 'I think I can be with you in about an hour.'

'Great! Look forward to seeing you, Rob!'

Rob put down the phone, wiped his eyes, and then,

heaving the canvas-bag off the kiosk floor, began the last walk he would ever make in his native town. He touched the overhanging lilacs and laburnums with sad fingers as he made his way downhill to the station where a train was already waiting.

'You don't seem to have much of an appetite,' said Dale to Laurie, 'and there's Mick and me been slaving over a hot stove, as old Mum used to say!'

'It was terrific!' said Laurie, wishing he could have chosen a slightly more appropriate adjective. Not that the heated-up steak-and-kidney pie with frozen-packet peas was much inferior to what Mum had been in the habit of serving up. 'The fact is, I'm feeling a bit down about something just now.'

'Women-trouble?' asked Mick almost eagerly.

'What makes you think that?'

'Well, when you're in the dumps, Laurie, isn't that what it usually is?'

'Is that how I seem?' mused Laurie. He could suddenly see with an outsider's eyes his life after breaking up with Polly; it would appear liberally strewn with emotional entanglements. And yet none of them had amounted to very much. 'Well, whatever the case *usually* is, what's depressed me today's nothing to do with women.' Though maybe indirectly it *is*, he silently corrected himself. He wasn't given to confiding in 'twins', but this evening he rather wanted to share the horrible episode with others, particularly with easy-going sanguine others such as his brothers. 'You see, an old pupil of mine came to see me. He's gone and got religion very badly, believes the most dreadful, cruel things about himself and me. It was hard to know what to say, but what I came out with wasn't the right thing, I'm afraid.'

He had travelled with Rob on his mind all the way back here to Tanbury. For most of the journey he'd remembered not Rob's violence but the appalling submissiveness of his departure. Of what seemed now like sacrilege against the pictures Laurie had not had the strength to think.

'Oh, that's bad, that is!' said Mick, 'sister of a girl I went out with got religion, and went clean off her rocker! Thought she was the Virgin Mary, and went out to one of the farms Foxton way, to look for a stable to have her baby in.'

'And if she'd seen her sister's boy-friend there,' put in Dale, 'she'd probably have thought him one of the cattle.'

When Mick had seen the point of this joke, he flicked a few bread pellets across the table. The twins appeared to enjoy nothing more than these amiable scorings-off of each other.

'Boys! Boys!' said Dad, half in remonstrance, half in gentle amusement at his sons' antics. These were the first words he'd spoken since the meal had begun. Laurie had all but forgotten his existence; if taciturnity can develop, Dad's had. . . . Of course, thought Laurie now, noticing the wry little smile on Dad's tired, drawn face, it's very good that he's so intensely – if undemonstratively – fond of twins. But he shouldn't really still be seeing them as 'boys'. They're men of twenty-seven now. Important years of their life have already gone by. And how? In aimless, if pleasant enough, mucking about.

Laurie said: 'Tomorrow, I'm going to take us all out to lunch. Yes, we'll find the snazziest restaurant in the neighbourhood, and celebrate my new job there. Which we haven't done yet!' He wondered, even as he spoke, if there was any point in his proposal: 'the good life' as boosted in, say, the colour supplements, clearly meant nothing to any of the persons at this dinner-table. But he'd committed himself now. 'Eh!' he exclaimed, as his father or mother, grandfathers or grandmothers might have done: 'What do you think Mum would say if she could know I was going to be Head of Art at my old school.'

'She'd be very pleased, I reckon,' said Mick loyally.

'You were always Mum's favourite, Laurie,' said Dale, quite without bitterness.

But what do I myself think about what's happened, about the turn my life's taken, Laurie asked himself, and by no means for the first time. He would have expected to be feeling far more joyful than he was. The preferment after all showed affection and respect for him – and for his work – and marked a return to people and places he loved and a farewell to somewhere where, through no fault of his own, he'd not been very happy, had been haunted by a distressing sense of incompleteness. And yet . . .

'But for now,' said Laurie, to prevent himself from further thought along these lines, 'I'm going to go over to Foxton shortly and have a chat with Jonathan West. He'd be a good person to talk to about this old pupil of mine. And we'll make tomorrow a real family day!'

The afterglow of sunset still lay on the Cotswolds, away in the Western distance, but Foxton was already wrapped in the shades of gentle summer night. Driving down the steep hill into the village, Laurie saw two bats flitting out of the barn by the church. Like little tea-trays in the sky, he thought, remembering the quotation from Lewis Carroll that had been one of Jonathan West's favourites. Outside the *Foxton Arms* a band of happy-faced young men were standing talking, tankards of glowing beer or cider in their hands. Laurie drove on, past the famous notice by the village pond which read: 'Careful: Ducks Crossing', and, as if for his benefit, a white waddle of ducks *did* walk across the road . . . Then a left turn, and the E-shaped Elizabethan manor house, Foxton Abbey, came splendidly into sight. Laurie saluted again the stern mysterious forms of the cedars that guarded the approach to it. Then down the lane towards Jonathan's cottage, above which the milky-coloured moon hung. Laurie parked the Renault, and walked a little further downhill to the cottage. Clematis spread and dangled along garden-walls. Twined honeysuckle and syringa luxuriant all over the Wests' porch emanated a heady fragrance that seemed to translate the entire night, up to the moon itself.

It was exactly as one would wish to approach the Wests' house, and how many times in similar circumstances – disquiet within, peace without – had Laurie done so! A sudden synthesis of memories filled him just as the scent of flowers did his nostrils, and Laurie found himself humming, as if to anticipate the happiness the Wests' home would bestow on him, one of those old music-hall songs (peculiarly appropriate for this evening) that he and Amanda and Lucy, Emma and Kate had sung round the old harmonium:

*'You are my honey, honeysuckle,
I am the bee;
I'd like to kiss those rosy-red lips of yours, you see!
I love you dearly, dearly,
And I hope that you love me:
You are my honey, honeysuckle, I am the bee!'*

The logic of these lines had always struck Laurie, even when he most enjoyed singing them, as somewhat shaky. But who cared? ...

'If it isn't my friend and successor!' said Jonathan West, affectionately, 'do you know, Lorna and I had a sort of hunch that you'd be coming over here this evening. So, together with some of our famous cherry-brandy, you can partake of Lorna's fresh cream trifle.'

'Wonderful!' said Laurie, and, after the afternoon's violence, he meant it.

How cheerful it was and yet how serene inside the Wests' sitting-room! A lamp threw light on Jonathan West's studies of ferns, bushes, undergrowth, hedges, tombstones and Abbey fish-ponds ... The sweetness of scent that drifted in from outside was complemented by that gently given forth by a bowl of pot-pourri on the table. Rob's hurling of glasses was all but unthinkable in this atmosphere, and yet Laurie *did* think about it, even to the point of an inane, repulsive fantasy, flickering in his head like some primitive film of *himself* dashing a glass – or even the pot-pourri bowl – just as Lorna handed him his cherry-brandy.

'All bearing up at home?' Jonathan was asking him.

'More or less, I think. Twins cooked a supper tonight,' disgustingly he could have added, 'and, though I know that they miss Mum a lot, they go on much as they always have done. But Dad – Dad is even more silent than before. He so obviously prefers *not* talking to talking, it's hard to know how to get through to him. I've always been a very talkative sort of bloke, what the French call a *bavard*, I suppose.'

'There's often the deepest communication between two people who accept each other's silence,' said Jonathan West, 'isn't part of the art of painting based on that assumption.

One person's quietness proffered to another's. Remember that always, Laurie!'

But what if there's something that one of those persons desperately needs to articulate to another, Laurie asked himself. But he couldn't quite bring himself to say this aloud. The Wests had made argument, even of the lightest kind, into a species of blasphemy. Perhaps, however, *his* silence would speak his disagreement for him . . .

' "Study to be quiet!" ' said Lorna West, spooning out trifle. It was obviously a quotation, but Laurie did not ask from whom.

'It's so good being here,' he said, as if to compensaste for the disloyalty of his reflections, 'especially today after a very unpleasant experience. With that old pupil of mine, Rob Peters, whom I've told you so much about.'

While this last statement was perfectly true, Laurie had, for obvious reasons omitted a very good deal from his accounts of Rob and their friendship. He'd told them that Rob had behaved 'very strangely and badly' on a visit to Saxingham Enfrith. But had not given them much of a clue as to wherein that strangeness, that badness lay. . . . Consequently, now, when he wanted to tell as full a tale about Rob as possible, he was compelled to edit, implying unmentionable things here, skating over distressing difficult matter there. It did justice neither to himself nor to poor possessed Rob. However one point came over well enough, that the youth had got religion in a very serious and dangerous way. He was creating a Hell inside himself, would surely create Hell in the lives of others. Undoubtedly the most honest part of Laurie's narrative was his presentation of his own misgivings. Had he done right to refuse to listen to Rob's attempts at salvationist proselytising? Had he done right to try to make him see the psychological foundations of his present stand? Had he done right to dismiss him as thoroughly as he had? . . . But he didn't tell them about the outrage upon the pictures, nor about the cries of 'blood!'. He was simply unable.

It was Lorna who spoke first: 'What a terrible story!' she sighed, 'for a boy – because he *is* still a boy – to be in the grip of pernicious nonsense like that! It really makes me *shudder*.'

And though she had not really shed any of her Vermeer-like calm, it did almost seem as if she might do as her last sentence suggested.

'As you know, Laurie,' said Jonathan West, speaking with a sort of measured indignation, 'I am not one who believes in punitive action. Few people could have signed as many petitions against our penal system than myself. But when I hear of the doings of a preacher-fellow like this – his lust for power, his unscrupulousness – well, perhaps I *do* think that imprisonment is the only – and the most effective – solution. What did you say his name was? Bill Bentley! I shall not forget that. To corrupt a young mind! . . .' Perhaps he was also about to shudder.

'A young man of eighteen having his head filled with ideas of Satan and Hell and eternal fire!' said Lorna West. Certainly, thought Laurie, these three terrible things appeared to have no hold over Foxton. Lorna spoke louder than was her custom, and her breath disturbed some dried petals in the pot-pourri bowl.

'Talking about becoming a friend of Jesus!' Jonathan exclaimed – indeed Laurie had never seen him more roused, 'of course, one has to see all this in context. Your young friend's clearly not at all intelligent, is lacking in any talents or security of culture. Foswich has come a long way from any kind of *organic* condition; the lad has a fractured mind, and so someone like this, this *rogue* can come in and fill the gaps. It's the rankest, most vicious exploitation of weakness, that's what it is!'

'Exploitation!' echoed Lorna fervently, and she shook her head in protest at the wickedness of which mankind was capable – at any rate beyond the serenity of the Oxfordshire countryside.

But just suppose, thought Laurie, surprising himself, and not liking the surprise, just suppose that this Bill Bentley has been acting out of sincere conviction. He took a sip, which turned into a swig, of the cherry-brandy that had won Lorna so many prizes at village fêtes. Let's for a minute assume that this Bill really, firmly and fearfully, believes in a moment of salvation, of knowing the Lord, that rescues you from sin and damnation. If he does believe this, it'd be irresponsible of him not to try to win over others. So he's paid! is part of an organisation! (For surely it would be the Greater Glory Tabernacle, Inc?) Don't we all need payment? Jonathan West, for instance, has been paid really quite a good salary – as I know, for it'll be my own – for many years for presenting his own particular creed, his reverence for the still and gentle. Paid by a state he can't approve of and who, more likely than not, can't approve of him. Does that invalidate his stance? No – though perhaps he shouldn't, in the light of its ambiguity, be quite so quick to condemn. Bill Bentley could easily be getting a deal of money for his work *and* be convinced of the righteousness of his words and actions.

Laurie did not like these thoughts of his one bit!

'It's a sad affair!' he said aloud, agreeing with his audience, but half-regretting that he had told them about it.

And then came another whisper in the caves of his head, the strangest, the most horrible he'd ever had. *How can you be so sure that Bill Bentley and Rob are wrong? What makes you so certain that the Wests – and yourself, and all those like you – have arrived at the true vision of life, the only one?*

A feeling, Laurie answered whatever-it-was that was speaking inside him: an instinct. Fine, fine! said the whisper. And Bill Bentley and Rob doubtless have *their* feelings and instinctual knowledge too.

'And what . . . what do you think of how I treated Rob this afternoon?' Laurie asked, almost as much to repress these inner whispers as to hear opinions about a matter he would now like to drop.

'You did absolutely the right thing!' said Lorna West, with a gentle smile of certainty. 'Don't have any doubts on *that* score, Laurie, dear! You must never, but never, encourage hysteria. It cannot lead to anything good. Smashing glasses indeed! . . .' She delivered these words as if she could envisage few more unpalatable crimes . . .

'You did him a *service*, Laurie,' said Jonathan West, 'I know how kindly and amiable you are by nature – that's why we're all so fond of you – but there are times, alas! when we have to act severely, uncompromisingly. The sordid little incident of this afternoon, in your flat in Foswich, was undoubtedly one of them. You handled it well, and we're proud of you.' Lorna nodded her head in agreement. 'Thanks to you, and your refusal to have truck with him, Rob may very probably come to his senses, and purge himself of this cruel – yes, and ridiculous – set of notions that have been forced upon him.'

'Thank you, thank you!' said Laurie, 'I'm so grateful for your support. The whole thing has been bothering me a lot.'

But no sooner had he spoken than he could see, coming between him and those green Ruskinesque studies of Jonathan West's upon the cottage walls, his former pupil hunched up like a trapped animal . . . Then in his head there reverberated again the dreadful scream of accusation Rob had given before throwing the first glass at the wall in religious wrath. And then, hardly aware that the Wests were offering him a delicious cream trifle, he saw the kingfisher again – rising from the Fase in independent, privately triumphant flight, blue as heaven itself.

By the time that Rob stepped on to the Circle Line train at Liverpool Street Station, the recently acquired vision of existence that had been possesing him and urging him to proselytise faded to no more than that smear of light Laurie had seen upon the Cotswolds to the west of Foxton.

The train out of Foswich had taken him through a succession of rather familiar stations, bringing back memories of expeditions to London made with Neil Ferris and others from St John's School, all of whom he'd probably never see again. The Woodfords, Leytonstone, Leyton, Stratford East! Somehow the sight of countless unknown persons on platforms that had presented themselves to him before acted against Bill Bentley's vision of life as nothing else could have done. Were *all* these people, the young, the old, the black, the brown, the white, destined for destruction unless someone like Bill brought them to salvation? Or was the situation quite other, that they – at least most of them – found life so absorbing that they didn't need to bother with visions of blackness and fire, of worrying what happened beyond a grave they knew perfectly well would be theirs? Out in the isolation of an Atlantic cargo-boat it had been comparatively easy to see yourself alone on some terrifying test-course which God had seen fit to arrange. But here . . . But now . . . Rob was left, as Liverpool Street came at him, with a picture of himself as seen by some invisible eye from above, an angel's maybe, but one not interested in great battles called Armageddon. The eye saw an unhappy, unwanted young man who'd behaved badly to a good friend, an over-packed canvas-bag at his side and a look on his face that showed he didn't know what to do with himself tomorrow, let alone all the time ahead of him. He tried to think of Norfolk, Virginia.

Really, he couldn't help feeling glad that the wager had been lost! And Laurie? If only he could see him one more time, and make it all right between them. But that could never be now.

Opposite him three young men were sitting; they were about his own age, and probably a glance told him, the same sort of person, though in far better spirits. All were wearing very tight jeans, all showed fully forth their blue-cased crotches. I like that, said Rob to himself, I like getting hints of what's between the legs. Yes, in all this mental misery, at this very moment when he should be bemoaning the diminution of the light of faith, he had the strongest urge to lean over and zip open one of their flies, to get a stiff cock between his fingers again, and then move them down to desire-plumped balls. What a wish! What sort of bloke did that make him? As he realized himself, there were thousands upon thousands of boys who felt like he was doing now – and followed their urges too. As he himself had done, with the friend he was bound for. Pete had been right, right about desire versus salvation. Perhaps secretly Rob had been really proud to be singled out by Bill Bentley for redemption, rather than accept his lot as a member of vast humanity, as a rag-bag of wishes and longings, who'd one day – and without the peals of judgement – fade away into the great over-crowded nothingness of death.

And now he saw himself back in Laurie's flat; Laurie was

suggesting to him that he looked on his behaviour of late summer as a symbol, but this time he did not yell out, still less threaten his friend in any way. No, no! He looked Laurie in the eyes, smiled at him, and said: 'You're right of course!'

How long had he known what Laurie suggested? Probably before he committed the crime, he'd known it. Maybe as early even as that afternoon he'd encountered him on the Japanese half-moon bridge and had accepted the invitation back to the flat, to have tea. Had known that he was in love with Laurie, and not merely loved him but wanted to *make* love to him. All hot summer long, last year, he'd pined for Laurie, burned for him, and yet had never had quite the courage to name that pining, that burning. He'd preferred not to match images and words.

One of the youths opposite him – who'd doubtless watched the direction of Rob's eyes – winked at him. Rob hesitated, then winked back. It was a good moment.

And then he let precisely those images swamp him to which he'd so long dreaded affixing labels. In the fug of the train, they became almost tangible: Laurie lying naked on top of him, Laurie working his tongue in the shell of his ear, Laurie biting his neck, slipping a hand under his body to grasp him in the groin, Laurie slowly, and accompanying the act with passionate kisses, thrusting his prick up his arse.

Always he'd felt alone: alone in the family, the classroom, the playground, the Youth Club, alone at parties like Mike Carter's stupid 'orgy', alone when trailing unwanted after Laurie and Polly, alone when shitting in fury on altar and bed, alone when appearing – the hero of some fairy-story – at the offices of Wolfgang Ludendorff in Hamburg. And it was to this that Bill Bentley had appealed, and it was in aloneness, standing on the bridge-deck below empty sky and above empty sea, that he'd received this vision, new to him but old to the world, about life under God.

But that wasn't the whole of the story. Under those brightly starry heavens, above that deep black ocean, beside him, on the bridge-deck, had been another young traveller, another bereft youth, someone as like himself as made no matter. Pete, Pete Rodriguez! With whom he'd come together, a union of bodies that seemed like a union of souls. With him all notions of making for Heaven and Hell had ceased. Why then had he allowed himself to be seduced back by Bill Bentley to so terrible a universe, where only a few were to escape punishment, a few such as Bill, who had refused to see Rob, had omitted him from some snobbish list he'd made.

The carriage of the tube-train had filled up. Now it seemed crammed with people, and the majority were young men of . . . well, his own *kind*. Some in black squeezing leather, some fetchingly ear-ringed and henna'ed, some crew-cutted and hungry-jawed, some merry and lithe in chic bi-coloured Italian shirts and little lockets depending from chains round their necks. There were even some who wore badges or carried magazines proclaiming their membership of this bright, and apparently confident band. Rob felt that as far as he was concerned the train could have journeyed from Gloucester Road to Earl's Court for ever, just so that he could feast his eyes on *others* who were yet versions of *himself*.

It was a tall, thin, shabby house in which Pete was staying, in a particularly tatty stretch of the Earl's Court Road, not far from the dirty mouth of the Underground Station. The ground floor was taken over by the Tagalog Tourist Agency, an organisation which, under the direction of Pete's uncle, catered for those wanting to visit the Philippines, Indonesia, Malaysia and Thailand. The principal offices were orderly enough, and on their walls were such gaudy posters of sun-kissed seas and palms as had decorated Pete's little cabin on board the *Egon Ludendorff*. Above the Agency's premises, though, order, bit by bit, ended. Off ramshackle stairway and landings ill-painted doors led into dingy rooms. However many people were living in the building? 'It's Liberty Hall here, Bob,' said Pete's moon-faced, shambling uncle, whose kindly manner was at once perky and wistful, 'Liberty Hall!'

'Rob!' said Pete.

'I'm sorry?'

'My friend's name is Rob not Bob.'

'Rob, Bob; Bob, Rob,' said Pete's uncle musically, with an

air of sad wisdom, 'what can one consonant matter in a name, either to me or the Divine Mind?'

Behind his back his nephew tapped his own forehead significantly.

'It's very kind of you to let me stay here for a while,' said Rob in his best voice. He wanted to establish – or re-establish – the fact of his temporary residence here; not for three days, not for three *hours*, could he go back to Foswich. His own had known him not, but then maybe they *weren't* his own. His own were here, in this forlorn house in a busy, populous street.

'It's very kind of Mother Earth to have us on the planet,' said the weird uncle, giving Rob a large, sweet smile, 'you will find yourself but one of many in this house. But in my Father's house there are many mansions; isn't that what your Christianity tells you?' This was a subject Rob did *not* wish pursued. 'Yes, in this house you will encounter a *great* diversity of types, I am happy to say.' He bent his head to meet Rob's intimately: 'Why, I even have a stockbroker who has taken two rooms right at the top. And it's for him that I feel most sorry. Sometimes he is so bowed down by work that he forgets the Divine Mind altogether . . .'

'Quite a lot of the people in this house are keen on the Divine *body*,' put in Pete, 'even that stockbroker. I saw him yesterday eyeing all the boys in that big pub in – what's it called, the Old Brompton Road? *I* saw him! Maybe, Uncle, you're exaggerating the diversity a bit.'

The room where, on a couch-bed, Pete slept was dark though very high-ceilinged. Its one window – curtained with a brown blanket – gave onto a drabness of back-walls and scrap-laden yards that the evening sunshine did little to redeem. A pair of tattered rag-rugs lay on the linoleum floor, but upon the walls Eastern objects hung: shadow-puppets from Bali stretched snaky necks to distance mis-shapen, huge-nosed faces from winged and taloned bodies; there were several shawls draped from nails, flowers and boughs patterned on the silk, while above the couch-bed itself a sword, a Javanese *kris*, had been placed, its curved sheath gleaming with mother-of-pearl studs.

It was not a room to feel at home in, but Rob realised, entering it, that he didn't want to feel at home. Home was where you were humiliated, where your own received you not and were proud of it; home was where you were imprisoned, despised. Worst of all home was where you could not be yourself. (And anyway this room would not shelter them for so very long. In a few days' time he and Pete, bound in all ways together, would be at sea once more, and from then on, nothing, not even Jesus and his self-appointed prophets, could come between them again.)

'Thank God we're alone!' said Pete, voicing Rob's own sentiments. 'Thank God I've got you to myself. Little sweetheart' (though in truth Rob was the taller of the two), 'so folks haven't been too nice to you in your home-town . . .'

Desire took possesssion of Rob, like the Holy Ghost descended.

'Which is it to be, the two of us together, as we know how? Or a dive into London's gayest quarter?'

Rob had no doubts. 'The two of us together,' he said softly but promptly, 'as we know how!'

'You've said it,' said Pete, 'and who's little old Pete Rodriguez to disagree?'

He began, with those beautifully practised hands of his, to undress Rob.

And then peeled off his own clothes.

Looking at Pete, naked, with his cock so erect and eager, Rob wanted to weep with tenderness for him. He said: 'Do me a favour, Pete! Before we go any further, dance that bird-dance for me.'

'You liked it?'

'Liked it nothing. I'll remember the first time you danced it for me until the day we die.' "We" – he'd spoken as if their lives were twined.

'I don't do it – in private, that is – for many people; you understand that, don't you? I danced it for *you* that time, for you, Rob Peters, as if you'd been the only guy in the world. I think that's what you were for me then.'

'And you for me!' said Rob happily – yes, *happily*, a condition he'd begun to think could never be his.

'And this time I dance with my cock stiff and a nude body; that's the best way of all. But . . .' And here Pete's saurian eyes looked all in an instant troubled, 'but there's something I'd like to tell you, something I'd like you to know. You ought to, I think.'

'Ought to?' A snake's tongue of fear shot out within him.

'Something about how I went on even when we were . . . when we were going together!' Pete's giggle may have been apologetic, nervous, but it was not without a sauciness, a vanity, which made Rob tremble a little. He wanted a Pete perfect.

'I guess,' Pete was saying, 'I'm not the faithful type.'

'You will be, Pete, you will be,' said Rob, with an irrational, desperate, rhetorical certainty. He wanted to hear not a sentence more. 'Dance, Pete, dance!' He thought of all he'd endured in Cabin Number Five, all those awful confessional sessions, and added, pleadingly: 'I guess I've had just about enough of talking-over the sins of the past.'

'What I'd tell you might make you think differently about me.'

All the more reason why I shouldn't hear it, thought Rob. Pete had put his hands on Rob's shoulders and their cocks stood against one another, like sheaves placed together in some harvest ritual.

Rob replied by kissing his friend full and lingeringly on the lips; then, drawing back a bit, he slipped his hand down to Pete's crutch to fondle his prick. It was the most effective way possible of banishing unpleasant topics of conversation.

'Dance, Pete, dance!' he said again, 'and after the dance we fuck.'

So Pete with those swift agile movements of his, detached himself from Rob and crouched down on the floor, between the shabby rag-rugs. Yes, he was a baby-bird again, all bony, busy head and inquisitive, grasping mouth, all valiant efforts to find his feet and discover his wings. Music swam like a shoal of fishes into Rob's head – polyphonous, to match the self-awakening of this pretty-boy bird. And the music was that too, surely, of mutually acknowledged love. Pete, his feathered adolescence having now arrived, was strutting very close to Rob, his bum muscular and lovely, his torso shining in the room's eerie fusion of the exotic and the dreary. And suddenly Rob – climax at hand – began to hear percussion instruments, rhythmic bangings and thumpings and clatterings. They could well be the sounds of someone opening first the front door, then others, and looking vigorously, roughly, through a succession of rooms. But who cared? Wasn't it Liberty Hall here? Let anyone who chooses, come in, said Rob defiantly to himself, nothing can break the spell of Pete's dance of joy – joy in himself, joy in me, joy in the whole wonderful world of free creatures. In his corner at the foot of the couch-bed he felt quite safe.

'It's courtship now?' he asked, having to shout as if above loud music.

'I fly from one bank to another,' said Pete, with surprising breath control.

And of course now Rob knew where he was being transported to; back he was on that Japanese-style half-moon bridge, and Pete was the kingfisher, a moment of blue and a moment of gold brought together, a glorious victory over time and space . . .

'*What* have we here?' came a breezy, coarse, voice, alien yet intensely familiar. And in a trice it smashed the perfect moment – into splinters that could pierce both head and heart. And Rob knew as soon as he heard it, before he'd seen its owner, that the Saviour had returned, maybe to claim him, and that he must be resisted. Best for the time being not to leave his corner, his spectator's sanctuary. The man was dressed in smart, summery clothes, and had a greedy look on his plump, tanned face. He most certainly wasn't wearing a white robe, nor was he carrying a broom.

The bird had abruptly ended his dance now. He was never going to move forward from adolescence. The Saviour shut the door behind him; Pete absurdly had picked up a shawl to disguise his nakedness, but it only made him seem the more naked. Not that this bothered the Saviour who was now leering at him, with a leer that grew and spread to the eyes. Strange to see the usually so composed Pete nervous, defensive, uncertain.

The Saviour's grin now turned into words. 'Pete, you're certainly a great guy for surprises,' he told him, 'I didn't think I'd arrive here, in this funny place you've set yourself up in, to find you so good and ready.'

The pause before Pete's reply was dreadfully long – enough for those splinters to hit Rob with their sharp truths. Still unseen he managed to grab the clothes of which Pete had so accomplishedly and amorously stripped him only a few minutes back.

'Bill,' said Pete, so uneasily poised (as if unsure which bank to make for), 'I'm not alone. I've got company!'

Warm though the evening was (indeed the room was positively stuffy) Rob's whole body had turned cold. Neither shirt nor trousers could protect him; exposure felt total.

'The old voyeur syndrome, huh?' said Bill Bentley. 'Well, I wouldn't put anything past *you*, Pete.' And with a ghastly knowing grin he lunged a hand towards Pete's member – that which had been standing up so joyously and particularly for Rob himself.

Now the obscene Saviour must be *forced* to take notice of him. Rob jumped on to the couch-bed. And what savage pleasure there was in watching Bill Bentley turn round to face him and in seeing, unmistakeable on his bland and apparently nerveless face, the marks of astonishment, guilt and – best of all – panic.

But it was not Bill who was addressing him now, it was Pete. 'Rob,' he was saying, with a crack in his voice, 'I *tried* to tell you. But you wouldn't listen!' The eyes he was turning up at Rob were pleading, welling with tears. 'You can't ever say,' he continued 'that I didn't try.'

'I don't know,' said Rob, 'that I shall ever say *any*thing to you, again!' Because everything's over now, thought Rob. Standing above the two of them as he was now doing was the best position to be in at the terrible point he'd reached in his life. *He* was judge now; it was lonely being judge, of course, even lonelier than being an unwanted guest at Saxingham Enfrith, or a rejected apostle in Foswich. Nevertheless there was satisfaction in the power, satisfaction in knowing that at last God had let him occupy a place where he could dispense his will.

Words came into his mouth, and it was to Bill Bentley that they delivered themselves:

> *'Even as Sodom and Gomorrha and the cities about them in like manner, giving themselves over to fornication, and going after strange flesh, are set forth for an example, suffering the vengeance of eternal fire.'*

'What do you think about all that *now* Bill?'

But what on earth could be the point of speaking about Sodom and Gomorrha from right in the middle of them, and when one of its declared enemies turned out to be a leading citizen?

'You've got to act like a *man*,' Bill Bentley was saying to him, 'you can't stay a hysterical little brat for ever.'

They were stupid words, stupid and cruel. He must not be forgiven them. Pete had sunk down to the floor again, was not crouching but sitting, cross-legged, his head seemingly bowed before a confrontation he'd probably already been dreading. For, of course, everything was clear to Rob now. He'd been blind but it was apparently not permitted him to remain in blindness. He saw it all – that Bill had been having it off with Pete, maybe all the time he'd been trying to convince Rob of the measureless torment awaiting him if he followed his inclinations. Saw too that all the while Pete had been allowing him to believe that there was something special, something unprecedentedly tender, between the two of them, he'd been trotting down to Cabin Number Five, not to hear God's words, but for a sly and senseless fuck.

Why, on Bill's face, as he tried to stand there confident and unashamed did something very similar to terror show itself. Because he *knew* that his own judgement was at hand? Because, too, he'd seen Rob reaching out for the *kris* that hung on the wall and, in his position of physical superiority and command, unsheathing it.

He drew back towards the door. 'Careful, Pete,' he said, 'the boy's a nutter!'

'Rob, Rob,' cried Pete, 'what are you doing? Like Bill says, you've got to be more realistic about things! Look at things more clearly!'

But Rob could look at nothing clearly. Never any more! The room itself was blurry, with just a few objects showing themselves through the haze. The grotesque forms of the Balinese puppets twitched, necks, wings, talons; the shawls shook their branches and gaudy flowers; the mother-of-pearl studs on the sheath of the *kris* winked brilliantly.

Bill Bentley – who could care about *him*? He belonged to that darkness with which he'd been threatening Rob on board the *Egon Ludendorff*. He was to be spurned, ignored. But Pete, Rob's own bird-boy, his bird-lover, his *real* deliverer – whom he'd given up for Christ's sake and with whom, Christ having failed him, he had been blissfully reunited ... Pete was a different story.

He was yelling out now: 'Rob! Rob!'

'Leave the room,' said Bill Bentley, 'this is getting dangerous!'

'*You* leave the room,' Rob cried, brandishing the sword. 'If you don't, you can guess what might happen to you! Pete and I have got to have a little chat.'

So he waited for the craven, pampered-faced preacher to leave the room before turning to Pete and saying, still from the heights of the couch: 'No sword could be as cruel as what *you*'ve made me suffer, Pete. No blade could be as deadly!'

'Have a heart,' said Pete, blubbering now, 'it was only a bit of fun!'

But Rob could feel nothing – or rather Nothing – in his heart, and as for fun, when had it ever had any appeal for him? It was supremely irrelevant now.

Nevertheless he managed to smile. Then brought down the *kris* upon a neck that, only moments ago, had been craning forward for knowledge of the burgeoning world. Rob felt as though he were the sword's instrument; he was carrying out its orders. He struck with great force, though this tired him.

Cries of agony were blood, but the blood was song, movement, flight, the blessed rising of kingfishers from the rushes of countless streams the world over.

Bill Bentley made his getaway with all the stealth and speed he could summon up. At the junction of the Earl's Court Road and the Old Brompton Road he got a taxi; the cab-driver didn't appear to notice his trembling hands or his shortness of breath. 'The Hilton,' he said, and to the Hilton he was taken. Bill tipped the man very handsomely, and then walked rather dazedly up Park Lane to The Dorchester. Back in his own hotel he took a long shower while he pondered what to do. It was quite a while before he sat down to pray to the Lord God for guidance. What had that crazy boy done after he'd left the room? He had only too good an idea ... Of course there could be no proof that he, Bill Bentley, had ever been near the Earl's Court address of a silly little Filipino bum-boy, whose erotic talents he'd – very briefly – availed himself of while getting on with the Lord's business on board the *Egon Ludendorff*?

If he cancelled his rooms at The Dorchester now, and went on to the house of his dismal, contemptible parents in Polhamsted, wouldn't he be very considerably safer? He'd ring up Greater Glory in Jackson, Mississippi, and tell them that he'd decided not to stay in a London hotel after all. That he wanted – as every rightminded man did – to be back in the bosom of his family. And he was sure that that family – if properly appealed to and buttered up – would testify that he'd been there, in his prosperous Chilterns home, ever since disembarcation. If anything arose, that is. If the worst had happened.

Laurie just could not fall asleep, and yet here, in this dull little room that had been his throughout adolescence he'd never found sleep hard before. What was troubling him? What indeed had been troubling him ever since that moment in the Wests' cottage when he'd fancied Rob's eyes hanging pleadingly before him?

'It is,' he'd written to the Headmaster of what was now called simply Tanbury School, 'with both pride and pleasure that I accept the position you've been good enough to offer me, and which Mr Jonathan West has occupied with such distinction for so many years.'

But each successive sleepless hour brought Laurie against a perverse-seeming sentence: 'I do not *want* to be Jonathan West'; it was one towards which, however, his resistance grew palpably ever weaker. At last he had to give it full hospitality, and it drove out many another more welcome guest from his head and underwent unexpected but irrefutable mutations: from 'I do not *want* to be Jonathan West!' to 'I *can't* be Jonathan West' and 'I *won't* be Jonathan West'. He lay first on one side, then on another, then finally upon his back. However much he tried to soothe himself with certain pictures that he'd been living with for some time now – walking through Tanbury streets to the very Art Block where he'd first become interested in painting; living peacefully (perhaps even with Polly) in a golden-stone Foxton cottage, honeysuckle and clematis all over the porch – he remained strangely agitated. Stomach was knotted, temples screwed up against any tranquility.

Rob, Rob Peters was the cause.

And here again his imagination defied his will. He wanted to see Rob as a curse, as the desecrator of Saxingham Enfrith, as the histrionic religious convert who'd menaced him and dashed glasses against loved and treasured pictures. But instead he saw and heard the young man (for Rob *was* that now) as he'd sat only that afternoon in the sunshine of a Foswich bay-window telling his traveller's tales. Of whales humping their backs in the North Atlantic wastes; of trees in the Carolina swamps hung with Spanish moss; of sportive 'gators in muddy Louisiana bayous.

And he could not but think of himself, in the days before Tanbury and Jonathan West, a self-possessed but nonetheless excited boy watching the flat rocky coast of Denmark draw ever nearer.

That memory doubtless brought him the dream which was to stay with him for so long afterwards. He was again on the Japanese-style half-moon bridge and yet saw coming towards him the *William Wilberforce*, smooth and effortless like a bird in flight. Indeed the more Laurie fixed his gaze upon her, the more similar to a bird she appeared. Funnel or beak? Portholes or shining scales on wings? Was that Rob riding her back? No, of course not: Rob was Assistant Ship's Cook. And this had to be the ocean, not the River Fase. And now he was surveying it all, from within the ship, from another kind of bridge, one on which was an office where he and his dad were poring over maps of Skaggerak and the Kattegat. Ahead of him he could see the rising sun, suggesting the further Baltic, with Leningrad, and all Russia itself beyond, and, bathed in its light, his own self, like an effigy only one far more animated, far more human than his present form from which tired eyes looked out.

And when the actual sun had risen, and Laurie opened lids drenched in its red light upon his adolescence-haunted room, he found more sentences in his head; they seemed to him to dance out of it into the day like motes in the morning air:

> *'I am very appreciative of the honour done me by your offer of the post of Senior Art Master. But regretfully I feel I must turn it down, and would like to apologise for any embarrassment or difficulty that this rather late decision may cause you. Personal factors which I didn't anticipate have made me realise that it would not ultimately suit me, and that I must pursue other courses . . .'*

But he needed time before the moment of daring when he actually wrote such a letter, time when his mind roved over new territory that the difficult night behind him seemed to have – alarmingly but enticingly – opened up. Ideally, he would have liked to have driven straight back to Foswich and brooded upon it all, both during the journey and in the solitude of his own flat. But he remembered his promise to Dad and twins that he'd take them out to lunch; Dad probably wouldn't have cared one way or another about it, but Mick and Dale reminded him of his offer, and Laurie felt that he'd better defer his return until the afternoon.

Lunch – at *The Silver Nutmeg* – was good and expensive enough to have pleased Polly herself, but really it was rather a pointless procedure. Dad, while occasionally mumbling words of gratitude, took, as always, very little interest in what there was to eat and drink, and Mick and Dale, elated though they had at first seemed, looked (and clearly felt) remarkably out-of-place. The rising young executives and their girl-friends, the stray Americans and Germans subdued them, and they resorted to low-toned banter between each other such as they would have indulged in every ordinary meal-time at home.

Ordering brandies Laurie said to Dad, somewhat to his own surprise:

'Do you think I'd make a good sailor?'

Dad answered from far-away: 'Oh, I'm sure you would, Laurie!'

'Really? You remember those voyages to Denmark I made with you? They've begun to haunt me a little.' And he thought sadly of the desecrated pictures in his Foswich room, and wondered if the reason for the memories and dreams lay *there*.

Dad said: 'Of course I remember them, Laurie. They were good times, weren't they? I always thought you had a feeling for the sea.'

'Did you, Dad?' said Laurie, suddenly moved, 'why did you never tell me that before?'

'Hey, what's all this about?' said Mick, 'you're not thinking of turning sailor, are you, Laurie?'

'"Every nice girl loves a sailor,"' said Dale.

'"Every nice girl loves a tar,"' capped Mick.

'"For there's something about a sailor,"' finished Dale, '"well, you know what sailors are!"'

'"I never allow a sailor six inches above my knee,"' said Mick.

Laurie, made nervous by this tomfoolery, deemed it best to change the subject. Later he could revive it for himself, in the long quiet drive eastwards. And he did. Sometimes it seemed to him that the flat farmland was a great expanse of ocean, and during this, as it seemed, voyage his mother died many times and Rob was clinging to him, crying, as he had done that memorable evening walk up to the bridge over the Fase, and he had already told Jonathan West about his change of mind and he was watching gulls wheel, wheel, wheel, until he himself partook of their effortless freedom.

242

By half-past six he was back home, and sitting in the bay window with a mug of tea. So intensely had his daydreams possessed him during the ride to Essex that he found, when he reviewed it, that the prospect of his teaching art in his old school had already become the past – a past over and done with. Perhaps, he now thought, that move down south, from Hull to Tanbury, was more significant, more of an upheaval of self than he had realised. The Laurie who'd arrived at the Grammar School with a broad East Riding accent, and been mocked out of it, had been forced to die; but sooner or later the old, buried Laurie had to resurrect himself.

The phone rang. 'Yes, Mr Williams is in, I'll get him for you,' he heard Mrs Hargreaves say.

Who? could it be? Polly? Dad, to see if he had arrived home safely?

Certainly he didn't recognise the voice on the other end of the line, had never heard it before. 'I'm glad you're in,' it was saying – a woman in latish middle age, he'd guess, 'I was so afraid you wouldn't be, and I've someone here who wants to see you really badly.'

She sounded quite agitated, and her manner of speaking was a curious one: she seemed to be banging her tongue about all over her mouth.

'I'm afraid I didn't catch your name,' said Laurie, guardedly; he knew, of course, that she'd not yet given it him.

'Coolidge. Nesta Coolidge of Chipping Ongar. Well-known in some quarters, but an obscure sort of person really.'

'And who is it who badly wants to see me?'

He hardly dared to hazard an answer himself. The one that came, however, astonished him.

'Jonathan West!'

'*Jonathan West!*' Why, if he were in Chipping Ongar today, hadn't he said last night that he was going to Essex, to Laurie's present part of the world? On the other hand, why *should* he have done? 'But I saw Jonathan only yesterday?'

'Yes, he's told me all about it.'

And then a possible explanation occurred to Laurie, and after he'd put the phone down, it seemed to him not just possible but probable. Jonathan West had, his old friend and mentor's knowledge bringing this about, understood Laurie's ambivalence (and more) about the post, and wanted, away from the memory-dominated atmosphere of Oxfordshire to talk to him about it again, to give him an opportunity for dignified retreat, an opportunity he'd surely now take.

'I think I understand,' said Laurie slowly, 'does he want me to come over?'

'Well, of course,' the tongue began to bang about like fury now, '*right* away. Just as *soon* as you possibly can!'

It surely can't be that urgent, thought Laurie, but Nesta Coolidge is clearly the kind of cracked officious gentlewoman, who's determined to 'do everything' for people. Perhaps some relation of Jonathan's, one it's not too surprising he's kept dark.

'And now I must give you address and directions, mustn't I?' said Nesta Coolidge, 'I take it that you don't belong to – what shall I call it? – the Charmed Circle, and that the very syllables, *The Hatchery*, mean nothing to you.'

'I'm afraid they don't,' said Laurie, wondering what on earth the Charmed Circle could be.

'Well, I presumed as much,' said his strange caller, 'so kindly take a pencil and paper and jot down instructions. There are many who think that Nesta Coolidge is a pretty odd bird, but when she comes to telling drivers how to find her house, she is better than the mightiest computer invented. So here goes . . .'

The walls of the room in which Rob was lying were covered in a faded rose-patterned paper and were hung (like most other rooms in The Hatchery) with framed photographs of various prize-winning goats, almost all beribboned and rosetted. Their long and, truth to tell, slightly foolish faces looked out behind glass in a kindly enough fashion, and kindliness was something infinitely precious to Rob just now. The bed itself was a large, feather-mattressed one, with a brass-knobbed frame, and its spread was a pretty, tattered patchwork quilt that smelt quite strongly of damp and possibly too of goats' urine. A mostly threadbare carpet lay on the floor, and, in the corner, was a tall-boy in the drawers of which Nesta had put away his clothes. Only *some* of them, in fact, – Rob had managed in the terrible, pursuing moments of his get-away from Pete's house to find a public lavatory in the Earl's Court Road and change into clean garments. The blood-flecked trousers he'd dropped later, in a carrier-bag, onto an Essex stretch of railway-line: the *kris* itself still lay in the canvas-bag, put beside his bed: Nesta had *not* seen it, it was carefully enough wrapped-up, but if she did? – well, what could happen? There was nothing to connect him (who was Jonathan West, after all) with any squalid and horrible happening in an Earls Court house.

The room had come, during his hours in it, soon to seem part of forever; he could hardly believe that Time could enter it. The shabby furniture and hangings would surely keep him safe, and the framed goats too. Besides . . . things didn't seem now to matter the way they'd done before. Even whether Pete Rodriguez were alive or dead. Rob had not permitted himself to examine the bleeding body he'd struck. It could be that he'd not actually killed him, though it seemed to Rob more likely than not that he had. But was *he* the right word? It seemed to him that just as it was Bill Bentley who'd spoiled Laurie's pictures, so it was he who'd taken Pete's life.

Rob could remember the exact minute when the idea of contacting Nesta Coolidge occurred to him. He'd bought his underground ticket and boarded the train at Earl's Court station like a sleepwalker. Neither the vaults of the station roof nor its crowded platforms had seemed to have any substance; the tubetrain had glided along almost like a carapace of his own body, moving towards its tomb. Then at South Kensington Station – only two stops along – he'd seen a woman laden with plants. How had she come to buy so many, when she obviously was incapable of carrying them all? She was waiting for the westward train; there was no point in his getting out to help her. But she'd put him in mind of 'funny Nesta', the one person in his recent life to have shown him unqualified benevolence.

At the next station he'd got out and telephoned her. She hadn't even sounded surprised to hear him. And yes, she'd said, if he could get a train to Chipping Ongar that night and he really had nowhere else to go, then she'd gladly put him up. Fat Anna would be pleased; she'd enjoyed that day out in the country when they'd met one another.

Rob thought he'd never been more tired than when he'd wielded the *kris* against Pete, but now, almost twenty-four hours later, he was yet more intensely weary. He'd got up late, and had taken a light lunch with Nesta Coolidge in her untidy kitchen. Knives and forks had shaken in his hands, his glass of water had seemed to defy holding – and anyway he'd had no appetite. Then Nesta had suggested that he helped her in the stables. The day was a perfect May one, just the kind you dreamed of when there were gale-force winds out in the Atlantic. Harmony everywhere, woods and fields fragrant, sky a gentle, pure, arching blue. But in order to savour such delights, perhaps it is necessary not to have killed someone, particularly someone whom you went out to in sexual need and ecstasy. Even if you feel it wasn't you but your adversary who did the killing . . .

Inside the stables it was dark and rank; goats bleated and butted. Rob began to feel sick, though shovelling out dung and changing straw were not tasks at which he baulked. The spade would not stay in his hand, stable-walls began quiveringly to move in on him.

He left the stable but not to walk across the yard. Instead he found himself on the gravel in almost exactly the position, the attitude that he'd left Pete in back in Earl's Court. He'd started to shiver – to shiver as if he could never stop.

'I suppose you've got yourself in trouble, eh?' said Nesta Coolidge.

Rob nodded, and then tried to raise himself up: temporarily he was in control of his body again.

Looking round him at the yard framed with flowering currant bushes, now-distant words and scenes came to him. 'You could say,' he said, 'that I'm *in sorrow*.' The expression struck him as almost insanely funny, and he began to laugh and laugh until he reached a point when shuddering began, and each peal of mirth was all but indistinguishable from bodily convulsions.

'Jonathan,' Nesta said, 'perhaps you'd better go back to bed!'

Rob clutched the woman's trousered legs. 'You won't get rid of me, will you? Promise me that! I don't want to leave The Hatchery, I mustn't, I can't.'

'Jonathan,' Nesta's tongue bounced about almost angrily, 'when Nesta Coolidge says that someone is welcome in her house – and she doesn't say it so very often – she *means* it. Ask Fat Anna, ask His Goatly Highness Prince Theobald of Saffron Walden. *They* know that Nesta's word is her bond. Whatever it is, *whoever* it is, that you're hiding from, you're perfectly safe with me.'

For a moment Rob wondered if somehow Nesta could have divined what had happened; it was hard not to scream out at this possibility, but then he understood that it couldn't be, that Nesta was probably imagining no offence more serious than a compromising situation with a girl or a putting of the hand into some cash-till. Nevertheless she led him upstairs with strong, solicitous hands.

Back in bed Rob felt tossed again on the ocean, the ocean that Pete and he would never cross together. 'Raging waves of the sea . . .' He allowed them now underneath him, to heave, and then subside from the feather-mattress. He slipped into a dreamless little sleep, not so different perhaps from the blackness of darkness, a foretaste of it even . . . When he emerged from it, all energies spent, Nesta was standing over him with a tea-tray.

'Drink a mug of this with a *lot* of sugar!' she was advising him, 'it'll be better than most of the tea you've taken. All that dreadful *cow's* muck inside it. No wonder so many people have problems these days!'

Rob tried to smile gratitude. His hands didn't tremble too much as he took the tray. But they'd never be steady enough to handle a sword again . . .

'Jonathan?'

'Yes, Nesta?'

'Isn't there someone you'd like to see. I mean I know funny Nesta's pretty wonderful – all my friends, my goatly friends – have told me so, but I can't help feeling there ought to be someone else for you. If you can think of that someone, I could ring him or her up.'

Rob scarcely paused before replying: 'Nesta, there *is* someone! He's called Laurie Williams, and he lives in Foswich. He's not in the phone-book but I know his number – like I do my own birthday.'

It was only after Nesta had left the room that he remembered that she thought of him as Jonathan West. And anyway wasn't Laurie in Tanbury this weekend? Far more to the point was the blackness of darkness slowly rolling down over him, even though the early evening outside was so sunny, so fair. Birds were starting up in the bushes; from the paddock behind the stable came the bleating of a kid-goat, and down in the hall below Nesta was humming an air from her musical, 'Oklagoata'. Soon the blackness of darkness would also include silence. As it was, it was pleasant that it was heralded by sounds so humdrum, innocuous and cheerful.

Jonathan could never be here, thought Laurie as the red-brick villa, announced by signs as standing at the bottom of this long bumpy unmade-up lane, came into view. 'The Hatchery', a notice proclaimed, 'where they don't divide the sheep from the goats'. 'The Hatchery', stated another, 'where you can play the goat to your heart's content;' (and underneath this in squiggly letters the price of goats' milk by the pint, by the quart, and in the translated forms of butter and cheese). There's some mistake somewhere, but what? Something is not as it would seem. And he thought this even more strongly when the doorbell produced the proprietress of the Hatchery, though she did look very like how he'd imagined while talking on the phone. Face wrenched, hair straggly, feet a little splayed, and clothes that wouldn't have been incongruous on a scarecrow.

'How did you like the lane leading to my house?' she was asking him, 'I like to call it Puncture Drive. Or after it's been raining, One Way Track. 'Cause your car's apt to get stuck, and wild horses wouldn't be able to get you out, let alone tame goats.' She laughed a little wildly, and Laurie could actually see how her long-looking tongue bounced about.

'Jonathan West?' he asked, almost nervously.

'Upstairs! In my spare-bedroom, the *best* one, the one with only the *faintest* aroma of goats' pee. Quite comfortable, all things considering!'

'Is Jonathan – ill?' Laurie asked. It hadn't perhaps, then, been simple officiousness that had made it Nesta, not his old teacher, who'd asked him here.

'Not in the usual sense of the word, no!' said Nesta, and a decidedly troubled look came over her contorted, asymmetrical face. 'But in another sense, I'd say, yes – ill from the heart outwards.'

'Is Lorna with him?' Laurie was following Nesta Coolidge into a hall that even on this sweet May evening stank – of animals, unwashed corners, mildew, damp.

'Lorna?' There was genuine ignorance in both voice and facial expression. 'I don't know about any Lorna, I'm afraid. Jonathan has never spoken about her.'

'But,' Laurie almost shouted the word; the confusion in his head now was nothing to the confusion he felt emanating from The Hatchery itself, where what he'd expected to find was somehow going to elude him and be replaced – by *what*? 'how could Jonathan *never* have spoken about her? She's his wife.'

'You all there?' asked Nesta stopping at the foot of the staircase, her face twitching, 'people have sometimes said *I'm* doolally-tap, but that remark takes the biscuit. How could a boy that age have a *wife*?'

'A boy?' said Laurie, (talk about 'doolally-tap'!), 'you call Jonathan West a *boy*?'

'Of course I do,' Nesta began to walk up the stairway rather angrily now, 'I know what you're thinking – here's a rum bird who's done nothing but look after goats most of her life; I'll *show* her that she's a bit missing, that she doesn't see people properly. I shall torment her by making her think she's suffering from delusions. But I'm not, I tell you. Funny Nesta has her times of 'clarity'!'

'You've got me all wrong,' said Laurie, 'and that's not the only thing that's wrong either, I think!' He tried to make the words sound conciliatory, offerings of his own perplexity, but to no avail. Nesta flung open a door, her face burning with discomposure.'

'And that is not a boy, I suppose!' she said, with a brief look of wild triumph, 'not a boy at all!'

Laurie looked ahead of him and saw Rob, pale as death upon the huge old-fashioned bed. Well, he should have guessed.

'An old man, eh?' said Nesta, 'an old married man.'

'No,' said Laurie quietly, 'that's a boy all right!'

'Hullo, Rob,' said Laurie.

'Hullo, Laurie,' said Rob.

A smile irradiated his face, which, could, just for that moment, have been that of a year ago, that of the days of their friendship. 'I *knew* you'd come. I *knew* I'd see you again,' he said.

Our comings and goings, *from* one another, *to* one another, are like smiles that appear and then fade on faces, thought Laurie . . . Nesta was watching the pair of them, as she might have done a couple of uncertain-natured goats. 'So why did you pretend you didn't know him?' she said to Laurie, to whom she didn't seem to have taken, 'and why all this *Rob* stuff?'

'Just a habit we once slipped into,' Laurie replied.

'I'd imagined someone *quite* different from you,' Nesta was pleased to say, 'if you don't mind my saying so, you've got a very weak chin. You look saturated with cows' milk too!'

'Laurie has always been a good friend to me,' said Rob. It was almost painful watching him trying to force himself into a conventional upright position, 'together with *you*, Nesta, the best friend I've ever had. It's *me* who's been weak, *me* who failed *him*.'

Nesta was a little mollified by this. 'I expect you'll be wanting some refreshment, Mr Williams,' she said, in an effort to be less *farouche*. I can bring you a better mug of tea than you'll have been used to, I wager. And then there c'd be a cake or two, I'd think.'

After lunch at *The Silver Nutmeg* Laurie didn't feel like further food, but he judged that assenting to the offer would be the only way of getting the 'rum bird' out of the room. And when she departed, Laurie felt he was entering both the time and space of lost intimacies. Nevertheless there was one mystery of the present he had to clear up. 'Jonathan West?' he queried.

'I told her I was called Jonathan West the very first time I met her; it was after that terrible time at Saxingham Enfrith,' Rob explained, looking away from Laurie, 'I suppose I thought "Rob Peters" would never do again, was too bad for use. Don't know why I didn't stick to that notion.'

And their eyes did meet now – and what vacancy, what despair inhabited them. Laurie sat down on the bed, as if smitten by their dull light. The bed was very, very soft. And – he suddenly and rather ashamedly thought – if this room is the one in The Hatchery with the faintest smell of goats' pee, what can the others be like?

'Rob,' he said, 'I'm very pleased to see you again!'

'How could you be?' Rob said faintly, 'after yesterday?'

'Yesterday!' said Laurie, 'was a mistake.'

Rob's laugh was rather a dreadful one.

'Yes,' he said, 'yesterday was a mistake all right. But I reckon there are some folks that yesterday's more than just a mistake for.' He tried again to smile but could not do so.

He was talking about something specific but Laurie couldn't grasp what it could be.

'I'm glad to tell you anyway,' Rob said in a low voice, such as surely he'd never used before, 'that yesterday is not going to have a tomorrow, Laurie. Like I just said, I'm glad to be able to tell you that myself.'

It was all nonsense, but what did that matter? Compared with the emotion sweeping Laurie now – a love for this tormented young sailor 'home from sea' so strong that it made all other feelings he'd had for people feeble and invalid.

'Rob,' he said, 'what's the matter? Something is! Tell me!'

'Why should you want to know, Laurie? You of all people,' said Rob, 'when I've brought you nothing but suffering and problems.'

'That's not true,' said Laurie, 'last night I couldn't sleep, and I started going over things. I've probably made *you* suffer more than *you* and *me*, I reckon, and I'm sorry for it.'

It was that late afternoon by the Fase, and more, because this time it was Laurie who clasped Rob to him, who felt tears in his eyes, who wanted to rest his troubled head against the others.

'Another thing I was thinking,' he now whispered into Rob's tensed but responsive body, 'was that I can't take Jonathan West's job. Don't ask me why not; I just know that it isn't for me, that I'm in need of something else. You remember my telling you about those voyages I made with my dad?'

'How could I not?' said Rob, 'it's partly what set me off on my life, isn't it? What made me want to leave Foswich!'

'I've been seeing all the sights of those days again,' said Laurie, 'I'm probably much more like my dad than I've ever thought. I'd like to go to sea myself – how I'm not sure, but with these longings inside me, I can't do anything else? We could go together, Rob?'

'We could go together,' echoed Rob, withdrawing from Laurie's embrace, 'Oh, Laurie, how could that ever be possible?'

'You wouldn't want it?' said Laurie, almost wounded, for it now seemed to be what he himself desired most in the world; the two of them would rescue one another from whatever forces were oppressing them.

'Wouldn't want it?' said Rob, 'don't you understand, that it's what I've dreamt of ever since I got to know you. But it wouldn't work – it couldn't work.'

'I don't see why not,' said Laurie. He let his glance wander out of the window, out over the yard with the red-brick stables at the end and beyond these the fields, edged in cow-parsley, and full of tangles of flowering grasses. He tried to make them – as he had the flatlands of this afternoon's car-journey – into a sea that he and Rob Peters were looking out upon together.

'Because – because,' Rob began, but he didn't finish the sentence, 'Laurie, why, *why* couldn't this have happened at the beginning? Why had I got to go through so many tests and trials? Which I wasn't up to; I've never been the test-passing type.'

'Who of us is?' said Laurie, thinking of himself, 'last night I told myself again and again: I've failed, I've failed in all I didn't realise I had to do!'

'I was thinking of something else,' said Rob, 'you try for something, and then there comes between them – shit and blood. Just like I told you about that afternoon last summer. They're real, they're very real. But other things are too, and I haven't been strong enough to follow them. And now it's too late.'

'How can it be too late?' said Laurie, 'you're so young, Rob; perhaps you've forgotten that?'

'Being young has nothing to do with it,' said Rob, 'once you've fallen . . .'

There was, Laurie now realised, terror in his eyes, and the body he was holding was suddenly convulsed by shudders. I have never really known him, perhaps never *could* know him, Laurie thought. And yet I still would like to voyage in his company – forward from all that's imprisoned us both. 'Rob,' said Laurie, 'please let me know what's troubling you. Is it impossible to tell me about? Perhaps I haven't seemed as sympathetic to you as I should have. Give me the chance now – even if it's only for once, even if it's the one-and-only time!'

Once again – as with Nesta – Rob broke out into laughs that were indistinguishable from spasms; ones so violent that Laurie was forced to let go of him. 'If I *did* tell you,' he said, 'it *would* be the one and only time.'

It was not possible to see any comic element in the remark, and anyway the terror stayed in his eyes.

Then, the shudders diminishing, Rob said: 'Hey, Laurie, tell you what! Why don't you go downstairs to see whether you can give Nesta a hand with those refreshments she's getting ready for you. She's a strange creature, as she'd be the first to tell you, but she's *good* – very *good*!'

Laurie, interpreting correctly that Rob wished to be alone for a few minutes, to recover from the seizure more fully, assented. He got off the bed, left the room and entered the landing. On the walls were yet more framed portraits of goats, and these extended down a long corridor.

'Mrs Coolidge,' he called down the stairwell, 'can I be of any help?'

'Well, I never say "no" to offers!' came up Nesta's voice, 'except from certain *dairies*, of course! Decided that I wasn't over polite to you, so I'm making you a bigger snack than I said.'

'That's certainly very kind,' said Laurie. He descended the stairwell, remarking to himself how the stench of goat got stronger as he did so. Not surprisingly: goats appeared to roam at will through the kitchen quarters. This afternoon, he reflected, I'd never so much as heard of The Hatchery, Chipping Ongar, and yet I've a feeling it may well turn out to be one of the most important places of my life.

Rob was thinking how in this strange, unkempt house he'd at last seen Laurie as he had always wanted him. It had been very beautiful.

Laurie had suggested what Rob had talked of last year, the two of them together upon the sea.

But now there were other things to come between dream and realisation. The malice of Jesus, his Saviour cruelly and greedily at large in the world, and Pete Rodriguez murdered.

The blackness of darkness would be sweeter than any confrontation with these, and besides how could he inflict more pain on Laurie? This moment with him, like that other by the Fase, had been perfect. Best to kept it that way.

He reached over for his canvas-bag and carefully took from it the wrapped-up *kris*. The magic it had so terribly performed yesterday could be exercised again, and the mother-of-pearl studs winked at him in the shadows cast by the four poster. He was sorry only for the pain he would cause Laurie and Nesta when they found him.

GMP books can be ordered from any bookshop in the UK, and from specialised bookshops overseas. If you prefer to order by mail, a comprehensive catalogue is available on request, from:
GMP Publishers Ltd (GB), P O Box 247, London N17 9QR.

Name and Address in block letters please:

Name _____

Address _____

_____

_____